WELSH
SHORT STORIES

*

AN ANTHOLOGY

FABER & FABER LIMITED
24 Russell Square
London

FIRST PUBLISHED IN SEPTEMBER MCMXXXVII
BY FABER AND FABER LIMITED
24 RUSSELL SQUARE LONDON W.C.1
PRINTED IN GREAT BRITAIN BY
LATIMER TREND AND CO LTD PLYMOUTH

PUBLISHER'S NOTE

The publishers express their sincere gratitude to all those who have assisted in the compilation of this book: especially Miss Elisabeth Inglis Jones, Mr. Llewelyn Wyn Griffith, Mr. James Hanley, and Mr. Arthur Jones.

The authors represented in this collection, with the exception of Dorothy Edwards, Allen Raine, and Richard Hughes Williams, are all living: the publishers wish to thank them for permitting their stories to be reprinted.

The publishers also wish to make grateful acknowledgement to the following for allowing stories to be republished in this volume: Messrs. Arthur Barker Ltd., the original publishers in book form of "Country Dance" by Margiad Evans; Messrs. Lovat Dickson Ltd., the original publishers in book form of "A Thing of Nought" by Hilda Vaughan; Messrs. Chatto & Windus for "The Stranger" by Richard Hughes from *A Moment of Time*; Messrs. Lawrence & Wishart Ltd. for "The Conquered" by Dorothy Edwards from *Rhapsody*; Messrs. Martin Secker & Warburg Ltd. for "The Shining Pyramid" from the volume of that name; Messrs. Hutchinson & Co. (Publishers) Ltd. for "A Life's Chase" by Allen

Raine from *All in a Month*; Messrs. Andrew Melrose Ltd. for "The Way of the Earth" by Caradoc Evans from *My People*; Messrs. Jonathan Cape Ltd. for "Wil Thomas" by Glyn Jones from *The Blue Bed*, and for "Janet Ifans' Donkey" by Geraint Goodwin from *The White Farm*; Messrs. Hughes & Son, Publishers, Wrexham, for "Siôn William" from *Storiau Richard Hughes Williams*, and for "The Strange Apeman" by E. Tegla Davies from *Y Llwybr Arian*; the Aberystwyth Press for "A Summer Day" by Kate Roberts from *Rhigolau Bywyd*; Messrs. Hugh Evans & Sons for "Big Business" by J. Ellis Williams from *Sglodion*; the Editor of *New Stories* for "Something to be Thankful For" by Jack Griffith; the National Eisteddfod Association for "A Good Year" by D. J. Williams.

The stories by E. Tegla Davies, D. J. Williams and Richard Hughes Williams have been translated for this volume by Ll. Wyn Griffith; the story by Kate Roberts has been translated by Dafydd Jenkins.

The story by Frank Richards, "The Black Rat", is from that author's book, *Old Soldiers Never Die*, published by Messrs. Faber & Faber Ltd.

6

CONTENTS

by

RICHARD HUGHES

⋆

THE STRANGER

I

The street in Cylfant was so steep that if you took a middling jump from the top of the village you would not touch ground again till you reached the bottom: but you would probably hurt yourself. The houses sat each on other's left shoulder, all the way up, so that the smoke from Mrs. Grocery-Jones's chimney blew in at Mrs. Boot-Jones's basement, and out through her top windows into the cellar of the Post Office, and out through the Post Office Daughter's little bedroom casement into that of the Butchery Aunt (who was paralysed and lived downstairs): and so on, up the whole line like a flue, till it left soot on the stomachs of the sheep grazing on the hillside above.

But that does not explain why the stranger came to Cylfant village, unless it was through curiosity: nor, indeed, what he was doing in such a Sabbath-keeping little Anabaptist hamlet at all, where he might have known he would meet with an accident: nor what he was doing so far from home.

9

Mr. Williams was the rector of Cylfant, and perhaps thirty miles round: such an old fat man that he had difficulty in walking between his different churches on Sundays. His face was heavy, his eyes small but with a dream in them, and he kept sticky sweet things ready in his pocket. He was stone deaf, so that now he roared like a bull, now whispered like a young lover. He might be heard roaring across a valley. He had one black suit, with patches on it, and one surplice, that he darned sometimes. He lived by letting the rectory in the summer: and when the Disestablishment Bill wiped away his stipend of eight pounds, he made up for it by taking in washing: you would see him in front of the rectory, legs set well apart, both heavy arms plunged up to the elbows in suds, a towel pinned to each shoulder to save his black coat, roaring a greeting to all who might pass.

Cylfant was very proud of the smallness of his congregation: for in Wales to have many church-people in a village is a great disgrace. They are always the scallywags, the folk who have been expelled from their chapels; and who hope, even if they cannot expect heaven, that things will not be quite so uncomfortable for them in the next world as if they gave up religion altogether. There were only three families, except for the Squire's governess, that ever came to Cylfant church. Mr. Williams hated verse, but he preached them pure poetry: he had such an imagination that if he meditated on the anatomy of angels there seemed to be strange flying things about his head; and the passionate roaring and whispering of his voice could hang Christ even on the polished brass altar-cross.

Presently he married the girl who played the harmonium: but she had one leg.

It was she, Minnie, that took in the Stranger. They were sitting one night in the rectory parlour, and Mr. Williams was reading a book of sermons with great fixity of mind, in order to forget his Loss: for that day the little ring on his watch-chain had opened, and he had lost the gold cross that he had always carried. Minnie was sure that it had been there when they started to climb the village: but they had no lantern: the wind was a fleet howling darkness, so they could not search till the morning, even if it lay on their very doorstep. Mr. Williams read three sermons at a gulp, and closed the book. It was always a thing of amazement that a man who read such dull sermons with such avidity could put so much thrill and beauty, so little of the moralities, into his own preaching.

He shut the book, and, giving a great sigh, puffed out his cheeks, while he squinted along the broad shirt-front under his chin. Minnie went to turn down the lamp—as she always did, for reasons of thrift, when her husband was not actually reading; and all at once she heard a cry in the night, sharp as a child's, and full of terror and innocence. She opened the door, and saw a small huddled figure in the roadway. There was a little light shining from it, bluish and fitful: and she knew at once it was something more than natural. She set her wooden leg firmly against the doorstep, and, bending down, caught the Stranger up in her arms, and lifted him over the threshold. He lay there, blinking in the lamplight: a grotesque thing, with misshapen ears and a broad, flat nose. His limbs were knotted, but the skin at his joints was yellow and delicate as a snake's belly. He had crumpled wings, as fine as petrol upon water: even thus battered, their beauty could not but be seen. He seemed in pain: and there was a small cross-shaped weal burnt on his side, as if he had stumbled on a little red-hot iron.

"Poor little thing," said Mr. Williams, looking at it sideways from his chair. "What is it?"

"It is more ugly than anything I have ever seen," said Minnie. "Perhaps it is an angel: for it was never born of woman."

"We should be more humble, Minnie," said her husband. "Who are we that God should send His angels to try us?"

"At any rate, I think it is not," said Minnie. "We will see."

She took up the book of sermons, and touched him on the forehead with it. He gave a shrill yell of pain.

"God forgive me for my cruelty," she exclaimed. "It must be a———"

"It is a Stranger," said Mr. Williams quickly.

Minnie turned and looked at him.

"What shall we do?" she shouted in his ear. "For if we harbour it we shall surely be damned. We must not help God's enemies."

"We are taught to love our enemies," whispered Mr. Williams. "And who is God's enemy is ours too."

"But it can feel no gratitude," said Minnie. "It will return us evil for good."

"If we do good in the hope of gratitude we have our reward," roared Mr. Williams.

"You mean you will keep him?" said Minnie.

"I mean"—the old man groaned—"I do not know what to do, indeed, whatever."

But the visitor settled that question for them himself. He crawled over to the fireplace, and sitting himself on one of the reddest coals, smiled out at them with a grin that stretched from ear to ear.

II

That was how the little devil came to Cylfant rectory. He had great natural charm, and when the cross-shaped weal on his side was better—for it healed quickly under the action of fire—his spirits returned to him. One was led to forget the grotesque beauty of his form by the generous amiability of his expression. He took to the old rector at once; and Mr. Williams himself could not but feel a secret liking for him. That night he followed them up to bed: Mr. Williams had to shut and lock the bedroom door on him. But hardly were they inside when they saw a bluish light on the panel: and presently the little devil was sitting perched upon the bed-rail, watching with a sober interest Minnie unstrap her wooden leg: and even when she said her prayers—which she did in a shamefast fashion, for fear of giving him pain—he showed no embarrassment whatever. When they were both fast asleep, he took down Minnie's old peg from the shelf where she had laid it, and did something to it in the corner. He then lay down in a pool of moonlight, and was still sleeping soundly when the rector heaved himself out of bed in the morning. The old man woke Minnie, who scrambled out of bed, and began to strap on her leg preparatory to getting the breakfast; but a wonderful thing happened, for no sooner had she fitted her scarred stump into the leather socket than the leather changed to flesh, and the wood to flesh, and there she was with the most elegant and seductive leg that ever troubled a man's eye: and, moreover, there was a silk stocking on it, and a high-heeled Paris shoe on it, before she could recover from her surprise. As she drew on her old ringed black-and-white cotton oddment over the other stocky red ankle she thought that never had such a pair of legs been seen together on one body. She looked round in a guilty fashion: but her husband was balanced in front of the looking-

glass shaving himself. He had not seen. She pulled
on her dress all in a hurry and danced away downstairs. She let up the blinds and swept the floor; and
all the time her new leg behaved as well as if she had
known it all her life: but directly she flung open the
front door to shake the mat, it began all at once to
drag, and jib: she got pins and needles in it: it
jumped and kicked like a thing quite out of control.
And she saw the reason: for there in the roadway,
where she had found the Stranger the night before,
was the rector's gold cross.

"There is no mistaking", said Minnie to herself,
"where *that* leg came from."

And, indeed, there was not. She sidled up to the
cross with difficulty, and recovered it: and all at once
heard steps on the cobbles. It was Scraggy Evan, the
postman. Minnie's first thought was to hide the leg,
for it would take some explaining away. But it would
not be hidden: the shameless thing thrust the delicate
turn of its ankle right under Scraggy Evan's nose.
Scraggy's cheery "bore da!" was lost in a gasp, and
poor Minnie fled into the house scarlet with shame,
the damnable leg giving coquettish little kicks into
the air as she went.

What Scraggy told the village we can only guess:
but he must have told them something, or why should
Mrs. Williams have received so many callers that
morning? The first came when breakfast was hardly
over: and the Stranger was sitting quietly on the hob

picking his teeth with his tail. Minnie had great presence of mind. She ran to her work-box, and taking from it a red-flannel petticoat that she had been mending, wrapped the Stranger in it and crammed him quickly into a wooden box, begging him in a staccato whisper to lie still. Upon the face of Mr. Williams there was a look of much courage and resignation. Devil or no, he was prepared to justify his guest to all comers. Minnie opened the door, and Mrs. Grocery-Jones stood there.

"Good morning," said she. "I was calling to ask if you are driving over to Ynysllanbedrbachdeudraethgerylan to-day."

She paused and sniffed; then sniffed again.

There was no doubt of it: somewhere sulphur was burning.

"We are not," said Minnie. "We are too busy here, indeed, with the plaguy wasps. Mr. Williams has hardly smoked out one nest, but bad are they as they were before, indeed."

Mrs. Jones gave a gasp of surprise.

"Wasps in the winter-time?" she said.

"I did not say *wasps*," said Minnie, "I said the *wallpaper*, which the doctor thinks may have the scarlet fever lurking in it, so have we fumigated the whole house."

It was lucky, thought Minnie, that her husband was so deaf. He would never have forgiven her.

"Well, good gracious!" said Mrs. Jones. As her

eyes got used to the dim light she caught sight of a broad head with two beady yellow eyes, peering at her from a soap-box. "And is that a cat you have there, Mrs. Williams?"

"It is a *pig*!" she cried with sudden heat; for her new leg showed an obvious desire to kick Mrs. Jones out of the house. "It has the wind," she explained, "so we thought it would be best in the house, indeed."

"Well, good gracious me!" repeated Mrs. Jones.

Minnie's leg was quivering, but she managed to control it. Mrs. Jones was staring past her at the pig, as if she could not take her eyes off it. As, indeed, she could not: for suddenly she shot half across the road, backwards, with the force of a bullet: and when released she scrambled down the street, as she herself explained it, "as if the devil was after me": and there was the Stranger, wrapped still in the red-flannel petticoat sitting on the window-sill and grinning amiably at her back.

III

If Mr. Williams had lived longer, a few curious things might have happened in Cylfant village: but he did not. There was a buzzing feeling in his head all that day, and when he went to bed at night he lay quietly on his back staring at the ceiling. It had turned a bright green. Presently, with his eyes open still, he began to snore. Minnie did not notice anything queer; and in the small hours of the morning, after two or three loud snorts, he stopped altogether.

When he felt better, he found that his soul was outside his body. It was not at all the kind of thing he had expected it to be, but was fairly round, and made of some stuff like white of egg. He gathered it gently into his arms, and began to float about: his body had disappeared. Presently he was aware that the Stranger was still watching him.

"You'll be damned for this: double-damned even, for giving place to the devil—and you a priest." He sighed. "It is so hard," he went on seriously, "even for devils to conquer their better nature. Oh, I *try* hard enough. I surely try. The seeds of goodness have lurked in us ever since the Fall; try as we will, they *sprout*.

> " '*With a fork drive Nature out,
> She will ever yet return.*'

"Temptation is always lurking ready for us: it is a long and a hard fight: the Forces of Evil against the Forces of Good. But we shall conquer in the end: with Wrong on our side, we *must* conquer." There was an elation in his face that transcended all earthly ugliness. "At last", he went on, "I have done a really immoral act: an act with no trace of good in it, either in motive or effect. You will be damned, and Minnie will be damned too, even if she has to hop to hell on the leg I gave her. But it was hard, hard."

Old Williams floated over on to the other side.

"I am a sinful man," he said; "a very sinful man. Heaven was never my deserts, whatever."

The devil looked at him in surprise.

"Oh, you were not!" he said earnestly. "Indeed, you were not! You were the truest——"

He stopped suddenly. Williams was aware of the presence of some very unpleasant personality. He looked round: and behind him stood a tall figure with thin, tight lips and watery eyes, who began speaking at once—rapidly, as if by rote.

"As a matter of form," said he, "I claim this soul."

"As a matter of form," replied the devil in a sing-song voice, "he is mine."

The angel rapped out: "De qua causa?"

"De diabolo consortando," chaunted the little devil, in even worse Latin.

"Quæ sit evidentia?"

"Tuos voco oculos ipsos."

"Quod vidi, vero, atque affirmo.—Satis," continued the angel. "Tuumst." And he turned to go.

"Stop!" cried the Stranger suddenly, all his bad resolutions breaking down.

"Stop!" he cried, and began speaking rapidly. "I'm a backslider, I know, but the strain is too much: there's no true devilry in me. Take him: take him: there never was better Christian in Wales, I swear it: and to that alone his damnation is due: pure charity——"

"What are you talking about?" snapped the angel

petulantly. "The case is settled: I have withdrawn my claim."

"So do I!" cried the devil excitedly. "I withdraw mine."

The angel shrugged his wings.

"What's the use of making a scene?" he said. "Never, in all my office, have I known a fiend break down and forget himself like this before. You are making an exhibition of yourself, sir! Besides, if we both withdraw, he can't go anywhere. It's none of my business."

He shrugged his wings and soared away.

"*Heaven or Hell or the Land of Whipperginny,*" murmured Williams to himself, vague memories of Nashe rising to the surface of his astonishment. Together they watched the angel's purple pinions bearing him from sight: the Stranger cocked a snook at his straight back.

"Where now?" asked the rector.

"Where now? Heaven! Wait till he's out of sight."

He turned and winked broadly at Williams, making a motion on his bare shanks as if to thrust his hand in a pocket.

"You come with me," he said. "I know how I can get things fixed for you!"

by

DOROTHY EDWARDS

*

THE CONQUERED

Last summer, just before my proper holiday, I
went to stay with an aunt who lives on the borders
of Wales, where there are so many orchards. I must
say I went there simply as a duty, because I used to
stay a lot with her when I was a boy, and she was, in
those days, very good to me. However, I took plenty
of books down so that it should not be waste of time.

Of course, when I got there it was really not so
bad. They made a great fuss of me. My aunt was as
tolerant as she used to be in the old days, leaving me
to do exactly as I liked. My cousin, Jessica, who is
just my age, had hardly changed at all, though they
both looked different with their hair up; but my
younger cousin Ruth, who used to be very lively and
something of a tomboy, had altered quite a lot. She
had become very quiet; at least, on the day I arrived
she was lively enough, and talked about the fun we
used to have there, but afterwards she became more
quiet every day, or perhaps it was that I noticed it
more. She remembered far more about what we used

to do than I did; but I suppose that is only natural, since she had been there all the time in between, and I do not suppose anything very exciting had happened to her, whereas I have been nearly everywhere.

But what I wanted to say is, that not far from my aunt's house, on the top of a little slope, on which there was an apple orchard, was a house with french windows and a large green lawn in front, and in this lived a very charming Welsh lady whom my cousins knew. Her grandfather had the house built, and it was his own design. It is said that he had been quite a friend of the Prince Consort, who once, I believe, actually stayed there for a night.

I knew the house very well, but I had never met any of the family, because they had not always occupied it, and, in any case, they would have been away at the times that I went to my aunt for holidays. Now only this one granddaughter was left of the family; her father and mother were dead, and she had just come back to live there. I found out all this at breakfast the morning after I came, when Jessica said, "Ruthie, we must take Frederick to see Gwyneth."

"Oh yes," said Ruthie. "Let's go to-day."

"And who is Gwyneth?"

Jessica laughed. "You will be most impressed. Won't he, Mother?"

"Yes," said my aunt, categorically.

However, we did not call on her that afternoon, because it poured with rain all day, and it did not seem worth while, though Ruthie appeared in her mackintosh and goloshes ready to go, and Jessica and I had some difficulty in dissuading her.

I did not think it was necessary to do any reading the first day, so I just sat and talked to the girls, and after tea Jessica and I even played duets on the piano, which had not been tuned lately, while Ruthie turned over the pages.

The next morning, though the grass was wet and every movement of the trees sent down a shower of rain, the sun began to shine brightly through the clouds. I should certainly have been taken to see their wonderful friend in the afternoon, only she herself called in the morning. I was sitting at one end of the dining-room, reading Tourguêniev, with a dictionary and about three grammars, and I dare say I looked very busy. I do not know where my aunt was when she came, and the girls were upstairs. I heard a most beautiful voice, that was very high pitched though, not low, say:

"All right I will wait for them in here," and she came into the room. Of course I had expected her to be nice, because my cousins liked her so much, but still they do not meet many people down there, and I thought they would be impressed with the sort of person I would be quite used to. But she really was charming.

She was not very young—older, I should say, than Jessica. She was very tall, and she had very fair hair.

23

But the chief thing about her was her finely carved features, which gave to her face the coolness of stone and a certain appearance of immobility, though she laughed very often and talked a lot. When she laughed she raised her chin a little, and looked down her nose in a bantering way. And she had a really perfect nose. If I had been a sculptor I should have put it on every one of my statues. When she saw me she laughed and said, "Ah! I am disturbing you," and she sat down, smiling to herself.

I did not have time to say anything to her before my cousins came in. She kissed Jessica and Ruthie, and kept Ruthie by her side.

"This is our cousin Frederick," said Jessica.

"We have told you about him," said Ruthie gravely.

Gwyneth laughed. "Oh, I recognized him, but how could I interrupt so busy a person! Let me tell you what I have come for. Will you come to tea to-morrow and bring Mr. Trenier?" She laughed at me again.

We thanked her, and then my aunt came in.

"How do you do, Gwyneth?" she said. "Will you stay to lunch?"

"No, thank you so much, Mrs. Haslett," she answered. "I only came to ask Jessica and Ruthie to tea to-morrow, and, of course, to see your wonderful nephew. You will come too, won't you?"

"Yes, thank you," said my aunt. "You and

Frederick ought to find many things to talk about together."

Gwyneth looked at me and laughed.

Ruthie went out to make some coffee, and afterwards Gwyneth sat in the window-seat drinking it and talking.

"What were you working at so busily when I came in?" she asked me.

"I was only trying to read Tourguéniev in the original," I said.

"Do you like Tourguéniev very much?" she asked, laughing.

"Yes," I said. "Do you?"

"Oh, I have only read one, *Fumé*."

She stayed for about an hour, laughing and talking all the time. I really found her very charming. She was like a personification, in a restrained manner, of Gaiety. Yes, really, very much like Milton's *L'Allegro*.

The moment she was gone Jessica said excitedly: "Now, Frederick, weren't you impressed?"

And Ruthie looked at me anxiously until I answered: "Yes, I really think I was."

The next day we went there to tea. It was a beautiful warm day, and we took the short cut across the fields and down a road now overgrown with grass to the bottom of the little slope on which her house was built. There is an old Roman road not far from here, and I am not quite sure whether that road is not part of it. We did not go into the house, but were taken at once to the orchard at the back, where she was sitting near a table, and we all sat down with her. The orchard was not very big, and, of course, the trees were no longer in flower, but the fruit on them was just beginning to grow and look like tiny apples and pears. At the other end some white chickens strutted about in the sunlight. We had tea outside.

She talked a lot, but I cannot remember now what she said; when she spoke to me it was nearly always to tell me about her grandfather, and the interesting people who used to come to visit him.

When it began to get cool we went into the house across the flat green lawn and through the french window. We went to a charming room; on the wall above the piano were some Japanese prints on silk, which were really beautiful. Outside it was just beginning to get dark.

She sang to us in a very nice high soprano voice, and she chose always gay, light songs which suited her excellently. She sang that song of Schumann's, *Der Nussbaum*; but then it is possible to sing that lightly and happily, though it is more often sung with a trace of sadness in it. Jessica played for her. She is a rather good accompanist. I never could accompany singers. But I played afterwards; I played some Schumann too.

"Has Ruthie told you I am teaching her to sing?" said Gwyneth. "I don't know much about it, and her voice is not like mine, but I remember more or less what my master taught me."

"No," I said, looking at Ruthie. "Sing for us now and let me hear."

"No," said Ruthie, and blushed a little. She never used to be shy.

Gwyneth pulled Ruthie towards her. "Now do sing. The fact is you are ashamed of your teacher."

"No," said Ruthie; "only you know I can't sing your songs."

Gwyneth laughed. "You would hardly believe what a melancholy little creature she is. She won't sing anything that is not tearful."

"But surely," I said, "in the whole of Schubert and Schumann you can find something sad enough for you?"

"No," said Ruthie, looking at the carpet, "I don't know any Schumann, and Schubert is never sad even in the sad songs. Really I can't sing what Gwyneth sings."

"Then you won't?" I said, feeling rather annoyed with her.

"No," she said, flushing, and she looked out of the window.

Ruthie and Jessica are quite different. Jessica is, of course, like her mother, but Ruthie is like her father, whom I never knew very well.

Next morning, immediately after breakfast, I went for a walk by myself and though I went by a very roundabout way, I soon found myself near Gwyneth's house, and perhaps that was not very surprising. I came out by a large bush of traveller's-nightshade. I believe that is its name. At least it is called old man's beard too, but that does not describe it when it is in flower at all. You know that it has tiny white waxen flowers, of which the buds look quite different from the open flower, so that it looks as though there are two different kinds of flowers on one stem. But what I wanted to say was, I came out by this bush, and there, below me, was the grass-covered road, with new cart-wheel ruts in it, which made two brown lines along the green where the earth showed. Naturally I walked down it, and stood by the fence of the orchard below her house. I looked up between the trees and there she was coming down towards me.

"Good morning, Mr. Trenier," she said, laughing. "Why are you deserting Tourguêniev?"

"It is such a lovely morning," I said, opening the gate for her; "and if I had known I should meet you, I should have felt even less hesitation."

She laughed, and we walked slowly across the grass, which was still wet with dew. It was a perfectly lovely day, with a soft pale-blue sky and little white clouds in it, and the grass was wet enough to be bright green.

"Oh, look!" she said suddenly, and pointed to two enormous mushrooms, like dinner-plates, growing at our feet.

28

"Do you want them?" I asked, stooping to pick them.

"Oh yes," she said; "when they are as big as that they make excellent sauces. Fancy such monsters growing in a night! They were not here yesterday."

"And last week I had not met you," I said, smiling.

She laughed, and took the mushrooms from me.

"Now we must take them to the cook," she said, "and then you shall come for a little walk with me."

As we crossed the lawn to the house she was carrying the pink-lined mushrooms by their little stalks.

"They look like the sunshades of Victorian ladies," I said.

She laughed, and said: "Did you know that Jenny Lind came here once?"

Afterwards we walked along the real Roman road, now only a pathway with grass growing up between the stones, and tall trees overshadowing it. On the right is a hill where the ancient Britons made a great stand against the Romans, and were defeated.

"Did you know this was a Roman road?" she asked. "Just think of the charming Romans who must have walked here! And I expect they developed a taste for apples. Does it shock you to know that I like the Romans better than the Greeks?"

I said "No", but now, when I think of it, I believe I *was* a little shocked, although, when I think of the Romans as the Silver Age, I see that silver was more appropriate to her than gold.

She was really very beautiful, and it was a great pleasure to be with her, because she walked in such a lovely way. She moved quickly, but she somehow preserved that same immobility which, though she laughed and smiled so often, made her face cool like stone, and calm.

After this we went for many walks and picnics. Sometimes the girls came too, but sometimes we went together. We climbed the old battle hill, and she stood at the top looking all around at the orchards on the plain below.

I had meant to stay only a week, but I decided to stay a little longer, or, rather, I stayed on without thinking about it at all. I had not told my aunt and the girls that I was going at the end of the week, so it did not make any difference, and I knew they would expect me to stay longer. The only difference it made was to my holiday, and, after all, I was going for the holiday to enjoy myself, and I could not have been happier than I was there.

I remember how one night I went out by myself down in the direction of her house, where my steps always seemed to take me. When I reached the traveller's-nightshade it was growing dark. For a moment I looked towards her house and a flood of joy came into my soul, and I began to think how strange it was that, although I have met so many interesting people, I should come there simply by chance and meet her. I walked towards the entrance of a little wood, and, full of a profound joy and happiness, I walked in between the trees. I stayed there for a long time imagining her coming gaily into the wood where the moonlight shone through the branches. And I remember thinking suddenly how we have grown used to believing night to be a sad and melancholy time, not romantic and exciting as it used to be. I kept longing for some miracle to bring her there to me, but she did not come, and I had to go home.

Then, one evening, we all went to her house for music and conversation. On the way there Ruthie came round to my side and said: "Frederick, I have brought with me a song that I can sing, and I will sing this time if you want me to."

"Yes, I certainly want you to," I said, walking on with her. "I want to see how she teaches."

"Yes," said Ruthie. "You do see that I could not sing her songs, don't you?"

In the old days Ruthie and I used to get on very well, better than I got on with Jessica, who was inclined to keep us in order then, and I must say it was very difficult for her to do so.

When we got there, right at the beginning of the evening Gwyneth sang a little Welsh song. And I felt suddenly disappointed. I always thought that the Welsh were melancholy in their music, but if she sang it sadly at all it was with the gossipy sadness of the tea after a funeral. However, afterwards

31

we talked and I forgot the momentary impression.

During the evening Ruthie sang. She sang Brahms' *An die Nachtigall*, which was really very foolish of her, because I am sure it is not an easy thing to sing, with its melting softness and its sudden cries of ecstasy and despair. Her voice was very unsteady, of a deeper tone than Gwyneth's, and sometimes it became quite hoarse from nervousness.

Gwyneth drew her down to the sofa beside her. She laughed: "I told you nothing was sad enough for her."

Ruthie was quite pale from the ordeal of singing before us.

"It is rather difficult, isn't it?" I said.

"Yes," said Ruthie, flushing.

"Have you ever heard a nightingale?" asked Gwyneth of me.

"No," I said.

"Why, there is one in the wood across here; I have heard it myself," said Jessica. "On just such a night as this," she added, laughing, and looking out of the window at the darkness coming to lie on the tops of the apple trees beyond the green lawn.

"Ah! you must hear a nightingale as well as read Tourguéniev, you know," said Gwyneth.

I laughed.

But later on in the evening I was sitting near the piano looking over a pile of music by my side. Suddenly I came across Chopin's *Polnische Lieder*. It is not often that one finds them. I looked up in excitement and said: "Oh, do you know the *Polens' Grabgesang*? I implore you to sing it."

She laughed a little at my excitement and said: "Yes, I know it. But I can't sing it. It does not suit me at all. Mrs. Haslett, your nephew actually wants me to sing a funeral march."

"Oh, please do sing it!" I said. "I have only heard it once before in my life. Nobody ever sings it. I have been longing to hear it again."

"It does not belong to me you know," she said. "I found it here; it must have belonged to my father." She smiled at me over the edge of some music she was putting on the piano. "No, I can't sing it. That is really decisive."

I was so much excited about the song, because I shall never forget the occasion on which I first heard it. I have a great friend, a very wonderful man, a perfect genius, in fact, and a very strong personality, and we have evenings at his house, and we talk about nearly everything, and have music too, sometimes. Often, when I used to go, there was a woman there, who never spoke much but always sat near my friend. She was not particularly beautiful and had a rather unhappy face, but one evening my friend turned to her suddenly and put his hand on her shoulder and said, "Sing for us."

She obeyed without a word. Everybody obeys him at once. And she sang this song. I shall never forget all the sorrow and pity for the sorrows of Poland that she put into it. And the song, too, is wonderful. I do not think I have ever heard in my life anything so terribly moving as the part, "O Polen, mein Polen," which is repeated several times. Everyone in the room was stirred, and, after she had sung it, we talked about nothing but politics and the Revolution for the whole of the evening. I do not think she was Polish either. After a few more times she did not come to the evenings any more, and I have never had the opportunity of asking him about her. And although, as I said, she was not beautiful, when I looked at Gwyneth again it seemed to me that some of her beauty had gone, and I thought to myself quite angrily: "No, of course she could not sing that song. She would have been on the side of the conquerors!"

And I felt like this all the evening until we began to walk home. Before we had gone far Jessica said: "Wouldn't you like to stay and listen for the nightingale, Frederick? We can find our way home without you."

"Yes," I said. "Where can I hear her?"

"The best place", said Jessica, "is to sit on the fallen tree—that is where I heard it. Go into the wood by the wild-rose bush with pink roses on it. Do you know it?"

"Yes."

"Don't be very late," said my aunt.

"No," I answered, and left them.

I went into the little wood and sat down on the fallen tree looking up and waiting, but there was no sound. I felt that there was nothing I wanted so much as to hear her sad notes. I remember thinking how Nietzsche said that Brahms' melancholy was the melancholy of impotence, not of power, and I remember feeling that there was much truth in it when I thought of his *Nachtigall* and then of Keats. And I sat and waited for the song that came to

"*. . . the sad heart of Ruth, when, sick for home,*
She stood in tears amid the alien corn."

Suddenly I heard a sound, and, looking round, I saw Gwyneth coming through the trees. She caught sight of me and laughed.

"You are here too," she said. "I came to hear Jessica's nightingale."

"So did I," I said; "but I do not think she will sing to-night."

"It is a beautiful night," she said. "Anybody should want to sing on such a lovely night."

I took her back to her gate, and I said good night and closed the gate behind her. But, all the same, I shall remember always how beautiful she looked standing under the apple trees by the gate in the moonlight, her smile resting like the reflection of light on her carved face. Then, however, I walked home, feeling angry and annoyed with her; but of course that was foolish. Because it seems to me now that the world is made up of gay people and sad people, and however charming and beautiful the gay people are, their souls can never really meet the souls of those who are born for suffering and melancholy, simply because they are made in a different mould. Of course I see that this is a sort of dualism, but still it seems to me to be the truth, and I believe my friend, of whom I spoke, is a dualist, too, in some things.

I did not stay more than a day or two after this, though my aunt and the girls begged me to do so. I did not see Gwyneth again, only something took place which was a little ridiculous in the circumstances.

The evening before I went Ruthie came and said, half in an anxious whisper: "Frederick, will you do something very important for me?"

"Yes, if I can," I said. "What is it?"

"Well, it is Gwyneth's birthday to-morrow, and she is so rich it is hard to think of something to give her."

"Yes," I said, without much interest.

"But do you know what I thought of? I have bought an almond tree—the man has just left it out in the shed—and I am going to plant it at the edge of the lawn so that she will see it to-morrow morning. So it will have to be planted in the middle of the night, and I wondered if you would come and help me."

"But is it the right time of the year to plant an almond tree—in August?"

"I don't know," said Ruthie; "but surely the man in the nursery would have said if it were not. You can sleep in the train, you know. You used always to do things with me."

"All right, I will," I said, "only we need not go in the middle of the night—early in the morning will do, before it is quite light."

"Oh, thank you so much," said Ruthie, trembling with gratitude and excitement. "But don't tell anyone, will you—not even Jessica?"

"No," I said.

Exceedingly early in the morning, long before it was light, Ruthie came into my room in her dressing-gown to wake me, looking exactly as she used to do. We went quietly downstairs and through the wet grass to Gwyneth's house, Ruthie carrying the spade and I the tree. It was still rather dark when we reached there, but Ruthie had planned the exact place before.

We hurried with the work. I did the digging, and Ruthie stood with the tree in her hand looking up at the house. We hardly spoke.

Ruthie whispered: "We must be quiet. That is her window. She will be able to see it as soon as she looks out. She is asleep now."

"Look here," I said, "don't tell her that I planted it, because it may not grow. I can't see very well."

37

"Oh, but she must never know that either of us did it."

"But are you going to give her a present and never let her know who it is from?"

"Yes," said Ruthie.

"I think that is rather silly," I said.

Ruthie turned away.

We put the tree in. I have never heard whether it grew or not. Just as the sun was rising we walked back, and that morning I went away.

by

RHYS DAVIES

★

RESURRECTION
From *The Things Men Do*

Half a day before the lid was to be screwed down on her, Meg rose in her coffin and faintly asked for a glass of water. Her two sisters were bustling about the room, tidying and dusting and admiring the flowers, and both, after a few moments of terrified shock, looked at the recently deceased with a bitter anger. Once again she was doing something improper.

"Water!" stuttered Bertha. "Go on with you now, what you want with water?" Gathering strength at the sound of her own voice, she went on sternly and as if speaking to a nuisance: "Lie back there, lie back. Dead you are."

"Yes, indeed," breathed Ellen, "dead these four days, and the mourning ordered."

Meg, nice in a new shiny white satin nightdress, trimmed with lace, stared back. But her gaze still had something of the marbled hardness of the dead. There seemed an awful weariness in the hang of her

39

head. Her shoulders gave little clutching jumps. Suddenly she lay back in her coffin, sighing, and without further speech.

"Ha!" cried Bertha in relief, "a bit of life there was left in her nerves and made her body rise up like that. Funny thing! Just like some chickens run round the yard after you've chopped off their heads." She sat down and her face was eased again. "But a nasty turn it gave me, Ellen. Just like her it would have been, to do a trick on us, making us spend money on mourning and that five-guinea coffin."

"Yes, indeed," cried Ellen, her face still very grey from retreating hysteria, but relieved too, "and eighty-five coming to the funeral to-morrow and an announcement in the newspaper." She turned her head away from the coffin. "A fine disgrace it would have been for us."

And both sisters thought of the hours that must elapse before the undertaker arrived that afternoon to shut up the coffin safely. Meg might rise again and frighten them with a bit of second-hand life. Why, the next time something awful might happen—perhaps she would be jolted back entirely into the land of the living.

"He won't come till five o'clock," said Bertha. "He's busy burying Samson Lewis this afternoon."

"Can't we screw the lid down ourselves?" Ellen quavered. "Not right is it for us to have shocks like this. My heart's going pit-a-pat."

40

"Talk there might be if we shut her up before the time arranged," Bertha answered, shaking her head. "People will say we was in a hurry. You know", she reminded her sister, "that two or three are coming at tea-time to mourn with us while the job is being done."

"Oh!" exclaimed Ellen, remembering at this, "I didn't buy the cold ham at the shop this morning."

"Sardines", said Bertha definitely, reverting to a debate of that morning, "will be enough, I tell you again. On toast. You can't give cold ham to-day *and* to-morrow."

"When Ceinwen Roberts was buried", Ellen, who was not quite so mean as Bertha, remarked, "they had baron of beef, leg of pork and veal pie. *One* meat is not enough for to-morrow, Bertha. Those there are who don't like cold ham."

"Then the tinned salmon they must have," Bertha grumbled. "Haven't we spent enough on clothes! Twelve pounds fifteen in the draper's. No one can say we've stinted decent burial for her."

"Most of it", said Ellen, with sudden sisterly sourness, "on our backs." Occasionally the sisters quarrelled.

"If *we* had died," Bertha brooded, "as cheap as possible *she'd* have put us away."

"Well," Ellen said, in the manner of one generously overlooking a fault, "she was never a one to enjoy a funeral."

41

"No," continued Bertha with a surprising depth of bitterness, "men and whisky was *her* bent."

"Hush, Bertha, hush. So many years ago that was."

"Ha, craving she had for them always. If she hadn't been obliged to take to her bed and lie there helpless, she'd have been out in the world disgracing herself and us to her dying day."

"Well," soothed Ellen, "safe she is now."

But they both glanced apprehensively towards the coffin. Bleak and raddled and wintry, the sisters, who were in the fifties, pursed their lips. They were twins. Both wore a piled-up mass of coarse dour hair in which were jabbed small combs and tortoiseshell prongs. Their faces were tuckered-in, secretive and proud. In chapel and street they liked to swank; they liked people to think they were well-off and to treat them with ceremony. They were daughters of a semi-successful builder, and in a hole behind some loose bricks in the cellar was the money he had made, for he had trusted no bank: his daughters thought like-wise. A widower, he had died five years ago and since then no event of importance had happened to the twins. But now the maladies of their younger sister Meg had culminated in a death too long delayed. They had looked on her as their cross. But they told themselves that they loved her, and indeed sometimes they had brought her a baked apple with clotted cream, her favourite, and showed affection. On the

42

day she had lain back and stiffened, they thought it was for the best, all things considered. They began to fluff and preen themselves, for death is important and brings ceremony, display and a great going out into public.

"She", Ellen had wept at intervals, "wasn't bad now and again, our poor Meg. After all, she didn't ought to have gone so young."

"No," agreed Bertha, who at intervals had been gloomy too, "she didn't ought to have gone before she tried to tidy up her life a bit. But now it's happened——"

"Yes," said Ellen, "yes indeed."

And after an hour or so of indulgence in the magic of grief they would bestir themselves, realizing that a rare opportunity had come to them. Like royalty they would ride in a procession for two miles to the cemetery; at every corner between the rows of houses knots of people would be gathered, craning their heads to see.

And then again it seemed they were to be thwarted. An hour or so later in that afternoon Meg sat up once more and peered round with dreadful stare, her white lips pulled back and showing her naked gums—for the sisters had removed her ten-guinea set of false teeth. And again she murmured for water. Ellen was alone in the room, Bertha having gone downstairs to prepare the food for the visitors; and realizing this time that something remarkable had happened to the

43

deceased, she tottered to the door and shrieked for her sister. Bertha came bustling upstairs, a half-cut loaf still clutched in her hand. "What now, what now?" she demanded, her suspicious fury ready.

"Come back again she has, asking for water," moaned Ellen. And she added despairingly: "Not dead at all is she."

"Rubbish now, rubbish." Bertha stood in the doorway like a snorting roused mare. "Hasn't the doctor signed the certificate! Dead he said she was." But there, undoubtedly, was the starkly upraised Meg, now looking round with vague and pathetic appeal. "But if not dead she is," breathed Bertha further, "damages the doctor will have to pay us. Close on twenty pounds," she suddenly screamed in shrill hysteria towards the menacing body, "have we spent on you."

The sisters advanced together towards the coffin, creeping, but angry now.

"Lie back." Ellen also began shouting in the wrath of despair, "lie back. Your funeral is to-morrow. At half-past two. Eighty-five are coming."

Bertha laid her hand restrainingly on Ellen's bristling arm. She began to speak in a cunningly entreating voice, coaxing: "Go you back, Meg, only half alive you'll be indeed if you don't. Not fit to live you are with your bladder and kidneys. And what if we go before you, who'll look after you then! The workhouse it'll be. Not worth living is life, Meg fach. A dirty business it is. Black is the future. Go you now, please, and follow soon we will, true enough. Better company in the other world than in this."

"Five guineas for your coffin alone!" Ellen took the coaxing cue from her sister, but added a whine to her voice. "Look you how lovely it is. Polished oak. Die now, there's a nice girl, die now."

But Meg's whitish eyes were fixed on the loaf of bread that was clutched in Bertha's hand: their dullness passed into a greedy gleam.

"Bread," she mumbled, "bread." And with a pleased sigh she eagerly stretched forth her trembling hands.

Wholly convinced at last, the sisters cried out in fury and horror. The clamour brought neighbours running into the house. The foaming and stuttering twins were attended to by sympathetic women while others stood in awe round the coffin. None attempted to lift the weak Meg out of her coffin or supply her with the refreshment she craved. Mrs. Williams, a strident and dominant woman, took charge and declared that a policeman must be informed before anything could be done. After some delay P.C. Johns appeared downstairs and in a stern disapproving voice asked:

"What's this I hear about a corpse coming to life, Bertha Evans?"

"It's upstairs," quavered Bertha. But at sight of the policeman she began to bounce back into energy, aware of the drama that was being offered her.

The policeman tramped heavily upstairs. Ellen had recovered some while before and was repeating over and over again how Meg had sat up twice. Exhausted with her futile demands for refreshment, Meg was now lying back amid the pleated mauve satin folds. There was no doubt, however, that life was flushing back into her features. The policeman gazed at her in the suspicious and convicting manner of his kind. At sight of him Meg gave a slight whimper, as if frightened. At one time in her young and gay days she had been arrested for drunkenness.

"A doctor must see her," declared P.C. Johns, after ten minutes' cogitation. "Nothing for me is there here." And sullenly he went away.

After further delay and searching the doctor was found. It was now late evening and still Meg had not been removed from the coffin. As the news spread, people kept on trooping into the house from near and far. Bertha and Ellen, recovered, were the centre of much enquiry. Sympathy was lavished on them. What would be done with the black clothes now, and the coffin? And no ride to the cemetery to-morrow. Someone suggested that they should take a week at the seaside as recompense. Doctor Miskin himself, befuddled with whisky as usual, glared at Meg so angrily that onlookers thought he was going to strike her. For a few moments he would not believe that she was living; he roughly pushed one of her already blinking eyelids up and down, prodded her, and spitefully gripped her limp wrist. Finally he declared her living, told Bertha that in England such things often happened, and left instructions that Meg was to receive only milk and water for three days: he spoke as if she deserved such punishment. Bertha looked back at him malevolently:

"Dead you said she was and signed certificate. Damages I ask you. What we've spent on mourning and the oak coffin. The food for the funeral tea to-morrow I leave out."

The doctor spat and left the house. Bertha and Ellen began to weep in rage; several women loosened their tears too, in sympathy. The undertaker, sweating in his haste, arrived and declared that contract had been made for the funeral to-morrow—he would keep it and at two o'clock the hearse and carriages would be outside the house: no business of his was it if the corpse was not in the coffin. He was very agitated and spoke wildly: trade had been bad all the winter. Bertha and Ellen, already incensed by the doctor, screamed and threatened until he went flying down the stairs. At the front door he turned and shouted back:

"On your hands the coffin will be. However. Made for you it was and I will not take it back now."

Bertha and Ellen had to admit defeat. A neighbour consoled them by saying that the coffin could be kept under a bed until required and would make a good cupboard for blankets and such-like.

Then once again Meg rose stark from her narrow bed and began whimpering:

"A bit of brandy," she begged. "And give me my teeth back, please, now."

Bertha and Ellen looked at each other numbly. The teeth had already been sold to the pawnbroker, but this they did not want to admit before the neighbours. They went over to their sister and lay her back in the coffin.

"Hush now, Meg fach. Rest, be quiet, take time. The pump in your heart is not working proper yet. Soon it will be."

"My teeth," whispered Meg, "give me my teeth ——"

The twins were saved further explanation by the arrival of a reporter from the newspaper, Tommy Thomas, a brisk young man. After glancing at Meg, he took out his notebook and asked for particulars.

Bertha and Ellen began speaking together. Excitement shone from their eyes now. Never had they been in the newspapers. When Tommy asked for a photograph of Meg, Bertha declared flatly:

"No photo is there of her. But one of Ellen and myself I will give you: taken in Swansea."

Tommy sucked his pencil. He asked the sisters if they had any special comment to make on the event.

Bertha's sense of grievance again got the upper hand
and she answered bitterly:

"Yes indeed. This now. What she want to come
back for? A fathead she was always. In life night-
mares she was always having. Peace she had a chance
of. Back she is now, the fool, where a lot of worries
bite at her like a plague of evil rats. Fathead twice
over. That put in your paper, young man, and let a
bit of truth be told for once. Now then, Ellen, fetch
you the photo."

In her coffin Meg still whimpered, as if in weary
distress. When all the visitors had gone, weakly she
managed to lift her head yet again. She asked to be
taken out of the coffin. The twins pursed their lips:
both, now that the excitement of the drama was over,
felt flat, as if something had been filched from them.
Ellen looked dangerously vexed. Bertha approached
the coffin and said maliciously:

"What for you want to get out! Not many people
is it get a chance to spend a night in a coffin. Comfortable it is surely? Clean and dry as the inside of a
nut. You stay there, Meg. Stripped your bed is, and
no sheets aired. And too weak you are to be shifted.
Yes indeed. To-morrow we'll lift you out, yes, perhaps. Settle down now and rest. . . ."

by

KATE ROBERTS
Translated from the Welsh by DAFYDD JENKINS

*

A SUMMER DAY

We were sitting, we three girls, on a stone wall outside a farmhouse, drinking milk. I am not fond of milk, but I can drink it on a hot day after walking for a long time, not because it quenches thirst, but because it is one of the things that go with walking in the country on a hot day. To see it conveys something of the cool atmosphere of a dairy. And so it was with this milk; we became a little cooler as we drank, though its flat taste made us more thirsty. The farmhouse had a cool look; it was newly white-washed, and there had been no rain to wash away the spots of white-wash which had fallen at the foot of the walls. The house looked quiet and calm as newly white-washed houses do. The people of the house were sitting near the door with their hands folded; they had the quiet look of people overpowered by the first sudden heat of summer. The garden too showed signs of spring-cleaning; the potatoes newly banked up, and the dark fresh earth which had been below

50

the surface showing now, with a strip of the old dry light-coloured earth to be seen here and there. There was neatness in the straight furrow and in the level beds of onions. The young gooseberries hung on the bushes like hundreds of little teats.

Refreshed after drinking the milk, we set off again on our journey; from the porch the farmer's wife looked at us going, with her hand shading her eyes, and a look on her face that said "I'd rather you were walking than I".

Outside the gate there was a stagnant pond; in it some ducks and a sow and piglets were enjoying themselves immensely. The sow was up to her belly in mud, and no swimmer in the sea ever looked happier. Some geese were feeding at the edge of the pond; they stretched out their necks after us. Then came a voice from somewhere behind the house, crying "chick, chick, chick", and fowls without number and geese and ducks and pigs rose up and ran to answer the call like a crowd of townspeople running to a fight. We stood astonished at the power of words to move animals.

We went on along the cart-track over the shoulder of the hill. An occasional stream ran between white sandy banks across our path, and many times we knelt to drink the cold water from our hands. Then we washed our hands with the gravel, so as to make them feel soft.

We came to a clearing under the shadow of the

trees, and lay down on the grass. To a casual glance, the world around us looked as though it were autumn; the young leaves of some of the trees were greenish yellow, and last year's dead bracken lay there, thick and brown. But a second look showed us the young bracken beginning to grow, grey-green in colour, with the tops of the shoots curling towards the ground. But it was no time for looking at things minutely, as we lay there on our backs like that. We saw everything with lazy eyes; so everything looked like one thing, and not like separate things. On the birch trees there were little leaves, grey on the under-side; but to us they looked like snow on the trees. The rim of the sky was far off, too far off for us to think of it for long without losing our senses; its colour was that blue you have so often wanted to have in a frock, but in vain. It was as though there were three rings of mountains about us, their black colour paling to a feeble grey on the horizon. We lay there literally warming ourselves in the sun. We gave our bodies, which had been shrinking in knitted coats throughout the winter, to that god. Uncomplaining, we let his rays fall on our faces. From the distance came the unbroken sound of waterfalls, a far-off, soft sound. But not indeed an unbroken sound; for our hearing would deceive us again. The sound seemed to stop with a gasp, and then to go on as before. The sound sent us to sleep. The three of us awoke with a single thought—tea.

We went down to the village. There was no tea-shop there; but as we always did, we decided to knock at the door of some house and ask them to make tea for us. There were not many people at home, for it was a holiday. We saw an open door, and made for it although that house had been our goal since we set it in the morning. A magnificent woman came to the door. A big rosy woman, with black eyes and hair. Her hair was tied in a knot on the top of her head. She must have been a beautiful woman when she was slighter. She was wearing high stays which drove her breast almost up to her chin. She had on a clean blouse with a high collar; the blouse was too small for her in every direction, and it made us feel better than we were. There was a certain cheerfulness about her and her house. She had a kind, open face and she granted our request.

"Yes, of course, in a minute, as soon as the kettle boils."

We went into the house and sat down. Soon our eyes became accustomed to furniture instead of the trees and sky. The furniture was full of china, inside and out; there was hardly a square inch that had not some piece of china or other; and the surprising thing was that there was no dust there, and that everything was shining. There was a fire, with a lot of bright fire-irons around it. The fire had decayed into a pile of black lumps, with white dust along their edges, in the heat of the sun. Sitting beside the

fire in an arm-chair was a young boy of about eighteen or twenty. It was some time before we saw him;
for it took a little while for our eyes to get used to
objects under the big chimney. My first feeling was
surprise at seeing a young man sleeping by the fire
in a hot kitchen on a holiday. Then came curiosy,
the curiosity of a person waiting for tea, and without
anything better to do. What sort of boy was this?
What sort of eyes had he, if he were to open them?
Was he intelligent? What if he were to wake up, and
to prove to be feeble-minded? How awkward it
would be!

The woman was moving about busily, and there
came to me the happiness that you feel in the sound
of china when you want your tea badly. She put
clean cloth on the table, and smoothed the f
down with her hand; the cloth made a sound
was harsh to the ear. And at the same time t
came from the woman a question that I never
hearing:

"And where do you come from, if I may mal
bold as to ask?" Whenever I hear the question
myself I will tell a lie when I answer; and every
I am asked, I am caught so much without war
that the truth is out before I have time to think
suitable lie.

"From B——" said I.

"Heavens!" said the woman, opening her
and showing unusual interest, "that's the name

been spoken oftenest in this house for a month now."
A shadow crossed her brow. "Do you know Miss
Jones from B—— who's a barmaid at the 'Three
Funnels'?"

"No indeed."

Without looking at the boy asleep in the chair, but
giving her head a certain scornful shake in his direction, she said:

"*He's* got married to that barmaid at the 'Three
Funnels'. He *has* done a pretty trick. He got the girl
into trouble, and he married her three weeks ago;
and he hasn't been near her since, and she hasn't
been near him either. And he doesn't mean to go
near her again ever, says he."

I turned my head unconsciously towards the boy.
I could not turn back, once I had begun to look at
him. He was still sleeping. I noticed his mouth and
jaw. They were very weak. It was a flabby, slack,
wet, dribbling mouth. His face had an innocent look,
but I thought to myself that a rake could look innocent in sleep. "I wish he'd wake up," I said to myself,
"so that I could see his eyes. Perhaps his face is
strong when he's awake. The eyes make so much
difference."

His mother was going on:

"He was eighteen last November, and his pay's a
pound a week. How he thought he was going to keep
a barmaid on a pound I do not know. But he didn't
mean to marry her. He didn't know her six months

ago. But he began to go pub-crawling with people older than himself, and this is the result."

She sighed.

"Why the boy couldn't see the value of a home I do not know. He's brought great sorrow on this house. We're respectable people, you know, and his father's an elder in the chapel. Since this business happened, his father and he haven't spoken a word to each other. And I have to live with the two of them and try to keep the peace."

She looked at her son sadly, and with more tenderness she said:

"Here he is to-day, moving here from one chair to the other without washing himself or putting a collar on, instead of going to the ploughing match with the boys as he did a year ago. The wenches have come to something indeed, they don't think of anything but how to trap innocent lads."

For the life of me I could not take my eyes off the boy. I wanted him to wake up, so that I could see what sort of boy he was. Was he as innocent as his mother wanted to make out? Perhaps he had a rake's eyes.

But what if he were to open his eyes and hear his mother talking to strangers about him? And I was the only one who understood his mother, for my two friends were English. To all intents and purposes, there were three deaf and dumb people in the room.

I do not know how long the mother would have

gone on if I had stayed to listen. To me, the house was quite different from what it was when we went in. Then, it was a bright house full of china. It was a heavy house by now.

As I turned to the porch, I turned my head to look again at the boy and his flabby mouth. He was still sleeping on. I hoped he would wake up.

I thought for a moment he was going to wake up. No, he turned over on his side, sighed, and slept on. When we went out, we heard the sound of the waterfalls again. The pavement was white in the sunlight, and the burning stones dazzled us. I turned my head back again, and saw the mother looking after us with a dazed and dreamy look upon her face.

by

SIAN EVANS

*

DAVIS

Fred Davis opened the back door and spat on the manure heap thrown up against the kitchen wall.

"It's no use following me about," he called into the hollow of the passage. "Nagging night and day, it ain't my fault, damn you."

He sighed heavily; his fat, sullen face sagged over a dirty, white rag tied round his throat in lieu of a collar, his hands picked at the edges of his pockets; his hair, yellow and plentiful, hung in tags over a flat red brow.

A shrill voice answered like an echo. "That's what you always say, you're lazy *and* you know it. Just look at the garden."

Voice and wife approached through the shadows; a woman thrust her face over the man's shoulder, at the same time pointing with a bony arm so that the fingers only appeared round the lintel of the door.

"Call that a garden, look at that hedge, I'd be ashamed to see my wife doing all the work."

Davis shook himself and turning round, muttered an oath.

"You clear off, leave me alone, can't you?"

His wife now stood on the weedy path from which vantage point she poured forth a string of invective and abuse.

"What's happening to us? Bills, no money, no beasts, the place rotting over our heads. Oh you lazy pig, I wish to God I'd never married you. Too idle to mend the hedge or move the horse manure from off the path. God, the place is worse than a slum and *yet* you won't do anything. I can't even find any vegetables to cook but have to buy what I want. Look at all this garden, wasted, while you lean about all day. It makes me sick. I'm through."

Her voice rose to a shriek, cracked and was silent.

Davis started to shamble off towards the pigsties, standing at the far end of the path.

"You drive me crazy," he mumbled. "My life's hell."

His wife tore at her hair as though with one frantic gesture to release all her bitterness.

"Hell, that's your destination all right, this ain't a patch on what God'll make you suffer in the world to come."

She turned and disappeared into the house, slamming the door behind her. Davis leaned on the pigsty wall.

He noticed the cracks in the bricks and how the rotten gate swung from one hinge only.

Moss grew like slime on the walls, the roof leaked, stale pig manure and straw sprouting grass littered the floor.

Again he sighed and the sound seemed ominous as though by his own breath he stood accused.

God, he was tired. Couldn't she see what an added burden it was to think?

Of course she could, the bitch, that's why she kept goading him. Facing him with his demon till his hands were at his own throat.

He groaned; only with an effort could he bring himself to look at the house.

What had happened? The place was going to ruin.

He remembered how it had looked before his father, old Davis, died. White walls, clean paint, plants in the windows, thick doors fitting without the tremor of a draught, flower-beds under the windows, vegetables in neatly dug patches, pigsties with proper roofs.

The yard, too, looked different, in those days a gate divided the cowsheds, stable and ricks from the open patch in front of the house; now yard and garden mingled in a puddly mess of straw, rotten stumps of cabbage and manure.

It had been a prosperous enough place.

Well, something had happened, that was all. A gradual decay.

The garden full of weeds, that large hole in the hedge that made his wife so angry, the patch of horse manure in the middle of the path left when the horse broke in and finished the last of the vegetables, the cracking doors tied together with string.

The yard, unkempt as the garden, standing deserted save for a scraggy horse pulling out tufts of hay from the two remaining ricks, hens scratching in the flower-beds, turning over old tins, cans and putrid scraps.

Yes, something had happened.

Davis made up his mind to remove the horse manure so that his wife shouldn't see it and scream at him every time she came to the door. He pulled out a cigarette and while he stood smoking watched the sun disappear beneath the rim of the fields.

Another day gone, too late to do anything now. To-morrow he'd tidy up the place and mend the hedge.

For a moment his heart seemed to lift in his side, his mind sprang lightly towards the future.

He'd get everything straight, he'd start work seriously.

Again his wife appeared at the door; a lighted candle burned in the passage throwing a beam that revealed her shape and her thin, attenuated arms waving like feelers towards the yard.

"Really!" she screamed, emphasizing each word with a fresh gesture. "Can't you see that horse eating it's head off in the yard? Anyone would think we'd got a dozen ricks to waste. Why don't you put it in the stable or shut it in the field? You've been standing out there for nearly an hour. I warn you, I've had about enough."

Davis looked at her, at her small body that even when still appeared possessed by a demon of energy, at her hands rapidly unwrapping a scrap of bandage from round her wrist and her face moving round words that poured from her lips in an endless stream.

"Why can't you do your share? Are you ill or what? You don't care about anything, no pride . . . no nothing."

He bellowed suddenly in a voice choking with anger. "It's your bloody tongue, you take the relish out of anything, work or pleasure. I'm going out, you've driven me out. You do everything yourself then you can't complain, you always know best, nothing I do's right, you make a man mad." He turned his back on her, setting off towards the road in a great hurry. His blood beat in his temples like pistons, he clutched at his chest uneasily. All this noise and excitement day in, day out, supposing he had a heart attack?

The thought made him feel sickish. When he had turned a corner in the lane he sat down on the roadside and held his head in his hands. No man could stand it.

A great depression fell on him. He kept asking

himself questions although the answers tormented him.

"What shall I do?"

"Work," came the reply like a stone hurled at his head.

"What's the use?"

"Do you want to die then?"

"No by God!"

"If everything rots over your head how will you live?"

"I don't know, something'll happen."

"No it won't."

He began to groan and mumble out loud.

"Things aren't so bad, I'll soon pull them round. I've seen many worse places about."

Then he heard his wife's voice: "You're lazy . . . bone lazy."

He jumped to his feet. "That's a lie, a damned lie. Nobody but a bitch would say a thing like that."

He stopped shouting as suddenly as he had commenced.

It was nearly dark, a light mist covered the surrounding fields, standing back the hills were black against a thickening sky. It looked like rain.

Davis turned and stared at the bank where he had been sitting. A distinct patch where the grass lay flattened revealed the spot.

He looked at it with surprise. "I'm going dotty, anyone would think I'd been drinking. . . ."

63

He walked about for some time unable to make up his mind to go down to "The Angel" for a pint. At last he made for home.

He remembered angrily that he had forgotten to milk the cows.

Never mind, it wouldn't be the first time, they'd have to wait a bit.

When he reached home his wife was washing the milking pails in the back kitchen.

He poked his head round the door but she kept her head obstinately turned from him. Her tightly compressed lips showed that her silence was the silence of anger and contempt.

He returned to the kitchen and sat warming his feet by the fire. Presently he slept.

His wife woke him. "Your supper's ready."

It was late, nearly nine o'clock; he sat up with a start.

"All right, you needn't pretend to be surprised it's so late. You needn't say: 'Why didn't you remind me about the cows', because you knew all along I'd do it like I always do."

The woman set his plate down as she spoke. There were two red spots burning in her cheeks.

She polished the forks on a cloth and then they started to eat. Neither spoke. While she was making the tea Davis watched his wife sulkily, pulling at his hair with his hands and watching her every movement through half-closed eyes.

As soon as the meal was over she hurried out to the sink and started to wash up.

That night Davis couldn't sleep but lay on his back staring at the chink of light showing through the bedroom window.

Outside he could hear the rustle of rain mixed with the lifting and falling of branches blowing in the wind.

If only with one sweep of his hand he could put everything right, if only from nothing wealth rose up like a thing solid to the touch, a thing one could snatch without effort and keep locked behind doors while one slept, ate, idled. . . .

His thoughts drifted; he stirred and looked at his wife lying straight and stark beside him; the pallor of her face divided her from the surrounding gloom, her dark hair, braided in two plaits hung outside the bedclothes.

He felt a dim desire, which, as his thoughts lingered grew in urgency; he leaned over and touched her with his hands. "Mary, let's be friends for God's sake."

As though through her sleep she had realized his passion, she at once drew away and answered harshly: "It's useless, quite useless, we can't go on like this."

He seized her arm and ran his fingers up to her bare shoulders; he could feel the blood beating slowly under his touch. There was a clanging in his veins, all his senses seemed gathering for a final revelation; everything was hastening, hastening. . . .

He muttered thickly. "I'm sorry, Mary, don't be hard; I've thought it all out how I'll start to-morrow; I'll mend the hedge, tidy the garden, in a week I'll get the place straight, honest to God I will."

His hands enclosed her breast, dimly he heard her cry. "It's no good . . . no good."

The lace curtains rustled, swept the fringe of the bed then lay with a shudder, flat against the window.

Davis swore slowly, half asleep. "I swear it, just you see in the morning."

His wife answered with a kind of wild intensity. "I don't mean to be hard. I try to believe in you but you make me so bitter."

Her voice broke; Davis fell asleep to the sound of her crying.

He awoke and at once he was depressed.

Daylight filtered through the window, it fell on the bed, wide, flat and tousled, on the white counterpane dipping to the floor, on peeling wallpaper and the washbasin half full of dirty water, standing in the far corner of the room.

He yawned and closed his eyes. Why did the days come on him like a burden?

Downstairs he could hear his wife lighting the fire.

What had he said last night? Something about lighting the fire himself. Well, anyway it was too late now.

With a groan he remembered other promises. He

66

closed his eyes; the warmth in the bed was like the heat from burning logs.

He heard his wife calling out that breakfast was ready. He must have slept again. He turned the clock with it's face to the wall and again shut his eyes. His limbs felt like logs.

Drowsily he heard the cows passing under the window on their way to the cowsheds, their feet splashed in the mud, splash, splash, splash.

"Another minute," he started to count slowly. Nearly sixty. What a fool he was to set a limit on time.

Rain ran down the windows and danced in bubbles on the aerial. One, two, three, no man could work in such weather.

Words ran in fragments to the tune of falling rain, they passed through his head and the pulsing of his blood set a rhythm to utterance. "Lazy, bone lazy, one, two, three. What were words?"

He buried his face deeper into the pillows. Once more he slept.

by

GERAINT GOODWIN

★

JANET IFANS' DONKEY

He heard the heavy steps crunch up the gravel drive. It was the Sergeant coming with the summonses—he always came about this time. The Sergeant would leave him in peace at his dinner, and give him time for his cigar and then come in, very deferential, as clumsy as a horse in his hobnail boots, carrying his helmet under his arm like a bowl.

He cocked his ear to listen, though he knew the step. Yes, the Sergeant had gone round to the side door as was his wont: there would be a bit of chaff with the housekeeper and then the solid, measured step down the corridor.

He pushed the things nearest him away, clearing the end of the table, and felt in his fob for his fountain pen. Then he shouted "come in" in a mixture of pleasantness and irritation.

The Sergeant took his seat beside the fire and spread his hands out over his knees. He was a big man, coarse cut, with a big, florid face and a moustache like a brush, which he kept swiping with his hand. He was very Welsh.

68

The little man raised his lack-lustre eyes in inquiry. He was never sure that the Sergeant was not laughing at him in some way. That was why he made such a show of authority. He was always glad when it was all over, when he had affixed "Thomas Williamson", in his neat, business-like hand, at the bottom of these blue documents, and the Sergeant had gathered them up again like shares, and tied them up with the bit of string he kept twiddling about in his hand. There were other magistrates who could have done it just as well, he told himself, and yet the Sergeant came to him night after night. And that was not because he was chairman of the Bench, but because his house was nearest the police station; he knew that perfectly well: and he had a good idea that the Sergeant knew that he knew, in spite of his dumb show of deference.

"That all?" looking up, at the last summons.

"Yes, sirr."

The Sergeant had his eyes on the decanter on the table, and, although he felt that it ought not to become a habit, he poured him out a glass. He always did.

"There is just *wan* thing, sirr. . . ."

"Yes: yes?" he broke in irritably. He was not irritable; he was very pleased with himself, and with the day, but he wanted to show the Sergeant that he could not be trifled with and that his time was precious.

69

"About old Janet Ifans," he went on. He brought a big hand backways across his moustache, gave a heavy sigh, and then bent the glass back over his nose.

"What!" said the little man, bristling.

"No—nothing, sirr. Nothing like that. Dead sirr—yess, yess. All over now, sirr."

"And . . . what has that to do with me?" he asked tartly.

He was not sure the Sergeant was not laughing at him. He looked uneasily into those thin, clear blue eyes in the florid face around them: they gave nothing away.

"No, sirr. Quite, sirr," he broke in hurriedly. "I understand, sirr."

He had given himself away in spite of all. And he knew at once. He took another gulp at the port and swiped his moustaches as was his way when no words came.

The little man got up and walked to the big bay window, his back turned.

"Perhaps you had better explain," he added drily.

"Not her, sirr. It's that bad old donkey—*ach y fi*. You don't mind me saying, sirr?"

"What *is* it?" he turned from the window. He was beside himself.

"Don't mind me saying, sirr?"

"Sergeant! *Please*. Will you please make yourself plain?"

"Yess, sirr." He began at the beginning again. He looked down at his feet and stroked his moustache.

"The old woman go, sirr." He waved his hand up briefly and then wagged his head. "Time too! Time for donkey too—but he very much alive. P.C. Jenkins go up there—go to shed. *Iesu mawr*—he kick. He try again. Eks-cuse me, sirr—he bite him in the backside. P.C. Jenkins come out."

"Well?" said the little man, fuming.

"P.C. Jenkins—fery kind man. He throw in carrots."

"What *do* you mean?" said the little man, very white.

"Well, sirr. What we do now? More carrots: then after, more carrots. From where? Policeman's allotments! How long? Ten, twenty years maybe. He a naughty donkey, sirr—he live for ever."

"Sergeant," he said, dropping his voice and wagging his head in his hurt. "Really, Sergeant, I *must* ask. . . ."

"Two things," said the Sergeant, forced to the point. "He live: he die. He live—where? He die—how?"

"I am afraid I have not the *slightest* idea of what you are talking about," said the little magistrate, turning round to the light. He had set his face in his prim way, the smooth, round, little face like a white apple, with a hurt, petulant, little mouth and eyes wide and anxious, with blue rings round them like a macaw's. They called him Tommy Titt in the town, because of his sprightly little walk: when he had his hands in his trouser pockets and sent the tails of his frock-coat out he looked like a tit, and when he was excited his voice went up high and shrill in a titter. He was an Englishman, and very wealthy, and they liked him more than most Englishmen, but he was sure they were always laughing at him. But then these Welsh people were altogether. . . .

"Not the *slightest*," he said again, shooting his hands out.

"All right, sirr," said the Sergeant with a final nod, as he fumbled with the summonses. "The old devil goes home to-morrow—to be sure."

The little man raised his eyebrows in question. And the Sergeant rubbed his nose pensively and moved his feet about.

"A dirty job, sirr—*ach y fi*. How would you be getting a human killer up again him, sirr? No, sirr. We got to pop a shotgun through the window."

"No, no, no," broke in the little man, raising his hands in horror.

"I was thinking, sirr? . . ."

"Yes, yes?" he said in his exasperation.

"As perhaps a home might be found."

"No doubt. We will see." He nodded his head grimly. "Is that all?" he asked.

"That's all, sirr." The Sergeant made a great show of going.

"A poor old soul, sirr. No harm in her, like."

"Yes, yes," he said, hurrying him out in his anxiety.

"A bit of a character, if you understand, sirr."

"Yes, yes," he said again, waving his hands in his hurry.

"You remember, sirr? . . ."

"Yes. Perfectly. Perfectly," he said and went on saying "perfectly, perfectly" as he strutted down the corridor. "I will see what can be done. Come back later." He only wanted to cut the Sergeant short, to get him out of the house.

The Sergeant was laughing at him: they were all laughing at him. He came back into the dining-room, his little white face strained and his eyes popping in his anger. No doubt the Sergeant had had his joke in the kitchen already. He was being laughed at in his own house. A vulgar, obscene old woman had dogged him ever since that time—ten years before— would always dog him.

He went over to the decanter for another glass of the old port. But he drank it at a gulp, not as he was wont to do in his happy, mellow, after-dinner mood, a sip at a time and a heavy sigh. He was very proud of the port, proud of his judgment in it; he was proud of the house, of the layout of the gardens, of the shrubberies: he was proud of everything he saw—if he were only left to himself.

It was these outside things, like the visit of the

Sergeant and this talk about the old woman, these things beyond him like the noises "off" in a theatre, that upset him and left him bewildered. Life could be so very easy and pleasant—the old room, frayed and mellow, and the De Wint that he had picked up at a Shrewsbury auction: the glow of the fire and the book he had and the cigar waiting him, and a few details of the day's business which drifted across his mind quietly and placidly like the cigar smoke. Everything was so easy and comfortable as he liked it to be—as it ought to be—if one could only shut the door, shut out the outside. But then one had to do one's duty: that ominous word, duty, frightened him. He would not be without his sense of duty but the thought of it frightened him. Why all these foolish things happened he did not know—but they did happen, and they kept on happening.

He walked over to pull the bell-cord in his agitation, but his hand stopped in the act. He did not want that woman laughing at him: they had probably had a good giggle below stairs. And here was he, a Justice of the Peace, and the wealthiest man in the town —yet a donkey could do this for him! It was absurd, he told himself—absurd. He walked about the room, his hands on his belly, saying absurd, absurd, many times over.

And then, as his mind went jumping about, he thought of her as he was bound to do. Things were better as they were, he told himself. They would never have got on together: it was just as well that they never tried.

But he had the image of her now—the clear, flame-like beauty of her, and the laughing impudent eyes. She had gone through his life like a shooting star—a divinity that had brushed him with its wings. It was all so bewildering—it was all over before it started. It had never really happened. And, as he knew now, it could *not* have happened. She was not for him. But supposing . . . supposing—he kept turning it over in his own mind.

Supposing there had been no donkey, no vulgar old woman in the police court that day? She would have been here, a part of him, have come into his life, have broken it and irradiated it, like the colours on a spectrum. That bright bewildering life—the life that might have been—frightened him and then excited him. But he wanted to feel that it could not have been, and he was sure that it could not have been.

There would have been no beginning and no end to that life: and he liked a beginning and he liked an end. All his life he had liked to know just where things were: and with her there was no knowing where things were—the sight of her, the sound of her laughter, was enough to send everything into a tumble.

"No, no," he said out loud, wagging his head backwards and forwards. It would not do: it could not do. He went over to the sideboard for his cigar and bit the end off viciously, and then spat it into the fire. He looked for his book on some Assyrian excavations and then threw it down again: he did not feel like reading.

He had turned fifty now, and he was a bachelor. But he had always been a bachelor—then, when he might have married. He had been born a bachelor, and would die a bachelor, and he did not really care so very much. At that time he was forty—it was ten years ago—and he was as much a bachelor then as he was now. He could not think of any incursion into that prim, precise world that he had made his own.

How it had all happened he could never rightly remember: it was that "county" dance that was the beginning of it. He was not "county" but it was the first year of his mayoralty and he was very wealthy, and he was let in on sufferance. Elsewhere, they would have called it the hunt ball, but in Wales, where everyone rode who could ride and had anything to ride, it would have been no better than letting in a troupe of beggars. So the county people had to get up an affair of their own which they called by some other name. It was held in the next town— it was always held in the next town, for there was a little pocket of county people round about, and it lay half-way over into Shropshire.

It was always the same—the old town hall, garlanded with flags and flowers, the band from Shrewsbury and the two hundred people, on and about the stairs, sipping claret cup and eating ices: the hot laughing crowd and the parquet floor and the noise and the chatter.

That was when he met her—very suddenly on the stairs with her laughing, wide-open violet eyes and the straight contemptuous stare at him as he stood there, transfixed. That was how it all began. She was the youngest daughter of a Welsh squire—they were as poor as church mice—and somehow or another things went on from that time. It was a "match" before he had ever hoped that it might be: but the slightly amused, contemptuous stare never left her.

That was the beginning of it. He had then been in the county some ten or twelve years, the son of a business man in the Midlands, who had bought out one of the flannel mills on the Severn and put his son in as manager. That was in the days when there was a run on Welsh flannel, and within ten years the business had doubled its capital. It was now one of the biggest mills in the district and was his own.

He was already a rich man. He had begun by being rich and there was nothing more for him to do than become richer. He was an only son, and it seemed that everything came to him; but sometimes he felt that everything passed him by. And yet all his life had been an orderly progress, but for this one thing that had tumbled him about so. He had never got over it, though he had told himself many times since that he had not been in love—that things would have been bound to go wrong. And now, as always, it left that ache, that sense of emptiness, of a life seen and never entered, like a small boy looking over a wall.

He was feeling it badly just now, all because of the Sergeant's visit, and mention of that confounded donkey and the old woman and all the rest of it. It puzzled and bewildered him—this sense of a life without, like the wind around the house, so wild and wayward, so wilful with no sense nor direction to it. He often felt like that on the Bench—that sort of peepshow view of a life that had no sense nor order. It was real enough, but it was very disturbing. He could never understand why people did the things they did.

He shuffled his feet into his carpet slippers and sank back into his easy-chair, trying to remember all about it—as much as he dare—about old Janet Ifans and her donkey, and about the woman who might have been his wife.

Janet Ifans was an old woman who lived alone, a mile or two away from the town, in a little stone and slate cottage, perched like a toy over a dingle. Whenever she turned out the ash pan it fell down two or three hundred feet to the torrent below, and everyone said that some day Janet would go with it. But she never did, and she died in her bed.

78

She was a very old woman with a light blue eye, a very wicked eye, and a shrill, high voice, which you could hear fields away, like a jay screeching. She was always shouting at the poor old donkey who was her only companion. His name was Ebenezer, but he was always called Ebbe. She was the widow of an old soldier in the South Wales Borderers who had died from wounds received in some foreign war, and the Dandy Fifth had a guard of honour when he went, and fired a round over his grave.

They were very happy together, except that on Saturday nights he used to unscrew his cork leg and beat her with it, but she did not seem to mind very much, and they were always in chapel again on Sundays billing and cooing like a pair of turtle doves. They had both come from somewhere down South, in the heyday of the little town, and Janet was a very vulgar woman indeed when she liked, though, as the Sergeant had said, there was no harm in her, and she kept herself and the little house as bright as could be.

Every Saturday she went into the market with two baskets across the donkey, like panniers, filled with stuff from her little garden, and herbs that she sold in the town—mandrakes and dandelion roots, and such like. The journey in was easy enough, for it was downhill, but it was a different story coming back. And every Saturday night Janet was drunk, her wisp of grey hair blown across her face and her eyes wild, whacking the poor donkey across his rump and shouting abuse at him. He would trot for a few paces and then wait for her, and at the steep pitch she had to get her shoulder to him and give him a hoist up. And every Saturday he would always stop at the same place, with the old woman beating him with her umbrella, a crowd of little boys from the town behind her, shouting and laughing and throwing stones.

In the end people began to complain, because her language was very bad, but no one would do anything, for the old woman was ribald in her cups and she had a very quick wit. But when the Methodist minister intervened the story went round the town. She was a very strong Methodist, and she respected the cloth as nothing else in this world, but she was Janet Ifans, and that was all there was to it.

"Hush, hush, Janet, *fach*. For shame on you," he said, discovering her at the worst bit of the journey, using a lot of words in Welsh and English that he did not want to hear. He turned round and drove the naughty boys off with his stick and then came back to try and coax the donkey. But the donkey would not move, however much he tried, and he had to get his shoulder to it alongside Janet. And then it was that the donkey, not caring for this added persuasion behind him, gave a sudden start and they both fell down in the road—Janet with her legs in the air and her red petticoats down over her head and the minister hard on his haunches.

"*Uffern dan*! You old sow!" called out Janet after

80

the donkey. She caught him by the tail and was for bringing him back to say he was sorry to Mr. Edwards.

"Come back," she shouted. "Come back you naughty old sow. Come back and say you're sorry to Mr. Edwards *bach*. Haf a look and see the mess he iss in," she shouted, helping the reverend gentleman to his feet. "Take no notice, Mr. Edwards *bach*. A shame on me, the naughty boy!"

The minister, who was a great heavy man with big feet like a policeman's, was the son of a farmer. He knew that drink and bad language were wicked, but he did not mind them very much if no one was about. And he had a big round, raddled face that made one want to laugh. But the tip that he gave Janet was to prove his undoing. He told her that the next time Ebbe jibbed at the pitch she was to press the half of a lemon under his tail. This was said in the kindness of his heart, and to save Ebenezer unnecessary beatings. But a week or two later the old woman, having had her little drop, found him in the High Street after the week-night service, with his deacons round him like a ring of nodding crows.

"Mister Edwards; Mister Edwards *bach*. . . ."

She came rolling down the Street, her umbrella raised.

"*Stopia*, Janet," said the minister, raising his hand gently and calling on her to desist. He had no idea what was to come next.

81

"Oh fine, Mr. Edwards!" she went on in her glory. "I put the lemon—as you say" she dropped her voice confidentially, her gin-laden breath going into their faces. She gave the old minister a playful nudge to show they understood one another. "Up he goes!" she shot out her hands in sudden emphasis. "Mis-terr Edwards—like a streak! *Iesu mawr* and I not keep half a lemon to use myself Mister Edwards and I neffer could catch him."

That went to show what a rude old woman she was: her goings on were a byword. But no one ever thought of summoning her because she was just Janet Ifans, and everyone knew what Janet Ifans was. And she would never have been summoned at all, but for the donkey, and then it was not the donkey's fault. It was a silly joke that they played on her, and no one knew how far the joke was going to go.

After the market, when she had sold her little bits of vegetables and eggs, it was her custom to go round doing her shopping, and she always took Ebenezer with her, loading him up as she went. And on this particular Saturday she had cause to go into the china market, which was a place apart, with straw on the concrete floor, and all the china laid about, from the best Staffordshire sets to the ordinary things in everyday use—a cheapjack among them like a hen among the eggs.

The old donkey was eating out of his nosebag, quite happy in the rest, when some of the urchins of the town began playing tricks while the old woman's back was turned. They had sticks with pins on the end and they began prodding the donkey, one or two at a time, and then began to pull hairs out of his tail. At first he only scraped a hoof and lifted his head inquiringly, but as the torment increased he grew restive. And then they dropped a lighted jack-jumper under him and as the squib exploded he leapt in the air, bent in a buck, and with panic in his eyes made his way across the china.

But there was no way out and he went on in a wild stampede, crunching over dinner plates and sending mugs and china pots flying with his hoofs. Within five minutes he had wrecked the whole place: the floor was strewn with china splinters like confetti after a wedding; women were shrieking and the cheapjacks shouting. When the Sergeant and another policeman arrived there was only the old lady left, chasing him round and round with her umbrella and trying to snatch at the bridle, all the while using the most foul language.

That was how she came to be summoned. It was the cheapjacks who kept the Sergeant up to it, and he had no choice. She was charged with creating, or causing to be created, a breach of the peace and word of it went round. The whole town was behind Janet, who was a Welshwoman, and had never done anyone any harm, and why should the Salford Jews go and make trouble? No one asked them to come.

It was a gala day in the town on the Monday. There was going to be a bit of fun—besides, feeling ran very high. The sessions opened at eleven o'clock, but an hour before that the silver band had gone up the lane to meet her. The old lady came down in her tight black bodice with the stays showing, like a head out of an egg-cup, and Ebenezer, hung about with garlands, braying at the trombones and showing his teeth.

It was the first day of the new chairman on the Bench. It was the one honour that was to come to him after the mayoralty—and it had come. It was the day of his life, and at his express wish his fiancée had come down to share his triumph. She had a seat beside the solicitors' table and she sat there with a faintly amused stare and the curl of a smile on her white oval face, at all the bustle and ceremonial.

It was the little man's day of triumph—the way he strutted out after the other magistrates and took the centre seat, after a little bow to right and left and a wan smile at his fiancée. The oak seat was far too big for him; the varnished back of it stuck up behind him and he was lost in it. And before him the bar, separating the bench from the well of the court, was far too high, cutting him off at the collar so that he looked like a white-faced little boy peering over a fence. But he was as pleased as could be as the chief constable on behalf of the police, and then representatives of the law and the Press, made their speeches of welcome.

Then began that ominous fanfare up the street, as the silver band approached and with it the procession and the confused murmur of voices. They had formed a ring outside the court and the band was ending up with "The Cossacks", drowning every other sound within and without. The Sergeant went rushing out of the court, but he could do nothing: the music had to have its way. They had got the old woman tipsy and she was doing a jig in the street with her red petticoats lifted.

Within the court there was an inquisitive stare, as from one to another—all but the little man. Borne along on the crest of his triumph, he had some idea that the band was for him. He smiled down graciously at the astonished faces below him and was surprised at the lack of response.

A moment or two later, when the doors were thrown open, the crowd swilled into the Town Hall and within a minute the court-room was filled to the doors.

The clerk read through the first charge on the sheet; the Sergeant roared out "Janet Ifans" and then walking to the door, shouted down the stone corridor "Janet Ifans".

And then the fun began. It started the minute she entered the room, with her old shawl about her, the white hair blown across her face in a wisp and her eyes shining. As they walked down the gangway in the centre of the court, she caught hold of the Sergeant's arm and he could not shake her free. Then she shook her shawl over her head like a veil and went pattering along and simpering to the pews of people until there was uproar. As she went up into the dock she hitched up her petticoat, like a lady getting into a carriage, and then, once inside, waved her hand coyly to the Bench. There was uproar again.

The little man leaned over to the clerk, his face white and strained.

"Is she fit to plead?" he asked nervously. But things had now gone too far, and there was no going back. And the laughter never stopped: there was something fresh all the time. It was one long guffaw. The old woman had no idea what all the fuss was about and she kept questioning the Sergeant in Welsh, whilst he pointed to the Bench, trying to keep his face straight.

"How plead you—guilty or not guilty?" sang out the clerk.

The old woman leaned forward and he repeated the question.

"There's daft!" she said and made to get out of the dock in her annoyance, but the Sergeant held on to the door.

"What's he want, then?" she shouted.

"What are you?" bellowed the Sergeant. "You hearr what he says."

"What am I?" she shrieked and then turned to the Bench with her umbrella raised. "I give you what for.

86

No one says one word to me since Seth go. No back doors for me, Mr. Benbow: no indeed. I know!" She wagged her finger viciously at the little cross-eyed clerk below her.

"Guilty or not guilty: yes or no?" roared the Sergeant, helping her out.

"What the matter with *you*—you old bullock?" she said, turning on him.

"She pleads guilty, your worships," explained the Sergeant after a lot of bother.

"Worships!" she broke in. "What worships? I know every wan of them."

She began making an inventory from left to right, touching up their private lives with many rude and bawdy details until they managed to stop her.

But it was hopeless, and they could do nothing with her. They had got her in the dock and they could not get her out—not without going on with it all. And all the time the court was in an uproar.

The little man sat there, his fingers laced and his round head sunk forward on his chest. It could be no worse, he felt. He had never known such humiliation as this in all his life. He dared not look up. But he felt that *she* was laughing too. He knew that she was laughing without looking at her. And this knowledge —that she would be bound to laugh, was not beside him in his humiliation—hurt him more than the humiliation itself. There was a great distance between them—how great he did not know. But he felt it now—the hopelessness of it.

That ribald crowd below him—that was one thing. To them law and justice and the decencies of life—it was something to get fun out of, some sort of a game. But he felt that she ought to know better. And yet he knew it was not a question of knowing better: it was a different world that he could not enter—and he had no wish to enter. He felt alone, absolutely alone, among these people: they had their own way of doing things and they ought to be left to themselves.

It was in all this uproar that he heard her speak. She had stood up at the table, in that impulsive way of hers, but her large, lustrous eyes, with that impudent gleam in them had suddenly clouded. She was sorry—but she was not sorry for him.

"May I try?" she asked.

She looked along the Bench from one to another and then her eyes came to rest on him, waiting for the nod. But the others had nodded all along the row before him, and his nod was only a matter of form. He knew, as he nodded, that it had nothing to do with him.

Then she stood up and faced the old woman, her face set and resolute. As though at a command, the tumult stopped. The Vaughans were a very old family and one of themselves. And the old lady became as docile as a lamb. If Miss Vaughan had something to say it was different.

The young woman spoke in Welsh, pleading with her and sounding her lovely lilting voice through all shades of expression, anger, reproach and then a half-hidden command.

The little man raised his eyes in wonder: he had never heard her like this—that something in the voice that transformed it. He could not understand a word that she said, and yet, in a way, he was able to follow her. There was a loving, intimate touch to it all that confounded him; the aristocrat and the peasant, the vulgar old woman in the dock, engaged in this pleasant preliminary banter.

What she said was something like this:

"Janet, dear. You must not be naughty. No indeed! The gentlemen don't want to harm you. They only want to know how it was that Ebenezer kicked the plates. That is all. Don't be afraid, Janet, for we are all with you. Just say what happened and how the naughty boys gave him a fright. *Ach*, naughty boys they were. Tell the little man in the middle all about it—just in your own words—and everything will be all right. Now be a good girl, Janet, and do as I tell."

The old woman nodded approvingly, called her a little dear, and began to say how she knew all the family and what a fine family they were, and then the young woman put her fingers to her lips and pointed to the chairman.

"In your own words," she said in English.

89

The old woman turned herself round to the Bench and coughed into her hand once or twice. Then she turned to the young woman again:

"Where to start?" she asked.

"At the beginning," nodded the chairman, trying to smile. "Just how it happened."

"Happen!" she shouted. "Indeed, sirr, there wass no happen. It end before it happen—so there!"

She was beginning to get truculent again but the young woman once more put her finger to her lips and Janet just as suddenly subsided. In the blank row of faces on the Bench she saw only the little man offering comfort, so she addressed herself to him.

"No, sirr. I tell you. Ebbe—a good boy, Ebbe. Fery good boy. No one say anything bad about Ebbe. No *indeed*, sirr."

She began to wag her head backwards and forwards at the memory.

"Poor lit-tel boy," she said, her voice warming to it. Then she looked straight at the magistrate, her thin blue eyes alight.

"Now I ask, sirr, I ask you straight. Suppose, sirr, as how naughty boys go put a cracker under your bottom, sirr. What you do, ay? I bet you kick sirr—right and left!"

"Silence!" roared the Sergeant, running down the court. He kept sweeping his hands downwards trying to get the people to their seats. No one heard what he said: no one cared. Roar on roar filled the room. The

Bench sat there, glum and silent, smirking into their hands. The little man, his head bowed, his face bloodless, waited to be heard.

"Case dismissed," he got out at last.

Even so, no one heard him. The Sergeant ran forward and leaned his head over.

"Case dismissed!" he roared, opening the dock gate and shooing the old woman out. Then he went on to clear the court, driving them before him like a flock of sheep.

The old woman stepped primly out of the dock and then preened herself in the court. She was a bit bewildered by it all—only knowing that in some miraculous way it was all over, and that she could go home. And she was sure that Miss Vaughan was at the bottom of it—the nice lady that she was.

"*Diolch yn fawr, Miss Vaughan bach,*" she said with great fervour, wringing her by the hand.

But the young lady was very serious now.

"You be a good woman, Janet, and go straight home," she said with a wan little smile.

He waited until the other magistrates had left the court before he came out of the retiring-room. The big Town Hall was empty now, save for the Sergeant, busying himself with pens and pencils at the table at the far end. She was there, waiting for him.

"I am . . . sorry," he said. It came out in a little gulp. He could say no more. He kept his eyes on the floor.

91

"No," she broke in, during the long silence. "I am sorry."

"Thank you," he said, and then again, "thank you."

He knew that she was sorry for him—sorry in her heart. And he knew, too, that she had always been sorry for him.

"I suppose . . ." he began as they walked towards the door. He searched his heart in his misery, but no words came.

"Oh," she said, "*that* can wait. Some other time," she added, trying to lighten the load.

But he knew then that it was all over.

He awoke with a start when the Sergeant returned, and looked round the room in bewilderment. The book lay spread out on the floor beside him and the fire had burned low. He must have had a nap—a most unusual thing for him. But he could not quite remember whether he had slept or not—whether he had dreamt or not. He knew that he had been thinking of her in some sort of a way. And it seemed to him now that she belonged to a dream—that she had never entered his life, and never could have entered it. It seemed to him stranger than ever that such things could happen, that such and such a thing was really within his grasp when it was always beyond it. And yet. . . .

"You told me, sirr . . . to come back."

The Sergeant was standing there, large and florid, half in and half out, of the door. The maid had taken him up.

"Yes: yes," he said petulantly. "What is it now?"

"The donkey, sirr—as belonged to old Janet Ifans."

The little man rubbed his eyes awake.

"Yes, yes. Of course."

He straightened himself in his chair and beckoned the Sergeant in.

"Well? . . ." he went on acidly. "What about this . . . this confounded donkey?"

"I told you, sirr," said the Sergeant reproachfully.

"Well then. I forget."

"Well, sirr. The old boy must go. Pity, sirr—but there it is."

"Then why ask *me*?" answered the little man, nettled.

"Well, sirr; it's not nice: no indeed. To blow a hole in the old thing. And for why?"

"Oh no, no," broke in the little man at the horror of it. "Not *that*—surely not that."

"Well, sirr. That's how it is," went on the Sergeant placidly.

"But surely . . . surely you can find someone to take it?"

"Who?" The Sergeant fixed him with his raw eye.

"Well!" he said, shocked. "There's not a great deal of Christian charity about—seemingly."

93

"No, sirr—not for donkeys."

"All right," he said with a final heave. He waved the Sergeant to the door. And he was sure that the Sergeant had known all along what would happen.

by

ARTHUR MACHEN

★

THE SHINING PYRAMID

I

"Haunted, you said?"

"Yes, haunted. Don't you remember, when I saw you three years ago, you told me about your place in the west with the ancient woods hanging all about it, and the wild, domed hills, and the ragged land? It has always remained a sort of enchanted picture in my mind as I sit at my desk and hear the traffic rattling in the street in the midst of whirling London. But when did you come up?"

"The fact is, Dyson, I have only just got out of the train. I drove to the station early this morning and caught the 10.45."

"Well, I am very glad you looked in on me. How have you been getting on since we last met? There is no Mrs. Vaughan, I suppose?"

"No," said Vaughan, "I am still a hermit, like yourself. I have done nothing but loaf about."

Vaughan had lit his pipe and sat in the elbow chair, fidgeting and glancing about him in a somewhat dazed and restless manner. Dyson had wheeled round

95

his chair when his visitor entered and sat with one arm fondly reclining on the desk of his bureau, and touching the litter of manuscript.

"And you are still engaged in the old task?" said Vaughan, pointing to the pile of papers and the teeming pigeon-holes.

"Yes, the vain pursuit of literature, as idle as alchemy, and as entrancing. But you have come to town for some time I suppose; what shall we do to-night?"

"Well, I rather wanted you to try a few days with me down in the west. It would do you a lot of good, I'm sure."

"You are very kind, Vaughan, but London in September is hard to leave. Doré could not have designed anything more wonderful and mystic than Oxford Street as I saw it the other evening; the sunset flaming, the blue haze transmuting the plain street into a road 'far in the spiritual city'."

"I should like you to come down though. You would enjoy roaming over our hills. Does this racket go on all day and all night? It quite bewilders me; I wonder how you can work through it. I am sure you would revel in the great peace of my old home among the woods."

Vaughan lit his pipe again, and looked anxiously at Dyson to see if his inducements had had any effect, but the man of letters shook his head, smiling, and vowed in his heart a firm allegiance to the streets.

"You cannot tempt me," he said.

"Well, you may be right. Perhaps, after all, I was wrong to speak of the peace of the country. There, when a tragedy does occur, it is like a stone thrown into a pond; the circles of disturbance keep on widening, and it seems as if the water would never be still again."

"Have you ever any tragedies where you are?"

"I can hardly say that. But I was a good deal disturbed about a month ago by something that happened; it may or may not have been a tragedy in the usual sense of the word."

"What was the occurrence?"

"Well, the fact is a girl disappeared in a way which seems highly mysterious. Her parents, people of the name of Trevor, are well-to-do farmers, and their eldest daughter Annie was a sort of village beauty; she was really remarkably handsome. One afternoon she thought she would go and see her aunt, a widow who farms her own land, and as the two houses are only about five or six miles apart, she started off, telling her parents she would take the short cut over the hills. She never got to her aunt's. She's still missing. That's putting it in a few words."

"What an extraordinary thing! I suppose there are no disused mines, are there, on the hills? I don't think you quite run to anything so formidable as a precipice?"

"No; the path the girl must have taken had no pitfalls of any description; it is just a track over wild, bare hillside, far, even, from a by-road. One may walk for miles without meeting a soul, but it is all perfectly safe."

"And what do people say about it?"

"Oh, they talk nonsense—among themselves. You have no notion as to how superstitious cottagers are in out-of-the-way parts like mine. They are as bad as the Irish, every whit, and even more secretive."

"But what do they say?"

"Oh, the poor girl is supposed to have 'gone with the fairies', or to have been 'taken by the fairies'. Such stuff!" he went on, "one would laugh if it were not for the real tragedy of the case."

Dyson looked somewhat interested.

"Yes," he said, " 'fairies' certainly strike a little curiously on the ear in these days. But what do the police say? I presume they do not accept the fairy-tale hypothesis?"

"No; but they seem quite at fault. What I am afraid of is that Annie Trevor must have fallen in with some scoundrels on her way. Castletown is a large seaport, you know, and some of the worst of the foreign sailors occasionally desert their ships and go on the tramp up and down the country. Not many years ago a Spanish sailor named Garcia murdered a whole family for the sake of plunder that was not worth sixpence. They are hardly human, some of these fellows, and I am dreadfully afraid the poor girl must have come to an awful end."

"But no foreign sailor was seen by anyone about the country?"

"No; there is certainly that; and of course country people are quick to notice anyone whose appearance and dress are a little out of the common. Still it seems as if my theory were the only possible explanation."

"There are no data to go upon," said Dyson, thoughtfully. "There was no question of a love affair, or anything of the kind, I suppose?"

"Oh, no, not a hint of such a thing. I am sure if Annie were alive she would have contrived to let her mother know of her safety."

"No doubt, no doubt. Still it is barely possible that she is alive and yet unable to communicate with her friends. But all this must have disturbed you a good deal."

"Yes, it did; I hate a mystery, and especially a mystery which is probably the veil of horror. But frankly, Dyson, I want to make a clean breast of it; I did not come here to tell you all this."

"Of course not," said Dyson, a little surprised at Vaughan's uneasy manner. "You came to have a chat on more cheerful topics."

"No, I did not. What I have been telling you about happened a month ago, but something which seems likely to affect me more personally has happened

99

within the last few days, and to be quite plain, I came up to town with the idea that you might be able to help me. You recollect that curious case you spoke to me about at our last meeting; something about a spectacle-maker."

"Oh, yes, I remember that. I know I was quite proud of my acumen at the time; even to this day the police have no idea why those peculiar yellow spectacles were wanted. But, Vaughan, you really look quite put out; I hope there is nothing serious?"

"No, I think I have been exaggerating, and I want you to reassure me. But what has happened is very odd."

"And what has happened?"

"I am sure that you will laugh at me, but this is the story. You must know there is a path, a right of way, that goes through my land, and to be precise, close to the wall of the kitchen garden. It is not used by many people; a woodman now and again finds it useful, and five or six children who go to school in the village pass twice a day. Well, a few days ago I was taking a walk about the place before breakfast, and I happened to stop to fill my pipe just by the large doors in the garden wall. The wood, I must tell you, comes to within a few feet of the wall, and the track I spoke of runs right in the shadow of the trees. I thought the shelter from a brisk wind that was blowing rather pleasant, and I stood there smoking with my eyes on the ground. Then something caught

THE SHINING PYRAMID

my attention. Just under the wall, on the short grass, a number of small flints were arranged in a pattern; something like this": and Mr. Vaughan caught at a pencil and piece of paper, and dotted down a few strokes.

"You see," he went on, "there were, I should think, twelve little stones neatly arranged in lines, and spaced at equal distances as I have shewn it on the paper. They were pointed stones and the points were very carefully directed one way."

"Yes," said Dyson, without much interest, "no doubt the children you have mentioned had been playing there on their way from school. Children, as you know, are very fond of making such devices with oyster shells or flints or flowers, or with whatever comes in their way."

"So I thought; I just noticed these flints were arranged in a sort of pattern and then went on. But the next morning I was taking the same round, which, as a matter of fact, is habitual with me, and again I saw at the same spot a device in flints. This time it was really a curious pattern; something like the spokes of a wheel, all meeting at a common centre, and this centre formed by a device which looked like a bowl; all, you understand, done in flints."

"You are right," said Dyson, "that seems odd enough. Still it is reasonable that your half a dozen school children are responsible for these fantasies in stone."

"Well, I thought I would set the matter at rest. The children pass the gate every evening at half-past five, and I walked by at six, and found the device just as I had left it in the morning. The next day I was up and about at a quarter to seven, and I found the whole thing had been changed. There was a pyramid outlined in flints upon the grass. The children I saw going by an hour and a half later, and they ran past the spot without glancing to right or left. In the evening I watched them going home, and this morning when I got to the gate at six o'clock there was a thing like a half-moon waiting for me."

"So then the series runs thus: firstly ordered lines, then the device of the spokes and the bowl, then the pyramid, and finally, this morning, the half-moon. That is the order, isn't it?"

"Yes; that is right. But do you know it has made me feel very uneasy? I suppose it seems absurd, but I can't help thinking that some kind of signalling is going on under my nose, and that sort of thing is disquieting."

"But what have you to dread? You have no enemies?"

"No; but I have some very valuable old plate."

"You are thinking of burglars then?" said Dyson, with an accent of considerable interest, "but you must know your neighbours. Are there any suspicious characters about?"

"Not that I am aware of. But you remember what I told you of the sailors."

"Can you trust your servants?"

"Oh, perfectly. The plate is preserved in a strong-room; the butler, an old family servant, alone knows where the key is kept. There is nothing wrong there. Still, everybody is aware that I have a lot of old silver, and all country folks are given to gossip. In that way information may have got abroad in very undesirable quarters."

"Yes, but I confess there seems something a little unsatisfactory in the burglar theory. Who is signalling to whom? I cannot see my way to accepting such an explanation. What put the plate into your head in connection with these flint signs, or whatever one may call them?"

"It was the figure of the bowl," said Vaughan. "I happen to possess a very large and very valuable Charles II punch-bowl. The chasing is really exquisite, and the thing is worth a lot of money. The sign I described to you was exactly the same shape as my punch-bowl."

"A queer coincidence certainly. But the other figures or devices: you have nothing shaped like a pyramid?"

"Ah, you will think that queerer. As it happens, this punch-bowl of mine, together with a set of rare old ladles, is kept in a mahogany chest of a pyramidal shape. The four sides slope upwards, the narrow towards the top."

"I confess all this interests me a good deal," said Dyson. "Let us go on then. What about the other figures; how about the Army, as we may call the first sign, and the Crescent or Half-moon?"

"Ah, there is no reference that I can make out of these two. Still, you see I have some excuse for curiosity at all events. I should be very vexed to lose any of the old plate; nearly all the pieces have been in the family for generations. And I cannot get it out of my head that some scoundrels mean to rob me, and are communicating with one another every night."

"Frankly," said Dyson, "I can make nothing of it; I am as much in the dark as yourself. Your theory seems certainly the only possible explanation, and yet the difficulties are immense."

He leaned back in his chair, and the two men faced each other, frowning, and perplexed by so bizarre a problem.

"By the way," said Dyson, after a long pause, "what is your geological formation down there?"

Mr. Vaughan looked up, a good deal surprised by the question.

"Old red sandstone and limestone, I believe," he said. "We are just beyond the coal measures, you know."

"But surely there are no flints either in the sandstone or the limestone?"

"No, I never see any flints in the fields. I confess that did strike me as a little curious."

"I should think so! It is very important. By the way, what size were the flints used in making these devices?"

"I happen to have brought one with me; I took it this morning."

"From the Half-moon?"

"Exactly. Here it is."

He handed over a small flint, tapering to a point, and about three inches in length.

Dyson's face blazed up with excitement as he took the thing from Vaughan.

"Certainly," he said, after a moment's pause, "you have some curious neighbours in your country. I hardly think they can harbour any designs on your punch-bowl. Do you know this is a flint arrow-head of vast antiquity, and not only that, but an arrow-head of a unique kind? I have seen specimens from all parts of the world, but there are features about this thing that are quite peculiar."

He laid down his pipe, and took out a book from a drawer.

"We shall just have time to catch the 5.45 to Castletown, he said."

<h2 style="text-align:center">II</h2>

Mr. Dyson drew in a long breath of the air of the hills and felt all the enchantment of the scene about him. It was very early morning, and he stood on the terrace in the front of the house. Vaughan's ancestor

had built on the lower slope of a great hill, in the
shelter of a deep and ancient wood that gathered on
three sides about the house, and on the fourth side,
the south-west, the land fell gently away and sank to
the valley, where a brook wound in and out in mystic
esses, and the dark and gleaming alders tracked the
stream's course to the eye. On the terrace in that
sheltered place no wind blew, and far beyond the
trees were still. Only one sound broke in upon the
silence, and Dyson heard the noise of the brook singing far below, the song of clear and shining water
rippling over the stones, whispering and murmuring
as it sank to dark deep pools. Across the stream, just
below the house, rose a grey stone bridge, vaulted
and buttressed, a fragment of the Middle Ages, and
then beyond the bridge the hills rose again, vast and
rounded like bastions, covered here and there with
dark woods and thickets of undergrowth, but the
heights were all bare of trees, showing only grey turf
and patches of bracken, touched here and there with
the gold of fading fronds. Dyson looked to the north
and south, and still he saw the wall of the hills, and
the ancient woods, and the stream drawn in and out
between them; all grey and dim with morning mist
beneath a grey sky in a hushed and haunted air.

Mr. Vaughan's voice broke in upon the silence.

"I thought you would be too tired to be about so
early," he said. "I see you are admiring the view. It
is very pretty, isn't it, though I suppose old Meyrick

Vaughan didn't think much about the scenery when he built the house. A queer grey, old place, isn't it?"

"Yes, and how it fits into the surroundings; it seems of a piece with the grey hills and the grey bridge below."

"I am afraid I have brought you down on false pretences, Dyson," said Vaughan, as they began to walk up and down the terrace. "I have been to the place, and there is not a sign of anything this morning."

"Ah, indeed. Well, suppose we go round together."

They walked across the lawn and went by a path through the ilex shrubbery to the back of the house. There Vaughan pointed out the track leading down to the valley and up to the heights above the wood, and presently they stood beneath the garden wall, by the door.

"Here, you see, it was," said Vaughan, pointing to a spot on the turf. "I was standing just where you are now that morning I first saw the flints."

"Yes, quite so. That morning it was the Army, as I call it; then the Bowl, then the Pyramid, and, yesterday, the Half-moon. What a queer old stone that is," he went on, pointing to a block of limestone rising out of the turf just beneath the wall. "It looks like a sort of dwarf pillar, but I suppose it is natural."

"Oh, yes, I think so. I imagine it was brought here, though, as we stand on the red sandstone. No doubt it was used as a foundation stone for some older building."

"Very likely." Dyson was peering about him attentively, looking from the ground to the wall, and from the wall to the deep wood that hung almost over the garden and made the place dark even in the morning.

"Look here," said Dyson at length, "it is certainly a case of children this time. Look at that."

He was bending down and staring at the dull red surface of the mellowed bricks of the wall. Vaughan came up and looked hard where Dyson's finger was pointing, and could scarcely distinguish a faint mark in deeper red.

"What is it?" he said. "I can make nothing of it."

"Look a little more closely. Don't you see it is an attempt to draw the human eye?"

"Ah, now I see what you mean. My sight is not very sharp. Yes, so it is, it is meant for an eye, no doubt, as you say. I thought the children learnt drawing at school."

"Well, it is an odd eye enough. Do you notice the peculiar almond shape; almost like the eye of a Chinaman?"

Dyson looked meditatively at the work of the undeveloped artist, and scanned the wall again, going down on his knees in the minuteness of his inquisition.

"I should like very much", he said at length, "to know how a child in this out-of-the-way place could have any idea of the shape of the Mongolian eye. You see the average child has a very distinct impression of the subject; he draws a circle, or something like a circle, and puts a dot in the centre. I don't think any child imagines that the eye is really made like that; it's just a convention of infantile art. But this almond-shaped thing puzzles me extremely. Perhaps it may be derived from a gilt Chinaman on a tea-canister in the grocer's shop. Still that's hardly likely."

"But why are you so sure it was done by a child?"

"Why! Look at the height. These old-fashioned bricks are little more than two inches thick; there are twenty courses from the ground to the sketch if we call it so; that gives a height of three and a half feet. Now, just imagine you are going to draw something on this wall. Exactly; your pencil, if you had one, would touch the wall somewhere on the level with your eyes, that is, more than five feet from the ground. It seems, therefore, a very simple deduction to conclude that this eye on the wall was drawn by a child about ten years old."

"Yes, I had not thought of that. Of course one of the children must have done it."

"I suppose so; and yet as I said, there is something singularly unchildlike about those two lines, and the eyeball itself, you see, is almost an oval. To my mind, the thing has an odd, ancient air; and a touch that is not altogether pleasant. I cannot help fancying that if we could see a whole face from the same hand it would not be altogether agreeable. However, that is nonsense, after all, and we are not getting further in our investigations. It is odd that the flint series has come to such an abrupt end."

The two men walked away towards the house, and as they went in at the porch there was a break in the grey sky, and a gleam of sunshine on the grey hill before them.

All the day Dyson prowled meditatively about the fields and woods surrounding the house. He was thoroughly and completely puzzled by the trivial circumstances he proposed to elucidate, and now he again took the flint arrow-head from his pocket, turning it over and examining it with deep attention. There was something about the thing that was altogether different from the specimens he had seen at the museums and private collections; the shape was of a distinct type, and around the edge there was a line of little punctured dots, apparently a suggestion of ornament. Who, thought Dyson, could possess such things in so remote a place; and who, possessing the flints, could have put them to the fantastic use of designing meaningless figures under Vaughan's garden wall? The rank absurdity of the whole affair offended him unutterably; and as one theory after another rose in his mind only to be rejected, he felt strongly tempted to take the next train back to town. He had seen the silver plate which Vaughan treasured, and had inspected the punch-bowl, the gem of

the collection, with close attention; and what he saw
and his interview with the butler convinced him that
a plot to rob the strong-box was out of the limits of
enquiry. The chest in which the bowl was kept, a
heavy piece of mahogany, evidently dating from the
beginning of the century, was certainly strongly sug-
gestive of a pyramid, and Dyson was at first inclined
to the inept manœuvres of the detective, but a little
sober thought convinced him of the impossibility of
the burglary hypothesis, and he cast wildly about for
something more satisfying. He asked Vaughan if
there were any gypsies in the neighbourhood, and
heard that the Romany had not been seen for years.
This dashed him a good deal, as he knew the gypsy
habit of leaving queer hieroglyphics on the line of
march, and had been much elated when the thought
occurred to him. He was facing Vaughan by the
old-fashioned hearth when he put the question, and
leaned back in his chair in disgust at the destruction
of his theory.

"It is odd," said Vaughan, "but the gypsies never
trouble us here. Now and then the farmers find traces
of fires in the wildest part of the hills, but nobody
seems to know who the fire-lighters are."

"Surely that looks like gypsies?"

"No, not in such places as those. Tinkers and
gypsies and wanderers of all sorts stick to the roads
and don't go very far from the farmhouses."

"Well, I can make nothing of it. I saw the children

going by this afternoon, and, as you say, they ran straight on. So we shall have no more eyes on the wall at all events."

"No, I must waylay them one of these days and find out who is the artist."

The next morning when Vaughan strolled in his usual course from the lawn to the back of the house he found Dyson already awaiting him by the garden door, and evidently in a state of high excitement, for he beckoned furiously with his hand, and gesticulated violently.

"What is it?" asked Vaughan. "The flints again?"

"No; but look here, look at the wall. There; don't you see it?"

"There's another of those eyes!"

"Exactly. Drawn, you see, at a little distance from the first, almost on the same level, but slightly lower."

"What on earth is one to make of it? It couldn't have been done by the children; it wasn't there last night, and they won't pass for another hour. What can it mean?"

"I think the very devil is at the bottom of all this," said Dyson. "Of course, one cannot resist the conclusion that these infernal almond eyes are to be set down to the same agency as the devices in the arrowheads; and where that conclusion is to lead us is more than I can tell. For my part, I have to put a strong check on my imagination, or it would run wild."

"Vaughan," he said, as they turned away from the

wall, "has it struck you that there is one point—a very curious point—in common between the figures done in flints and the eyes drawn on the wall?"

"What is that?" asked Vaughan, on whose face there had fallen a certain shadow of indefinite dread.

"It is this. We know that the signs of the Army, the Bowl, the Pyramid, and the Half-moon must have been done at night. Presumably they were meant to be seen at night. Well, precisely the same reasoning applies to those eyes on the wall."

"I do not quite see your point."

"Oh, surely. The nights are dark just now, and have been very cloudy, I know, since I came down. Moreover, those overhanging trees would throw that wall into deep shadow even on a clear night."

"Well?"

"What struck me was this. What very peculiarly sharp eyesight they, whoever 'they' are, must have to be able to arrange arrow-heads in intricate order in the blackest shadow of the wood, and then draw the eyes on the wall without a trace of bungling, or a false line."

"I have read of persons confined in dungeons for many years who have been able to see quite well in the dark," said Vaughan.

"Yes," said Dyson, "there was the abbé in *Monte Cristo*. But it is a singular point."

III

"Who was that old man that touched his hat to you just now?" said Dyson, as they came to the bend of the lane near the house.

"Oh, that was old Trevor. He looks very broken, poor old fellow."

"Who is Trevor?"

"Don't you remember? I told you the story that afternoon I came to your rooms—about a girl named Annie Trevor, who disappeared in the most inexplicable manner about five weeks ago. That was her father."

"Yes, yes, I recollect now. To tell the truth I had forgotten all about it. And nothing has been heard of the girl?"

"Nothing whatever. The police are quite at fault."

"I am afraid I did not pay very much attention to the details you gave me. Which way did the girl go?"

"Her path would take her right across those wild hills above the house; the nearest point in the track must be about two miles from here."

"Is it near that little hamlet I saw yesterday?"

"You mean Croesyceiliog, where the children come from? No; it goes more to the north."

"Ah, I have never been that way."

They went into the house, and Dyson shut himself up in his room, sunk deep in doubtful thought, but yet with the shadow of a suspicion growing within him that for a while haunted his brain, all vague and fantastic, refusing to take definite form. He was sitting by the open window and looking out on the valley and saw, as if in a picture, the intricate winding of the brook, the grey bridge, and the vast hills rising beyond; all still and without a breath of wind to stir the mystic hanging woods, and the evening sunshine glowed warm on the bracken, and down below a faint mist, pure white, began to rise from the stream. Dyson sat by the window as the day darkened and the huge bastioned hills loomed vast and vague, and the woods became dim and more shadowy; and the fancy that had seized him no longer appeared altogether impossible. He passed the rest of the evening in a reverie, hardly hearing what Vaughan said; and when he took his candle in the hall, he paused a moment before bidding his friend good night.

"I want a good rest," he said. "I have got some work to do to-morrow."

"Some writing, you mean?"

"No. I am going to look for the Bowl."

"The Bowl! If you mean my punch-bowl, that is safe in the chest."

"I don't mean the punch-bowl. You may take my word for it that your plate has never been threatened. No; I will not bother you with any suppositions. We shall in all probability have something much stronger than suppositions before long. Good night, Vaughan."

The next morning Dyson set off after breakfast.

He took the path by the garden wall, and noted that there were now eight of the weird almond eyes dimly outlined on the brick.

"Six days more," he said to himself, but as he thought over the theory he had formed, he shrank, in spite of strong conviction, from such a wildly incredible fancy. He struck up through the dense shadows of the wood, and at length came out on the bare hillside, and climbed higher and higher over the slippery turf, keeping well to the north, and following the indications given him by Vaughan. As he went on, he seemed to mount ever higher above the world of human life and customary things; to his right he looked at a fringe of orchard and saw a faint blue smoke rising like a pillar; there was the hamlet from which the children came to school, and there the only sign of life, for the woods embowered and concealed Vaughan's old grey house. As he reached what seemed the summit of the hill, he realized for the first time the desolate loneliness and strangeness of the land; there was nothing but grey sky and grey hill, a high, vast plain that seemed to stretch on for ever and ever, and a faint glimpse of a blue-peaked mountain far away and to the north. At length he came to the path, a slight track scarcely noticeable, and from its position and by what Vaughan had told him he knew that it was the way the lost girl, Annie Trevor, must have taken. He followed the path on the bare hill-top, noticing the great limestone rocks

116

that cropped out of the turf, grim and hideous, and of an aspect as forbidding as an idol of the South Seas; and suddenly he halted, astonished, although he had found what he searched for. Almost without warning the ground shelved suddenly away on all sides, and Dyson looked down into a circular depression, which might well have been a Roman amphitheatre, and the ugly crags of limestone rimmed it round as if with a broken wall. Dyson walked round the hollow, and noted the position of the stones, and then turned on his way home.

"This", he thought to himself, "is more than curious. The Bowl is discovered, but where is the Pyramid?"

"My dear Vaughan," he said, when he got back, "I may tell you that I have found the Bowl, and that is all I shall tell you for the present. We have six days of absolute inaction before us; there is really nothing to be done."

IV

"I have just been round the garden," said Vaughan one morning. "I have been counting those infernal eyes, and I find there are fourteen of them. For heaven's sake, Dyson, tell me what the meaning of it all is."

"I should be very sorry to attempt to do so. I may have guessed this or that, but I always make it a principle to keep my guesses to myself. Besides, it is really not worth while anticipating events; you will remember my telling you that we had six days of inaction before us? Well, this is the sixth day, and the last of idleness. To-night I propose we take a stroll."

"A stroll! Is that all the action you mean to take?"

"Well, it may show you some very curious things. To be plain, I want you to start with me at nine o'clock this evening for the hills. We may have to be out all night, so you had better wrap up well, and bring some of that brandy."

"Is it a joke?" asked Vaughan, who was bewildered with strange events and strange surmises.

"No, I don't think there is much joke in it. Unless I am much mistaken we shall find a very serious explanation of the puzzle. You will come with me, I am sure?"

"Very good. Which way do you want to go?"

"By the path you told me of; the path Annie Trevor is supposed to have taken."

Vaughan looked white at the mention of the girl's name.

"I did not think you were on that track," he said. "I thought it was the affair of those devices in flint and of the eyes on the wall that you were engaged on. It's no good saying any more, but I will go with you."

At a quarter to nine that evening the two men set out, taking the path through the wood, and up the hillside. It was a dark and heavy night, the sky was thick with clouds, and the valley full of mist, and all the way they seemed to walk in a world of shadow and gloom, hardly speaking, and afraid to break the haunted silence. They came out at last on the steep hillside, and instead of the oppression of the wood there was the long, dim sweep of the turf, and higher, the fantastic limestone rocks hinted horror through the darkness, and the wind sighed as it passed across the mountain to the sea, and in its passage beat chill about their hearts. They seemed to walk on and on for hours, and the dim outline of the hill still stretched before them, and the haggard rocks still loomed through the darkness, when suddenly Dyson whispered, drawing his breath quickly, and coming close to his companion.

"Here," he said, "we will lie down. I do not think there is anything yet."

"I know the place," said Vaughan, after a moment. "I have often been by in the daytime. The country people are afraid to come here, I believe; it is supposed to be a fairies' castle, or something of the kind. But why on earth have we come here?"

"Speak a little lower," said Dyson. "It might not do us any good if we are overheard."

"Overheard here! There is not a soul within three miles of us."

"Possibly not; indeed, I should say certainly not. But there might be a body somewhat nearer."

"I don't understand you in the least," said Vaughan, whispering to humour Dyson, "but why have we come here?"

"Well, you see this hollow before us is the Bowl. I think we had better not talk even in whispers."

They lay full length upon the turf; the rock between their faces and the Bowl, and now and again, Dyson, slouching his dark, soft hat over his forehead, put out the glint of an eye, and in a moment drew back, not daring to take a prolonged view. Again he laid an ear to the ground and listened, and the hours went by, and the darkness seemed to blacken, and the faint sigh of the wind was the only sound.

Vaughan grew impatient with this heaviness of silence, this watching for indefinite terror; for to him there was no shape or form of apprehension, and he began to think the whole vigil a dreary farce.

"How much longer is this to last?" he whispered to Dyson, and Dyson who had been holding his breath in the agony of attention put his mouth to Vaughan's ear and said:

"Will you listen?" with pauses between each syllable, and in the voice with which the priest pronounces the awful words.

Vaughan caught the ground with his hands, and stretched forward, wondering what he was to hear. At first there was nothing, and then a low and gentle noise came very softly from the Bowl, a faint sound, almost indescribable, but as if one held the tongue against the roof of the mouth and expelled the breath. He listened eagerly and presently the noise grew louder, and became a strident and horrible hissing as if the pit beneath boiled with fervent heat, and Vaughan, unable to remain in suspense any longer, drew his cap half over his face in imitation of Dyson, and looked down to the hollow below.

It did, in truth, stir and seethe like an infernal caldron. The whole of the sides and bottom tossed and writhed with vague and restless forms that passed to and fro without the sound of feet, and gathered thick here and there and seemed to speak to one another in those tones of horrible sibilance, like the hissing of snakes, that he had heard. It was as if the sweet turf and the cleanly earth had suddenly become quickened with some foul writhing growth. Vaughan could not draw back his face, though he felt Dyson's finger touch him, but he peered into the quaking mass and saw faintly that there were things like faces and human limbs, and yet he felt his inmost soul chill with the sure belief that no fellow soul or human thing stirred in all that tossing and hissing host. He looked aghast, choking back sobs of horror, and at length the loathsome forms gathered thickest about some vague object in the middle of the hollow and the hissing of their speech grew more venomous, and he saw in the uncertain light the abominable limbs, vague and yet too plainly seen, writhe and intertwine, and he thought he heard, very faint, a low human moan striking through the noise of speech that was not of man. At his heart something seemed to whisper ever "the worm of corruption, the worm that dieth not," and grotesquely the image was pictured to his imagination of a piece of putrid offal stirring through and through with bloated and horrible creeping things. The writhing of the dusky limbs continued, they seemed clustered round the dark form in the middle of the hollow, and the sweat dripped and poured off Vaughan's forehead, and fell cold on his hand beneath his face.

Then, it seemed done in an instant, the loathsome mass melted and fell away to the sides of the Bowl, and for a moment Vaughan saw in the middle of the hollow the tossing of human arms. But a spark gleamed beneath, a fire kindled, and as the voice of a woman cried out loud in a shrill scream of utter anguish and terror, a great pyramid of flame spired up like a bursting of a pent fountain, and threw a blaze of light upon the whole mountain. In that instant Vaughan saw the myriads beneath; the things made in the form of men but stunted like children hideously deformed, the faces with the almond eyes burning with evil and unspeakable lusts; the ghastly yellow of the mass of naked flesh; and then as if by magic the place was empty, while the fire roared and crackled, and the flames shone abroad.

"You have seen the Pyramid," said Dyson in his ear, "the Pyramid of fire."

V

"Then you recognize the thing?"

"Certainly. It is a brooch that Annie Trevor used to wear on Sundays; I remember the pattern. But where did you find it? You don't mean to say that you have discovered the girl?"

"My dear Vaughan, I wonder you have not guessed where I found the brooch. You have not forgotten last night already?"

"Dyson," said the other, speaking very seriously, "I have been turning it over in my mind this morning while you have been out. I have thought about what I saw, or perhaps I should say about what I thought I saw, and the only conclusion I can come to is this, that the thing won't bear recollection. As men live, I have lived soberly and honestly, in the fear of God, all my days, and all I can do is believe that I suffered from some monstrous delusion, from some phantasmagoria of the bewildered senses. You know we went home together in silence, not a word passed between us as to what I fancied I saw; had we not better agree to keep silence on the subject? When I took my walk in the peaceful morning sunshine, I thought all the earth seemed full of praise, and passing by that wall I noticed there were no more signs recorded, and I blotted out those that remained. The mystery is over, and we can live quietly again. I think some poison has been working for the last few weeks; I have trodden on the verge of madness, but I am sane now."

Mr. Vaughan had spoken earnestly, and bent forward in his chair and glanced at Dyson with something of entreaty.

"My dear Vaughan," said the other, after a pause, "what's the use of this? it is much too late to take that tone; we have gone too deep. Besides you know as well as I that there is no delusion in the case; I wish there were with all my heart. No, in justice to myself I must tell you the whole story, so far as I know it."

"Very good," said Vaughan with a sigh, "if you must, you must."

"Then," said Dyson, "we will begin with the end if you please. I found this brooch you have just identified in the place we have called the Bowl. There was a heap of grey ashes, as if a fire had been burning, indeed, the embers were still hot, and this brooch was lying on the ground, just outside the range of the flame. It must have dropped accidentally from the dress of the person who was wearing it. No, don't interrupt me; we can pass now to the beginning, as we have had the end. Let us go back to that day you came to see me in my rooms in London. So far as I can remember, soon after you came in you mentioned, in a somewhat casual manner, that an unfortunate and mysterious incident had occurred in your part of the country; a girl named Annie Trevor had gone to see a relative, and had disappeared. I confess freely that what you said did not greatly interest me;

there are so many reasons which may make it extremely convenient for a man and more especially a woman to vanish from the circle of their relations and friends. I suppose, if we were to consult the police, one would find that in London somebody disappears mysteriously every other week, and the officers would no doubt shrug their shoulders, and tell you that by the law of averages it could not be otherwise. So I was very culpably careless to your story, and besides, there is another reason for my lack of interest; your tale was inexplicable. You could only suggest a blackguard sailor on the tramp, but I discarded the explanation immediately. For many reasons, but chiefly because the occasional criminal, the amateur in brutal crime, is always found out, especially if he selects the country as the scene of his operations. You will remember the case of that Garcia you mentioned; he strolled into a railway station the day after the murder, his trousers covered with blood, and the works of the Dutch clock, his loot, tied in a neat parcel. So rejecting this, your only suggestion, the whole tale became, as I say, inexplicable, and, therefore, profoundly uninteresting. Yes, *therefore*, it is a perfectly valid conclusion. Do you ever trouble your head about problems which you know to be insoluble? Did you ever bestow much thought on the old puzzle of Achilles and the Tortoise? Of course not, because you knew it was a hopeless quest, and so when you told me the story of a country girl who had disappeared I simply placed the whole thing down in the category of the insoluble, and thought no more about the matter. I was mistaken, so it has turned out; but if you remember, you immediately passed on to an affair which interested you more intensely, because personally. I need not go over the very singular narrative of the flint signs; at first I thought it all trivial, probably some children's game, and if not that a hoax of some sort; but your showing me the arrow-head awoke my acute interest. Here, I saw, there was something widely removed from the commonplace, and matter of real curiosity; and as soon as I came here I set to work to find the solution, repeating to myself again and again the signs you had described. First came the sign we have agreed to call the Army; a number of serried lines of flints, all pointing in the same way. Then the lines, like the spokes of a wheel, all converging towards the figure of a Bowl, then the triangle or Pyramid, and last of all the Half-moon. I confess that I exhausted conjecture in my efforts to unveil this mystery, and as you will understand it was a duplex or rather triplex problem. For I had not merely to ask myself: what do these figures mean? but also, who can possibly be responsible for the designing of them? And again, who can possibly possess such valuable things, and knowing their value thus throw them down by the wayside? This line of thought led me to suppose that the person or persons in question did not know the value of unique flint arrow-heads, and yet this did not lead me far, for a well-educated man might easily be ignorant on such a subject. Then came the complication of the eye on the wall, and you remember that we could not avoid the conclusion that in the two cases the same agency was at work. The peculiar position of these eyes on the wall made me enquire if there was such a thing as a dwarf anywhere in the neighbourhood, but I found that there was not, and I knew that the children who pass by every day had nothing to do with the matter. Yet I felt convinced that whoever drew the eyes must be from three and a half to four feet high, since, as I pointed out at the time, anyone who draws on a perpendicular surface chooses by instinct a spot about level with his face. Then again, there was the question of the peculiar shape of the eyes; that marked Mongolian character of which the English countryman could have no conception, and for a final cause of confusion the obvious fact that the designer or designers must be able practically to see in the dark. As you remarked, a man who has been confined for many years in an extremely dark cell or dungeon might acquire that power; but since the days of Edmond Dantés, where would such a prison be found in Europe? A sailor, who had been immured for a considerable period in some horrible Chinese *oubliette*, seemed the individual I was in search of, and though it looked improbable, it was not absolutely impossible that a sailor or, let us say, a man employed on shipboard, should be a dwarf. But how to account for my imaginary sailor being in possession of prehistoric arrow-heads? And the possession granted, what was the meaning and object of these mysterious signs of flint, and the almond-shaped eyes? Your theory of a contemplated burglary I saw, nearly from the first, to be quite untenable, and I confess I was utterly at a loss for a working hypothesis. It was a mere accident which put me on the track; we passed poor old Trevor, and your mention of his name and of the disappearance of his daughter, recalled the story which I had forgotten, or which remained unheeded. Here, then, I said to myself, is another problem, uninteresting, it is true, by itself; but what if it prove to be in relation with all these enigmas which torture me? I shut myself in my room, and endeavoured to dismiss all prejudice from my mind, and I went over everything *de novo*, assuming for theory's sake that the disappearance of Annie Trevor had some connection with the flint signs and the eyes on the wall. This assumption did not lead me very far, and I was on the point of giving the whole problem up in despair, when a possible significance of the Bowl struck me. As you know there is a 'Devil's Punch-bowl' in Surrey, and I saw that the symbol might refer to some feature in the country. Putting the two extremes together, I determined to look for the Bowl near the path which the lost girl had taken, and you know how I found it. I interpreted the sign

by what I knew, and read the first, the Army, thus:
'there is to be a gathering or assembly at the Bowl in
a fortnight (that is the Half-moon) to see the Pyramid, or to build the Pyramid.' The eyes, drawn one
by one, day by day, evidently checked off the days,
and I knew that there would be fourteen and no
more. Thus far the way seemed pretty plain; I would
not trouble myself to enquire as to the nature of the
assembly, or as to who was to assemble in the loneliest
and most dreaded place among these lonely hills. In
Ireland or China or the west of America the question
would have been easily answered; a muster of the dis-
affected, the meeting of a secret society, Vigilantes
summoned to report: the thing would be simplicity
itself; but in this quiet corner of England, inhabited
by quiet folk, no such suppositions were possible for
a moment. But I knew that I should have an opportunity of seeing and watching the assembly, and I
did not care to perplex myself with hopeless research;
and in place of reasoning a wild fancy entered into
judgment; I remembered what people had said about
Annie Trevor's disappearance, that she had been
'taken by the fairies'. I tell you, Vaughan, I am a sane
man as you are, my brain is not, I trust, mere vacant
space to let to any wild improbability, and I tried my
best to thrust the fantasy away. And the hint came of
the old name of fairies, 'the little people', and the
very probable belief that they represent a tradition of
the prehistoric Turanian inhabitants of the country,

who were cave dwellers: and then I realized with a shock that I was looking for a being under four feet in height, accustomed to live in darkness, possessing stone instruments, and familiar with the Mongolian cast of features! I say this, Vaughan, that I should be ashamed to hint at such visionary stuff to you, if it were not for that which you saw with your very eyes last night, and I say that I might doubt the evidence of my senses, if they were not confirmed by yours. But you and I cannot look each other in the face and pretend delusion; as you lay on the turf beside me I felt your flesh shrink and quiver, and I saw your eyes in the light of the flame. And so I tell you without any shame what was in my mind last night as we went through the wood and climbed the hill, and lay hidden beneath the rock.

"There was one thing that should have been most evident that puzzled me to the very last. I told you how I read the sign of the Pyramid; the assembly was to see a pyramid, and the true meaning of the symbol escaped me to the last moment. The old derivation from πυρ, fire, though false, should have set me on the track, but it never occurred to me.

"I think I need say very little more. You know we were quite helpless, even if we had foreseen what was to come. Ah, the particular place where these signs were displayed? Yes, that is a curious question. But this house, is, so far as I can judge, in a pretty central situation amongst the hills; and possibly, who can say yes or no, that queer, old limestone pillar by your garden wall was a place of meeting before the Celt set foot in Britain. But there is one thing I must add: I don't regret our inability to rescue the wretched girl. You saw the appearance of those things that gathered thick and writhed in the Bowl; you may be sure that what lay bound in the midst of them was no longer fit for earth."

"So?" said Vaughan.

"So she passed in the Pyramid of Fire," said Dyson, "and they passed again to the underworld, to the places beneath the hills."

by

GWYN JONES

★

SHACKI THOMAS

Shacki Thomas was fifty-two, shortish, and bandy from working underground. Unemployment was straitening his means but could do nothing with his legs. But play the white man, he would say—though I'm bandy, I'm straight. It was his one witticism, and he was not using it so frequently now that his missis was in hospital.

He was going to see her this afternoon. He gave a two-handed pluck at his white silk muffler, a tug at the broken nose of his tweed cap, and so went out the back way to the street slanting sharply from High Street to the river. The houses were part soft stone, part yellow brick, and grimy; the roadway between them was decorated with dogs and children and three new-painted lamp-posts, and each parlour window showed a china flower-pot nesting an aspidistra or rock fern. He passed his own window, and saw that the fern was doing famous though he'd forgotten to water it since Gwenny—oh, Gwenny, Gwenny, he was saying, if only you was home in our house again!

Twenty yards in front he saw Jinkins the Oil and hurried to catch him up. Owbe, they said.

" 'Orse gets more human every day," said Jinkins from the cart, and to forget his troubles Shacki made a long speech, addressing the horse's hindquarters:

"Some horses is marvellous. Pony I used to know underground, see—you never seen nothing like that pony at the end of a shift. Used to rip down the road, mun, if there'd a-been anything in the way he'd a-hit his brains out ten times over. Intelligent, Mr. Jinkins? You never seen nothing like him!"

As they approached the railway bridge, the two-ten to Cwmcawl went whitely over. The horse raised his head.

"Now, now, you old fool," cried Jinkins. "It's under you got to go, not over." He turned to Shacki and apologized for the dumb creature. " 'Orse do get more human every day, see."

But Shacki couldn't laugh. It was Gwenny, Gwenny, if only you was home with me, my gel; and fear was gnawing him, wormlike.

Turning away beyond the bridge into High Street, he found the old sweats around the Cenotaph. For a minute or two he would take his place in the congregation. A lady angel spread her wings over them, but her eyes were fixed on the door of the Griffin opposite. GWELL ANGAU NA CHYWILYDD said the inscription, "Better death than dishonour", and as Shacki arrived the conversation was of death. "I once hear tell", said Ianto Evans, "about a farmer in the Vale who quarrelled summut shocking with his daughter after his old woman died. Well, p'raps she give him arsenic—I donno nothing 'bout that—but he went off at last, and they stuck him in the deep hole and went back to hear the will. Lawyer chap, all chops and whiskers like a balled tomcat, he reads it out, and everything in the safe goes to Mary Anne and the other stuff to his sister. So they has a look at the safe, and what's inside it? Sweet fanny adams, boys, that's what." By pointing a finger at him, Ianto brought Shacki into his audience. " 'And what'll you do with the safe, my pretty?' asks the sister—like sugar on lemon, so I hear. Mary Anne thinks a bit and then brings it out very slow. 'If it wasn't for my poor old mam as is in heaven,' she says, 'I'd stick it up over the old bugger for a tombstone.' " He scratched his big nose. "What's think of that, uh?"

His brother Ivor picked his teeth. "Funny things do happen at funedrals. I once hear tell about a chap as travelled from Wrexham to the Rhondda to spit into another chap's grave."

"Might a-brought the flowers up," said Ianto.

"No, not this chap's spit wouldn't."

"I mean, there's spit and spit," said Tommy Sayce. "I mean, f'rinstance——" A moist starfish splashed on the dust, and he changed the subject. "How's the missis, Shacki?"

Shacki looked from Ivor to the lady angel, but she

was intent on the Griffin. "Thass what I going to see, chaps. Fine I do hope, ay."

They all hoped so, and confessed as much. But they were all fools, and the worm fear was at Shacki's heart like a maggot in a swede. "I got to go this afternoon, see," he said, hoping for a chorus of re-assurance and brave words, but—— "I remember," Tommy Sayce took up the tale, "when little Sammy Jones had his leg took off at the hip. 'How do a chap with only one peg on him get about, doctor?' he asks old Dr. Combes. 'Why, mun,' doctor tells him, 'we'll get you a nice wooden leg, Sammy.' 'Ay, but will I be safe with him, doctor?' asks Sammy. 'Safe? Good God, mun, you'll be timber right to the face!' Thass what doctor told him."

"Ah, they'm marvellous places, them hospitals," Shacki assured them, to assure himself at the same time. "Look at the good they do do."

"Ay, and look at the good they don't do! Didn't they let Johnny James's mam out 'cos she had cancer and they was too dull to cure it? And Johnny think-ing she was better—the devils!"

The worm went ahead with his tunnelling. "I carn stop, anyway," said Shacki, and low-spiritedly he left them to their talk. Not fifty yards away he cursed them bitterly. Death, death, death, cancer, cancer, cancer—by God he'd like to see that big-nosed bas-tard Ianto Evans on his back there, and that brother of his, and Tommy Sayce, and every other knackerpant as hadn't more feeling than a tram of rippings. From the bend of the street he looked back and saw the lady angel's head and benedictory right arm and cursed her too, the scut of hell, the flat-faced sow she was! Nobody have pain, or everybody—that was the thing. He cleared his throat savagely and spat into the gutter as though between the eyes of the world. Self-pity for his loneliness brought too big a lump to his throat before he could curse again, and then once more it was all Gwenny fach, oh Gwenny fach, he'd like to tear the sky in pieces to get her home again. If only she was better, if only she was home, he'd do the washing, he'd blacklead the grate, he'd scrub through every day, he'd water that fern the minute he got back—he was shaking his head in disgust. Ay, he was a fine one, he was.

Then he went into the greengrocer's, where the air smelled so much a pound.

"Nice bunch of chrysanths," he was offered, but they were white and he rejected them. "I ain't enamelled of them white ones. Something with a bit of colour, look."

He bought a bunch of flowers and three fresh eggs for a shilling and fivepence, and carried them as carefully as one-tenth his dole deserved to the Red Lion bus stop. Soon the bus came, chocolate and white, with chromium fittings. He found the conductor struggling with a small table brought on by a hill farm-woman at the Deri. "Watch my eggs, butty," he begged, and stood on the step till at last they fixed it in the gangway, where it lay on its back with its legs up in the air like a live thing dead. Through the back window Shacki saw a youngster running after the bus. "Oi, mate——" "Behind time," said the conductor hotly. "This here blasted table——" He came for his fare and to mutter to Shacki. "I never had this woman on board yet she hadn't a table or a hantimacassar or a chest in drawers or a frail of pickled onions or summut. Moving by instalments I reckon she is, or doing a moonlight flit. Iss a 'ell of a life this!"

As the bus went on up the valley, Shacki made a gloomy attempt to put in proper order what he had to tell Gwenny. The house was going on fine, he himself was feeling in the pink, there was a new baby at number five, he'd watered the fern—and he must tell her summut cheerful. Like what Jinkins said to the horse, and this here conductor chap—proper devil-may-care this conductor, you could see that with half an eye. Near Pensarn he saw lime on the bulging fields, like salt on a fat woman's lap. The grass under it looked the colour of a sick dog's nose. He saw farming as a thin-lined circle. If you hadn't the grass, you couldn't feed the beasts; if you couldn't feed the beasts, you didn't get manure; if you didn't get manure, you had to buy fertilizer—which brought you back to grass. All flesh is grass, he heard the preacher say, and all the goodliness thereof is as the flower of the field. The grass withereth, the flower fadeth—duw, duw, what a thought! It made a fellow think, indeed now it did. Yesterday a kid, to-day a man of fifty, to-morrow they're buying you eight pound ten's worth of elm with brass handles. Oh death, death, death, and in life pain and trouble—away, away, the wall of his belly trembled with the trembling of the bus, and the worm drove a roadway through his heart.

At Pensarn a girl stood at the bus stop and said: "Did a young man leave a message for me at the Red Lion?"

"Yes, my dear," said the conductor. "He told me special you was to let me give you a nice kiss."

"Cheeky flamer!" said the hill farm-woman, but the girl looked down in the mouth, and Shacki felt sorry for her. He explained that a young man had run after the bus at the Red Lion. Ay, he did rather fancy he was a fairish sort of chap 'bout as big as the conductor, so——— "It must a-been Harry," the girl concluded. "Thank you," said Shacki, as though she had done him a favour. Indeed, she had, for he could talk about this to Gwenny.

Later a collier got on. "Where you been then?" the conductor asked. "Why you so dirty, mun?"

"I been picking you a bag of nuts." He took the conductor's measurements, aggressively. "Monkey nuts," he added. He did not enter the bus and sit down, but stood on the step for his twopenny ride.

"We got to draw the line somewhere," the conductor pointed out.

Shacki was cheered by the undoubted circumstance that all the wit of the Goytre Valley was being poured out for his and Gwenny's benefit. What Jinkins said about the horse now—— And this about the nuts —— And that gel at Pensarn—— What funny chaps there was about if you only came to think of it. He began to think hard, hoping for a witticism of his own, a personal offering for Gwenny. She had heard the bandy-straight one before, just once or twice or fifty times or a hundred, or maybe oftener than that. Something new was wanted. A fellow like this conductor, of course, he could turn them off like lightning. Here he was, looking at the flowers. Shacki waited for his sally. They were his flowers, weren't they? Diawl, anything said about um was as good as his, too.

"I like a nice lily, myself," said the conductor.

"You look more you'd like a nice pansy," said the collier. He grinned, the slaver glistening on his red gums, and winked at the hill farm-woman. "Cheeky flamer!" she called him.

"You askin' for a fight? 'Cos if you are——"

"Sorry, can't stop now." Still grinning, he narrowed his coaly eyes. "But any time you want me, butty, I'm Jack Powell, Mutton Tump. That's me —Jack Powell." He prepared to drop off, and the conductor kept his finger on the bell, hoping to fetch him a cropper. "Oh, no you don't, butty!" They heard his nailed boots braking on the road and then through the back window saw him fall away behind them, his knees jerking very fast. "I'll be up here Sunday," threatened the conductor, but Shacki didn't believe him. He'd lay two-to-one Jack Powell any day, and was glad a collier could lick a bus conductor.

"Don't forget to stop at the hospital," he said by way of reminder, and the conductor, as though to recover face, told a tale about the patient who wouldn't take a black draught unless the sister took one too. To please him, Shacki smiled grimly and wagged his head and said what chaps there was about, but he now thought less highly of the humorist, and as they came nearer the stopping place he could feel that same old disturbance, just as though he wanted to go out the back. Bump, bump, bump, the driver must be doing it deliberate, but try to forget, for he might be going to hear good news. She might even be coming home. He grovelled. Home, like Johnny James's mother, hopeless case, cancer of the womb— not that for you, Gwenny fach, he prayed, and Ianto Evans, for speaking of it, he thrust into the devil's baking oven. Bump, bump, bump, if he didn't get off this bus soon, he'd be all turned up, only too sure. He felt rotten in the belly, and the worm turned a new heading in his heart.

He alighted.

Inside the hall, he found from the clock that as

usual he was five minutes too early for the women's ward. "Would you like to see anyone in the men's ward?" He thought he would, if only to pass the time. So down the corridor he went, for it was a tiny hospital, run on the pennies of colliers like himself. The men's ward had a wireless set, and the patients were a lively lot. Bill Williams the Cwm borrowed Shacki's flowers. "Oi, nurse," he shouted; " 'ow'll I look with a bunch of these on me chest?"

It was the sporty probationer. "Like a big fat pig with a happle in his mouth," she suggested.

"There's a fine bloody thing to say, nurse! Don't I look better'n a pig, boys?"

"Ay," said Shacki, thinking of the flowers of the field. "You looks like a lily in the mouth of 'ell."

Bill started to laugh, and the other men started to laugh, and, seeing this, Shacki became quite convulsed at his second witticism. The blue smallcoal pitting his face grew less noticeable as his scars grew redder. It was a laugh to do a man's heart good, and it came down on that tunnelling worm like a hob-nailed boot. "You'll have matron along," the probationer warned them.

Then Shacki took his flowers from Bill, and grinning all over his face went back through the corridor to the entrance hall. He'd make his lovely gel laugh an' all! He felt fine now, he did, and everything was going to be all right. He knew it. Tell her he'd cleaned the house, and about the baby at number five, and about Jinkins and the collier and the girl and the conductor and Bill Williams the Cwm and him—it'd be better'n a circus for Gwenny.

Into the women's ward. Nod here, nod there, straight across to Gwenny with all the news on the end of his tongue. Then he swore under his breath. Matron was standing by Gwenny's bed, looking like a change of pillowcases. She was so clean and stiff and starched and grand that he felt small and mean and shabby before her, and frightened, and something of a fool. Respectfully, he greeted her even before he greeted his wife, and when she returned his good day, thanked her.

"We've got good news for you, Mr. Thomas. You'll be able to have Mrs. Thomas home very soon now."

"Oh," he said. He was looking down at Gwenny's white smile. A murderous hate and rage against all living things filled his heart, and he would have had no one free of suffering. " 'Cos she's better?"

"Of course. Why else?"

He put the eggs down carefully, and the flowers. Then he fell on his knees at the bedside. "My gel!" he cried out hoarsely. "Oh, my lovely gel!" With her right hand she touched his hair. "There, there, little Shacki bach! Don't take on, look!"

"You are upsetting the patient," the pillowcase said severely, "and you are disturbing the ward. I shall have to ask you to go outside."

It was a quarter of a minute before he got to his feet, and then he was ashamed to look anyone in the face. He snuffled a bit and rubbed under his eyes. "All right, matron," he managed to say. "You can send for the pleece, if you like. I'm that happy, mun!"

He saw his old Gwenny looking an absolute picture there in bed, and thought these would be her last tears, and such happy ones. And with the thought he looked proudly around, and could tell that no one in the ward thought him an old softy. He didn't hate anyone any longer. He was all love, and gave old Gwenny a kiss as bold as brass before he walked outside. He knew they'd let him in again soon.

by

E. TEGLA DAVIES

*

THE STRANGE APEMAN

Translated from the Welsh by
Ll. Wyn Griffith

A day of teeming rain in the great forest, the ape-men hunched up against the tree-trunks, so close to the trees that they seemed part of them, their arms like branches in shape and colour. There they squatted, watching the heavy raindrops falling lifelessly to the ground. The water formed into pools under the trees, and the pools rose and met, until the marshy ground became a lake and each apeman stood on a small island little larger than his foot.

At times a light puff of wind rustled the leaves and a rush of water fell from them: here and there an apeman climbed the trunk of his tree as his island vanished under him. Soon there remained but one upon the ground—the strange apeman whose behaviour troubled them all. As his island shrank, they watched him bend down to reach a large stone still above the water-level, dragging it towards him and thrusting it against the tree-trunk, standing upon it when his island disappeared. They parted the leaves and stared at him vacantly. Whenever they were in trouble, his actions were inexplicably strange to them. Sometimes they showed their gratitude by rubbing their cheeks against his, but more frequently he roused a feeling of perplexity and imminent danger, and then they sought his blood. His skill in devising a new way of escape or defence saved him.

One day, when the monster was pursuing them closely and they had neither refuge nor forest at hand, nor were they numerous enough to attack tooth and limb, it was he who scaled a crag quickly to loosen a great boulder so that it fell on the head of the beast and killed him. They had not imagined that boulder and crag could help them, nor did they understand how it happened then. They knew that the stone this strange apeman had loosened fell upon the monster's head and saved them, and that the fall of the stone came after his climb. For a while, they expected this to happen each time he scaled the crag, and as it did not take place, they grew more confused and avoided him whenever possible.

Now that they saw him standing on the stone instead of climbing the trunk, they feared him and they crept each to the other side of his own tree, so that the trees that sheltered them might protect them from him. As the rain fell, they peered past the trunks and through the large heavy leaves at this strange apeman on his stone. But the water rose and covered

145

the stone, and he was compelled, against his will, to
climb his tree. They were relieved when they saw that
he had to do as they had done, and they moved once
more towards him and made him one of themselves
again. There they sheltered, each in his tree, mute
and still as images, listening to the rain, with no sign
of life but an occasional blink as a stray raindrop fell
between the leaves and on their heads.

In spite of the downpour the leaves stood firm and
unbent, giving good shelter: rarely did any drops
penetrate, but in the gaps between the trees the rain
fell straight to the ground in a mighty deluge. For a
long time the leaves withstood the tempest although
the water accumulated in them, but in the end they
gave way, for all their strength, and they began to
droop and the water to fall upon the creatures below.
This continued until there was little to choose between tree and open ground, the one with its steady
rain and the other with its periodical drenching.
Gradually the leaves took the shape of the wings of
giant birds, wounded in their joints, hanging limply,
rain pouring from their tips: the trees ceased to give
shelter and the apemen closed into the places where
the boughs branched most thickly.

Terrified at their helplessness, they forgot the
strange apeman until one of them chanced to look in
his direction and saw him seizing the leaf-stalks and
shaking them free of water, plaiting them clumsily
into a fairish roof above his head, stout enough to

shelter him. The watcher's grunt of surprise drew the attention of the rest, and they stared at him in amazement, pressing against the tree-trunks, closely following his movements as he plaited until at last he was content to rest and gaze at the downpour. They began to scowl, their hands to twitch with desire to rend him could they venture near: a few gnashed their teeth, and others were so bemused that they left their shelters and moved to the ends of the boughs nearest to him, until the sagging of the thinner boughs beneath their weight and the weight of the water on the leaves brought a deluge on their heads and roused them to retreat.

Thus they remained, closing in to the trees for shelter while the rain fell down the leaves and into the lake below. No rustle, no cry, no sound but the sad drip of water on the trees, dripping again from tree to lake, until the very sound of it became silence in their ears. Suddenly it was broken by the uneasy stir of a great bird sheltering near by and shrinking from the rain that penetrated the leaves, flapping its wings when a large leaf emptied its burden. A viper rustled its way out of the dust that was turning into mud, and swam in the lake to clean itself. The apemen, even the strange apeman, looked disconsolate and cowardly as they stared at the falling rain, the lake rising round the trees, the great birds and the vipers growing restless.

The strange apeman began to sniff and to look this

way and that, the others following him, their chests rising and falling quickly, sniffing frantically until the noise rivalled the sound of the rain. A heavy stench of mud reached them and brought new terror to them. Their eyes opened wide and turned red, and they scowled in their panic as they vainly sought another refuge. For they were creatures of the ground, clumsy in their movements upon the trees to which they resorted in emergency only.

The monster roamed in search of prey, and the stench arose from the deep mud of the marsh as his feet squelched through the crust, wave after wave of stench as he lifted his feet. The apemen sniffed violently, for the strange apeman had located the source of the odour, and a new fear came upon them with the new sound, the vile sound of feet in the mud. They forgot the rain and began to descend, but the lake lay below and they turned back into their shelters on the trees. If the monster reached the trees, it would be hard to hold to the branches when he began to shake a tree, as he had so often done in the past, until he uprooted it, and then woe betide whoever trusted to the tree. In days gone by, escape would have been easier, but now the ground below had become a lake, and the unsubmerged land was a bog more dangerous than the lake.

Drenched and despondent, the apemen looked at each other in their fear, barely able to grip the slippery branches. The strange apeman, they observed, rose and shook himself, looked at them and then leapt on to another tree in spite of the danger of slipping: as he landed, a torrent of water fell from the leaves. They were afraid to do likewise, until they saw him leap again a moment later, and after he had leapt several times in safety, they ventured to follow his example. For this was their only means of escape, and they dared not take to the lake below them. He leapt from tree to tree, and they followed him. A screech re-echoed through the forest, and in their sudden panic they clung to the nearest branch. But one of them fell and sank until they saw nothing but his head and arms vainly striving to reach the trunk of his tree: the strange apeman leapt upon one of its branches and forced it down within reach of the creature until he seized it and climbed up again, the others staring confusedly at him and at each other. A glimmer in their eyes showed that they relied upon him for salvation.

As the water fell from the trees after each leap, the hideous cry of the monster tore through the air until the forest seemed to quake in terror, for the falling water revealed their position and he drew nearer to them, the stench rising and the sound of his squelching feet growing louder. The strange apeman leapt forward from tree to tree steadily and safely, ever in the same direction, and they followed him heedless of the wet and of the danger of slipping, so great was their desire to escape.

Soon they reached open country with rising ground a short distance ahead, and from the last tree the strange apeman leapt on to a knoll. They followed him up a rocky spur on to a high crag, climbing from ledge to ledge, crossing the many torrents, quickly disappearing into a cave half-way up its face. There they tried to shake themselves free of water, looking now at the strange apeman who led them, now at one another, with a trace of something not unlike a smile on their faces. They stood at the mouth of the cave watching the heavy and monotonous rain falling life-lessly, with nothing to break the monotony but the occasional fall of a stone loosened from the crag and hurtling down from ledge to ledge until it reached the water below, for all the land from the crag to the forest and beyond was one vast sea. They squatted at the cave-mouth in long and sullen silence, listening intently.

When at length the rain stopped, the silence was profound, for there was no wind blowing. But the dread sound rose up again, the squelching feet of the monster approaching, the stench of mud heavy on the air. Huddled together, they were still as the dead, listening to every movement as the monster sniffed about at the foot of the crag uncertain of their position and half submerged in the water.

The sky cleared, and the sun was setting. Towards the horizon, the tints merged their beauty and wisps of cloud crossed the sky. The apemen saw it all, unmoved and uncomprehending, as they had watched the falling rain. But the strange apeman looked upon this beauty open-eyed, stirring uneasily as if lost in contemplation, while the others glared at him angrily each time he moved, although he made no noise in moving. Under the spell of this new marvel of colour changing before his eyes, he forgot his scowling companions, the monster sniffing to and fro below the crag, the terror awakened by the squelching feet, and he stepped forward.

Suddenly, forgetting his peril, oblivious of his surroundings, the strangest "Oh!" that apeman ever uttered burst from his lips, and the monster bellowed in reply to this betraying cry. His companions turned upon him and tore him limb from limb and cast him down; they fled from the cave, rushed up the crag into safety, leaving his limbs to the monster to devour. Each in his own crevice in the rock-face, they stared contentedly at the vain efforts of the monster to climb towards them, rid of their peril and of the strange apeman. On their faces, as they sucked their fingers and licked their chops, was a look of ease; the world turned bright.

So died the first man, and a myriad years passed before a second man appeared.

by

EILUNED LEWIS

*

THE POACHER

Mr. Richard Woodly was a bachelor who flattered himself on never interfering in other people's affairs. Having inherited a pleasant estate in Wiltshire with enough money to carry out the improvements it needed, he was free to indulge his taste for gardening and ecclesiastical archæology. There was not a church in the county on which he was not an authority, while his glowing herbaceous borders, expensively-run greenhouses and a new water-garden of his own plan ning, bore witness to a love of flowers.

Every spring or, to put it more precisely, between the time of the bulbs and the flowering shrubs, Mr. Woodly would inform his housekeeper and his head gardener that he was going away for a few weeks. As a young man these journeys led him to Italy, Spain or Greece, but with the approach of middle-age, he found himself more and more affected by the beauty of an English landscape and inclined to remain at home.

One April, he had gone to stay in Gloucestershire,

and on a certain fine, sunny morning he walked from his inn through the fields where the larks were singing, to visit a neighbouring church.

While he stood in the chancel examining the carved miserere seats of the choir stalls a conversation forced itself on his hearing through the open door of the vestry.

"Well, I reckon we needn't trespass on your time any longer." The man's voice was unmistakably American, and Mr. Woodly, who didn't care for Americans, continued to give his attention to the choir stalls.

"It's very good of you to have taken so much trouble," a woman's voice chimed in and was cut short by, "Not at all! Not at all!" The words of the last speaker—full-throated, English and parsonic—boomed under the vaulted roof.

"I only wish I could throw some light on the subject. It's a most interesting story. As you see, there were Lovells in the parish as lately as ten years ago, but none, it seems, who fit into your tale. If ever I do discover anything——"

The speakers came out through the vestry door—a smartly dressed woman, holding a little girl by the hand, a tall man, wearing tortoiseshell spectacles, and the grey-haired vicar. As they passed down the aisle the child turned and looked at Mr. Woodly, who was now studying an almost obliterated wall-painting of the Day of Judgment over the chancel arch. She had, he thought, an elfish face and remarkably large, dark eyes. For a minute or two he stood watching the little creature, with her thin legs and black curls, on her way from the dark church to the sunshine outside.

Perhaps it was the child who made him inclined to be more sociable than usual when the same family appeared at his inn that morning, driving up to the door in a large, closed car, just as Mr. Woodly reached it by way of field paths.

In the coffee-room at lunch time they sat at an opposite table, and the child, restless and unwilling to eat, slipped down from her chair before the end of the meal to examine a stuffed fox in a glass case at one end of the room.

She slid past Mr. Woodly with a quick grace of movement, and suddenly he wanted to speak to her.

"He looks a wily old fox, don't you think?"

There now! He had startled her. For a fraction of a second the child hesitated, her dark brown eyes fixed on Mr. Woodly; then she fled back to her parents. They were apologizing to him now, with little smiles and gestures. Later, the man strolled over to where Mr. Woodly was sitting and introduced himself.

"I'm Ernest P. Wilbur," he announced. "Didn't we see you in that li'l old church this morning? I wonder now, could you tell me the exact age of all these churches round here?"

He had come to the right authority in Mr. Woodly.

"I guess you know a lot about ancient monuments," said Ernest P. Wilbur, when Mr. Woodly had finished his short history of the Cotswold churches, followed by a few scholarly remarks on the Norman, Transitional and Perpendicular styles of architecture.

"And ancient families, too, I dare say. May I ask you if this is your part of the country? No? Well, then I reckon you won't be able to help me over a problem I've been trying to figure out lately. It's about our li'l girl here."

Mr. Woodly expressed well-bred surprise, adding that he had never seen a more attractive child.

"Yes, sir!" agreed Mr. Wilbur proudly. "In another few years she'll be doing some damage with those eyes of hers, but she didn't get them from either Mrs. Wilbur or me." The big American paused to fill his pipe and with another glance at the quiet face of the Englishman opposite him, leant back in his chair.

"If I may, I'll tell you the story. My wife and I lost our own li'l girl when she was a baby." He was silent for a moment, trying, it seemed, to get his pipe to draw. Then he went on.

"I thought Mrs. Wilbur would never leave off fretting, but after a time we went up into Canada for a change, for she'd been very ill, and in the shack next to where we were staying for the fishing, there was a German family—just poor emigrants, with a whole heap of children. The youngest of the lot was a baby a few months old. The mother was an English-woman who had come there one night and died in giving birth to the child, and the German woman had taken it in and brought it up along with her own children, though she didn't know anything about its history. She told us that the mother was a delicate, soft-spoken lady, and she was so darned sorry for her that she promised to look after the child though there was no money and she had six of her own."

"And her father?" asked Mr. Woodly.

"No, sir. She couldn't find out anything about her father—only that his name was Lovell. I guess he'd gone off with another dame. Well, I expect you've seen the end of my story. I saw it myself after a few days. Mrs. Wilbur was only happy when she was looking after that child. It just seemed as though we'd been sent straight to care for her, and she's been like our own daughter ever since, or pretty near. Not just exactly the same perhaps, but there are some things you can't have over again."

"It's a strange story," said Mr. Woodly. He was more interested than he would have thought possible by the confidence of this complete stranger. So this dark-eyed changeling did not belong to theAmerican couple. She was the child of English parents, of some runaway couple perhaps.

"You said the name was Lovell?"

"Yeah! And I can't discover a darn thing about the family. It sounds a kind of aristocratic name to me, and there's nothing about that child that would make you think it wasn't. She's sensitive—and wild. I guess there was something dare-devil about those Lovells. All this time I've been waiting for a chance to come to England and find things out for myself. I thought it would be easy but it seems it's like searching for——"

"What led you to think of this place?" asked Mr. Woodly.

"A man on the ship coming over said he'd known of some Lovells in this part of Gloucestershire, and I found the name in the parish register where you saw us this morning; but that dug-out old parson had never heard of any of 'em going to America."

"Well, I wish you luck," said Mr. Woodly. "But I shouldn't be too keen on finding the family. They might want to keep her, you know."

Next morning the Wilburs left. Over his kidney and bacon Mr. Woodly saw the car drive up to the door and Ernest P. Wilbur—very large in his overcoat—distribute tips to the boots, the chambermaid and the red-cheeked waitress. Mr. Woodly found himself watching their departure with interest, hoping at the last that the brown-eyed child would turn her head in his direction.

"If they do find her relations," he remarked to

himself, "I hope for Ernest P. Wilbur's sake they'll be aristocratic." And, smiling gently, Mr. Woodly helped himself to the marmalade.

I have said that Mr. Woodly prided himself upon not interfering in other people's affairs. The sentimental quest of Ernest P. Wilbur slipped into a pigeon-hole of his mind; it was of considerably less importance than the stone effigies and fourteenth-century wall paintings in the Gloucestershire churches, and the flowering of his azaleas next month.

The summer that followed was fine and Mr. Woodly's herbaceous borders had never looked better. But, by the time the October sunshine was slanting through his beech woods, he had grown restive. This time he chose to visit the Welsh Marches, where an Archæological Society claimed to have laid bare fresh Roman remains.

Sending his luggage on ahead, Mr. Woodly left the train at a border station and walked a dozen miles across the hills. The rich colours of October surrounded him: the scarlet berries of the mountain ash, the tips of the bilberry leaves and the rust-coloured bracken at his feet. There was autumn, too, in the sunset which flamed before him beyond the rugged country cut by innumerable dingles and the dark hills rising one behind the other. The blue smoke of the "Pencader Arms" rising from the valley was a welcome sight to Mr. Woodly as he scrambled down the last hillside and over a stile into a muddy lane.

Mrs. Evans, the landlady, received him with the natural courtesy of her race. She was a woman of forty, with dark eyes, a slightly aquiline nose and a soft Welsh voice. The "Pencader Arms" was a hostelry noted in the district for the comfort of its beds, the superiority of its fishing and the excellence of its bacon and eggs. Mr. Woodly found that he was the sole guest, with ample opportunity of relishing Mrs. Evans's conversation as well as her cooking.

Next morning the weather broke. Mr. Woodly decided that it was too wet to visit the Roman camp with enjoyment, and found his way instead to the village of Aberdulas, where he purchased tobacco at the general store and examined the church with its square wooden tower and sixteenth-century rood screen.

Mrs. Evans was distressed at his reappearance.

"Well, well, there's wet you are!" she exclaimed. Then calling to the little maid: "Quick, Polly, take Mr. Woodly's coat. Better take off your boots at once. Sit you down there and ketch into your dinner. I'll make you a nice cup of hot tea."

The inn parlour where Mr. Woodly spent the afternoon was a long, low room where the scent of wood smoke and beeswax mingled with the penetrating flavour of dry rot. Past the distorted glass of the window panes the leaves of the yellowing damson trees whirled by in gusts of rain. Mr. Woodly settled himself by the fire with a book on Celtic civilization, but found his attention straying to the rugs which covered the floor round his feet.

They were, it appeared, all that was left of Mrs. Evans's late domestic pets. Across the middle of the floor caracoled a white pony skin; near the door lay the fleecy coat of a pet lamb; and something that looked very like a sheepdog crouched at the foot of the tall-boy. From the opposite wall a squirrel in a glass case regarded him with a glassy eye, and a stuffed white ferret bared its teeth in a snarl. At the end of an hour Mr. Woodly was in a state of fidgets, and decided to see how the weather looked from the front door.

The bar of the "Pencader Arms" was far more cheerful than the parlour and Mrs. Evans herself, knitting by the fire, was a pleasant sight. She welcomed him to the seat opposite—"though indeed that old settle isn't very comfortable".

It was distinctly better than the parlour and the company of the dead, Mr. Woodly reflected, crossing his legs before the comfortable blaze, and then the outer door was suddenly and violently opened, and a gust of cold wind and wet whirling leaves blew into the room as a man stepped in.

"If you're coming in, Ned, shut that door behind you," called out Mrs. Evans, with a sharper tone than Mr. Woodly had heard her use before. The intruder turned and closed the door, then faced the room, pulling off his hat that was black with rain, and raising a finger to his forehead in salutation. He had the brown eyes, set rather close together, of a gipsy and a quick smile, though his teeth were dark with decay.

"Good day, marm! Good day to you, sir! I've brought you a chub, Mrs. Evans fach, caught in the Dulas this morning. Look at the lovely creature."

He opened his basket and laid a slippery fish on the table where it lay catching the firelight on its steely scales.

"Maybe you'll be coming out one of these days, sir," the fisherman leaned across the table and smiled at Mr. Woodly. "There's not much in a chub, now, once you've caught it. They're rubbishy fish to be eating—no offence to you, Mrs. Evans—but pretty enough to catch if you've the mind and the wrist that way. Now, if you was to be here when the salmon is up——"

"Dear to goodness, Ned," cried Mrs. Evans. "D'ye think the gentleman has nothing to think of but your old fishing?"

"Not when you're around, marm, I dare say he hasn't," said Ned with a sly look and a wink at Mr. Woodly.

"There's foolish you talk!" remarked Mrs. Evans and stepped from the room.

Ned meanwhile had removed his wet boots and padded across the floor in his socks. His lean, wiry frame was clad in the wreck of a tweed jacket and a much-patched pair of corduroy trousers; the red handkerchief at his throat suited his gipsy face. Leaning against the chimney-piece, he pulled out a pipe and set to filling it, one eye cocked in Mr. Woodly's direction.

"You've not been to Aberdulas before, have you, sir?"

"No, this is my first visit. It's a pretty country, this of yours."

"Beautiful, sir. Nothing like these old hills." The pipe was alight now and giving out a strong smell of rank tobacco.

"I've travelled a bit," he went on, "and I've never seen anything to touch them. No, not even the Rocky Mountains, though they're grand enough in their way."

"Ah, so you've been to America, have you?"

"Canada, it was, sir. Been all over it. I have seen the Falls of Niagara and the Prairies and the Great Lakes—big as the sea. We travelled across them for days—me and my lady wife."

The outer door opened once more and two farmers stepped in. They were on their way home from market and at sight of Ned their joy was evident.

"How are you, man?" cried one, a red-faced young fellow. "Get out, dog!" he added, aiming a kick at a nimble little collie that had followed him in; then, nodding to Mr. Woodly, he called for drinks in which Ned was invited to join.

The second farmer, an older man with a sallow skin and a cast in one eye, emptied the rain water out of his hat with deliberation, and leaned on the bar. His eye rested on the chub.

"Thee's been up to thy old games again," he said slyly. "Where d'ee find that fellow, Ned?"

Ned jerked his thumb behind him and winked.

"Diawl, man," cried the young fellow, "tell us about the trout you caught in the brook and old Squire Lloyd watching 'ee through a little small hole in the bank."

There was a roar of laughter at this sally. Mr. Woodly, beginning to think more kindly of his book and the silence of solitude, walked from the room and back to the parlour.

In the gathering dark he read a chapter and rang for a light. Mrs. Evans herself brought in the lamp.

"I hope, sir," she said, placing it on the table, "that you haven't been disturbed by any noise." Mr. Woodly assured her that he had not.

"Well, I'm glad of that. It's that Ned Lovell again. A glass goes straight to his head and William Jones Pentre is leading him on, as though he wasn't wild enough already."

"He's an attractive looking rascal," said Mr. Woodly. "Rather gipsy-looking, perhaps."

"Half gipsy he is," replied Mrs. Evans, adding: "Lovell's a gipsy name in these parts."

At the sound of the name something stirred in Mr. Woodly's memory and he asked sharply: "What was that he said about a visit to Canada and his lady wife?"

"Did he tell you that?" Mrs. Evans was startled. "Why that was poor Miss Frances Lloyd who ran away with him."

Mr. Woodly closed his book firmly. "I'd be very much obliged to you if you'd tell the story," he said. "I have a particular reason for wanting to hear it, as a matter of fact."

"It's queer you should ask, for I'm the one that can tell you best. I was housekeeper to Jasper Lloyd at Pencader."

"And these Lloyds," asked Mr. Woodly, "what were they like?"

Mrs. Evans drew a chair up to the table and examined the wick of the lamp.

"They were all of them a bit queer, as you might say, but Jasper Lloyd was the meanest and worst of the lot. Everyone was sorry for his wife, poor lady, but she died when Miss Frances was a little thing. It was a strange house for a child to grow up in. I lived there for three years as housekeeper and I never could abide the place, with the trees crowding close all round and the plaster peeling off the walls. The river runs through the garden, so near that it's no use at all calling to anyone at the farther end; your voice is lost in the rushing of the water over the stones. And at night the noise of it seemed to get into the

house. I'd often lie awake listening to it and not able
to sleep.

"Old Mrs. Lloyd, Jasper's mother, was still living
there. She'd been a beauty in her time, but her poor
old brain had run all to seed till she forgot the faces
of her own family. She'd a liking for raw eggs—'to
clear her throat,' she used to say. She would steal
about the outhouses looking for them and hoard
them all about the place in chests and old cupboards.

"Then there was Miss Hetty, Jasper's sister. She's
never been right in the head, poor thing, thinking
she was still seventeen and always talking of going to
her first ball. She'd spend hours of the day at a big
old chest up in the attic trying on her grandmother's
frocks.

"The Lloyds had been big people in the old days,
and there'd been fine goings-on. Old Jasper's father
always kept good horses and was fond of driving
tandem.

"There were a lot of old dresses up in that cupboard, and Miss Hetty would pull them out and
sweep up and down in them—all rustling bombazine
and satin, though she was a little bit of a thing. I
remember a stiff yellow silk with a sprig on it, and a
claret silk shawl with a long fringe, and little old
high-heeled satin slippers and a brown parasol with a
jointed handle.

"Poor creature, it did her no harm! But Miss
Frances, she couldn't abide to see her aunt bedizened

in that way. She'd lock the cupboard and hide the key till Miss Hetty would come whimpering to her for it.

"All the rest of the day Miss Hetty would sit curled in front of the fire. She'd a way of covering her face with her hands when she was talking, and then peeping at you between her fingers. She wore a heap of bangles, and if ever it happened that someone came to call—which wasn't often—Miss Hetty would skip upstairs and put on a locket or a bit of lace at her throat, and then she'd trip into the drawing-room, seemingly astonished to find anyone there.

"As for old Jasper, he was the worst landlord in the county, letting his farms fall down before he'd do any repairs, so much as mend a gate or put a slate on a roof. He used to drive about in a high, rickety dog-cart, and all through the winter he hunted once or twice a week on a big old chestnut horse.

"Miss Frances didn't care for hunting—which was just as well, for her father would never have spent the money on her. He didn't part with a penny more than he could help; wore a greasy old green coat and wouldn't buy any new top-boots. His own were so tight that old Sam, the coachman, had a job to pull them off every hunting day; the Squire's language was something shocking.

"Maybe you're wondering what Ned Lovell had to do with all this. Well, every now and then he'd come round to the back door with his fishing tackle and ask if missie (as he called Miss Frances) would like to come out with him. The fish would be rising nicely, he'd say, and he'd seen a big trout as he passed the pool.

"Ned was half gipsy, and he was a young fellow in those days with brown eyes and a way of smiling. He walked loose and springy, like a collie dog.

"He was the best fisherman in these parts and he taught Miss Frances to cast a fly. She'd be out with him for hours and come back wet through, as often as not, and with a spot of colour in her cheeks. 'Look what Ned and I have caught for you, Mrs. Evans,' she'd say, coming in with a basket of fish.

"I blame myself that I didn't suspect anything in those days, but somehow I never did, for Miss Frances had a haughty way with her.

"Yet there was no one else to look after the child, Miss Hetty being so foolish and old Mrs. Lloyd getting queerer every day. Why, one evening at dinner she looks down the table at the Squire and says sudden-like: 'I seem to know your face. Tell me, who was your father?'

"Old Jasper gives a nasty sort of laugh: 'Well, mother,' he says, 'if you can't tell me, I don't know who can!'

"Miss Frances turned very red, but Miss Hetty goes on counting her cherry stones: 'This year, next year, sometime——'

"I went away about that time to take over the inn

here for my brother and his children, and glad I was to leave that daft house.

"It seems that soon after—one warm evening in May when the fish were rising nicely—Ned Lovell comes to the door. 'I've come to catch a trout,' says he. 'A pretty silver one.' (He was always poetical in his way of talking.) 'Will you tell Miss Frances I've gone to the river?'

"The servant girl takes the message to Miss Frances.

" 'Thank you, Clara,' says she, very quiet. And that's the last time she was ever seen or heard of in that house. She and Ned Lovell slipped off together that evening and he must have led her a feckless life, for he was no mate for the likes of her. They went to America, and it seems she died when a child was born, but no one ever knew where or how they lived.

"As for Ned Lovell, he came drifting back in four or five years. He was never any use for anything but fishing and drinking, and it's when he's had a glass too much that he'll tell you of his lady wife.

"And now, sir," finished Mrs. Evans, "you'll be wanting your supper. It's late, but you've let me run on so."

Mr. Woodly stood for some time, looking into the fire. He was thinking of the dark eyes of a little ten-year-old girl, and of a cheerful American voice that said: "I haven't discovered a darn thing about the family, but it sounds to me an aristocratic kind of a name."

by

FRANK RICHARDS

*

THE BLACK RAT
From *Old Soldiers Never Die*

We were in the trenches at Hulloch, and a Battalion Headquarters' signaller came in our dug-out and handed me Battalion Orders to give to the Company Commander; of course, Dann and I read it before handing it over. It consisted mainly of orders sent by the Lieutenant-General commanding the corps we were now in, and ran something like this: "It has been brought to my notice that a pessimistic feeling prevails amongst the officers, N.C.O.s and men in my corps; such expressions as 'We will never shift the enemy out of their entrenched positions' and 'The war has now become a stalemate', are frequently made. Officers must eradicate this feeling from their minds and from the minds of the men serving under them, and remember that it is only a question of time before the enemy will be driven headlong out of the lines that they now occupy." There was also too much swearing in the corps for his liking, and the officers were worse than the men: "This practice must also cease." I took the message to the Company-Commander, and his language for the rest of the day was delightful to listen to: it would have done that Lieutenant-General a heap of good if he could have heard it.

The Corps Commander was right about the pessimistic feeling prevailing: since the Battle of Loos, all along this front from Cambrin to Hulloch and as far as the eye could see, our dead were still lying out in front of us, and looking through the periscopes by day we could see the rats crawling over their bodies. They had a good picking along this front and were as fat as prize porkers. We also knew that from now on any attack that was made by us would involve huge casualties. We old hands were always hoping that the enemy would atttack us, so that we could get a bit of our own back for the Loos battle. It was all very well for the Corps General to be so optimistic: he was living in a château or mansion many many miles behind the front line from where he issued his orders, which went from him to divisions then to brigades then to battalion commanders, from them to company commanders and platoon officers who with the men had to do the real dirty work. If he had been in a front-line trench on a dark or dirty night, and going around a traverse had been knocked head over heels on his back in the deep mud by someone carrying a roll of barbed wire, or by the burst of a shell, I expect his language would have been a little stronger than what he used back in his abode of luxury. A few weeks previously he had inspected the Battalion in Montmorency Barracks and noticed that the men's brasses were not polished. He gave orders that all men in his corps when out of action must polish their brasses the same as if they were at home. Up to this time it had been a standing order in the Battalion to keep the brasses dull, but after that inspection our brasses were polished good enough to shave in. Many prayers were offered up for his soul, and a few days later when we marched down the main road towards the line with the sun shining brightly and striking on our polished brasses, the enemy in their observation balloons must have thought that hundreds of small heliographs were moving into action. One man called Duffy swore that the Corps Commander was a chief director in one of the large metal-polish companies and another remarked that the old sinner would sooner lose his trenches than his button-sticks.

During one spell in the line at Hulloch, Dann and I came out of our little dug-out, which was about fifteen yards behind the front-line trench, to clean our rifles and bayonets. We were just about to begin when there appeared, on the back of the trench we were in, the largest rat that I ever saw in my life. It was jet black and was looking intently at Dann, who threw a clod of earth at it but missed, and it didn't even attempt to dodge it. I threw a clod at it then; it sprang out of the way, but not far, and began staring at Dann again. This got on Dann's nerves; he threw another clod but missed again, and it never even flinched. I had my bayonet fixed and made a lunge at it; it sprang out of the way for me all right but had another intent look at Dann before it disappeared over the top. I would have shot it, for I had a round in the breach, but we were not allowed to fire over the top to the rear of us for fear of hitting men in the support trench; one or two men had been hit this way by men shooting at rats, and orders were very strict regarding it.

Dann had gone very pale; I asked him if he were ill. He said that he wasn't but the rat had made him feel queer. I burst out laughing. He said: "It's all right, you laughing, but I know my number is up. You saw how that rat never even flinched when I threw at it, and I saw something besides that you didn't see or you wouldn't be laughing at me. Mark my words, when I do go West that rat will be close by." I told him not to talk so wet and that we may be a hundred miles from this part of the front in a week's time. He said: "That don't matter: if it's two hundred miles off or a thousand, that rat will still be knocking around when I go West." Dann was a very brave and cheery fellow, but from that day he was a changed man. He still did his work the same as the rest of us, and never shirked a dangerous job, but all his former cheeriness had left him. Old soldiers who knew him well often asked me what was wrong with him. But I never told them; they might have chaffed him about it. Neither I nor Dann ever made any reference about the rat from that day on, and though we two had passed many hours together shooting at rats for sport in those trenches, especially along at Givenchy by the canal bank, he never went shooting them again.

A few months later we arrived on the Somme by a six days' march from the railhead, and early in the morning of the 15th July passed through Fricourt, where our First Battalion had broken through on 1st July, and arrived at the end of Mametz Wood which had been captured some days before by the 38th Welsh Division which included four of our new service battalions. The enemy had been sending over tear-gas and the valley was thick with it. It smelt like strong onions which made our eyes and noses run very badly; we were soon coughing, sneezing and cursing. We rested in shell-holes, the ground all around us being thick with dead of the troops who had been attacking Mametz Wood. The fighting was going on about three-quarters of a mile ahead of us.

Dann, a young signaller named Thomas, and I, were posted to A Company. The three of us were dozing when Thomas gave a shout: a spent bullet with sufficient force to penetrate had hit him in the knee—our first casualty on the Somme. Dann said: "I don't suppose it will be my luck to get hit with a spent bullet; it will be one at short range through the head or a twelve-inch shell all on my own." I replied, as usual, that he would be damned lucky if he stopped either, and that he wouldn't be able to grouse much afterwards. "You're right enough about that, Dick," he said.

A few hours later the battalion moved around the corner of the wood, the company occupying a shallow trench which was only knee-deep. Dann and I were by ourselves in one part of this trench, the Company Commander being about ten yards below us. The majority of the company were soon in the wood on the scrounge; we had been told that we were likely to stay where we were for a day or two. I told Dann that I was going in the wood on the scrounge and that I would try and get a couple of German topcoats and some food if I could find any. The topcoats would be very handy as we were in fighting order, and the nights were cold for July. Just inside the wood, which was a great tangle of broken trees and branches, was a German trench, and all around it our dead and theirs were lying. I was in luck's way; I got two tins of Maconochies and half a loaf of bread, also two topcoats. The bread was very stale and it was a wonder the rats hadn't got at it. Although gas destroyed large numbers of them there were plenty of them left skipping about. I returned to Dann telling him how lucky I had been, and that we would have a feed. "Righto," he replied, "but I think I'll write out a couple of quickfirers first." (Quickfirers were Field Service Postcards.)

Enemy shells were now coming over and a lot of spent machine-gun bullets were zipping about. He sat on the back of the trench writing his quickfirers, when—zip!—and he rolled over, clutching his neck. Then a terrified look came in his face as he pointed one hand behind me. I turned and just behind me on the back of the trench, saw the huge black rat that we had seen in Hulloch. It was looking straight past me at Dann. I was paralysed myself for a moment and without looking at me it turned and disappeared in a shell-hole behind. I turned around and instantly flattened myself on the bottom of the trench, a fraction of a second before a shell burst behind me. I picked myself up amid a shower of dirt and clods and looked at Dann, but he was dead. The spent bullet had sufficient force to penetrate his neck and touch the spinal column. And there by his side, also dead, was the large rat. The explosion of the shell had blown it up and it had dropped by the side of him. I seized hold of its tail and swung it back in the shell-hole it had blown from. I was getting the creeps. Although Mametz Wood, was, I dare say, over fifty miles as the crow flies from Hulloch, I had no doubt in my mind that it was the same rat that we had seen in the latter place. It was the only weird experience I had during the whole of the war. There was no one near us at the time, and men on the right and left of us did not know Dann was killed until I told them. If I hadn't handled that rat and flung it away, I should have thought that I had been seeing things, like many who saw things on the retirement from Mons.

by

CARADOC EVANS

*

THE WAY OF THE EARTH

Simon and Beca are waiting for Death. The ten acres of land over Penrhos—their peat-thatched cottage under the edge of the moor—grows wilder and weedier. For Simon and Beca can do nothing now. Often the mood comes on the broken, helpless old man to speak to his daughter of the only thing that troubles him.

"When the time comes, Sara Jane fach," he says, "don't you hire the old hearse. Go you down to Dai the son of Mali, and Isaac the Cobbler, and Dennis the larger servant of Dan, and Twm Tybach, and mouth you like this to them: 'Jasto now, my little father Simon has gone to wear the White Shirt in the Palace. Come you then and carry him on your shoulders nice into Sion.'"

"Yea, Sara fach," Beca says, "and speak you to Lias the Carpenter that you will give no more than ten over twenty shillings for the coffin."

Simon adds: "If we perish together, make you one coffin serve."

Neither Simon nor Beca has further use for life. Paralysis shattered the old man the day of Sara Jane's wedding; the right side of his face sags, and he is lame on both his feet. Beca is blind, and she gropes her way about. Worse than all, they stand without the gates of Capel Sion—the living sin of all the land: they were married after the birth of Sara Jane, and though in the years of their passion they were all that a man and woman can be to each other, they begat no children. But Sion, jealous that not even his errant sheep shall lie in the parish graveyard and swell in appearance those who have worshipped the fripperies of the heathen Church, will embrace them in Death.

The land attached to Penrhos was changed from sterile moorland into a fertile garden by Simon and Beca. Great toil went to the taming of these ten acres of heather into the most fruitful soil in the district. Sometimes now Simon drags himself out into the open and complains when he sees his garden; and he calls Beca to look how the fields are going back to heatherland. And Beca will rise from her chair and feel her way past the bed which stands against the wooden partition, and as she touches with her right hand the ashen post that holds up the forehead of the house she knows she is facing the fields, and she too will groan, for her strength and pride are mixed with the soil.

"Sober serious, little Simon," she says, "this is the way of the earth, man bach."

But she means that it is the way of mortal flesh . . . of her daughter Sara Jane, who will no longer give the land the labour it requires to keep it clean and good. Sara Jane has more than she can do in tending to her five-year-old twins and her dying parents, and she lets the fields pass back into wild moorland.

In the days of his sin and might Simon had been the useful man of Manteg. He was careless then that the gates of Sion were closed against him. He possessed himself of a cart and horse, and became the carrier between the cartless folk of Manteg and the townspeople of Castellybryn, eight miles down the valley. He and Beca saved; oil lamp nor candle never lit up their house, and they did not spend money on coal because peat was to be lifted just beyond their threshold. They stinted themselves in halfpennies, gathered the pennies till they amounted to shillings, put the silver in a box till they had five sovereigns' worth of it, and this sum Simon took to the bank in Castellybryn on his next carrier's journey. They looked to the time their riches would triumph over even Sion and so open for them the gates of the temple.

As soon as the Schoolin allowed her to leave the Board School, Sara Jane was made to help Beca in all the farm work, thus enabling Simon to devote himself almost entirely to his neighbours. The man was covetous, and there were murmurings that strange sheaves of wheat were threshed on his floor, that his pigs fattened on other people's meal.

In accordance with the manner of labouring women Sara Jane wore clogs which had iron rims beneath them, grey stockings of coarse wool that were patched on the heels and legs with artless darns, and short petticoats; in all seasons her hands were chapped and ugly. Still, with her auburn hair, her firm breast, and her white teeth, she was the desire of many. Farm servants ogled her in public places; farmers' sons lay in wait for her in lonely places. Men spoke to her frankly, and with counterfeit smiles in their faces; Sara Jane answered their lustful sayings with lewd laughter, and when the attack became too pressing she picked up her petticoats and ran home. Nor was she put out over the attentions she received: she was well favoured and she liked to be desired; and in the twilight of an evening her full-bosomed, ripe beauty struck Simon suddenly as he met her in the close. Her eyes were dancing with delight, and her breast heaving. Sadrach the Small had chased her right to Penrhos.

Simon and Beca discussed this that had happened, and became exceedingly afraid for her.

"There's an old boy, dear me, for you indeed!" said Simon. "The wench fach is four over twenty now, and fretful I feel."

"Iss, iss, Simon," said Beca.

"If she was wedded now, she would be out of harm."

"Wisdom you mouth, Simon. Good, serious me, to get her a male."

"How say you then about Josi Cwmtwrch?"

"Clap your old lips, little man. Josi Cwmtwrch! What has Josi to give her? What for you talk about Josi?"

"Well, well, then. Tidy wench she is, whatever. And when we go she'll have the nice little yellow sovereigns in the bank."

Beca interrupted. "The eggs fetched three and ten pennies. Another florin now, Simon, and we've got five yellow sovereigns."

"Don't say then! Pity that is. Am I not taking the old Schoolin's pig to Castellybryn on Friday, too? Went you to all the old nests, woman fach?"

"Iss, man."

"What is old Rhys giving for eggs now?"

"Five pennies for six. Big is the fortune the cheater is making."

Beca dropped off her outer petticoat and drew a shawl over her head, and she got into bed; an hour later she was followed by Simon. In the morning she took to Shop Rhys three shillings' worth of eggs.

This was the slack period between harvests, and Sara Jane went with Simon to Castellybryn; and while Simon was weighing the Schoolin's pig she wandered hither and thither, and going over the bridge which spans Avon Teify she paused at the window of Jenkins Shop General, attracted thereto

181

by the soaps and perfumes that were displayed.

"How you are?" said a young man at her side.

"Man bach, what for you fright me?" said Sara Jane. She was moved to step away, for she had heard read that the corners of streets are places of great temptation. The young man—a choice young man and comely: he wore spectacles, had the front of his hair trimmed in waves, and his moustaches ended in thin points—the young man seized her arm.

"Free you are, boy bach," Sara Jane cried. "Go you on now!"

"Come you in and take a small peep at my shop," said the young man. . . .

When Sara entered her father's cart she had hidden in the big pocket of her under-petticoat a cake of scented soap and a bottle of perfume.

That night she drew all the hobnails out of the soles of her Sabbath boots. That night also she collected the eggs, and for every three she gathered she concealed one. This she did for two more days, and the third day she purchased a blouse in Shop Rhys. For this wastefulness her parents' wrath was kindled against her. The next Sunday she secretly used scented soap on her face and hands and poured perfume on her garments; and towards evening she traversed to the gateway where the moorland road breaks into the tramping way which takes you to Morfa-on-the-Sea. William Jenkins was waiting for her, his bicycle against the hedge; he was cutting the letters of his name into the gatepost. On the fourth night Sara Jane lay awake in bed. She heard the sound of gravel falling on the window-pane, and she got up and let in the visitor.

The rumour began to be spread that Jenkins Shop General was courting in bed with the wench of Penrhos, and it got to the ears of Simon and Beca.

"What for you want to court Shinkins Shop General in bed for?" said Simon.

"There's bad you are," said Beca.

"Is not Bertha Daviss saying that he comes up here on his old iron horse?" said Simon.

"Indeed to goodness," answered Sara Jane, "what is old Bertha doing out so late for? Say she to you that Rhys Shop was with her?"

"Speak you with sense, wench fach," Beca said to her daughter.

"Is not William Shinkins going to wed me then?" said Sara Jane.

"Glad am I to hear that," said Simon. "Say you to the boy bach: 'Come you to Penrhos on the Sabbath, little Shinkins.'"

"Large gentleman is he," said Sara Jane.

"Of course, dear me," said Simon. "But voice you like that to him."

The Sabbath came, and people on their way to Capel Sion saw William Jenkins go up the narrow Roman road to Penrhos, and they said one to another:

"Close will be the bargaining." Simon was glad that Sara Jane had found favour in William's eyes: here was a godly man and one of substance; he owned Shop General, his coat was always dry, he wore a collar every day in the week, and he received many red pennies in the course of a day. Simon took him out on the moor.

"Shall we talk this business then at once?" Mishtir Jenkins observed. "Make plain Sara Jane's inheritance."

"Much, little boy."

"Penrhos will come to Sara Jane, then?"

"Iss, man."

"Right that is, Simon. Wealthy am I. Do I not own Shop General? Man bach, there's a grand business for you!"

"Don't say!"

"Move your tongue now about Sara Jane's wedding portion," said Mishtir Jenkins.

"Dear me then, talk will I to Beca about this thing," answered Simon.

Three months passed by. Sara Jane moaned because that her breast was hurtful. Beca brewed for her camomile tea, but the pains did not go away. Then at the end of a day Sara Jane told Beca and Simon how she had done.

"Concubine!" cried Beca.

"Harlot!" cried Simon.

"For sure me, disgrace is this," said Beca.

Sara Jane straightened her shoulders.

"Samplers bach nice you are!" she said maliciously. "Crafty goats you are. What did the old Schoolin use to say when he called the names in the morning? 'Sara Jane, the bastard of Simon and Beca.' Iss, that's the old Schoolin. But William Shinkins will wed me. I shan't be cut out of Sion."

Simon and Beca were distressed.

"Go you down, little Simon, and word to the boy," said Beca.

"I've nothing to go for," replied Simon.

"Hap Madlen Tybach need coal?"

"No-no. Has she not much left? Did I not look upon the coal when I fetched the eggs?"

"Sorrowful it is you can find no errand. Wise would be to speech to the male bach."

"Dear little me! I'll go round and ask the tailor if he is expecting parcels from the station."

"Do you now. You won't be losing money if you can find a little errand."

At dawn Simon rose and went to Castellybryn. In going over the bridge of Avon Teify he halted and closed his eyes and prayed. This is his prayer: "Powerful Big Man bach, deal you fair by your little servant. And if Shinkins Shop General says, 'I am not the father of your wench's child,' strike him dead. We know he is. Ask you Bertha Daviss. Have we not seen his name on the gatepost? This, Jesus bach, in the name of the little White Jesus."

185

Outside Shop General he called in a loud voice: "William Shinkins, where he is?" Then he came down and walked into the parlour where Mishtir Jenkins was eating.

Simon said: "Sara Jane is with child."

"And say you do that to me," said Mishtir Jenkins.

"Iss, iss, man. Sore is Beca about it."

"Don't you worry, Simon bach, the time is long."

"Mishtir Shinkins. There's religious he is," said Simon, addressing William Jenkins in the third person, as is the custom in West Wales when you are before your betters. "Put him up the banns now then."

"I will, Simon."

"Tell he me, when shall I say to Beca thus: 'On such and such a day is the wedding'? Say him a month this day?"

"All right, Simon. I'll send the old fly from the Drivers' Arms to bring you and Sara Jane. Much style there will be. Did you voice to Beca about the matter?"

"What was that now, indeed, Mishtir Shinkins?"

"Why was you so dull? Sara Jane's portion, old boy."

"Well-well, iss. Well-well, no. We're poor in Penrhos, Mishtir Shinkins. Poor."

"Grudging you are with your money, Simon Penrhos."

186

THE WAY OF THE EARTH

"Don't he say like that. Make speech will I again with Beca."

Mishtir Jenkins stretched his face towards Simon, and said:

"What would you say, Simon, if I asked you to give me Sara Jane's portion this one small minute?"

"Waggish is his way, little Shinkins bach," said Simon with pretended good-humour.

"My father had a farm and sovereigns and a cow when he wedded."

"Open my lips to Beca I will about this," answered Simon.

"Good, very," replied Mishtir Jenkins. "I will say about the wedding, man, when you bring me Beca's words."

"Shinkins! Shinkins!"

"Leave you me half a hundred of pounds of Sara Jane's portion and I'll stand by my agreement."

"Joking he is, William Shinkins. Deal well we will by Sara Jane on the day of her wedding."

William Shinkins spoke presently. "I am not a man to go back on my promise to Sara Jane," he said. "And am I not one of respect?"

Simon went home and gave thanks unto God Who had imparted understanding to the heart of William Jenkins. But folks in Manteg declared that designing men cross rivers in the search of females to wed. Sara Jane was no longer ashamed. She went about and abroad and wore daily the boots from which she had taken out the hobnails.

On the appointed day the fly came to Penrhos, and Simon and Sara Jane went away in it: and as they passed through Manteg Bertha Daviss cried: "People bach, tell you me where you are going."

Simon told her the glad news.

Bertha waved her hand, and she cried to the driver: "Boy nice, whip up, whip up, or you'll have another passenger to carry."

Mishtir Jenkins met Simon and Sara Jane at the door of the inn.

"Sara Jane," he said, "stop you outside while me and your father expound to each other."

He took Simon into the stable.

"Did you ask Beca about the yellow sovereigns?" he said.

"Iss, iss. Many sovereigns he will get."

"How many?"

"Shinkins bach, why for he hurry? Bad it looks."

"Sound the figures now, Simon."

"Ten yellow sovereigns, dear me."

"Simon Penrhos, you and your wench go home."

"William Shinkins, he knows that Sara Jane is full. I'll inform against him. The law of the Sessions I'll put on him. Indeed I will."

"Am I not making Sara Jane mistress of Shop General? Solemn me, serious it is to wed a woman with child!"

"There's hard he is, Shinkins. Take two over ten sovereigns and a little parcel of potatoes, and a few white cabbages, and many carrots."

"Is that your best offer, Simon?"

"It's all we have, little man. We're poor."

"Go with the wench. Costly the old fly is for me."

Simon seized Mishtir Jenkins's coat.

"William Shinkins bach," he cried, "don't he let his anger get the better of his goodness. Are we not poor? Accept he our daughter——"

"Simon Penrhos, one hundred of pounds you've got in the bank, man. Give me that one hundred this morning before the wedding. If you don't do that you shall see."

Simon shivered. He was parting from his life. It was his life and Beca's life. She had made it, turning over the heather, and wringing it penny by penny from the stubborn earth. He, too, had helped her. He had served his neighbours, and thieved from them. He wept.

"He asks too much," he cried. "Too much."

"Come now, indeed," said William Jenkins. "Do you act religious by the wench fach."

Simon went with him to the bank, and with a smudge and a cross blotted out his account. Then he witnessed the completion of the bargain in Capel Baptists, which is beyond the Sycamore Tree.

The bridegroom took the bride home to Shop General, and he gave half of the dowry to a broker's

man who had been put in possession. Some of the
remaining fifty sovereigns went to his landlord for
overdue rent, and on the rest William Jenkins and
Sara Jane lived for nearly a year. Then the broker's
man returned, wherefore William Jenkins gave over
the fight and fled out of the land.

by

ALLEN RAINE

*

A LIFE'S CHASE

I

In the soft twilight of a June evening, seventy years
ago, and far from the haunts of busy life, when the
hay was just fit to cut, Mistress Parry of Bryneidon
walked out to inspect for herself the state of the crops,
whether to-morrow or the next day should be fixed
upon for the mowing.

With her red flannel scarf drawn tightly over her
shoulders, the ends hanging down from the grip of
her elbows over her dress of red-and-black homespun,
her high muslin cap, very full at the top and fastened
at the sides under its broad band of black silk, her
gold-headed cane, and her high-heeled shoes, she
looked what she was—a very determined and capable
manager of her own affairs. She looked at the soft
clear sky, where the faint glow of the sunset still
lingered beyond the billowy blue hills, and nodded
her head; then she turned to the east, where one bril-
liant star looked serenely down, and nodded again.
"To-morrow it shall be," she said, and, returning
briskly through the darkening lane to the farmyard,

she saw before her the grey figure of a man who walked in a curious uneven fashion—hurrying, then halting, and continually looking over his shoulder as he went.

There was no workhouse or asylum in the whole county, and the parish authorities considered they had well discharged their duties when they made it compulsory upon every farmer to house and feed any tramps or beggars who might claim their shelter and charity for two nights and a day, after which they were expected to move on to the next parish. As a consequence, the county was infested with tramps, or "travellers", as they were called. The lazy, the incapable, and the insane roamed about unwatched and uncared for, and the farm-servants looked forward with pleasurable curiosity to the almost nightly "guests" whose arrival varied the monotony of their lives.

Mistress Parry, therefore, was not much surprised, on her return, to find the grey figure who had preceded her up the lane already sitting under the big chimney by the peat fire which burnt on the hearth in the old farm kitchen.

"Ach-y-fi! Is it thee, Cadifor, appearing like a ghost as usual?"

"Yes, it is me," said a trembling voice.

"It was thee, then, who walked up the dark lane before me like a bwcci as thou art."

"Yes, it was me," said the man, with a sigh.

192

Looking at him, Mistress Parry's irritation subsided, and her sharp tones changed to a pitiful tenderness. "Well! well! pwr fellow! Marged will give thee
a bowl of cawl there in the chimney corner."

With a groan of weariness the beggar accepted the
offered hospitality. About forty years of age, he
looked many years older; haggard and worn with
continual walking, weary and faint with hunger, and
ever haunted by some mysterious dread. His clothes
hung in tatters about his shrivelled form; his worn-
out shoes were white with the dust of travel; all his
worldly possessions he carried in a canvas wallet
which hung over his shoulders; in his right hand he
clutched a thick-headed staff, which he seemed reluc-
tant to part with even for a moment.

"Lay thy staff by, man! No one will hurt thee
here; and make haste with that cawl, Marged."

The man laid his staff aside, and stretched out his
legs, leaning back on the oak settle with another sigh,
which told a tale of weakness and weariness. His grey
eyes roamed incessantly into the dark corners of the
kitchen, his lips moved, though his words were in-
audible, and with a frightened look of some hunted
creature, he glanced continually towards the open
doorway.

"Where hast been the last three months?" said the
mistress.

"I have been," he said in a hollow voice, his eyes
fixed hungrily upon the bowl which Marged was fill-

ing for him—"I have been north, south, east, west. The winds blow cold over Llangefelach, and I have been there! The sun has been scorching the sandhills of Glamorgan, and I have been there! The snow lies deep on Cader Idris, and I have been there! But I have not found rest!"

Meanwhile, the farm-servants who had trooped in to their supper had hailed with glee the advent of the beggar, for it meant fun for them, and something to tease and laugh at.

"Hallo, Cadifor!" said Twm, the most boisterous and reckless of the company, "hast been to the market? Shôn Powell was singing his ballads there, and said he was coming here to-night."

Before he had finished speaking, the beggar had seized his wallet and staff, and rushed headlong through the open doorway, leaving the coveted "cawl" untasted. There was a roar of laughter as he disappeared through the doorway, Mistress Parry in vain calling him to return. Over the stubble in the yard, over the stream at the bottom, and through the gap into the dark lane, the wretched man fled, and neither by hedgerow nor bank did he rest, until many miles lay between him and Bryneidon.

"How darest thou, stupid lout?" said the mistress. "This is the second time thou hast frightened that poor wanderer away. Next time, thou wilt be turned from my door on the instant, remember!" And drawing her red scarf tightly round her shoulders, her heels and her walking-stick tapping the stone floor, she turned angrily away and left the servants to their supper.

II

Robin, the new shepherd, who was about to have his first meal at Bryneidon, forgot to sit down as he stared open-mouthed after the flying beggar.

"Dear God!" he said, "have I come so far to meet Cadifor Gwynne again?"

"Dost know him?" said Twm, with great interest. "He is one of the 'travellers' who comes here three or four times every year, always hiding from Shôn Powell and Shôn Powell always looking for him. Jar-i! I won't stand easy in my 'cloes'[1] till I have seen them meet, whatever the mistress says."

"Let me have my cawl first," said Robin, "and I will tell you about him." And, after supper, they sat round the fire, though it was June, Mistress Parry herself joining the circle and sitting in the high-backed beehive chair.

"I knew them both," said Robin, "when I was a lad, very little younger than they were, though I think time has dealt more hardly with Cadifor than with me. 'Twas up on the wool-mountains, where I worked on my father's little farm. Shôn Powell and Cadifor Gwynne were shepherds on two neighbouring farms; their sheep grazed on the same mountains,

[1] Wooden shoes.

and they were always together. Everyone talked of their strong friendship. Cadifor could play on the flute, and Shôn Powell made a harp for himself, and played on it, too. Dei anwl! How he played and won a prize at the Eisteddfod! Well, Arianwen Hughes lived down in the valley with her father and mother, and Shôn Powell, when he saw her at the 'Steddfod, fell in love with her, and she with him, for he looked a fine fellow in his new smock-frock and his gaiters, when he played his harp on the platform. Everybody shouted and cheered when one of the grand ladies hung the prize round his neck in a pretty silk bag, while Shôn bent his head before her.

"The lasses tied a wreath of flowers to his crook. Oh! It was a grand day for him! Well do I remember! He only laughed at the cheers, and the prize, and the wreath on his crook; but when Arianwen shook hands with him you could see him redden through his dark skin. No one rejoiced more than Cadifor that day, and they went up the sheep-paths together when the 'Steddfod was over."

"Oh Dei!" said Twm, "that could not be our Shôn Powell who storms and tears like a mad bull when the children crowd round him on Fair days, and tease him and call out, 'Shôn dwl! Hast caught Cadifor yet?' I have seen him white with rage, grinding his teeth at the children, his face wet with tears, for they never rest till they make him cry. I have joined in the fun many times myself."

"Silence, Twm," said Mistress Parry severely; "go on, Robin."

"Well, Shôn Powell's master had a son who married a rich lass from near Towyn, and her father bought a sheep farm for them far away in Scotland. The young man was not much of a farmer, and his father offered Shôn Powell twenty whole sovereigns if he would go with his son to Scotland for a year, to settle him into his farm and to see to the sheep and cattle for him.

"Shôn Powell had made his way with Arianwen by this time, and everyone knew they were to be wedded as soon as he could afford to stock a sheep farm for himself; so the twenty sovereigns tempted him.

"Arianwen promised to wait a year for him, and Cadifor undertook to watch over her at 'Steddfod and Fair, so that no other man should court her during Shôn's absence; but he was false to his friend— though, poor fellow, many people pitied him, for they said Arianwen was too fair a woman to be much in her company without loving her. Anyway, she often strayed up the hills and Cadifor met her on the sheep-paths, and talked about Shôn; but the meetings grew more frequent, and Cadifor's flute was even sweeter in her ears than Shôn's harp had been; and before Shôn came home at the end of the year she had married his false friend, and they lived together in a little thatched cottage on the mountainside.

"When Shôn, on his return, found out what had happened he grew mad with rage and love, and swore if he caught Cadifor by field or by ford, by wood or by mountain, he would kill him as he would kill a wolf—and everybody knew he would do so. But Cadifor fled for his life, and was nowhere to be seen on sheep-path or moor.

"Shôn Powell grew more and more furious, until at last he was tied with ropes, and carried away to a mad-house in Glamorgan, and then Cadifor came home, and before long a child was born to him and Arianwen. She had pined and fretted ever since Shôn's return, for Cadifor had lied to her, and had made her believe that his rival was false to her.

"When the baby was born she died, and the little one with her. So Cadifor lived alone on the wool-mountains; his flute was silent and his sheep went astray, and he grew thin and melancholy, until at last people were afraid to meet him as he roamed about the mountains like a spirit.

"One day news came that Shôn Powell was well again, and had come home to his own place. Dei anwl! There was a talk in every farm and in every village! But Cadifor never waited to hear it. He disappeared like the grey mist of the morning, and no one had ever seen him or heard of him on the wool-mountains since, and I never thought to see him again."

"God grant they may never meet," said the mistress. "Now I understand why the one should be always fleeing and the other always pursuing."

"It seems a pity, too," said Twm, "when they are so near meeting sometimes——"

"Twm, thou art a fool!" said the old dame, "and a cruel fool! Go to bed," and Twm shuffled off obediently, but with a mischievous twinkle in his eye.

III

A few weeks later on there was a "Fair" at Rhydavon, the little town which lay down by the river three miles from Bryneidon.

Twm was there, and Mari the milkmaid, and, in spite of the dust and heat, they had a happy day, visiting one gingerbread-stall after another, where Twm spent a fortune in "treating" his companion, who went home in the evening jubilant, her pocket-handkerchief full of nuts, cakes, and apples. But Twm loitered, for Shôn Powell, in a rich sonorous bass voice, was singing a ballad in the street which held the crowd around him enthralled.

Beyond the ring of listeners, however, there was gathering another crowd of boys, beggars, and idlers, with jibes and hootings, and even sticks and stones, prepared for the ballad-singer when his song should be over. Twm scented fun in the fray, and for that he would willingly sacrifice his supper.

"Shôn dwl! Shôn dwl!"[1] cried the children, "hast caught Cadifor yet?"

The ballad-singer's face changed; the expression of rapt enjoyment with which he had trolled out his song gave place to one of rage, as he turned in a mad rush upon his tormentors. "Cadifor! Cadifor!" reached his ears from every direction, mixed with shouts of derision, until he writhed and fell to the ground in the fury of his anger, and, losing all control over himself, rolled in the dust, his face wet with tears of mad passion. This was all the children wanted. After this, they knew from experience, there would be no more fun and Twm took his way home to Bryneidon well satisfied with his evening's entertainment.

In a few moments Shôn Powell seemed somewhat restored to calmness, and to have regained what senses he was possessed of, for, on rising from the dust, and seeing that his tormentors had dispersed, he picked up his wallet and his packet of ballads and took his way over the bridge and out towards the country, turning round sometimes to shake his fist at the cruel town, and to pour out imprecations and curses upon it through the darkening twilight.

When Twm returned from the Fair, it was to find Cadifor Gwynne already seated under the big chimney drinking his cawl, while Mistress Parry sat in the beehive chair, knitting, and endeavouring to gather

[1] "Dwl"=mad.

from the frightened beggar where his wanderings had led him since he had last sought the shelter of her roof and been so ruthlessly driven from it by Twm's thoughtless mischief.

Peering furtively into the corners, looking anxiously into the darkening farmyard, Cadifor answered her questions, and gradually, under her kindly sympathy, became less nervous and agitated. He drank his cawl and ate his bread and cheese hungrily, and at last Betto escorted him to the door of the hay-loft, and, closing it on the latch only, left the weary man to his rest in the sweet dry hay. No light was allowed the vagrants, but the moon was rising, and Cadifor knew his way well.

Later on in the evening, when all the farm servants had gathered round the hearth, and Mari was recounting the glories of the Fair, they heard a loud voice demanding admittance, and the thump of a heavy stick at the door.

"Open to me, I am Shôn Powell," and Twm opened the door eagerly.

Shôn entered like a blustering gale of wind, with his customary inquiry: "Where is Cadifor? Have you seen him?"

The usual answer to this question, given at all times, regardless of truth was: "Oh! Cadifor was here a week or fortnight ago. He is gone to Caer Madoc. Thou wilt find him there to-morrow." And, easily satisfied, Shôn would cast away wallet and staff, and give himself up to the enjoyment of a good meal and the comfort of a cheerful fire, solacing himself with the words: "To-morrow I'll catch him!"

"Sit thee down, Shôn bach," said the mistress kindly, and he leant his broad shoulders against the white-washed walls and stretched his long legs to the blazing peat. He glowered moodily at the fire while Marged filled for him a bowl of barley bread and buttermilk. When he had made a good supper and seemed more amenable to reason, Mistress Parry ventured to ask him a few questions, but they were received with stolid indifference. Getting no answer, the mistress at last rose and left the kitchen, calling Twm aside, and bidding him see that Shôn was safely housed in the barn—"The barn, dost hear, and not the hay-loft," she said, with a meaning look, remind-ing him that Cadifor was there; "and more," she added, "be sure that to-morrow morning the barn door is kept locked until Cadifor is well on his way; I would not have them meet here, and—remember, no smoking and no candle!"

"No, no, mem, the moon is as light as day," and Twm returned to the hearth where Shôn Powell still sat brooding over the fire.

"Thee's been to the Fair to-day, Shôn; I saw thee there. 'Twas a fine ballad thou wert singing—has any to sell?"

Shôn sulkily drew some long slips of printed verses from his wallet, and held them towards the company.

"Not for me," said Twm, "but I'll buy one for Mari, for she can read like a parson," and he paid a halfpenny for it and handed it to the girl, who, by the light of the rush candle held close to the paper, read out the words in a sing-song monotonous voice.

"Stop!" cried Shôn, "put music to it." And, with his chin in the air and his shoulders thrown back, he sang in a voice of such tender pathos, that Mistress Parry came and stood at the door to listen.

> *I'll ne'er forget that leafy shade!*
> *I'll ne'er forget that winsome maid!*
> *But there no more her form I see.*
> *So Berwen Banks are sad to me.*

"Didn't Cadifor once sing us that song?" said Twm, with that dangerous gleam in his eye which everyone knew meant "fun at any price".

In a moment Shôn's music had fled and the evil spirit was upon him again. "He can't sing," he shouted, "he can't sing! Give me his flute, and I'll smash it to pieces!" and, starting to his feet, he grew loud and boisterous, gradually working himself up into a fury. The servants, as was their wont, had at first laughed and followed Twm's lead, but presently, getting frightened, they endeavoured to pacify the frantic man with promises of revenge. "Cadifor is only gone to Caer Madoc. Thee'll catch him there to-morrow!" they said.

"What if he knew," whispered Mari to Betto, "that Cadifor is now asleep in the hay-loft?"

"It wouldn't take him long to cross the yard," said Betto. "But, indeed, I'm frightened of him; 'tis quite time to go to bed, whatever!"

"To bed all," said the mistress, and, under her firm rule, there was no loitering. The maids left their wooden shoes in the kitchen and ran softly up the bare stairs, the men retired to their beds over the stable, Twm alone lingering to help Shôn with his wallet and staff before leading him across the farmyard to his resting-place for the night.

The spirit of mischief once more took possession of Twm, and, passing the barn door, contrary to the mistress's orders, he opened that leading to the hay-loft. "Now—up the stairs, Shôn, and turn to the left; thee know'st the way"—for he knew that Cadifor had turned to the right, and he did not wish the two enemies to meet until the dawn should reveal to each the other's presence. He chuckled to himself as he recrossed the yard. "Jar-i!" he said, "I must get up early to-morrow if I want to see the fun. I wouldn't miss the sight for the world. There'll be a fine fight when they wake up and see each other! They can't be much hurt in the soft hay."

But he was disappointed, for, on rising early the next morning and peeping into the hay-loft he saw the two men, lying apparently quietly asleep at opposite ends of the loft.

"Beggars are always lazy," he thought, and at breakfast, when Shôn came in silently, and sat down with the servants to his milk-porridge and barley bread, Twm thought his manœuvres had fallen flat. Shôn ate his breakfast quietly.

"There's nice he is this morning!" whispered Mari to Betto; "nobody would think that he wasn't wise." Indeed, he seemed at peace with the whole world. Breakfast over, he prepared to start afresh on his endless tramps over moor and mountain. He shouldered his wallet, which, with her accustomed charity, Mistress Parry had ordered to be well filled with sufficient bread and cheese for a day's travel. Bowing low to the mistress, he delivered himself in a loud voice of his usual parting greeting: "Well, da bo chi! Good betide you till I come again," and, staff in hand, he crossed the farmyard and disappeared through the gap into the shady lane. As he passed the hay-loft door, he administered to it three thundering blows with the knobbed head of his thick staff, a freak which caused the servants much amusement.

"Cadifor has gone, as usual, without breakfast, I suppose," said Mistress Parry, "pwr fellow! I hope he and Shôn have not taken the same road."

Later on in the day, Mari went searching for eggs in the hay-loft, but returned quickly, white and trembling. "Oh! Mestress fach!" she sobbed, "Cadifor is not gone, he is lying still in the hay. I think he is dead!" and when Mistress Parry herself walked up to the hay-loft, followed by the gaping and horrified servants, they found the beggar lying stiff and cold on the hay. The hunted and frightened look which he had worn during lifetime had fled, and a calm and restful expression had settled down on the harassed face; there was almost a smile upon the lips.

"He was dreaming that he was playing his flute on the mountainside to Arianwen, I should think," said Mari.

"Anyway, he died suddenly," said Mistress Parry, "and, to all appearance, Death has been kinder to him than Life was."

Robin pointed silently to a purple mark on the temple, and Twm felt as if he were shrivelling up in his "cloes".

"A fall, no doubt," said the mistress; "you know he had fits sometimes."

Her word was law, and no more was said about the purple mark; but in her own clear clever mind, Mistress Parry made a shrewd guess as to the cause of Cadifor's death; but, like a "cute" Welshwoman, she kept her suspicions to herself, and satisfied her conscience by dismissing Twm, who solaced himself by marrying Mari.

For many years Shôn Powell continued his periodical visits to Bryneidon, even till his strong form was bent and his black hair had turned to silver; but it was remarked that he never again heralded his arrival with the question, "Where is Cadifor?"

by

J. ELLIS WILLIAMS

*

BIG BUSINESS

A thrush sang on the cottage roof. On the wall below, a cat made other music.

John Jones woke, sat up, snorted, and cursed the cat. John would. Bird music did not affect him.

The sun had risen three or four hours earlier. This cheered John a little. It was right that the servant should rise before the master.

John reached for his trousers, sat gingerly on the edge of his rickety bed, and stretched out his leg slowly and thoughtfully. By chance, or else by dint of long practice, his foot skilfully weaved its way past a dozen gaping holes into the one hole where it belonged. With equal deliberation, he raised the other leg.

Abruptly, he became motionless. His features darkened with thought, deep furrows ploughed his brow, his eyes shone like Jacob's Pool. And then, as suddenly, the mental struggle ceased. The black clouds vanished. And his face lightened a moment before resuming its normal dullness.

His foot was still in mid-air on its way into the trousers. He lowered it gently to the floor, and carefully withdrew the other leg. The ragged trousers were thrown on a chair. He rose, looked at his reflection in the mirror, and nodded his head.

John had come to a great decision. To-day he would wear his breeches.

From a tin box underneath the bed he took out his pair of cloth breeches. Usually he wore them only on Fair Days. He eyed them with the loving respect a politician's wife has for the O.B.E. John had been a nobody until he bought these breeches. It was to these breeches that he owed his reputation as a judge of cattle. For when the countryside saw that the check of John's breeches was larger even than the squire's, they knew then that John had a mind of his own.

His appearance downstairs startled his wife.

"John!" she gasped. "It's not Fair Day. Why is it you're wearing *the* breeches to-day?"

And then she remembered. It was the fifth anniversary of their marriage. She smiled fondly. How she had misjudged him! He had not forgotten the day. Perhaps he was taking her to. . . .

John wondered what she was smiling about. He cleared his throat importantly.

"I'm off on business," he said. "Big business."

She looked at him anxiously.

"John, you don't intend to spend, I hope? Sugar's eightpence a pound, tea's going up, and you can't get more than tuppence for an egg and three shillings for a pound of butter. We can't afford to take risks in war-time."

"Don't I know it as well as you do?" replied John. "Don't I know how dear is everything to buy, and how cheap when you want to sell? But this time I'm on to a good thing."

"What are you going to do?"

John hitched out his breeches.

"I'm going to buy a cow."

"What! Buy a cow? You can never afford another cow now! We only saved twenty pounds last month!"

"I know what I'm doing. I've got my eye on a cow I can get cheap."

"Where?"

"From old Huw Davis at Hendre. The old chap's down and out. Nothing but the workhouse in front of him."

"Poor soul! And he as kind a man as ever lived."

"Aye, I'm sorry for the old boy. Real sorry for him. Someone told me he'd a cow for sale. And it's easy to bargain with a man who's got to sell. I'll buy her cheap as dirt."

"We'll have four cows then, John."

She put his bacon on the table.

"I wish we kept a shop," she said as she watched him eat. "We'd get one and nine a pound for that bacon. And you eating it so thoughtlessly."

John reached Hendre at midday. He had timed

himself well. They were eating when he arrived.

After the meal, Huw Davis and he went out for a smoke. They talked, with long intervals of silence, about what farmers always talk about, the weather mostly. They shared their gossip, but each man smoked his own tobacco.

Tea-time drew near, and old Huw Davis's pouch was empty.

"Baccy finished, John. Can't get any more till to-morrow."

John looked at him sympathetically. He couldn't smoke with his old friend looking at him so hungrily.

"We'd better go in, Huw," he said as he put his pipe and pouch back in his pocket. "I think I hear your wife laying the table."

Tea over (he could have eaten more of that jam, but he didn't like to reach out for it a fourth time), John got up and said it was time for him to go home.

"Thank you for your kind welcome," he said. "I'll be round again one of these days, I suppose."

With his hand on the latch of the door, he turned round.

"Oh aye," said he. "I've just remembered. I heard something in the fair about your having a cow to sell."

There was no reply. The old man's head dropped slightly. His wife took a quick look at him, and turned away to clear the table. It was some time before Huw replied.

"Aye. Were you thinking of buying?"

"No no," replied John immediately. "I don't want a cow just now unless I can pick one up cheap."

Huw Davis stared at him for a while. All afternoon he had wondered what brought John to Hendre. Even a farmer does not walk fifteen miles to talk about the weather. And now . . . that last-minute trick of turning back which he himself had so often practised! Why had it to be John of all people? Thanks to the breeches, John now had such a reputation that he could fix the market price of the cow. What was to be done?

He paused to think.

"A fine cow she is," said he, slowly. "Worth her weight in gold, that cow is. Let's go and look at her."

She was an ordinary cow. She was the best cow the seller had ever known, the worst the buyer had ever seen.

Huw Davis demanded four times her worth. John offered a quarter of the price he was ultimately prepared to pay.

When night fell, there was still a shilling between them.

"That's my final offer," said John. "And it's more than she's worth. If I didn't know how things were with you, and you an old friend too, I wouldn't offer half as much."

John was well pleased with himself. He had delivered his ultimatum, so suggestively and so diplomatically that his threat could not hurt anybody's feelings. He had also brought the price down a good deal lower than he had hoped. Still, that was no reason why he should throw away a whole shilling.

"I'll walk a bit of the way with you," said Huw Davis. "Perhaps we can strike a bargain as we go."

They haggled as they walked. Mile by mile, penny by penny, the gap narrowed. There was eightpence between them.

And now John had a brain-wave. He pulled out his pipe, very very slowly filled it, and carefully lit it. Huw Davis put his hand in his pocket, and as soon as he touched his pipe he remembered that his pouch was empty.

The look in his eyes would have melted a rock.

John thought quickly. Ninepence an ounce. He had smoked six pipefuls. Say sixpenn'orth left.

He turned to Huw.

"I'll tell you what," he said. "You come down to my figure, and I'll share my baccy with you."

A cloud of tobacco smoke followed the old man on his way home.

by

GLYN JONES

*

WIL THOMAS

At the top of a disused incline running up the mountain stood a lonely row of ironworkers' cottages. In front of them were fields and rough heathland, but behind, the big black tips rose up into the height of perpendicular cliffs, crested and streaked with white clinker like the droppings of gigantic birds. On the doorstep of the end cottage a man called Wil Thomas stood looking down the incline towards the town in the valley, and watching the sun beginning to set in the clouds beyond as though it were going down behind yellow celluloid. He had a bottle in his hand and he was waiting for his wife to come home from the prayer meeting.

Wil was an ordinary enough chap to look at, being heavy and thickset with short legs, wearing a greenish suit and a white muffler. His body was egg-shaped, set diagonally from back to front, with the heavy end of the egg swelling out full behind the lower end of his tight waistcoat and the fly-buttons of his trousers, stretching them apart, and the small end rising in a

213

low hump between his shoulder-blades, lifting out his
coat a bit. He had no neck and his head fitted plumb
on to his body. His hair was white and cut short, and
for a nose he had a hook like a large soft beak, big
and fleshy, constellated all over with small equally
spaced blue blackheads like pencil dots. His heavy
jaw, wanting a shave, was like white velvet and his
eyes were noticeable, being khaki—his eye, more
like, because he had only one. The place where the
other had been looked sore, the raw lids hanging
loose, the flesh all round red as though the eye-hole
had been cut in his skin with a scissors. Usually he
wore a false eye but he hadn't had it in for the last
fortnight because he had been home from work with
a clout on the back, so that he hadn't been able to
leave the house at all.

After watching for a bit he grinned to himself
because he was able to make out his wife struggling
up the incline road with her breath in her fist. As she
got nearer he could tell by the explosive kind of way
she was walking, jerky, automatic, scattering her feet
and kicking her skirts out, that she wasn't very sweet,
and she wasn't either, although she had been to the
prayer meeting. Before going she put her coms
through the mangle and broke the buttons, and that
had upset her, and now her feet were beginning to
ache and her back-comb was sticking hard into her
head under her heavy best hat and giving her jip
every yard of the way. And she knew what Wil

would be after with his clowning as soon as she got
to the house. But she wasn't going until she'd had a
rest. He'd have to wait for his beer for once, that
was all about it.

When she got up to the doorstep Wil stopped her
and pointed towards the sunset with the flagon:
"Mari," he said, gazing before him, "what other
hand than His?"

She pushed past him into the kitchen. "I know
whàt you want," she snapped, "as long as you can
bathe your gums that's all you care about."

Wil shrugged his shoulders, grinning to himself.
He was a bit of a comic and he thought he would be
able to humour her saying something like that. But
she was a queer plant. She could be awkward when
she wanted to, Wil knew that, turning very spiteful
and touchy at times. She was a little woman dressed
in a big heavy hat of black velvet and a dark costume
with long wide skirts, and she had little steel glasses
on only just big enough to cover her eyes, with black
wool wound round the nose-piece. She was always
full of quick mechanical energy, her movements were
always a bit sudden and automatic-looking, and now
because of her boots and her heavy hat she was filled
up with spite and malice, vindictive, as fierce and
quarrelsome as a little bullfinch. Her face was a bit
purpler than usual, and her small tidy little features
looked snappish, disgusted with everything, and her
lips were tight too, and hard as a couple of pebbles,

215

evil-looking. But Wil wasn't a bit frightened by her
nasty little darting eyes or the dirty look she kept on
giving him as he followed her about carrying the
bottle. He only grinned behind her back and after a
lot of coaxing he got her to go for him. She put some
steak and onions in the oven and then went out wearing comfortable things, house shoes and a shawl and
one of his old caps on her head. She wasn't willing
but she couldn't refuse somehow.

"Well done little Mari," he said, and he came
with her to the doorstep. "You'll think of this in
years to come. Long after I have joined my eye, my
little pelican."

He grinned after her as she went down the pavement.

Soon it began to get dark in the house so Wil lit
the oil-lamp and put it on the table by the window.
Then he pulled the blind down and sat by the fire
feeling pretty good, taking an occasional look at
Mari's medicine bottle that was standing on the
window-sill, and enjoying the warmth and the steak-
smell, listening from time to time to the wind outside
beginning to rise over the mountains, moving uneasily in the belly of the darkness. His back was
comfortable too, and he was enjoying himself fine by
the fire in his low little kitchen, dreaming about his
eye which had dropped out like a pop-alley when he
was born or had been eaten by a rat that time he was
dull enough to work underground, he couldn't re-

member which, he had told so many different tales about it. No, that was sure to be wrong though, he wasn't any rat's leavings, he was sure of that. He had dug a fork into it when the woman next door ran out of the lavatory on fire, that was more like it. Yes that was it, she was Lissa Richards, number two, who used to smoke her husband's long-ends in the lavatory, but what she'd done was set her drawers on fire by accident, the wicked bitch and made Wil stick an old fork in his eye with excitement. But he felt pretty good waiting for Mari to come home with the beer.

Then the preacher knocked at the door.

"Cokes of hell," said Wil, "who can be there now?"

He got up and went to have a look, taking the lamp off the table with him because it had become quite dark outside. When he saw it was Evans he brought him in at once. "Come on in, come on in," he said, glad of company now that he had been feeling so shabby. "Damn it all, little Evans, come on in at once." The preacher stepped from the pavement into the kitchen, ducking as he came, thanking Wil in his big preaching voice.

'May the thumbs of the dragon never lift the latch of William Thomas," he said in his big voice, stopping just inside the door, towering above Wil with his hand aloft. "How do you feel, William?"

"Blessed, little Evans," said Wil, "blessed. Come

right in and sit your little bottom down on the stool over by here."

Evans was a queer-looking chap, tall and dark, dressed from head to foot in black clothes, having his mouth half-way up his face and filled with big false teeth that were broken in the plate and rattled when he was talking like a pocketful of taws. He had big nostrils too with tufts of black hairs sticking out of them, hooked and black like little bunches of candle-wicks. He always wore very thick glasses that made his black boot-button eyes look small and queer, with the glass in them as thick as a pop bottle, and his eye-brows were heavy and black, curving upwards, the shape of nail-parings.

"Come right over here by the fire," said Wil, noticing his funny strong smell. And when he had got him sitting he took his black hat off for him so that his ears sprang upright, and then he hung it on his knee. The preacher's forehead was the width of a good garter and his hair was like astrakhan.

Wil never went to chapel himself, he pretended he was too dense, but he wasn't embarrassed at all because of that. He was glad to have Evans in the house, hoping to be able to tease him a bit, because the preacher was supposed to be a bit simple and once he had cocked his leg over the pulpit to show the people Balaam riding on the donkey. But he wanted to make him feel at home as well.

"Have a cup of tea?" he said.

"No tea," said Evans, shaking his face.

"Small beer then?" said Wil.

"No small beer," said Evans.

"Whisky and water?" said Wil, moving towards the window-sill.

"No water," said Evans, and he sucked a line of fluid like a macaroni pipe back up into his nose.

Wil was glad he had shown willing anyway. He got down two cups and poured out some of the whisky Mari kept on the window-sill for her heartburn, and they enjoyed themselves nice and tidy. They sat at the table in the low comfortable little kitchen, one each side of the lamp, with Wil's nose throwing a huge shadow shaped like a rudder across his face and Evans turning his eyes up and muttering as the whisky was coming out of the bottle. Wil did most of the talking at first, he was glad to, living in that back-crack up the incline and not being able to go out at all, but he was watching Evans all the time trying to draw him out. He started to talk about the compo doctor not asking him how he felt but how soon he was going to start work again. He clowned a lot, imitating the doctor's classy English, and then he spat in the fire with disgust.

"There is none to hold up the arms of the needy, William," said Evans, solemn and important, and he drew through his nose again so that he could have a drink. His big face near the lamp-globe was full of edges under his thin skin and heavy looking with a lot of bone in it like a horse.

"There's no two ways about that," said Wil, convinced. "How are you shaping? Aren't you empty yet?"

Evans glanced down into his cup. "The Lord giveth and the Lord taketh away," he said, gazing at the ceiling boards as Wil poured out again.

And with a new drink in front of him and Wil encouraging him he cleared his throat and started to talk, letting Wil have one of his old sermons, the one about Samson and Delilah and the Dragon. "Like me," said Wil, interrupting him for devilment and wiping his eye with his coat-sleeve, "I dug a fork in mine."

Evans swallowed with a lot of noise, a bit impatient wanting to get on. "The scratches of the Dragon are stripes in the army of the Lord," he said, heavy and dramatic, starting off again.

"Quite right, quite right, little Evans," Wil broke out showing he was convinced, and nearly upsetting his whisky. "And when I'm in the bar of the Angel and I want to pass water, Evans, I haven't got to spit in my beer before I go out, see?" Evans nodded slowly, not very interested, anxious to have his own say. "I've only got to take my glass eye out," Wil went on acting the part, "and put it on the counter by my pint and everything is fine. I only say 'Watch here a bit little one', and it's as good as if I was there myself." He picked up his cup and held it to his lips grinning. "That's quite right what you said, little Evans."

Wil took a sip. But Evans waved his big hands before his face eager to have another go. He looked cunning and while Wil was swallowing his drink he took his chance and started off again.

"It is better to have one eye, William," he said, "than two and hell fire. . . ."

Wil brought his cup down smartly. "There was hell fire when I lost mine all right," he broke out in a hurry, and then he went on describing and acting how he had been on the back doorstep getting a cork out of a bottle with a fork when the woman next door ran out into the garden on fire.

"The roots of the tobacco tree are suckled in hell below," said Evans, poking his finger out at Wil with his thumb up like a trigger, determined to be listened to, "but I have come to speak comfort, William, if my arm is long enough. I ought to have said my tongue, that was a mistake." He boomed at Wil and lifted the lamp towards him. "I have brattice, William, against the blowings of the Dragon. I can make you a whole man again."

Wil grinned at him, thinking he'd got him well started now. "That's how you chaps are when you wear your collars arse-frontwards," he said, "you'll say anything." He just leaned back and let Evans have his say, preparing to enjoy himself. But what fascinated him after a bit was the preacher's nose. He was so interested he couldn't take his eyes off it. One of the huge black nostrils had dried up in the heat and left a narrow glistening line like a snail-track along his upper lip between his nostril and his mouth, but the other side was exciting to watch because it was still active, and a thin tube of whitish liquid was all the time creeping slyly out of his nose and advancing towards his mouth as he was talking. At times Wil got so excited he could hardly hear what he was saying, thinking it would tap him on the knee or the back of the hand, but always at the last minute Evans would sniff it up again out of sight. Then Wil would listen in comfort for a bit until it began to signal once more, wet and shiny among the growth of black hairs. He was so excited and amused, most of what Evans was getting on about was going right over his head and he didn't notice how he was working himself up. The chap was talking like the river, his broken teeth chattering as though there was a horse-bit in his mouth and his arms were exercising in front of his face like mad. Then he stood up suddenly, still talking in his double bass, and his hat fell off his knee to the rag rug, but he took no notice of it at all. Instead he stood towering above Wil in his black clothes with his glove-back hair up against the planks of the ceiling and his huge shadow flapping about on the wall like a big bat's umbrellas or the wings of a goody-hoo. Wil was a bit surprised at first, thinking it funny that the medicine was making him talk like this, but wishing all the same he'd go off the boil a bit and take it easy now before Mari got back. "Little Evans, little Evans," he said trying to soothe him, "sit down and be comfortable and don't stand up there, boy, bending like a black bluebell." But he took no notice and because of something or other he'd said he started emptying his tail pocket, babbling all the time about the dragon and taking things out of his pocket by the fistful, piling them on the table in the round pool of lamplight. "Well God knows," Wil grinned to himself, "there was supposed to be everything in the ark but there's sure to be more in this." Evans went on talking as fast as he could with his pointed Adam's apple working like a piston, but he wasn't getting any change out of Wil although he continued being dramatic, pulling things out of his pocket, string and papers and pins and camphor balls. "No doubt that's why he always smells like the cathedral," thought Wil wondering what was coming out next. And because the preacher looked as though he was going to tread on it, he picked up his hat off the rug for him and put it under the lamp where it looked, because of the dent across the top, like the round head of a big black screw driven into the table.

When he looked up again he had brought a human eye out of his pocket.

"Wonderful man," cried Wil jumping up, forgetting all his clowning, "what's that you've got there?"

It was a real eye, fresh and glistening in the lamp-light, with threads of thin steam rising from it and the nerve-roots hanging out between the preacher's fingers. It lay solid and big as a fine peeled egg, shining among the camphor balls on his shaking palm, polished like china in the lamplight with the pupil and the khaki iris gazing up at Wil in a fixed way he didn't like at all. There were no lids on it and it stared wickedly up at him all the time so that he couldn't avoid it whichever way he looked, fixing its clear shining pupil on his good eye, making him feel very uneasy, and although there was no face round it it seemed to be jeering at him all the time. He had seen plenty of scraps of bodies about after accidents in work, and when he was a boy he had carried the top of the lodger's finger about in a matchbox until it stunk too bad, but he had never seen anything like the eye before. He couldn't have touched it for a fortune although Evans was holding it out to him, asking him to take it, his arm going up and down under Wil's face like a pump handle. And he began to look so fierce, he was turning so curly that Wil thought he'd better take it into his hand to save trouble. It was cold and wet underneath, slimy like a peeled plum, heavy and moist as an egg-plum with the skin pulled off as the juices of the chilly wet flesh touched his unwilling palm.

Wil shivered from head to foot, and outside the loud wind stumbled over the house.

As Mari was coming up the dark lonely incline in the wind, carrying the beer, she said good night to some man she wasn't sure of. He reminded her of Evans the minister. "Poor fellow," she thought, "a year to-day he swam the Jordan." When she got back to the house the lamp had burnt out, and when she relit it she saw Wil lying on the sofa fast asleep on his back and looking pretty rough. She went through a little door that looked like a cupboard into the pantry to put the beer on the stone and when she came out she noticed her whisky bottle empty on the window-sill. That settled her. Without stopping to take off her things she pulled Wil's steak and onions out of the oven and ate them up with relish while Wil still lay fast asleep with his mouth open on the sofa behind her. Then she drank his beer. The gravy that was left over from the steak she spread around his mouth where it stuck well because he hadn't shaved for a few days. Then she took out a book called the *Grapes of Canaan* and adjusting her little steel glasses sat by the fire reading. Her face was innocent, white, round as a little coin.

At last Wil woke up. He wanted his beer. "Mari," he said, "let me have my supper."

"Supper," she snapped at him, "how many suppers do you want, you belly-dog?" She snatched the looking-glass off the wall and held it before him.

Will clapped his hand to his empty eye.

by

HERBERT M. VAUGHAN

*

AN IDYLL WITHOUT AN END

It was flaming June, and Miss Delia Ward, authoress in a small way, and owner of a small income, aged forty-two but looking some few years younger than her age, felt she required a holiday. During the war Miss Ward had worked conscientiously in the "Pap and Powder-Puff Department of the Ministry for Welfare of War Babies", drawing a salary which barely covered her expenses for her services. A year and a half after the Armistice this branch of public organization had been closed down, and Miss Ward was again free to follow her own devices; so as a preliminary measure, she decided to take a holiday after her late exertions. Shutting up her tiny flat in Kensington, she travelled down to Flemingston, which, as everybody knows, is a picturesque little watering-place on the Pembrokeshire coast. Here she led the quiet cultivated life, enjoying the views, the sea air, and a succession of volumes from the local circulating library. Except for the society of one or two elderly ladies at the St. David's private hotel, where she lodged for three guineas a week (out of season terms), Miss Ward was wholly dependent on her own internal resources. The time passed pleasantly enough, still she did now and again feel her solitude, and it brought a sense of melancholy with it.

One sunny afternoon, Miss Delia was sitting on a seat below the Castle ruins that overlook the Bristol Channel. She was dressed very simply, with a cheap shady hat, and she carried a volume of Mid-Victorian literary memoirs which she dipped into from time to time, dividing her attention between the book and the landscape. It was all very peaceful, but just a trifle dull. With her easy philosophy, she assured herself mentally it could not well be otherwise, and was content with this deduction. Still, it seemed all a little commonplace, a little empty.

As she sate thus with the Castle Hill all to herself except for a few children playing on the turf some distance off, she noticed a man walking slowly along the pathway that ran round the contour of the hill. She regarded him with idle curiosity, as his figure slowly came betwixt her vision and the background of sea. He was middle-aged, of moderate height, rather inclined to stoop and shamble, whilst his clothes, his air, and something indefinable in his appearance at once suggested the well-to-do artisan. When he came close to the seat occupied by Miss Delia, he paused, looked hard at the lady, and after some hesitancy, seated himself at the farther end of the bench. There he remained, looking alternately at the sea and at his companion. His attitude was quite respectful, yet there was certainly something in his manner that hinted a desire to open talk, did he dare. And somehow Miss Ward did long for the sound of a voice, especially a masculine voice, at this juncture. The wish to open conversation was in fact mutual.

Miss Delia was no prude, no snob, no devotee of the conventional. She had had a fair experience of the world, she had travelled, and she prided herself on her independence and her modernity. Why should not she address her neighbour, who was very properly too shy or too modest to make an opening? So, with just a little flutter at her heart, she hazarded a remark.

"How lovely the sea looks this afternoon! I suppose you often get days like this at Flemingston?"

"Yes," replied the man with evident embarrassment, yet clearly pleased at being spoken to, "them clouds are beautiful. I always likes that purple shadow they throws on the blue water."

Miss Delia was confirmed in her first estimate. He was an ill-educated artisan, though he evidently had a nice mind.

"Yes, the colouring, as you say, is lovely. And I do so love to watch those tall yellow flowers against the blue of the sea."

"They be the wild cabbages in bloom. It 'adn't struck me afore; but as you say, they du make a tidy show of colour. . . . You are a stranger in Flemingston, Miss?"

"Oh, yes, I am just a Cockney visitor," replied Miss Delia with a smile.

"You should come 'ere in August when the 'scursions are on," said the man, envisaging her with a rather puzzled look, for the shabby clothes and hat belied the refinement of the voice and manner, as he was now dimly aware.

"Oh, no, thank you!" cried Miss Delia with a laugh. "That's just what I wanted to avoid. I am a bit of an artist, and I like the quiet as well as the scenery and the colouring."

"Plenty of artis' comes here," observed the man dryly.

"You must enjoy living in such a pretty place," continued Miss Delia after a pause.

"Aye, I've nothing against poor old Flemingston. I was born and bred here, and here in Flemingston I am likes to die," he added with a sigh and a nervous little laugh. "Maybe you have to work hard in London?" he ventured boldly.

"No," said Miss Delia. "I'm afraid I don't work at all, now that the war is over."

It was beginning to dawn more clearly on the man that his new acquaintance was a real lady. He felt uncomfortable, and began to shuffle uneasily on the bench. Miss Delia was quick to perceive this, and at once decided to put him at his ease.

229

"We are both artists in the same sense, you and I," she said pleasantly. "We can both appreciate Nature. Perhaps you sketch?"

"No," he replied bluntly. "I am a carpenter on The Gryst, and I 'aven't the time, even if I 'ad the power, to go a-sketching, like them artis' chaps."

He blushed deeply, and then looked aside at the little town with the tall church spire piercing the blue sky.

"You have a very honourable trade, Mr.—Mr. ——" and she looked enquiringly at him.

"Thomas," he jerked out laconically.

"Remember, Mr. Thomas, the Blessed Virgin chose a carpenter for her husband, so I always consider a carpenter's is the first profession in the world."

In her way, Miss Ward was quite sincere if sententious, for she was very High Church and attended regularly at All Saints', Margaret Street.

This remark made Mr. Thomas feel more uncomfortable than before. But after some more fidgeting he blurted out:

"Yes, that's all very fine. I've heerd something of the same sort in St. Mary's here. But, ma'am, you're a lady, and I'se just a poor working man."

"I don't see what that's got to do with it," said Miss Delia decisively. "Surely two people, a man and a woman, can exchange an idea occasionally?"

"We've never been interdooced," objected Mr. Thomas with some coldness.

"Well, then, let me introduce myself—Miss Delia Ward, of Kensington, now staying at Flemingston."

Silence fell, and both regarded the sea all glittering before them, with paths of golden light joining Ynys Pir island to the mainland. Miss Ward was communing rapidly with herself. She liked the man, though she had been unaware of his existence half an hour ago. But what was he to her or she to him? Nevertheless, she could tell with unerring instinct that he had been attracted to her even as he walked past her on the bench. But for her simple dress he no doubt would have refrained from sitting beside her, but (so she gathered) he had been deceived by the outward appearance at first glance, and had followed his sudden fancy. Then it had broken on him that she was a lady, a condescending one perhaps, but all the same a lady, miles beyond his social and mental reach. Poor man! It was no wonder Miss Ward with her warm little heart and innocent vanity had been flattered, moved even, by the unequal conversation that had followed. And Mr. Thomas—what *was* his Christian name?— had natural refinement. It was all very charming but more than a trifle difficult.

Miss Ward felt she could not sustain any further talk, just yet. She wanted to think things over. *Solvitur ambulando*. She rose, and offering her hand to Mr. Thomas, said:

"Now, I have to hurry back. I often sit here on

231

this bench in the afternoon, and I hope we shall meet again. I see we have much in common, and I have enjoyed our little chat."

Mr. Thomas rose too, took off his hat, not without some natural grace, and shook the proffered hand with deference.

"You really mean it, ma'am?"

"I do indeed, Mr. Thomas. Remember, I am a stranger here, and it is nice to make a pleasant acquaintance in a strange place."

And, so saying, Miss Delia hurried off with a smile and a bow, and was quickly out of sight of the Flemingston carpenter, who stood staring dully after her retreating figure, which was soon lost behind a projecting bastion of the ruined castle.

Miss Ward owned the makings of a diplomatist. On returning to St. David's, the comfortable boarding-house on the South Cliff, she waited for a suitable chance of asking Miss Mason, the manageress, if she knew of any carpenter in Flemingston who could make her a copy of an old Welsh chair. After some reflection, Miss Mason gave her opinion that Clement Thomas, of The Gryst, was probably the most likely man for the purpose—"He is an oldish bachelor, a bit of a recluse, who lives in a mouldy old house with a bedridden mother," she informed her. And she added: "You get to The Gryst by passing through Barbican Lane and keeping to the left till you reach the Old Harbour. . . . Oh, it looks rather dirty, but it's all quite safe and respectable."

The following day Miss Delia made her way to The Gryst, feeling a little nervous and self-conscious on her expedition of discovery. On emerging from narrow medieval Barbican Lane, she found The Gryst to consist of a row of houses and gardens perched above a cliff gay with sea-cabbage and fennel which overhung the Old Harbour. Here, in distant Plantagenet days had been the chief seat of commerce; in these decaying warehouses on The Gryst and beside the shore were landed brandy and wines and spices and furs for the prosperous burgher families of Flemingston. Now all was quiet and moribund. But the fringe of valerian on the old wall—"Pretty Nancy", as the natives call it—stood out exquisitely against the blue background of the sea with its masses of blossom of a rich Florentine red.

Cautiously peeping around, Miss Delia soon espied the house and workshop of Mr. Clement Thomas. (Clement! What a nice name, and so unusual!) It was a gaunt grey stone building, faced with slates for protection against the gales. Out of the shed beside it issued sounds of sawing. From her sheltered corner Miss Delia watched patiently, though what she was waiting for she really did not know, certainly did not acknowledge, even to herself. By and by, she saw Clement Thomas come out of the open doorway in his working dress, covered with a long blue linen apron. He certainly struck her as interesting, yet she could have wished him ten years younger, for he looked well over fifty, whatever his actual age might chance to be. She also noticed he wore spectacles for his work. Mr. Thomas stood for a few moments in the open air, as though to inhale its freshness and the tang of the sea, and then disappeared. Once more there reached her the sound of sawing or planing, and then Miss Delia quietly threaded her way back to the St. David's Hotel.

A day or two later, towards sunset, Miss Delia was sitting on the seat below the Castle ruins, looking out to sea and half-hoping for, half-dreading, the arrival of Mr. Clement Thomas in response to her late invitation. Her uncertainty was not prolonged. A male figure advanced from behind the ruins and presently was standing opposite to her, hat in hand. Smothering some misgivings, Miss Ward welcomed him warmly. He looked quite nice in his blue serge; he wore no spectacles; his brown eyes and serious expression were pleasing. He seated himself beside her without a word.

"I am very glad to meet again, Mr. Thomas," began Miss Delia.

"It was very kind of you to invite me, ma'am," he replied.

"You mustn't call me ma'am," she corrected him. "You must call me Miss Ward."

234

"Thank you, ma'am—Miss Ward."

Miss Delia could see her companion was ill at ease, for he kept scanning the walks and lawns of the Castle Hill.

"Are you expecting anyone?" asked Miss Delia.

"N-no, not exactly. But people do come here sometimes."

"Well, Mr. Thomas, and what if they do?" said Miss Delia tartly. "Surely two middle-aged people like ourselves can sit and talk together on a bench without causing scandal?"

"I wasn't thinking of myself, ma—Miss Ward," he pleaded nervously.

Miss Delia was about to answer sharply, but she changed her mind and let the matter drop. The two sate on in silence contemplating the sunset.

Suddenly Mr. Thomas began.

"I wish I could travel! Far, far away. It might all be different then."

"What would be different? What do you mean?" asked Miss Delia.

"Oh, many things. I could sit and talk to you far away, and explain things I can't explain here, in Flemingston."

"You mean", said Miss Ward tenderly, "that in another place you and I might get to understand one another better? Isn't that it?"

Mr. Thomas nodded, and they both relapsed into silence. Miss Delia's mind was working furiously.

She could divine the man's thoughts better than he could himself. Somewhere far, far away. Somewhere in a freer, healthier atmosphere, where we could all of us be rated at our real and exact worth. "Man is worth just what he is in God's eyes; just that, nothing more and nothing less." So had written the author of the *Imitation* hundreds of years ago, and how true, yet how impracticable was his judgment. Miss Delia could feel through every fibre of her being that this silent, sad, shy middle-aged man was longing to make love to her, but he was too awestricken, too diffident, too uncouth to attempt to make the veriest beginning. She also realized that a heart of gold was at her disposal, if she cared to accept it. It lay with herself to seize it or leave it. It was a veritable dilemma, and she must choose, and choose quickly. Suppose she made the road easy for the advance of his love? What then? They might both be very happy? Yes, perhaps. It was clear they had both been baptized with the same spiritual baptism, and though their social differences might at times cause discord, yet surely their spiritual identities would compensate for any trouble in that quarter? Yet, on the other hand, was not any such alliance bound to result in failure? What could they have in common in everyday life? And strange apprehensions invaded Miss Delia, when she thought with a sudden pang of the criticism to be passed by her brother, the Canon, and (still worse) by her aunt, Lady Fraser. "A *mésalliance*! Never could have believed our Delia capable of demeaning herself, or of stooping so low as to marry a common carpenter! Always thought she had the instincts of a lady, etc. etc. etc." All very petty and spiteful and prejudiced, so argued Miss Delia to herself; but how galling, how saddening, and oh, how inevitable! Class distinction is no doubt a very cruel and a very reprehensible thing, but it is an evil that is deep-rooted in human nature itself, and it will only be eradicated at the call of the last trump. No champion of democracy, no Jack Cade, no Danton, no Lenin will ever be able to slay that dragon of caste. Miss Delia knew it, and had to confess it. They might go far, far away, as Clement Thomas had said so pathetically the very moment they met that afternoon. But was such a thing possible? We may change our sky, but never our inherent prejudices.

This is an age of compromise. Everybody compromises with everybody else, from the highest politician to the humblest wage-earner; we compromise equally over people and principles. Miss Delia must have picked up the germ of Compromise in the bureau of the Pap and Powder-Puff Department. The germ began to operate now in her mental system.

"I hope we shall continue good friends, as I feel we already understand one another," she began anxiously.

But Mr. Thomas would not or could not help her further with this new train of thought.

237

Miss Delia tried again. "I am very lonely," she said. "I am getting an old maid, and I never mean to marry."

Mr. Thomas gave a convulsive start, but controlled himself.

"Yes, I never will marry anybody. But I do want a friend, and I have no men friends. I should like to write to you. Will you let me?"

"I ain't much use with the pen, Miss Ward," was the rather dismal response.

"Oh, yes, but you will be," said Miss Delia, brightening with an effort. "I'll teach you to write as good a letter as I write myself. Now, do say Yes."

There was a look of displeasure, and Mr. Thomas hesitated. But he replied humbly enough.

"It is very good of you to teach me. I have always wanted to better me for a scholar. Yes, I will try to learn."

Miss Delia gave him her hand. Clement Thomas clasped it tightly for a moment and then relaxed his grasp awkwardly.

"Now we are real friends, aren't we?" cried Miss Delia, with an air of outward assurance she was far from feeling inwardly.

"Will you write first, ma—Miss Ward?"

"Of course I will. And you must answer me, not a stiff letter, you know, but just such a letter as you would write to a friend, to a lady friend."

"I ain't got no such thing," interjected Mr.

Thomas doggedly. Miss Delia felt some secret relief at this statement.

"Well, it comes to this, doesn't it? I have no gentleman to write to me, and you have no lady. So now we understand our position. We are friends, and we mean to keep friends through the post."

Mr. Thomas nodded, but his brown eyes had a watery look in them for just one moment.

They sate on, watching the sun sink into the sea, till only a small flaming arc remained. Clement Thomas's hand stole into Miss Delia's and she stroked its poor hard wrinkled skin.

"The sun is sinking like my hopes," he said, sadly but without any resentment.

"Dear friend, it will rise again for us both, and there is a promise of a glorious daybreak."

Mr. Thomas sighed, and gazed with a rapt look at the disappearing disc of gold. Miss Delia rose and took hold of both his hands, though he still kept his face averted.

"Look into my eyes," she said authoritatively, and the man instantly obeyed. "Look into my eyes, and you will trust me. We must make a beginning gently. I shall write to you, and you will write to me. We shall then both of us have something fresh and wholesome in our lives. Do you understand me?" And she shook both his hands with vigorous meaning.

The man was silent for a minute, and his face grew tense and white. Then he said simply, and with a sigh of relief: "Yes, Miss Delia—I may call you Miss Delia, mayn't I?—I do understand, just a bit. You must teach me to understand better."

"Now, I feel quite happy. That is just the answer I wanted. We shall begin this week. I am leaving, I must leave, Flemingston to-morrow. I shall write from London, and tell you *my* news, and you must write back and tell me *your* news."

"I ain't much of a scholar, as I said afore," he interposed doubtfully.

"No, but I'll make you one," retorted Miss Delia eagerly. "At least, I can teach you to write letters that will please me, and that's all I ask at present."

They sate still for a few moments longer, and then Miss Delia suddenly shook hands with him and rose.

"Stay here on the bench," she said with a tone of command, "till I am out of sight."

They parted, she walking back to the town, and he remaining seated in face of the afterglow.

It is a commonplace maxim that the pen is mightier than the sword of Mars; maybe it is mightier also than the treacherous arrow of Cupid.

by

MARGIAD EVANS

★

COUNTRY DANCE[1]

ANN'S BOOK: FIRST PART, 1850

Dod dy law ond wyd yn coelio
Dan fy mron a gwylia 'mrifo
Ti gei glywed os gwrandewi
Sŵn y galon fach yn torri.

(Place thy hand, unless thou believest me,
Under my breast and beware of hurting me;
Thou shalt hear if thou listen
The sound of the little heart breaking.)

OLD SONG

Gabriel gives me this book, telling me to write in it all I do, for him to see, until we shall be married. And when that will be I do not know, since I am to leave Twelve Poplars and look to my mother.

Owen Somers comes for me: Mary and I cry. I have lived with her for fifteen years. The morning is bitter cold and the horse will not stand still for me to get in. Owen wraps my feet in straw, but they are

[1] First published in book form by Arthur Barker Ltd.

frozen before we have gone very far. At first we talk, the last half of the way I sleep, and he wakes me at the foot of the hill: I stumble up half asleep. There is a light in the kitchen window and my father and mother are having their tea. Afterwards I wash up. My father says there are lambs about already; we are later in the hills. Even my mother is up at five, and when we have given my father his breakfast, he lights his lantern and goes off to his sheep. Evan ap Evans says that he is very content with them this year: my father says a wiser man would have waited before he spoke, with the lambing ahead, but the master can never hold his tongue or his temper.

I miss my dairy. With everything out of the way so soon there is a lot of time to spare. While I am sewing the new curtains for the kitchen I see the parson come up the hill in the snow. My mother goes to let him in, and he sits himself down before the fire to thaw a bit and drink the cup of tea we give him. My lap is full of snips and ends, which I drop all over the floor when I stand up.

"And this is your daughter? We have met before, I think?"

"Maybe," says my mother.

"And how does she like these parts after the hills?"

"She likes them well enough."

"And how long are you thinking of staying?" he asks me.

"Until she shall be married."

He laughs a little. I can see he thinks I have lost my tongue, leaving my mother to answer all the questions. She smiles at me.

"And whom are you marrying? Is it anyone here?"

"It's Gabriel Ford," says my mother.

"I don't know him. Is he English?"

"What else could he be with such a name?" cries my mother. "He is not from these parts, but where she has come from."

"The mountains, eh? It's a long way for a sweetheart."

"Shorter than for others, perhaps."

"Perhaps you are right, Mrs. Goodman. But the men hereabouts are well enough. Don't you think so?"

"Maybe, but my husband and Evan ap Evans are the only ones worth a look."

Parson gives her a sharp glance: "Ah, Evan ap Evans is a fine-looking man, I grant you, but he belongs to the chapel."

"He's a true Welshman," says my mother. "What else should he belong to?"

"Well, well," mutters Parson, pushing back his chair. "You will be better when the warmer weather comes, Mrs. Goodman."

"I hope so, I'm sure, but I'd rather be higher up."

"Why, what do you mean? You are on top of the hill as it is. It's quite a climb."

"Brenin Mawr! (Good Lord!) it's nothing but a pimple," cries my mother.

Parson laughs. "Have you met any neighbours yet, Ann?"

"Yes, sir. I met most of them before I went away, and I have seen them on visits."

"Ah, they do not change much. This is a quiet spot."

"My son was alive then," says my mother.

I often think of Rhys, who died grown up and married when I was no more than fifteen; my mother loved him heart and soul, for it seemed he was all her child. One hard winter like this he was out of nights with the early lambing and he took a chill and died, leaving Gwyneth to follow him two months later when their first child was born. They say seeing him with his sheep was like watching a man with his family; that comes from my father, who has shepherding in his blood.

Another person comes to-day. This is the sexton's daughter, all arms and legs, as thin as a hurdle. She comes to see if our hens are laying; her father will have eggs, and whence to find them this weather she does not know without going to Salus, and he will not let her half a mile from home. All the parish knows what a life he leads her.

The cold is in my very bones. I make such a great fire in the kitchen that the chimney catches: the smoke rushes out and goes away on the wind till everybody thinks we are burning. Half the parish comes running with pails of snow and sticks to beat it out: even the master is there to see his cottage burn. My mother runs out in her stockings; her feet are so swollen she cannot wear boots. Never was there such a scrimmage over a chimney!

I throw salt on the fire, and when my father comes it is out; he is very angry, and so is the master. He takes me by the shoulders before all the world. He has a Welsh voice that sings in speaking in English.

"Next time, look, my girl, what you are about."

I step back and say my sorrow, for I think of my father, but I hate Evan ap Evans from this day and wish Gabriel had been there to shake the life out of him.

Another heavy fall of snow and three of the lambs are dead. I am taking some sewing because the master is charging us with the cost of the chimney. And it is but scorched!

I find there is no yeast for Thursday's baking, so I leave my mother sitting before the fire with her knitting and the door locked, because my father will be late, and go to Salus to fetch some.

It is very dark and windy in the narrow lanes; when I cross the bridge I can hear the water is very near the top of the arches, and a glimmering here and there down in the meadows shows me the floods are out. Salus is empty, and well it may be on such a wild night; I get my yeast and am glad to set my feet on the way home, but the wind is dead against me and every inch is a struggle: the rain is falling in torrents so that it almost blinds me. I hear Tom Hill's cart coming; I know it by its one light and the clicking of the mare's hoofs. The light flickers over me, and Tom pulls up, calling me by name.

"What is wrong?" I shout above the din of the wind and rain.

"Sexton's missing—been off all day. We think he's in the river. Stop Olwen if you should meet her on your way back and take her home along with you."

"That child out alone to-night!"

"Ay. She wanted to come with me. I told her there was nothing she could do, but I believe she followed me."

"In the river!" I think of the awful sucking under the bridge, and the watery fields.

"I'll take her home. What are you going to do?" I ask.

"Going to Salus to find if anyone has seen him."

He drives off. Half-way home I find Olwen sitting on a gate, soaked to the bone, without shawl or bonnet: she gives a great start when she sees me.

"Come home with me," I says.

"Ann, I can't go farther, I'm too affeared. Have they found him in the river?"

"No, Olwen. Come home, and you shall sleep the night with me. You have no cause to be affeared with me."

"Ann, why did he do it? Last week, when he dug old Mr. Somers's grave, he laughed and said he would see all the parish underground."

"It may not be so bad, after all. Come with me. Come home out of the cold."

"Yes," she answers, "I'll go with you to-night, if Shepherd won't be vexed. I can't stay alone."

My father is out till early morning looking for Sexton with the rest of the men. I see lights going up and down, and the master's dog is howling loud, as he always does when he is left behind. I cannot sleep, though Olwen, tired out, goes off beside me the minute the candle is blown out, and when my father comes in I get up and make a cup of tea.

"There is seventeen foot of flood-water at the bridge," he says, "and the oak meadow is under. It's the highest for years. There's not a mite to be gained by searching. He'll turn up right in the morning."

But three days later they find him, when the floods have gone down, fast in the hedge where the waters have carried him. The coroner sits over him; he says he was mad when he did it, for it seems he was mortal ill and all the world hard on him for his bad temper.

Olwen is still with us, and my father begins to grumble about the girl being no kin of ours. Mrs.

Hill says she will have her at Baysham to mind the baby.

This morning, as I am walking at the bottom of the hill, there I catch the master shouting at the gypsies that are on his land. He is waving his stick, they are looking rough, and I hear him cry out:

"Get off my land, or I'll make you!"

The gypsies give a murmur among themselves.

"Those that won't work shan't live," shouts the master.

One of the women gives a sudden sharp screech: a knife flashes past him and falls at my feet. I pick it up. "Give that to me," orders Evan ap Evans very sharply. "I'll have the law on them for that. They shall sweat for it next assizes."

I give it to him; he puts it in his pocket.

"You are witness of attempted murder."

"I am no such thing," I says, not wishing to fall foul of the gypsies or get tangled up with the law. "I didn't see the knife flung. I was stood here and it falls at my feet."

"Then nobody flung it; it fell down from the clouds, I suppose?"

"*You* may have done, for aught I know," I bursts out, fairly furious, master or no master, "and it may have been meant for me."

His mouth falls open; I pass him and go on up the hill, leaving him hammer and tongs with the gypsies.

They seem to be getting the best of it, and well I wish they may.

How long is spring in coming!

The month has come in like a lion: four chimneys are blown down—one at Cotterill's, two at Baysham, where Olwen goes with many tears, and Mrs. Somers's copper chimney, which she says makes washing-day a nightmare.

I am close by Cotterill's when their chimney comes down with a noise like thunder; the bricks are scattered all over the yard, and the master runs out of the wagon-house. We stare at the broken chimney-stack.

"You bring ill-luck to chimneys," says the master. "Are you a witch, Ann Goodman?"

"I shall not have to pay for this one," I answer.

He scowls.

All the Somers family are busy sawing up the great elm that has fallen across their pigsties. Owen is going to help on his uncle's farm come midsummer; they say he is wiser than his father, who is a fool with animals and fears his wife.

Gabriel tells me I sing well, but this morning my father hears me and calls out: "Not so much concert, and get on with what you are doing."

It is a little hard that he should never open his mouth but to grumble and find fault with all I do. My mother is poorly too, and keeps to her bed. I

hang the new curtains in her window to-day, white
ones with red roses. When I pull them for her to
sleep, she says: "They are pretty, Ann, but I would
rather see the mountains. Indeed, they look a long
way off to-day." And I draws them back again.

Chimneys are a plague! We are sitting by the fire,
and a great lump of soot falls down among the cinders, scattering them in my father's cider that is
warming. He says it is loosened by the great wind,
but the chimney must be dirty, and I am to sweep it.

I am up early, cutting young hazel rods in which
the juice is rising; I tuft them well at their heads with
bits of bushy holly; when I have finished, I have
brushes supple as leather, but upright. With these I
sweep the chimney clean, and the fire burns clear and
hot. The dirt and soot on me forces me to take a bath
in the wash-tub. My mother is afraid of chills; it is a
backward spring and early for baths.

Evan ap Evans loses all his prize fowls last week,
stolen by the gypsies out of spite. What a black rage
he is in! Not a word to a soul for three days after
would he speak. My father says speak softly to
gypsies, but the master cannot do that; it is not in
his breed.

Parson comes, and I am busy in the garden with
my skirts tucked up almost to my knees out of the
dirt. He laughs; I am too ashamed to stand upright,
for I must look a sight, with my long legs and my

hair down on my shoulders. This man does seem to creep about.

"You are busy. How pretty your garden looks!"

I am pleased to hear that, for I have taken a deal of trouble with it.

"I have heard Mrs. Goodman isn't well. Is she in bed?"

"Yes, and has been this fortnight."

He looks at me sharply. I go on scratching among the plants with my head down and my hair all over my face.

"I am sorry for that. I would have come before if I had known."

"You should have known."

He bends down and says: "You are a queer woman. I don't think you are very civil, Ann; one can see you have lived in the mountains. Shall I go in and talk to your mother?"

My mother stares at my clothes; I am more than decent, but I burn with shame as Parson fixes his eyes on me. I go downstairs, let down my dress, and put up my hair; in my vexation I break the new brown teapot, banging about getting my father's tea. When Parson comes down, I offer him a cup.

"Why, where's the gypsy?" he asks.

"What gypsy?"

"The one I met in the garden."

"I am not a child, sir."

He stops his laughing.

"No, indeed, you are not. I did not mean to annoy you, and you need not look so angry."

I do not feel polite; as he goes out he has to unlatch the door himself; he turns back in the porch, saying over his shoulder:

"But you make a very pretty gypsy with your curls down."

My father calls him a fool. He and Evan ap Evans are two men I do hate.

The evenings do draw out. Mrs. Hill gives me some seeds, and I spend hours in the garden planting them and pulling up the weeds. Sometimes the master passes. He speaks to me always in Welsh, and often I make believe not to hear him. Then he comes, leans his elbows on the wall, and says in his tongue:

"Good day, my proud girl."

Laughing, he goes away. Why does he always speak to me in Welsh? I wish Gabriel would come! To-night all the parish is dancing in the Somers's big barn. I see the Morgans from Gillow, the Meredyths, and the Willets. The Lewises are there beside the folk, and Miss Evans has come with her brother. He has on a very fine waistcoat, with silk flowers, which he does not wear to chapel, although he goes very regular: perhaps his sister thinks it is not quiet enough for that, as they are so narrow in their ways. But the master pays no heeds to man or woman.

They have piled the hay into one corner: lamps

and flares hang from the beams. Will Williams and Harry Parry are playing the concertina, and a young woman they say comes from the forest has a violin. More for show than playing, for when the master asks her to dance, she just puts her hand in his and whirls away with the rest, leaving the poor violin to Tom Somers, who soon breaks a string and puts all our teeth on edge.

It is pretty to see them all go round in the light, but I do not dance. Mrs. Hill tells me she does not feel comfortable so close to a man so be he is not her husband. We are both surprised to hear the master laughing behind us, where he has been stood listening to every word we have said, like the Welshman he is. "Why, that's just it," he says; "if Ann will come along with me I'll soon teach her to dance."

"Will you go, my dear?" asks Mrs. Hill. "You will be cold stood still in that thin dress. Look at the lamps flickering."

"No," I says, "I'll stay here."

Evan ap Evans catches at my arm:

"Wilt thou dance with me, sweetheart?"

I answer him boldly in Welsh:

"No, for my heart goes with my feet," and I think of Gabriel.

"Then you shall dance with me, fy cariad anwyl (my dear love), until the day breaks."

"That I will not."

I sets my back against the wall.

253

"Very well, I am sorry," says he, turning away.

"Why do you speak Welsh to me?"

"Because I am a Welshman."

"But I am English."

"Half. No, not that even, for you have lived in the mountains."

He sings softly, in the voice that the English have not, an old Welsh song that I have sung round the fire at night.

Mrs. Hill smiles, for she cannot understand the tongue, but I feel the tears come smarting. I turn my head away.

"Ann, wilt thou dance?" repeats the master.

"You had better dance, Ann," Mrs. Hill whispers. "You can tread well on his toes."

"More likely he will tread on mine. No, sir, you must find someone else; I am not going to dance."

He goes away; I think I am to be left in peace, as the young lady from the forest clings to his arm like a bur to sheep's wool, but it seems I am mistaken. Old Somers calls out:

"Now for something a bit more old-fashioned, something the older folk can join in. We'll have 'Black Nag'."

The couples sort themselves out in a minute. Harry and Will begin swaying and playing as if they have just awoke; all the other tunes are sleepy and droning compared to this—my feet are tapping when the master slips up behind me, claps his arm round my

254

waist like a vice, and says: "Now, Nan, thou canst dance 'Black Nag' with me!"

Willy-nilly I am compelled, though I am not at all content. Afterwards we have "A-hunting we will go". He gallops me so fast up and down the line I have no breath left to tell him what I think of him, roaring out the words above everyone else.

I am fairly ashamed.

> *A-hunting we will go,*
> *A-hunting we will go,*
> *We'll catch a fox*
> *And put him in a box,*
> *And a-hunting we will go.*
> *Ta ra la, ta ra la, ta ra la,*
> *A-hunting we will go.*

If I could free my hands, I would box my master's ears before all the world.

Olwen is sitting up with my mother. I find her asleep in the kitchen with her head on the table, and her long hair twining round the candlestick, all among the grease. Such a beautiful face I have never seen. I carry her up, lay her on my bed and take off her clothes. She wakes:

"Oh, Ann," she says. "Good night," and sleeps again.

This morning Owen comes running to me: "Come

with me," he cries. "Tom would play with the scythe; he has cut his leg, and we have sent for the doctor to sew up the cut." I find Tom very white, and the kitchen floor very red with his blood. Mrs. Somers is shrieking and sobbing; she wrings her hands and says it is his fault.

"Scythes are not to play with, but he would not be warned. Oh, dear!"

I stop the bleeding with old towels and clean water until the doctor comes. He stitches it together.

"And who are you, my girl?"

"I am Shepherd's daughter from Cotterill's."

"You! Well, you have done right. You would make a good nurse."

Gabriel should be content to have a wife who can clean chimneys and stop bleeding.

Gabriel is coming to see me.

I am putting on a clean new calico cover on our book.

He rides so beautifully that I run down the hill to watch him come up the lane; I stand by the gate to wait for him, and truth to tell I am thirsty for the sight of him after so long. It seems so much time wasted to be stood there at midday doing nothing, so I tuck up my sleeves and stoop down to the brook to gather watercress for our tea.

256

There is my face staring back at me out of the brown water among the weeds, almost like a person drowned.

It looks so strange that for a minute I forget Gabriel, but I hear the horse and spring into the middle of the road. Gabriel shakes the whip at me, and calls my name loud; he jumps down, kisses me, and takes the horse by the bridle.

"Why, Ann, what have you? Your arms are wet and your feet all muddy. Sit on the gate, sweetheart, while I clean your shoes."

I sit on the gate and he takes a handful of grass to wipe the mud away. We hear a step. Evan ap Evans passes; he scowls at Gabriel and says to me:

"Good day, love."

"Who is that calling you dear names in Welsh, so friendly?"

"It is father's master, Evan ap Evans, and he is not friendly, but hard and sharp. He does that to vex me."

"If he were not your father's master, I would show him!"

"I wish you could," I says. "Many a time I would have liked it!"

"Many a time?" he says. "Many a time?"

Mrs. Somers is keeping my mother company. She is telling her how bad Tom's leg is, and how sure she is it is poisoned.

She is a very sad woman. We take this book out

with us to the little spinney. Gabriel laughs when I show him the new cover. "I hope the inside is as clean," he says.

We are sat on a log among the bushes, and I see his face grown dark as he reads. At last he rises up and flings the book away with all his strength into the brambles and nettles.

"I know Welsh," he cries, "I understand why you looked on the ground when that man passed you, speaking his dirty tongue. Get away, you little bitch, and find your Welshman!"

"My friends are in that book. Pull it out of the brambles, Gabriel Ford, or I'll have no more to do with you."

I take his arm and shake it. He pushes me on the ground. "I'll take you from your Welshman and keep you from the parson!"

I twist away from him and run; he catches me, but I dash my hand into his face and scream, for his look is fearful. I run and run; when I can no more I sit down upon a stone and cry till my face is sore. I see him go riding down our lane, lashing his horse and galloping hard. I get up and at home I tell my mother Gabriel had to be gone early.

"He is a fine man," says my mother, "but I wish, Ann, you would not marry an Englishman. If you lived in Wales I could go perhaps to stay a bit with you. I would wish to die in my own country."

In the dark I go out to the little spinney: my book

258

is lying in the bushes, and I bring it home. It is mine now. Farewell, Gabriel.

I watch them wash the sheep before the shearing comes on. The poor things struggle on the edge of the pool, tramping up the mud. The water is shallow and dirty, but in the middle it is still and very deep.

They are all round that bit of water in the shade: my father and Willy Preece are dipping with two young boys to help; the sheep are panting in the hurdles. I stand behind an elder bush that my father may not see me, and I hear the boys call Evan ap Evans a mean master.

"He works cripples on his farm because he can get them for less."

"But he doesn't give them less work."

"No, and they must put up with his curses."

"No man dare stand up to him save Shepherd, and he is near as bad himself."

"Never a shilling does he give his men at Christmas, nor Easter. Old Somers gives each man bacon and half a crown."

"Old Somers is a fool. Which is richest?"

"Evans, curse him! Mean men make the money and keep it. Come, shup. Come, shup, come, shup. Shepherd's ready for another pair."

We have had a dreadful storm. I did not know it

could be so bad here, where there are no hills worth speaking of to shut the lightning in.

I am on the way home from Salus, and I have to take shelter with the Somers; they are all in the kitchen watching the lightning.

"Now I do hope," says Mrs. Somers, "I do hope our Owen won't go sheltering under any trees."

"Don't you fret, mother. Owen is no fool," says her husband.

"But you never know, and fool or no fool is all the same with lightning, you are never safe from it. My uncle used to have a man on his farm—a full-grown man he was—who could only look after cows like a woman or help a little with the hay; no ploughing or harrowing or reaping. He had been struck by lightning when he was fifteen. In the leg it was."

"But there's very few folk that *are*," argues Mr. Somers, who should know better by now.

"And the lightning is so pretty, Mam," says Chrissie, who wants to go outside and watch it from the gate.

"I don't know, and as for being pretty, my word, I think it is terrible, and smells awful they say."

"Smells?" we all cry.

"That it does. I mind a dreadful storm once, oh, a very bad storm it was, but not so near as this, and a man I used to know when I was a girl went out with his brother to see if the cattle were safe. The lightning come down not fifty yards from them and burnt up a whole elm. They said it smelt awful. They were both big men, but they put their hands over their eyes and ran back to the house like children."

"But I'm not affeared, Mam!" laughs Chrissie.

"Your great-grandfather said that," says Mrs. Somers very solemnly.

"I like to watch it."

"Your great-grandfather said that too. And one day when he was sat in the porch watching it, down it come like a blue serpent and got him in the arm! Just you take warning, Chrissie! He wouldn't and it struck him three times until he stopped looking at it. I don't remember where he was struck each time, but there wasn't much left of him when I knew him. Your grandmother always put *her* head in the bread-pan, and it never got her."

Chrissie begins to cry; Mrs. Somers does not heed, or perhaps she cannot hear, for she has stuffed both ears with jeweller's cotton at the beginning of the storm and sits looking at her feet.

"There's nothing to be affeared for," says Mr. Somers. "Don't take on, child."

"And listen! There was another man my sister knew; he was hoeing turnips when the lightning come without any rain. He left his hoe and went into the garden because he was wise, but his cousin looked up at the sky and laughed, and *he* was struck. All they ever found was his buttons."

"Oh dear," says Chrissie, crying bitterly.

"I must go, the sun has come out," I says.

"I never thought to see it again," says Mrs. Somers, taking the wool out of her ears. "Go and get the tea, Chrissie. Whatever is the matter with the child? You will stay a bit, won't you, Ann? We don't see much of you, and it is so cheering to have a bit of talk."

"Have you told her the news, Mother?" asks Mr. Somers.

"No; fancy that! It went clean out of my head in the storm. Owen is going to his uncle's farm down at Monmouth next week. Oh, I do hope he hasn't been walking under any trees."

"I hope he will be happy," I says.

I wish I were.

Time is long in passing! I look at the clock and wonder how I shall get through to-morrow. My father asks me when I shall be married; I do not answer, and his look follows me.

Summer has come in: Mary's sheep will be up the mountains, and the master has begun to shear. Olwen comes over to-day. She puts her two hands to my face, turning it this way and that so that the light falls on it:

"Dear Ann," she says, "what have you?"

"Maybe I'm tired with the heat, Olwen."

"Never. Tell me what has happened to you."

She kneels down beside me.

"Gabriel and I have quarrelled. He has left me, Olwen; we shall not be married."

She takes my two hands and lays her cheek upon them.

"He heard the master speaking Welsh to me, and thought he spoke too friendly. He is jealous of Evan ap Evans, that loves neither man, woman, nor beast."

I take my father's dinner down to the big meadow, where they are all shearing under the elms. Olwen is there, sitting on a hurdle swinging her legs, with her hair out of plait; so is young Williams's new wife. She comes from a town, and watches him as he shears with all her eyes. The master is stood close, too, looking and holding his watch in his hand; he scowls at Williams, who has made two cuts in five minutes.

"Look at him," whispers Olwen; "he is vexed, but he will not say so."

"It is plain you don't know him," I says. "If he is vexed he will be out with the reason, and a double measure of cursing too."

Olwen laughs out loud; the master looks up and sees us together.

"Good day," he calls out, but he does not keep his eyes for long off the sheep that is struggling under Williams's shears. Suddenly he puts the watch back in his pocket. "You need not come again, you are too slow."

"Yes, sir," says Williams, though he is not pleased. His wife puts out her tongue at the master as he turns away; she bends down to stroke her dog that sits by her quietly all the time, and I can see she is crying. I make to slip away when I see Evan ap Evans coming.

"Don't run away," he says, "I want to speak to thee."

"I'm going back home. You cannot have anything to say to me."

"But I have, and I will say it—leastways, I'll shout it if thou wilt not stay to listen. Olwen can go closer to watch them shearing; she cannot see very well from here, I know."

"Not very well," she says, and is off like a flash.

"Now, Ann, art thou vexed with me?"

"I've reason to be."

He draws his brows together, as he does when he is angered.

"Thou art very saucy for a shepherd's daughter: very high and haughty thou art, Ann Goodman: had thy father not been such a good shepherd, thou mightst have had cause to rue it before now! But I am not here to quarrel. I'll ask thee a question. Wilt thou answer me straight like a man, since thou canst not speak to me like a woman?"

He fixes his eyes on me; I am not affeared at his black looks.

"Yes, I would like to answer you like a man if there were no folk here. But they might find it strange to see Evan ap Evans, farmer of Cotterill's, struck by a hired man's daughter!"

264

"What a tongue has our Nan!"

He walks a few steps from me, calling to the men to hurry. Suddenly he turns round:

"Answer me, or I'll bawl it for all the world to hear. Is it true that I have made trouble between thee and thy sweetheart?"

"Yes, you have done that."

"How should that be? I am thy father's master, he is my shepherd, and how should I have anything to do with his daughter?"

"You called me your love when he was by. What right had you? He understood."

He gives a kind of laugh, but I am nearer tears than I like for him to see.

"As good a right as any man!"

"No, no," I cry.

"Well, I will not speak Welsh now. I thought it might seem homely to thee, thou being from the mountains, and it's a sweeter tongue than English."

"No," I tell him, "I am English. I was with English folk in Wales, and I hate the Welsh and all their shifty ways of dealing. 'Taffy was a Welshman, Taffy was a thief.'"

"Ay, among Englishmen I'd cheat the log-heads out of every penny. Thou hatest the Welsh, dost thou? Is Myfanwy an English name?"

For once I cannot answer.

"I'll go to thy Gabriel."

"You'll do no such thing. You've done enough."

265

"I will. I will tell him that thou and I are nought but good enemies, and always have been. I shall tell him he is a fool—an English fool."

"I'm going home," I say. "You cannot undo what you have done, even with your Welsh tongue."

"I will, though," shouts the master.

"Gabriel Ford will never take your word," I answer back.

"Nor thine, or this would never have happened. How shalt thou marry him then? Ann, stay with me."

"I'm going home," I say again. "I hate you, and if I could work you harm for what you have done, I would."

I leave him standing stock-still; as I do I hear him whisper:

"There is a longing on me for my own country."

I have looked for furious rage.

I go straight to Olwen.

"You are a strange friend, giving me away to the man I hate most in the world. Now tell me what you said to him."

"Yes, I will. Only don't frown so, Ann."

"When did you tell him?"

"I went to Cotterill's yesterday. I felt like Daniel in the lions' den!"

"Does anyone know beside the master?"

"No."

Olwen tells me she ran off to Cotterill's the moment the baby was in bed.

266

"The yard was full of pigs, Ann, and when I opened the gate, because I could not climb over the spikes, a big sow ran out into the road. I run out after her, leaving the big gate open to drive her through; while I was chasing her, the rest came out and ran up the road the other way."

She hears them squealing and grunting and thinks whatever shall she do, and which way shall she go? In the end she chases the sow as far as Baysham Marsh, where she turns her. As she comes up the lane, very hot and out of breath, she meets Miss Evans with her back hair falling down and her cap all crooked.

"What are you doing with my sow, child?" she asks, giving it a whack with her stick.

Olwen makes a curtsey.

"Please, Miss, she got out when I opened the gate. I come to see the master, and please the others are all gone up Hentland way."

Olwen says Gwladys Evans goes up that lane like lightning, the sow galloping in front like a mad thing.

"Now pen her up, and come to help me with the others, since you let them out."

"I'm very sorry, Miss," says Olwen; "if you stand by the gate I think I can get them in."

"My dear, do you think I want to stay here all night while you go catching pigs all over the parish? I have to go out, so come along."

Olwen tells me she did want to laugh; Miss Evans

looked very odd with her hair streaming behind her, scampering up the lane, hallooing and calling to the pigs, and asking questions all the time.

"You work for Mrs. Hill, don't you? When is Mr. Hill going to haul that elm trunk across my brother's hedge? Why have you come to see him? And what are you going to say? How old are you?"

Olwen says she is fourteen come next July.

"I'm sure you're not. You are much older."

"No, I'm only that."

"Nonsense, I know you are fifteen at least. Brenin Mawr! (Good Lord!) there's my pigs over in Scudamore's orchard! Whatever will he say? Creep through the hedge and drive them out quick, before they are seen. Here's a hole."

As each pig comes through, Gwladys Evans gives it a whack.

"That's for leading me such a dance!"

Yet, Olwen says, she did not seem to be at all vexed.

"Well, now you had better come to the dairy and have a drink of milk. I am going out, so you shall sit in my kitchen and wait for the master. He'll be back in half an hour or so."

She takes Olwen through the back door, gives her cake and milk, and a bowl of gooseberries to top and tail.

"Put the tops and tails in the fire, and mind you don't throw any about; I cannot abide a dirty kitchen. And don't let the fire out."

She puts on her bonnet, takes a shawl from the drawer and goes out, leaving Olwen sitting there very contented. About an hour after, Olwen hears the outer dairy door bang; Evan ap Evans walks in whistling.

"Cythraul! what are you doing sitting here in the dusk? Are you a fairy?"

"Please, sir, I want to speak to you. I am Olwen Davies."

"You are welcome," says the master.

"Ann Goodman's sweetheart have left her because he heard you call her dear names in Welsh."

She is almost frightened to death then, for he breaks out into his own tongue, which she cannot understand.

"What are you staring at?" he cries after a while. "What do you want?"

Olwen bursts out crying.

"I want to go home, I am affeared, I wish I hadn't come!"

"Come back," the master calls, "come back, Olwen, I've something to ask you. Come back, and I'll give you some cake and a whole duck."

As Olwen tells me this, she puts her arm round me.

"I ran home, Ann, without another word. Are you still vexed with me?"

"Is that all?"

"Yes," she says.

"Well, it's nothing but truth, though I hadn't thought to tell him."

As I am stood in the kitchen, making a pudding, I hear my mother call out:

"Ann, wash your floury hands. The master is riding up the hill."

"He won't come here, never fear," I say.

She calls again:

"Quick! I can see him through the window; he is tying his horse to the gate."

It is too late to wash; I have the door open for coolness, and the master is stood in it looking at me.

"Good day," he says, "I am riding into Wales, Ann Goodman. What message have you for your sweetheart?"

"None by you," I answer.

There is something strange to me in his voice. He is speaking English. He flicks the lintel with his whip.

"Perhaps there'll be one to bring you."

"If you are going to Gabriel Ford, I cannot stay you. But you are more likely to bring back a bruised face than any message."

"Then you shall bathe it for me."

I make no answer.

"Ffarwel, Nan (Good-bye, Ann). Time brings ointment to every hurt."

He goes away. I wish we had never met!

My father says the master came home late last night. He has been away three days, and I have not heard his face was bruised.

I wish it had been!

He has brought no message.

I dream that I am in the kitchen at Twelve Poplars, sitting by the hearth. Mary touches me, she is stood close behind me.

"I can hear them coming, Ann," she says.

I too hear the sound of wagon wheels. I run to the door; the master's heavy wagon is coming up slowly under the trees with my father on the front by Willy Preece. The wheels are dripping with water. They draw up before the door, and I see there is a coffin in the wagon, covered with a cloth. They carry it into the house.

What does this mean?

A month has passed. This evening on the way home from Salus I meet Mr. Hill, staring over the gate into the bottom field, where every man that can be hired round here is carrying the master's hay.

He turns to me.

"Gamus is still uncut. A heavy crop, Ann! Most of it is flat on the ground. The grass in the Oak Meadow has been lying out untouched this fortnight. My hay is ruined."

"I've never known the weather so bad. Hay will be dear this year."

271

"Evans will sell it dear! He has every man in the place. Oh, he can pay well when there's money to be made by it. He saves enough on his cripples to pay for his harvesting, while we who pay a fair wage all the year round see our crops rot. Curse him!"

"Yes, it is all in safe; this is the last field."

"Mine is not fit for fodder. The Welsh hog!"

My father grunts when I tell him.

"Hill is too quick to mow, too slow to turn, too quick to carry. He has none to blame but himself."

ANN'S BOOK: SECOND PART, 1850

Gwyn ac oer yw marmor mynydd,
Gwyn ac oer yw ewyn nentydd,
Gwyn ac oer yw eira Berwyn,
Gwynnach oerach dwyfron Ann.

(*White and cold is the marble of the mountains,*
White and cold is the foam of the rivers,
White and cold is the snow on Berwyn,
Whiter, colder is the breast of Ann.)

My mother is dead.

I take my father his tea in the bottom meadow, where he is loading hay with the rest: when I come back there is my mother on the floor beside her bed, gasping for breath.

"What is it? What have you?" I cry, running to her.

"My heart!" she answers.

I lift her up in my arms and lay her on the bed. Her face is grey like ashes and damp with sweat; every minute her breath comes shorter, every minute it seems to me that she must die under my hands.

"Mae arnafeisian gweld John," she gasps. "I want to see John." She has fallen into her own tongue, that she has not spoken since she was married.

There is no time to lose: from the window I can see my father down in the meadow, working by the gate. I lean out with my fingers to my mouth and give the shepherd's whistle; he looks up. "Father!"

He throws down his fork. I wait but a moment to see him start on the way before going back to my mother, who is groaning.

"The pain, the pain," she cries.

I sponge her face and lift her up. My father shouts from the kitchen to know what is wrong.

"Send Willy Preece for the doctor. I think Mother is dying," I whisper down the stairs.

How long my father is away, and all the time my mother crying out to me to fetch him! But when he comes to her bed and tries to speak to her, she does not seem to know he is there.

"What is she saying? What does she want?"

"She is asking for you, Father."

"Myfanwy, Myfanwy, I am here. Speak to her, Ann! Can't you? Speak her own tongue!"

"Father is here," I tells her.

She grasps my wrists.

"Oh, be quick, Ann dear, be quick, I am dying."

"He is here," I cry over and over.

At last I tells my father to say:

"Rwaf yma wrtheich ymyl" (I am here beside thee).

He tries, word for word, after me, and she smiles as best she can.

"Will the doctor be long?"

"An hour maybe, if he is in."

"She will be gone before then," I says.

There is nothing we can do to hinder her, but she is still alive when the doctor comes into the room. He looks at her once, and a minute after we see that she is dead. Without a word or another glance my father pulls the curtains and goes away downstairs.

"What was it?"

"Angina pectoris—her heart. Had she ever been at all like this before?"

"Never, but she has been ailing this past year."

"Has she been crossed or thwarted to-day, or has she done anything different from her habit that might have upset her?"

"No, she has been in bed, knitting, like she always does."

"Have you left her alone at all?"

"I was ten minutes gone to the field with my father's tea. She was well and smiling when I looked back at the window, waving her hand to me."

He says that waving killed her.

After he has gone and it is quite dark, I go down to my father in the kitchen. He lights the candle and puts it on the table beside me with a piece of paper and a pen. "Sit down here. Write to your cousin."

"Not to-night, Father!"

"Yes—now. Tell her you will be going back to Wales, and Myfanwy too; it was a promise years gone by."

I takes the pen in my hand.

"In the morning you must find a woman to help get her ready."

I write: my father stands behind me, looking out of the window.

"I'll live alone," he says.

In a while he goes up the stairs to my mother, and I hear the bolt thrust.

Parson comes and begins to talk about the funeral:

"She was too frail to attend the services, but of course she will be buried according to our rites and ceremonies?"

"Whose rites?" asks my father. "Yours?"

"And yours," says Parson sharply.

My father laughs.

"If rites are religious fancies, I leave them to other

folk. Myfanwy had them: chapel and Wales was her wishes, and back over the Border she shall go, where she came from. I'll take her to Pentredwr, where I met her at a sheep fair, thirty years ago."

This morning my father goes to the doctor for the certificate, and Mrs. Hill and Mrs. Somers come in to help me dress her. Gwladys Evans sends flowers from her garden. Mary comes over to fetch me. She goes up to my mother. "Poor Myfanwy," she says when she comes down, "poor Myfanwy!"

My mother wears a long white shawl that I knitted for her in the spring to keep her warm in bed, and her face is younger than my memory of it. Mary and I walk to the bottom of the hill, where Morgan and the trap are waiting by the brook. The horse is fresh from standing; Cotterill's and our cottage are soon out of sight.

"Twelve Poplars is your home," says Mary; "your father is best left alone. My word, I could say something to him for making you write that letter with Myfanwy not cold, telling you to go the minute the breath is out of your mother's body!"

The master passes us, riding into Salus; he draws close in to my side.

"Art going back to the mountains for good, Ann?"

"I'm not coming back," I answer, with my eyes on the horse's ears.

He looses the reins.

"Ffarwel, Ann."

"Ffarwel," I says.

Mary stares after him.

"Who is that man calling you by name? He was over at Tan y Bryn one evening when I was there."

"It is the master."

The dream comes true in every way: my father and Willy Preece bring my mother from England in a wagon. They are more than an hour late for the funeral, and three hours over the time we were all to meet at Twelve Poplars. After this wet summer the river is very hard to ford; the wagon is wet to the axles, and the black cloth over the coffin is dripping at the edges.

My father gets down.

"Don't carry her in, we're late as it is. We'll start away now. Are you ready?"

Willy Preece, Owen Somers, and Harry Edwards are the other bearers. They are all waiting, but Mary pushes them back.

"Myfanwy is coming over my doorstep if I have to carry her myself!"

They take my mother into the parlour, where there are flowers for her; the curtains are drawn—my father will not wait above ten minutes, and for fear of trouble Mary gives in, though she sets her lips very tight.

It is a long way to the cemetery: Mary and I walk close behind the coffin, the rest follow us. We are the only kin, for my father would have none of our people at the funeral.

The minister reads:

"It is better to go to the house of mourning than to go to the house of feasting: for that is the end of all men; and the living will lay it to his heart. Sorrow is better than laughter: for by the sadness of the countenance the heart is made better."

He prays that strength and consolation may be dealt to us.

The mountains are black with rain: when the coffin is in the grave, the storm breaks, and on the way back home we take shelter.

Mary has beer and food spread, but my father will not touch a morsel. She asks him to rest the night.

"No," he says. "I have no time to waste. Come into the kitchen, Ann."

Mary's look follows us.

"See here, now your mother is dead I have no use for you; all you could do for me I could do a deal better for myself. You make trouble with the master, you would lose me my shepherding by your saucy ways. All the parish sees he is sweet with you; if you won't have him, stay here till his blood cools, but it is a fool of a woman that takes the man when she might have the master! Still, have it your own way, only don't you set foot over the Border without I sends for you. You will not be welcome. Maybe you could be useful later on when the lambing is on me."

He puts his hat on and turns away. Mary stops him in the doorway:

"What, you are never going back to-night?"

"I'm going to the Goat at Pentredwr. That's where I'll rest the night over."

Mary begins to look sharp.

"Very well, Shepherd Goodman, go to your old Goat! But the horses don't stir from here to-night. They will be a deal more comfortable than you, I know. A bug-bitten man *you* will be to-morrow. Shall we see you in the morning?"

"No."

"Well, let us be thankful for that! But I suppose you'll be over sometimes to keep an eye on your wife's grave?"

"Once I am out of Wales I stay out of Wales," says my father.

"You are a worthless fellow, and the best thing a woman can wish you is that your sheep keep you so busy with foot-rot and maggots that you have no time to think of your own wickedness."

My father goes out, banging the door. He shouts to Willy Preece through the window:

"Here you, swilling beer on a coffin, have the wagon down at the gate sharp at five."

After an hour or so the folk go away, save those that are to sleep here. Owen Somers and Willy Preece go up into the granary to give the children rides on the trolleys. They have been sliding on the grain all the afternoon. Charlie drives the cows into the yard, and, going to the dairy, I take my milking stool and pail off the hook.

In the morning, just after we are astir, I see the empty wagon go up the hill with my father and Willy Preece on the front. They are sitting on the black cloth that covered my mother's coffin. I watch them go crawling out of sight, hoping that wagon will be the last I see of them this many a day.

Owen Somers comes to me in the dairy, where I am skimming the milk: I ask him to have some before he goes: he takes the cup from my hands.

"Shepherd says we shall not be seeing you this side of Christmas, Ann. Shall you be away all those months? Mother will miss you sadly."

"It is no sorrow to me staying here, Owen; these parts are less strange to me than over the Border. Give my remembrances to your father and mother when you go home, and if you should see Olwen Davies, give her my dear love."

"Yes, Ann. I will do that. Good-bye to you."

Charlie and Georgie are holding his horse in the yard; he mounts and rides away, waving his hand to the children. My father would have no flowers on my mother's grave. Now that he is gone we carry roses and marigolds out of the garden to her. There are some bits of speedwell too, which Mary was used to tell me meant, "God be with you."

I am content to have my dairy to take my mind off other things.

Jenny is a strange child.

This evening she is sat in the kitchen window, holding the children's big Bible with the pictures open on her knees: beside her she has made a great pile of red and white rose petals. One by one she drops them between the pages.

"What are you doing, Jenny dear?"

"The red petals are for the happy pictures, and the white for the sad ones."

She holds up the Bible for me to see: there is a white petal on the raising of Lazarus from the dead.

"But that surely is a happy picture. Lazarus was dead, and was called back to life again."

Jenny shakes her head.

"No, it is a sad picture. Lazarus was asleep, and they woke him."

Mary takes the children to church in the morning. I was used to go with them, but this Sunday I go to the Welsh service in the evening. There are very few folk, for most of the Welsh-speaking people are chapel. It is for fear of meeting Gabriel that I go this evening. He will never go where the Welsh tongue is spoken, so be that he can help it; he finds it bitter to work at Tan y Bryn, although it is a good place with a kind master. He was born and bred in England, and he has no use for the Welsh, nor for their way of speaking.

There is a cold wind blowing for July, and a deal of spoilt hay lying out in the fields. I look up Graig Ddu. Gwen Powys's sheep are wandering about, but Gabriel is not with them. After the service I go to the cemetery. Looking down upon my mother's grave, it seems strange to think of life at Cotterill's, and while I stand there lost, there is a footstep by the gate. It is Gabriel, staring at me through the bars; without a word I turn away, and he does not follow.

Mary asks me:

"Ann, what is wrong between you and Gabriel?"

"We have quarrelled."

"Why?"

We are in the dairy, straining off the milk. I hold the muslin while she pours, and my hands tremble so that I let it slip.

"Careful," says Mary. "We'll have a bit of talk over this after we have done."

Long as I have lived with her I would be more content to keep it to myself. But she must be told; everybody must notice that he has stopped coming here after me.

"What was the trouble?" she asks in the kitchen.

"Gabriel was jealous of Evan ap Evans, my father's master."

"I fancy there are some things I could tell you about those two."

"Yes, you said you were at Tan y Bryn the time the master come."

"I was sitting in the kitchen with old Powys; Gwen and the girls were at Pentredwr. We had been having a lot of rain, and the spring had come through the floor again. There was the poor old man down on his hands and knees with a basin and saucer, saucering it up. When I come in at the door he threw them both against the wall, shouting:

" 'Diawl! An hour have I been on my knees, and no more will I do. Ah, ah, ah, with the crickets singing round the fire and the water between the stones, indeed, it is unpeaceful even with Gwen away at the market.'

" 'I'll do a bit,' I said. I had barely dipped up a saucerful when there came a knock on the door."

Mary stops and looks at me very solemnly.

"It was the man that overtook us riding to Salus," she says, "a big dark Welshman and looks sour."

"That's the master."

" 'Is Gabriel Ford a shepherd here?' he asked.

" 'Yes, he is,' we answered.

" 'I want to see him.'

"Old Powys told him he would have to climb Graig Ddu, unless he liked to wait until Gabriel came down to milk. Their sheep have had maggots badly this year, and Gabriel was up with them.

" 'I will climb Graig Ddu,' said your master.

"We asked him if he knew the way, but before we had finished pointing out the track Gabriel came into the yard; he had a bottle of Thorley's in his hand that he had been using on the sheep.

" 'That is Gabriel Ford over yonder,' I said.

"He went over at once: my word, Ann, you should have seen Gabriel's face when he saw your master coming!"

"I know well enough how he looked."

" 'There's going to be trouble; whatever can be amiss between those two?' I thought, seeing Gabriel's black scowl, and knowing him to be a stranger in these parts. I heard him ask in English:

" 'Are you Gabriel Ford?'

"Gabriel answered:

" 'I am, blast your soul!' and threw that bottle of Thorley's straight at your master's head: he ducked, but the bottle hit his shoulder and burst all over his coat. My word, Ann, that set things going!"

" 'Diawl!' your master yelled, and he caught Gabriel a clip which sent him reeling through the stable door, though Gabriel dealt him a slash with his crook that marked him under his clothes, I know."

"Did they harm each other?"

"Gabriel was hurt a bit, though not by the Welsh-man. That young mare they call Cadi was in the stable; whether she was frightened at Gabriel bump-

ing in on her so sudden I cannot say, because I was
right over by the kitchen door, only she kicked him
out of the stable on to the muck heap in the yard, and
for five minutes he was quiet enough—while we were
throwing cold water over him. Your master went
over very cool to the stream and washed off the
Thorley's with his handkerchief; he got on his horse
and rode off without another glance at us.

"Not very long after, Gwen Powys and the girls
came back; they wanted to know why Gabriel had a
black eye and a stiff leg, but he wouldn't say anything
beyond the mare had kicked him. He went on with
the milking as though nothing had happened, though
everybody could tell he was in a boiling passion.
Still, they were affeared to ask the reason, so to this
day Gwen Powys is none the wiser."

"Was that *all*? Didn't the master say why he had
come?"

"Not a word to a soul, my dear. He just went off
looking like murder."

"He told me he would go to Gabriel and make
him understand we were nought to each other."

Mary looks up sharply.

"Then there was some cause for Gabriel to be
jealous?"

"He heard the master calling me dear names in
Welsh one day when he was come over to see
me."

"So your master *was* sweet with you! He is a fine

man, Ann; it would be better for you than to marry a shepherd."

"Those were my father's words to me just after we buried my mother. Listen, Mary. I hate Evan ap Evans!"

"Perhaps, seeing you were his shepherd's daughter—though you are as good as he is by blood and better by behaviour—he thought nothing of a kiss here and there."

"There were no kisses."

"Well," says Mary, "there is no telling what a Welshman means by what he says."

And she calls the children in to their supper. I do not answer, for sometimes, since I have left Cotterill's, I have thought the master loved me.

When we are sat sewing in the porch, there comes a bang on the back door: it is a man in a black velvet coat and plaid trousers, with a jug in one hand and a gridiron in the other.

"What do you want?" says Mary.

"I am selling china and hardware."

"Well, if that is all your stock you will soon be sold out. Good afternoon to you."

She begins to shut the door, but he does not move off the step.

"Ah, it is good to hear English again! The folk here have a tongue that we cannot understand, me and my little girl out there."

We look past him into the yard, where we see a little donkey-cart and a child sucking an apple among a crowd of pots and pans.

"What else do you sell?"

"Brushes and buckets, funeral cards and syrups."

"Syrups!" cried Mary. "Have you any cough cures?"

He pulls a bottle out of his pocket.

"This mixture will cure any cough in a week. Not one of those railway-train cures, but a good steady reliable brew."

"How much is the bottle?"

"One shilling and sixpence. Give a teaspoonful after every cough, and mix it with water to make it last—it is very strong."

"Is it too strong for a little girl?"

"Oh, no, no, no. Bless you, no! It is the mixture I always give my own little girl out there."

Mary buys the mixture and a scrubbing brush. Ten minutes after he is gone, Margiad Powys runs into the kitchen all out of breath.

"Has a man selling china been to you?"

"Yes. He was here but a few minutes since."

"Cythraul! Which way did he go?"

"Oh, up the hill."

"Oh, it is too hot to run up there after him."

"Why, what is it?" I ask.

"He has stolen a drench Gabriel had for Cadi. He told Mother how happy he was to be among his own

287

people again, and asked her who won the prize for singing at the Eisteddfod this year. While she was gone to ask he must have put it in his pocket. It was on the table by the door."

Mary and I give a look at each other; she takes the bottle of cough mixture off the dresser and hands it to Margiad.

"The Welsh varmint!" she says.

How slowly the days go by without Gabriel coming to see me in the evenings and walk with me to church on Sundays. In England there was my mother to look to, and the master to vex and plague me; at Cotterill's I was not used to meet him in the fields like I was here, where we both grew up.

Yesterday, crossing the bridge, I see him fishing in the pool where I was used to go with him and vex him by throwing my fish back. He does not see me leaning on the bridge, watching him as he watched me through the gate.

This morning the sun comes out. We gather up all the dirty clothes and make a washing day of it, putting off the churning till to-morrow.

Mary calls Charlie to her.

"Here, come and get the copper ready. Mind you fill it up to the brim and then be off to play with Georgie and Jenny. Mind now what I am telling you, and keep them out of mischief."

Charlie is a good-hearted boy but stupid; in the

wash-house we find the copper filled but the fire unlit—we lose half an hour waiting for the water to boil. It is a big wash for two wet weeks: there are sheets and towels and blankets.

"I'll wash; you rinse and wring," says Mary.

We spread the things to dry over the blackberry bushes in the orchard, where it is sunny.

Jenny comes in crying just before dinner.

"I feel sick, Mam."

"What have you been eating?"

"Apples, Mam," says Jenny, sobbing and crying.

"Apples! They're as green as gooseberries. Who gave them to you?"

"Charlie did, to keep me out of mischief while he played up the tree with Georgie."

Mary carries her off to dose her well.

"Run down to the orchard, Ann, and see what those boys are up to," she says.

They are up the big tree playing sailors. One of our clean sheets is tied to a branch for a sail, flapping and torn, and George is waving one of his shirts tied to a stick by both arms.

Mary and I are very angry; Charlie has to go with bread for his dinner, and Georgie has to learn his duty to his neighbour. And we have to boil the sheet again and sew up the rents.

At sundown I pass through the Winllan on my way home from the cemetery. Gabriel is there, split-

ting logs, with Cadi and a cart; so we meet face to
face alone, and I can see he is my sweetheart still.

Without a word spoken I stand beside him, watching his dark face and the mallet falling on the wedge.
It is deep in the wood when there is a crack, the
mallet head flies past my ear, and strikes against a
tree behind me.

Gabriel drops the shaft, staring, and catches me in
his arms.

"Forgive me, Ann; it was in my heart to hurt you!
The head was coming loose with every blow, and yet
I would not tell you."

"I saw it, but I would not move for pride."

He stoops to kiss my mouth: I push him off.

"Loose me," I cry.

"Is your father's master sweet with you?"

"You would not take my word," I says slowly in
Welsh.

Gabriel scowls at the tongue.

"Loose me."

He lets me go on my way; a field beyond I hear
the rumble of the cart behind me, and turn my head:
Gabriel comes up with me, he stretches out his hand;
I take it, set my foot on the shaft, and stand up beside
him. He keeps me steady with an arm round my
waist.

Mary sees us come into the yard.

"What happened?" she asks me when we are
going to bed. I tell her.

"Ah, everything comes right in the end," she says, very content.

Our two black cows are sold at Pentredwr fair. Gabriel goes with Megan and Margiad against his will, because they have to leave before the fighting begins. Afterwards he comes to me.

"They pestered me to take them and buy them coloured handkerchiefs. I would have nought to say to them, but these are for you."

He gives me sweets in a box.

"Ann, what makes you look so different these days? What have you been doing to yourself? Is it your black frock?"

"A deal of sad things have happened since you left me, but it was you and the master worked this with me."

"Curse him!"

"All the world does that."

"Then there must be good reason for it. When will you marry me—when the mourning is done?"

"It is too soon to talk of that," I says.

While Gabriel and the girls are gone to the fair we go with Gwen Powys gathering whinberries up Graig Ddu. Gwen looks at her sheep.

"It's terrible to see them so lame and ailing. This has been a bad year: no fruit, all the hay lost, and by the looks of it the corn harvest may go the same way."

Mary looks very grave.

By midday we have all filled our baskets—Jenny's mouth is purple with juice, and she cannot eat her dinner. Just after we have finished the rain comes down like a flood and we are soaked to the bone long before we can reach the house. On the way down I fall, cutting my knee, and Jenny cries out at the sight of the blood, so that a person would think it was her own.

We have to give Gwen Powys all dry clothes, and when we put hers on the horse before the fire we cannot help but see that she goes with only two petticoats—a grey flannel and a pink cotton.

"Saves the washing," she says, seeing our surprise, that we cannot hide.

"One day she will take to wearing gloves to save her fingers," Mary whispers.

We make our whinberries into jam and two tarts; Gwen Powys tries to take more than her share.

In the evenings Gabriel comes to see me.

But it is not like old times together.

While I am in the dairy churning, Charlie passes the window as idle as a plough-boy in August. The butter has just come, and I am letting off the buttermilk.

"Charlie, fetch me a bucket of water," I say.

He takes the bucket I hand him through the window.

"Shall I put it in the churn?"

"Yes," I tells him, pouring the buttermilk into the pig-trough with my back turned.

When I look round there is a stream coming out of the churn; Charlie has put in boiling water from the copper, and though I rush to take out the bung, half the butter is melted.

Mary says Charlie must go. Last night the fox come and killed five ducks, because he forgot to shut them up.

The weather has come in hot and fine.

Gabriel goes to church with me this Sunday. Afterwards we walk on to my mother's grave with honeysuckle that we gather in the hedges. She was used to call it fairy's fingers.

Gabriel says: "Will you marry me in the spring, Ann?"

I cannot answer.

Sian Pritchard from Glanrafon (on the banks of the river) is married to Abel Daw in the chapel at Pentredwr to-day. He keeps a draper's shop in Salus. Her father is fair furious at the marriage, being a true Welshman that would have his daughter marry one of her own country, but her English mother is well content the girl should go back over the Border.

Five years ago this July, Abel comes to Glanrafon in the evening with a pack on his shoulders as a journeyman. Mrs. Pritchard was that overjoyed to make welcome one of her own country that she kept him the night over, and by candlelight he and Sian cast such looks at each other as they neither of them ever forgot. The next year Abel came again to ask Sian if she would be his wife, and she said she would. He had started his shop, but when her father came to hear of it he fell into a rage, and went at Abel with a flail before Sian, till he was all but dead had she not dropped down in a fit on the threshing floor. She was so mortal ill that her father swore he would never thwart her or cross her again, so be she got better. For years Abel never come near her; at last she sent him a letter, and now for his promise Mr. Pritchard must put up with the wedding.

These last evenings I have been making her lace for a present. Mary went to the chapel; she said the lace was sewn on the wedding dress.

When the sun is down and the day cools off towards nightfall, Gabriel and I go up to Graig Ddu. He has his dog and his crook with him, and in his hand is a bottle of Thorley's, which makes me think of the master.

"Ben is in for the trials at Pentredwr. You'll be coming, Ann? It's not like a celebration," says he.

"Yes. I'll be there."

"You shall see us win the cup from the Caernarvonshire bitch."

We stop at the pool where we was used to catch trout.

"Could you catch them in your hands now?" he asks.

It is already dusk when we are among the sheep. Ben fetches them together in the hollow called the Basin, and Gabriel and I sit down on a rock and wait for the moon to rise.

"Gwen Powys gives me but a scrap of candle for the lantern, so when there is free light I use it. She is the nearest woman in these parts, and many of them are near enough, God knows! She stints for food and light and firing. She keeps a sharp eye on the almanac too, and at full moon my candle is shorter by an inch, be the weather fair or foul. The mountain is well named Graig Ddu (Black Mountain). I have been up and down these paths on some dark nights, Ann."

"Have you seen the Roman soldiers marching through Craig Dinas and the White Lady that drowned herself in Llyn-tro?" (the turning pool).

"Never, and I have fished it many a night alone. All I heard was an otter splashing off the bank. It's a lonely place after dark under those trees, with the water rushing over the stones. There's never hardly much of a moon down there."

I cannot see his face, but his voice changes after a moment. He points down where we came from.

"There are no lights in Tan y Bryn, you see? Gwen Powys sits by the hearth knitting stockings in the dark to save candles, and if Megan and Margiad are not out visiting or courting, they have to go to bed. It's well for them they are handsome girls."

295

"You speak discontented, Gabriel," I says, thinking he has good reason for it.

"I have worked here fifteen years, and now I have done with Wales—done with it. Come spring we will be married. Perhaps I can find a place over the Border, where candle-ends count for less. Ah! if I can win the trials."

He sits there silent with his arm round my waist.

"Look," I say, "the moon is up, we can count the sheep."

"There's all the night before us. Now I can see you, Ann. How beautiful you are!"

He takes the pins from my hair and pulls it round my shoulders. I struggle to be free of him, but he holds me fast.

"Light the lantern for me, Gabriel, and let me go."

He scowls.

"You love that Welshman! Time was when you could bear to be beside me half an hour without whining to be off."

"Time never was when I would sit on the mountain till midnight. Loose me, I tell you."

"We are doing no wrong here together," says Gabriel angrily.

I am affeared. Suddenly I loose his arm and run from him down the path. He comes away after me, then stays at the edge of the Basin shouting and cursing.

In my heart I know now that we shall never marry.

August has come in hot and cloudy.

Early in the morning, before the others are awake, I go out mushrooming. It is not very long before I know someone has been through the meadows: there are footmarks in the dew and no rabbits feeding. And the home meadow is bare of mushrooms where last night I marked many for the picking. In the lower pastures I see a woman, thin as a crow, stooping with a basket in her hand.

"Good morning, Miss Powys," I says behind her. "What are you doing taking my cousin's mushrooms?"

Gwen Powys almost lets the basket fall in her fright. "I came out early to gather them for a little surprise to Mrs. Maddocks, and it was in my mind to leave them on the doorstep," she gabbles.

Margiad's head is bobbing above the hedgerow as she stoops and raises herself; Gwen's eyes go roving round the field while she is speaking.

"It was very kind of you. Myself, I haven't had the luck to find a mushroom. You have sharp eyes Miss Powys, but thank you all the same. I'll take the mushrooms with me to save you the walk."

And I goes off with my basket full of her gathering.

August is a bad month for beasts; our cows have been very vexing lately, kicking and wasting the milk. This evening our only Welsh Black kicks me when I am milking the shorthorn next her; she strikes the leg off the stool and drenches me with the milk.

Morgan comes running, thinking to find me on the way to death from a blow in the back, but the stool takes the most hurt, and the cow too, when he beats her for her hastiness. There is a black bruise on my leg which I shall feel for many a day to come. And when I loose them from the chains, the blue cow that Mary brought up by hand like a child, spoilt and petted, goes to horn me, and only Morgan going at her with a pitch-fork saves me from a hole in the thigh.

Gabriel was used to say kind words drive a cow beside her senses: they must always be used to hard ways and the whip. Every evening he is in the Lower Pastures, training his dog for the trials. Save only my father, he is the best shepherd known to me in England or Wales. His ways are quicker, but as yet he lacks the patience my father keeps only for his sheep. When Ben has finished work, Gabriel comes over to me. He shows me a red mark under his ear like a sore place, and tells me how he come by it. Last night the rain come through the roof on to his bed, so that he woke to find himself wet and shivering; he got up to dry himself in front of the embers in the kitchen, and while he was at it he fell asleep on the settle. Early, before it was light, he woke again with a weight on his shoulders and breast: it was Gwen's sandy tomcat curled up by his head, licking the skin over the great vein in his neck so that he might suck the blood. He was almost through when Gabriel thrust him off.

It seems it is never wise to sleep with a cat in the room, for their natures are as savage and bloodthirsty as any tiger's.

I take Jenny and Georgie down to the sheep-wash to bathe. For a time they are very good, till Georgie slips out through the hurdles, chasing a fish, and finds the river too strong for his little legs; it catches him up before he can grasp the hurdles, turns him round and round, and away he goes, kicking and rolling over among the rocks, sometimes on his face and sometimes on his back till the current carries him screaming and half-drowned into Llyn-tro, where the water turns on itself like a wheel and is very deep. Before I have the wits to do anything Charlie runs past me like a flash; he jumps into the pool without a stop, boots and all, and drags Georgie to the side by his hair: I give him my hand, and in a minute they are up the bank and out of the quiet black water, that has such an evil look, even by day, that the folk hereabouts shun it, for all the fine fish in it, save Gabriel, who has no fear of spirits, and swims like the salmon-trout he catches there.

For my part, I cannot see deep water, running or still, without a shiver, like some harm will come to me from it, and the sight and sound of a waterfall is full of terror. Now I cannot forget that if Charlie had not saved Georgie, I would never have done it.

His teeth are clicking with fear and cold. We wrap him in the children's clothes and my apron.

"Come back to the farm with me, Charlie," I say, "the mistress shall know what you have done."

Charlie shakes his head.

"No, I am affeared."

"Affeared? Have you been up to something? She'll forgive you. She'll want to thank you, Charlie."

But nothing will move Charlie, and we have to leave him, streaming with water, on the river bank.

Back at the house Mary and I put Georgie to bed in blankets and hot bricks to his feet.

"What!" cries Mary when I tell her, "Charlie pulled him out? Oh, Ann, I have sent the boy off home not a minute before and told him never to set his foot on my doorstep again, because not half an hour ago I told him to throw the stale buttermilk into the pigs' trough, and he went and poured away all this morning's milk, though I *said* the red crock, and the milk was in a yellow one. Dear, dear, and now he has been in the river after our Georgie! There's something in having an English boy about the place, even if he is thick-headed. A Welshman never would have gone in the river after the child."

"You mistake the Welsh, that's plain," I say; "they are a brave foolhardy lot, too apt at running into danger for no purpose at all. I have been told that father's master, Evan ap Evans, went into the river when it was in flood after a sheep, and this river here is but a runlet to ours at its lowest."

"A sheep, yes. A sheep's worth money. Mark my words, he would never have gone in after a little boy."

I laugh out loud: Mary looks at me sharply and smiles.

"But there, opinions differ," she says, "and lately I have been seeing your mother's blood in you, Ann —all that is good in it. Put on your bonnet, there's a good soul, and go down to Charlie's: tell him I am more than thankful to him, poor boy, and, from this day on, it is little scolding he will get at Twelve Poplars. Bring him back with you, for if he's a fool he's a brave one."

Charlie is sitting in his mother's doorway dressed in his Sunday clothes and eating his dinner with brown paper pinned over him to keep off the gravy. When I tell him Mary's words, he gets up with a smile, puts the bowl on the table, kisses the cat, and makes ready to follow me, brown paper and all.

Something possesses Gwen Powys to ask Mary and me to take supper at Tan y Bryn, and so that we may have a laugh together afterwards we say we will go. When we get there, we find she has a party of Welsh friends there, and at supper theirs is the tongue spoken. Mary looks quite pleasant, though at heart she is like Gabriel in thinking it strange that the folk here should prefer their own tongue to English, but Gabriel sits at the bottom of the table glowering on the company.

Gwen has put out her blackberry wine; it sets the men to singing reckless words from "Men of Harlech", despite his mutters and angry looks.

One of them jumps up from his place shouting:

"I drink to Wales!"

Gabriel roars:

"And I to England!" and stands facing the other across the table. Megan and Margiad clap their hands; Mary looks serious.

"There'll be trouble in a minute, the men are hot as coals," she whispers.

Gwen purses up her lips.

"I give the Border," she says, very quiet.

We all drink it down, and for once Mary and I have to forgo our laugh.

Gabriel hears me singing in the fields.

"Why do you sing in Welsh?"

"It is sweet for singing."

"What was that sad song?"

"An old one I heard a man sing months ago."

"It was your father's master sang it?"

"Yes, at a May dance."

"Do you love that Welshman?"

"No."

"When I hear you speak of him I tremble with rage."

"You have no need," I says; "one day your temper will work you harm."

"Do you love me?"

"*No.*" I answer him from my heart.

He draws in his breath and leaves my side.

Gabriel has taken up with Margiad: three times they walk slowly up and down beneath the poplars.

For years she has hated me for his sake.

Pentredwr is full of shepherds and their masters come for the trials to-morrow: there are English and South Welsh besides those from hereabouts, and some, they say, come all the way from Cumberland.

Two cows calved this week, so I take twelve pounds of butter to Mrs. Williams at the Goat. In the yard there are traps and carts of all sorts and colours; among them I see one high yellow two-wheeled cart with a liver-chestnut mare between the shafts that I have reason to know, and the lettering is plain, even from the other side of the road:

Evan Evans,
Cotterill's Farm, Salus.

My father comes down the street with the master's dog, Twm, at his heels. He takes hold of the mare's bridle and leads her off to the stables without seeing me watching him from the window.

The master has come to the trials!

Gabriel waylays me in the market-place.

"Did you mean what you said the other night in the meadows?"

I pull my arm from him, for I will not bear with his rough ways.

"Yes, I did. With all my soul."

"You will not have me for your sweetheart?"

"I have done with sweethearts."

He keeps pace with me, ranting and storming under his breath, till on a sudden he falls silent; across the street Evan ap Evans is walking slowly up and down, and Gabriel's eyes follow him.

The trials are held on the lower slopes of the mountains beyond Pentredwr; Mary and I go over in the afternoon, when the novices are out of the way.

It is days that Gabriel has not been near me. He is stood over among the shepherds, with Ben on a chain, the only English sheepdog there, and I think to myself that he will not be able to pick me out of the crowd; but I am mistaken: he turns his head, fastening his eyes on my face with all his black rage behind the look.

"Do you see who is there, Ann?" Mary says, taking hold of my arm between her finger and thumb. She points to my father, stood a little away from the others with Twm; beside him is the master, poking his head forward as he talks. He waves his stick and my father spits.

"Well, he is a hard unnatural man serving a ruffianly master," whispers Mary. "Just look at the pair of them quarrelling and disputing over there in the sight of all the world. They might settle their differences before they come among decent quiet folk."

By the looks of it they are still at odds when the trials begin, but when the first dog is off up the field the master folds his arms and watches as though his life hangs on it.

The sheep are loosed three at a time from the higher meadow: there are two of them and a this year's lamb as wild as they can find them. The dogs must bring them down towards the shepherd who stands by the judges' box, through a gap in the hedge into the meadow, where all the world is stood blaming and praising the man for his handling of the dog.

There are four trials before the penning, which is the hardest to do: the sheep are driven between two hurdles, turned and driven back through two more, turned again through a gate from left to right, and once more through another gate from right to left. The shepherd may not move a pace until his dog has been through all four, but both must do the penning, and it's strange to see that more often than not it is the shepherd that is at fault. Only seven minutes are given at Pentredwr for all the work, beginning to end.

There are half a dozen turns before the Caernarvonshire bitch that has been first in the trials all over

Wales. Some of them work well, but none under time, while she has them penned with half a minute to spare. She works without a fault; once the sheep break, but she turns them before much harm is done, and I can see Gabriel never takes his eyes off her.

"He'll find that hard to beat!" cries Mary. "More's the pity. My word, I would like to see an Englishman win—so be that it isn't John Goodman, with all respect to his daughter."

"But the master's Welsh," I says, "and the dog is his."

When it comes to Gabriel, there is a hush in the crowd, for folk are beginning to know him, and Ben works faster than I have ever seen him. In four minutes they are up with the pen, though the sheep are wild and like to break with the rushing; Gabriel comes down with a run, and we think it is all over when the lamb breaks. Ben is off up the field like a flash, he turns it before it gets to the boundary, and the two of them come down full tilt to Gabriel, who turns the lamb in its rush straight into the pen with a wave of the crook.

Everybody bursts out cheering. Mary is smiling all over her face.

"Half a minute less than the bitch. There's a bit of work for you! Now we shall see what your father can do; his master looks black as the inside of a cow." Indeed, he does, and well he may.

"My father is not used to the ways of the mountain sheep; he is a proper English shepherd that takes his time and the master must be mad to give him leave to put Twm in for the trials."

"Things are the other way, I think," says Mary, staring at my father that walks slowly to his place, cleaning his nose.

It seems I am right, and my father shows no knowledge of these sheep; he lets Twm go too far on the first drive, and they rush over the boundary in a panic. The judge blows his whistle.

"Another trial!" shouts Evan ap Evans above the laughing. My father throws down his crook cursing, and the master shakes his fist at him. I see Gabriel grinning, and it makes me fairly angry.

"Another trial!" I bursts out without a second thought that I am a fool.

"Ann, I am ashamed of you!" cries Mary, taking hold of me by the arm.

"Another trial! Another trial!" the master yells, getting a sight of me.

"I'll be damned if I'll do it," my father shouts so that all the world can hear. And he walks off with Twm.

Gabriel wins the cup, and I wish him joy of it.

This evening I do the milking alone; the cowshed door stands open, and with my head in the cow's flank I can hear nothing but the milk spurting into the bucket. When I look up I nearly loose it in my surprise, for there is the master stood beside me, smiling down like he was used to over the garden wall in the spring.

"Good day, Ann Goodman. Did you laugh at me at the trials?" I say nothing.

"As high as ever!" he mutters. "Gabriel Ford will be in a glory now he has won the silver cup."

"Yes, indeed, I am glad he won it. What made you put Twm in the trials?"

"The devil take you!" shouts the master.

The cow flicks her tail across my face, stinging like a whip and drawing the tears to my eyes; the master holds it while I milk her dry; she does not like it and tries to kick.

"The milk will all be wasted; I wish you would go," I says, nearer to tears than I can understand.

"I have news for you from Olwen Davies."

I will not ask him his news, and he bends over me looking into my face.

"Come, Ann, look up. Give me a sight of you to take back to England with me. I am not speaking Welsh, though indeed it is on the end of my tongue, cariad" (love).

I look up.

"What is the news?"

"Olwen sends you her dear love, and for that matter there could be no better man to carry it than myself——"

The iron bar falls into the socket with a crash; the door is fast, and Gabriel is stood inside it.

He says nothing; nor does the master: like two bulls they come together and I cannot stay them. There is blood on their mouths and running down their chins; their breath comes panting, their eyes are red. Charlie bangs on the door, the cows fling themselves from side to side, pulling at their chains.

My knees grow weak at the sight. I am affeared of them as I have never been when they have turned on me.

"Stop, stop!" I cry, almost out of my senses. "Master—Gabriel, I cannot bear it!"

It is only a matter of moments; the master knocks Gabriel against the wall; he falls on his knees, then full length, and there is blood among his hair.

"Is he dead?"

"No, beaten. Cymru am byth!" (Wales for ever!) The master laughs.

"Then open the door and let in some air."

Charlie and the master carry him into the house; he has a great cut in the head, long, but not deep, and his face is swollen and black. As I follow them from the cowhouse I see the silver cup lying among the straw with a dent in its side: they have trodden on it and twisted the stem. Charlie rides into Pentredwr for a doctor, but long before he returns, saying he cannot find the house, Gabriel is sitting up on the settle with a piece of old pillowslip round his head.

Mary is looking to him; I let her, for I never want to speak to him or touch him again.

The master is holding his head under the pump in the yard; his lip is cut and one eye is quite shut. I bathe it, I wipe his face.

"Ann, how thou didst cry!" he whispers.

I brush the dust and straw from his coat, and bring him buttermilk to drink. The silver cup comes first to my hand from my pocket where I have kept it. At first I throw it down, then pick it up and fill it to the brim. The master takes it, and my hand.

"Cariad, have I won the cup after all?"

"Drink," I answer, "and never come here again. I wish one of us three were dead!"

Mary calls me down to see Gabriel.

"Will you come, Ann?"

"Yes, this time, but never again," I says, my mind fixed to end it.

He is waiting for me in the threshing-room, and his face is still a painful sight.

I go up to him.

"Say what you want to say, and be done with it, for this is the last time I'll hold talk with you, so be that I can help it."

"Are you going to marry me, Ann?" he asks, twisting the flail in his fingers like a snake.

"Never in the world, Gabriel!"

"Are you going to marry your father's master?"

"Who gave you leave to question me?" I bursts out in my rage and shame, "you who look no farther than the doorstep for a woman to take the place you swore was mine until we both should die!"

"There never was another woman in that place, and there never will be."

"Margiad?"

"Margiad means nought to me."

"More shame to you then that you took up with her; you and the master have made me look a fine fool before folk with your fighting and brawling. Between the two of you you make my life a misery, and then you talk of marriage! Leave me alone; I hate both of you!"

"So that you hate him I'll leave him content till you come round to my way of thinking."

"If you are an Englishman, Gabriel Ford, then from this day I'll count myself as Welsh. You are a jealous, unreasonable man, and I pity the woman your choice falls on!"

"You'll have need to."

"You look now ripe for murder. Go away and never trouble me again."

For a minute it seems that he will strike at me with the flail. Throwing it down, he swallows his rage and seizes my wrists so that I cannot pull them away; stooping, he kisses me, and loosing me, leaves me standing half choked with rage.

Mary comes in to me with a cup of tea.

311

"Here, drink this. My word, Ann, you are well rid of that devil! I could hear him bellowing right over in the dairy. In your place I should keep clear of Gabriel Ford."

The countryside is full of talk; it is well for me my mourning keeps me close at home.

The other day Gwen Powys comes over to ask me why Gabriel's silver cup that he won at the trials is dented; people say he and the master fought for it.

"There might be something in it—you never know. I wonder," she says while her sharp eye wanders round. We are vexed and not over polite.

A day or two after Mrs. Pritchard walks all the way from Glanrafon to ask if there is a charge against the master, and when she has drunk three cups of tea Mary sends her off none the wiser but for the recipe which she wanted as an excuse for her visit.

The minister cannot come himself among the church folk that he has said are going to hell; he asks Jenny questions which she is far too young to understand.

"Ask Cousin Ann," she says; but when he meets me he looks the other way.

One afternoon, when I am at the cemetery, Mr. Davies comes to see me. He has been first to Twelve Poplars, and Mary, busy with the baking, tells him where to find me.

He fetches water from the stream to fill the jars, then he puts the flowers in. He talks in a harsh way that used to put me in mind of a raven when I was a child, but his words are kind enough.

"For fifteen years you have been coming to my church and I remember well the summer you spent at Twelve Poplars long before you lived there. If you are troubled, Ann, and I can be of any help to you, come to me and think of me as your friend."

Mr. Davies is an old bachelor, and for all I think well of him, I cannot tell him my heart. I thank him for his kindness; he sighs, and on the way home talks of the coming harvest.

A sight that is strange in my eyes is the hay lying out black and rotten in the fields while the corn stands ripe and ready to the harvest. Scythes are coming off the walls, and men are waiting for the hiring.

I wake in the night to find a red light shining through my window on the foot of my bed, clear enough for me to see my clothes on the chair.

I get up, and outside the door Mary calls that a rick has fired at Tan y Bryn, and she has sent Morgan off to lend a hand.

We watch the fire from her bedroom till the dawn puts out the glow in the sky. Mr. Powys was always one to gather his hay too soon; this way he has lost it as surely as Mary, whose crop is lying out in the fields.

"Well," she says, putting on her clothes as sharp as if she had slept all night, "this will give Gwen something new to talk about!"

I see Margiad alone in Pentredwr, looking as miserable as a moulting hen.

To-day we bake bread pies and tarts that we may go a week without cooking.

Mary has hired five men for the harvesting; they will do the mowing and we shall do the binding ourselves, all because the weather looks too bad to put it off any longer. Mary goes to see Mrs. Williams at the Goat, whose son died last week of consumption, and I tidy up the kitchen after our cooking. With the day so warm and fine I let the fire out and boil up the big kettle for tea under the copper. After my wash I think there will be a tidy place for me to sit sewing, but when I come down I find ashes on the hearth, the flagstones black with soot, and the embers raked out of the grate all over the floor. What is worse, a draught from the window to the open door has blown ash-dust on everything.

I hear the pump going in the yard, and there I catch Jenny and Georgie, smeared like chimney-sweeps, pumping and pouring water over Charlie, that is blacker by far than either of them, and soaking wet into the bargain.

"What have you been doing now?" I cry. "It seems I cannot turn my back a minute!"

"Georgie says the swallows live up the chimney in the winter, and Charlie went to have a look at their nests," says Jenny, half laughing and half crying.

"Then Charlie can go straight in and sweep up the kitchen after he has cleaned himself."

"And what will happen to Georgie?"

"I shall tan him well with my shoe for talking nonsense."

"And what will you do to me?"

"Wash your face with soap and give you a clean pinafore."

They all burst into howls, and I am forced to give them bread and treacle before they will stop. Mary comes in while I am on my hands and knees scrubbing the floor.

"We shall have to keep Charlie, I suppose, but oh, I could wish it had been another body pulled Georgie out of the water!"

The harvest has begun.

From morning till evening we are hard at it in the wake of the mowers, gathering up the swathes, binding them, and making them into sheaves because we are pressed for time. There is no sun to scorch our necks, but our backs ache enough to kill us with the stooping.

My place is behind Twm Williams; he never seems to tire, though he mows the widest swathe of all.

Towards sundown we cannot hold ourselves up for very weariness.

"Enough; if it must spoil, it must," says Mary.

We go in to supper: she is half asleep and I can hardly drag my feet. Even in bed our bones ache, and in the night we hear rain falling.

The barley is stood near a fortnight in the field with not a chance of drying. After a fine day comes a wet one; twice there are heavy showers in the night. Thank heaven we have no oats!

Gwen Powys comes over to talk a bit, bringing some stockings to knit. She uses such hard coarse wool that we are all very sorry for her poor brother, it must be like walking in canvas.

"I buy my wool for wear and not for show. Who sees Trefor's feet? And I knit very tight to make the wool go a long way."

One day she will take to knitting his stockings out of binding twine, for I see her looking very hard at a ball of it on the table.

She cannot hold her news for long.

"Did you know that Gabriel is leaving us at Christmas?" she bursts out.

"Is that so—after so many years?"

"Yes, Mrs. Maddocks, indeed; I could hardly believe my ears when he tell me. Ann bach, we shall look in the cups to see what will come for you."

"Look in the teacups to see what will come to the harvest," says Mary.

"Caton pawb! (Good gracious!) I know without the looking. First you will lose your barley, and

316

afterwards Trefor will lose his oats. That's how it is, you see."

When she had finished her tea Gwen swills her cup round three times and turns it upside-down in the saucer.

"To let the tears run down," she says.

Mary is rather particular in her ways; she looks sideways at this. Gwen foretells a present and a gentleman visitor for herself.

"Now we'll try Ann's cup. Ah, she does not know how to shake up a good fortune in the tealeaves!"

"It must be all nonsense if I make the fortune, good or bad, by shaking the cup."

"Indeed," says Gwen, looking very old-fashioned, "and don't we all make our own fortunes? In your cup there are tears, tears, tears, and a land journey with a great surprise to you. Beware of danger by night; you are standing near a great misfortune, and soon you shall hear of a death."

As she puts my cup down with a very solemn glance at me that makes us want to laugh, one of the hens outside gives a little crow like a young cockerel at dawn: Gwen begins to shake, and even Mary is a little pale.

"It is the truth that I have told you! Hark to the little bird, she knows best. When a hen crows in the yard, the time has come for one of the household to go through the dark."

Mary laughs out loud.

"It is only an old saying, Miss Powys."

"There is nothing so true as sayings, I tell you," says Gwen, who is very fanciful, like most of the Welsh folk.

"You are full of ideas," I tells her.

"Yes, ideas. Listen, and I will tell you about the idea I saw in our yard last week. I was shutting up the hens; Trefor, he is in bed, Gabriel on the mountain with the sheep, and the girls, they are sleeping away. It was a very dark night, I was alone, and what did I see but a great dog glaring at me between me and the kitchen door! Ah, indeed, Mrs. Maddocks, my hair got up with fear, for it was bigger than any dog that walks the world we live in.

" 'O Lord, save me from the devil,' I cried, and on the sound of my voice the creature goes from my sight. I went in and shut all the doors and windows until the light of dawn. All night I did not close my eyes. Ah! indeed."

"Perhaps it was a real dog," says Mary, who is having hard work not to laugh.

"No, no, it was the devil," answers Gwen.

"Well that may be, though myself I think the devil is too busy to have the doing of half that is laid to him. Folk speak badly of Llyn-tro; I have been there at night many a time and seen nothing."

"Not for much would I go, even in full daylight. There my old father saw the spirit of the pool, and there the white otter swims."

318

"And there my Georgie was nearly drowned."

"And there are the biggest fish hereabouts," I says.

And I thinks of the many times Gabriel and I have fished there together in the evenings when he was a boy just come to Tan y Bryn, and Wales was new to me.

I think the Welsh are fanciful folk that frighten none but themselves by their tales, and though most of them are brave as lions, there are some, like Morgan, who will not stir a step after dark without company so be he can help it. One night I meet him coming home from Pentredwr when there is no moon: from the noise a person would think that three men are out walking, but there is only himself talking questions and answers very loud in three voices. He tells me three men pass safely where harm would fall to one. I ask him what harm would come to anybody in these quiet parts. He answers that if he knew he would not be affeared.

We have long seen the bread goes very fast from the larder. Such plain fare will not tempt Georgie and Jenny, and Charlie, with all his faults, is no thief of means or money; but Mary catches Morgan leaving the larder with something under his smock besides his dinner. She calls him back.

"What have you hidden away there?"

"Nought."

"Let me see."

It is half a loaf. She is vexed to find him stealing.

"I did not think it of you."

Morgan mutters to himself, and at last he tells her that he is very affeared of dogs.

"They know when a man is like that," he says in English, that he learned years gone by at service in Liverpool. "When a dog see me she bark, bark like she was hungry, and would take a bite out of me. So every dog I meet her, I throw down a piece of bread."

Mary is content to hear him speak her tongue, which he will not often do, because, he says, it makes his blood rise to blow through his teeth in talking like we do. She cannot keep from laughing that a grown man who will tackle a bull with nought but a whip should go in fear of dogs. All she says is:

"Carry a stick, and don't you go stuffing all the hounds of the countryside with our baking."

She keeps a good heart, but this is a sad harvest with the barley sprouting in the fields.

We go down to open the sheaves and spread them about in the air.

Gabriel and I pass in the market without a word or a sign.

We begin to load the barley.

The barn doors are opened wide only at harvest time, now they are propped with great stones that the carts may go in and out, and the barn seems very large inside without the half being full of hay. I work with Mary and Williams on the stack while Morgan,

Charlie, and Lewis are loading in the fields. We have to keep Morgan and Lewis from each other, for whenever they get together they split words like two children. At night when we are at supper, we hear them at it hammer and tongs in the kitchen:

"What hast thou done to-day?" shouts one.

"Six times as much as thou!" answers the other, and the two of them would idle away the whole day without someone to eye them.

Charlie gives us all the fright of our lives: he is riding on the load when the wagon goes over a stone in the yard and with a yell he falls headfirst to the ground.

For a moment he does not move; we all rush to him, thinking to find him dead or dying, but his eyes are open and he smiles up at us. In a little while he gets upon his legs to go on with his work none the worse, as though his head were made of wood.

In the evening Mary has bread and cheese and beer laid out in the kitchen for the men—none eats so heartily as Charlie, and none looks so bright and humorous.

I have been to put my mother's grave straight after the high wind, and I walk back through the fields by moonlight. The wailing of the bull at Glanrafon comes to my ears while I am yet a field away; he smells a human being, though he is tied up in his pen, for the Pritchards are bound to be careful with a right-of-way running through their yard. When I

come to the gate I open it and go in, not at all affeared,
but I have hardly taken half a dozen steps when I see
something like a great black shadow coming slowly
to me. It is the bull, with his unfastened chain dragging on his neck, turning his head from side to side
and moaning as he walks. They are at the worst this
time of the year and with this in mind I lose no time
in getting to the other side of the gate. He seems
very quiet stood there, switching his tail, and staring
at me through the bars with his eyes glinting in the
moonlight, but I dare not pass through, for only last
week Mr. Pritchard tells me he is very savage. I run
round the front. There is a light upstairs and the
Pritchards are going to bed. I fling a handful of dirt
at the window, and Mrs. Pritchard puts her head out.

"Brenin Mawr! Is that Ann Goodman?"

"Yes, the bull is loose."

She calls her husband and he comes down with a
candle in his hand.

Not half an hour since, he says, the bull was safe
in the pen, chained and made fast by himself.

"To be sure I had a peep at him. Ah, he is wicked!
He looked at me. He never sleeps."

He takes a pitchfork—I hear him chasing the bull
into the pen, and the rattle of the chain.

When he comes back to me he is holding something in his hand: it is a shepherd's crook, and at
Glanrafon there are no sheep.

I go home by the longer way—affeared.

Mary goes to her brother's for two days, taking the children with her.

I slide the bolts very early, going to bed with a stocking to knit for company. After the candle is out I hear a cart come into the yard, and there is a loud knocking on the kitchen door. I put on my shawl and call from the window to know who is there.

"Willy Preece from Cotterill's. Shall I put the horse up and come in? The rain is teeming down."

I have time to dress and make up the fire, and wonder to myself what can have brought Willy over here, before he comes in, wet to the bone.

"I have a letter for you from the mistress."

Gwladys Evans has written to ask me if I will go home at once to help my father, as there is scab in the sheep, and he cannot manage for himself.

Scab in my father's sheep!

Willy eats the bacon I give him and warms himself at the fire, filling the place with steam.

"What makes you so late?"

"I would have been here by midday, but beyond Trelech the horse shied and put me in the ditch; we broke an axle. But what time will you be ready in the morning?" he asks, as though there is nothing for me to do but to leave Twelve Poplars at a word from Gwladys Evans.

"I am not free to leave to-morrow. My father must wait until the next day."

"Shepherd Goodman would wait till Domesday, but the mistress said to hurry."

"No help for that—Mrs. Maddocks is from home, and you must stay here over to-morrow."

Willy would argue, but I leave him a candle and go to bed. When Mary comes home, she is very angry, and the children cry.

"Why should you be for ever shifting yourself from pillar to post for the sake of a selfish old man that has no feeling for you at all? Stay here, Ann, and let his sheep go rotten with scab—his precious master can get help elsewhere."

"I have thought there's something more behind Miss Evans's letter. How should my father's sheep come to have the scab?"

"That's true. Have you asked Willy Preece?"

"He will tell me nothing beyond what's in the letter."

Mary makes a face.

"Well, Ann, if you feel you must go, you know you can come back when the wish takes you, and don't let yourself be put upon by John Goodman, father or no father. Not that you will, for you have his own temper hidden away. Maybe, too, it is better you should get away for a bit; there are some queer tales going about."

Willy Preece is ready before it is properly light, though he takes so long over his breakfast that I might have had another half-hour in bed. But once we are on the road we hurry. At Trelech we change the horse for the master's mare, that trots faster between the shafts than any animal I know. We are half-way home before I ask Willy if the scab has spread badly.

"Three hundred odd," he says, flicking the mare.

Three hundred! My breath is fairly taken away.

"How does it come to be so bad?" I ask, amazed. "Three hundred means that it has spread for weeks without checking."

Willy stares away over the mare's ears and says nothing, so that I could almost pinch him with vexation.

"Come, let me know what has happened. My father can tell the scab at a look; he would keep scabby sheep out of the flock."

"Ay, he could tell right enough if he could see."

"Willy Preece, do you mean my father is *blind*?"

"Often. Ann, Shepherd's taken to the bottle since your mother died."

After a while he goes on:

"Scudamore had scabby sheep, and he was never over-careful. They strayed over into the master's meadows through a gap where there should have been a hurdle."

"Is the master very vexed?"

"Ay, fair furious," says Willy, "but he hasn't said a word to Shepherd about going as far as I can make out."

MARGIAD EVANS

At Salus we stop to buy gunpowder for ointment.
Willy has pressed the mare on the last few miles, so
that she is black with sweat, and when I get home it
is still light enough for me to see my garden overgrown with weeds. Our kitchen is like a pigsty.

My father is out with the sheep; after I have had
something to eat I set to work to wash the pile of
dirty dishes on the table. He comes in with a lantern
about eleven.

"So you are back, after two days on the road. What
were you doing at night?" he says.

"Oh! be silent," I answer sharply, so vexed and
tired that I hardly know where to turn.

My father mutters to himself:

"Here, take this lard and help me to make the
ointment for the morning. Did you bring the pow-
der?"

"Yes. Shall I use the lot?"

"Ay, there are two hundred sheep that need it."

Willy made it out worse by a hundred, but this is
bad enough.

I set the place to rights.

My father is trying tobacco water on the sheep:
all day long there is a great cauldron over the fire,
and our kitchen reeks of lard ointment and carbolic.

The scabby sheep are in Kirkham and Katy Hop-
kins, away from the whole; it is a sad thing to see
them rubbing and picking at their wool with their
necks and shoulders raw and red from the sores.

326

Every day they are dressed by my father with Willy Preece and two young boys.

"Shall I come down to give you a hand?" I asks.

"Stay where you are," my father answers angrily, "and don't take so much on yourself."

I do not go out much, but Mrs. Hill comes up to see me when she hears I am home. She is all in black that is not widow's mourning, and she seems pleased to take a cup of tea. We go in and sit by the fire.

"This is the first time I have been near the place since Myfanwy died."

"A good thing, since my father kept it so dirty."

"Is that so? And you was used to have it spotless."

"There was enough cleaning out to do when I came back, and you must have seen the garden."

"Yes," says Mrs. Hill sadly, "in the spring it was a picture."

She looks down at her dress.

"Do you remember the May Dance, Ann? And now here we are sitting in black, the two of us. Have you heard about my poor little baby?"

"It is for her—the black?"

"Yes," she says, beginning to cry, "did no one tell you? And I thought my sorrow filled the world! She was taken poorly once or twice after you left home, and I see there was something wrong with her, for she was nothing more than a little bag of bones. Tom says, 'Oh, it is nought but the rain, the sun, the heat, the cold; don't think so much about the child.' He would not hear of the doctor. Ann, one night—the fifteenth of July it was—she had an awful fit and died before we could get a soul in to help. I put her in a warm bath and slapped her little hands and feet; it was no use, there was no life in her when Olwen brought the doctor."

Mrs. Hill wrings her hands together till the knuckles show white as bone.

"There was an inquest after, and some very hard words were spoken. Tom has been a different man ever since. Sometimes, though we have been married but three years and I pity him with all my heart, it is all I can do to keep from hating him. Poor Tom! He meant no harm. Oh, it is a sad world, Ann!"

After a time I ask for news of Olwen.

"She left us; there was nothing for her to do. She went to Cotterill's to work for Miss Evans that always had a fancy for her. It is a good place, for she is a kind woman; Olwen always looks very content when she comes over to see us."

So this was the master's news of Olwen!

Mrs. Hill will not stay long. She hurries off with her black frock fluttering round her, as thin as if she had half a mind to follow the baby.

All day long I am boiling, pounding, and mixing: my father uses gunpowder and lard for an ointment, tobacco water for a wash, and carbolic to stop the scab spreading. Every time he goes to Salus he brings more.

I help him to carry the bowls and buckets down to the pens; the men are waiting for us near the gates, and while they begin I go back again for the rest of the dressing. When I come back I start to work with them. One of them calls out to me:

"Don't you touch them, 'tisn't work for a woman —you might catch it yourself."

"No more than us. Get on with what you are doing and leave the girl to work if she pleases," says my father, without looking up.

We are at it until sundown, when we wash our hands and arms and go home. After supper there is more tobacco water to boil and more ointment to mix, and in my dreams I see a flock of scabby sheep driven into Llyn-tro by my father, who is waving a bottle.

Parson comes up in the rain with his umbrella, and his spaniel to keep him company. The wind is too strong for the umbrella; at the top of the hill, a step outside our gate, it is blown inside out. While he is pulling it right way about with one hand, and holding his hat on with the other, I bolt the door very quietly and hide at the back of the settle. After banging on the door three times loud enough to wake the dead, and peeping through every window, he goes away, leaving me in peace.

This afternoon it clears up a bit; Mrs. Somers, and I go blackberrying together. She gives me news of her family. "Owen is doing well in Monmouth, but

Tom is a flighty boy; I always tell his father we shall come to see him deported. As for Chrissie, young as she is, she is a real bad girl!"

"She is very pretty and seems handy."

"If she is pretty, what of that? So much the worse. It will be her undoing, I know, and as for handy, she is that; she has the makings of a thief."

Mrs. Somers picks blackberries very quick and eats most of them. When I find a good patch she leaves her own to strip mine bare. As fast as I move on she follows, talking all the time.

"What a deal of dying there has been this year! First Sexton drowned in the river back in the winter, then your mother goes off in June, though I am sure you would have hindered her if you could, and then little Elsie Hill, soon after. I should not wonder if Mrs. Hill herself went the next; she seems poorly. Half the parish looks ready for the grave with all the rain we've had."

"It might be our turn next," I says; Mrs. Somers goes on as if she has not heard me.

"And the different deaths people make! All my family go off very quiet, and I often wonder if I shall do the same. My father was a lovely man that died beautifully while carrying hay. He just dropped the fork and died. We were shorthanded that year too, and the morning before the funeral my sister and I were out in the meadow, doing his work."

I go to another bush; Mrs. Somers follows.

"My sister died at forty-five. She was singing like an angel when she went, without any pain or struggle. Very quiet."

And wherever I move she comes after me, telling me of the deaths in her family, till I know as much about them as if I had sat by all their bedsides and been to all their funerals. When it is time to go home she is surprised to find my basket quite full and her own more than half empty.

Olwen comes hurrying up the hill all out of breath, straight through the open door with her apron flying. She throws her arms round my neck tight enough to throttle me.

"Oh, Ann, my dear, I see Shepherd in the yard talking to the master, and I had the kitchen straight, so I ran up to you for a moment. I was affeared to come before lest he should be here," she pants out.

Her hair, that she was used to keep in plaits down her back when I left Cotterill's, is twisted round her head and she wears a cap.

"Miss Evans makes me look like a grandmother!"

"No, Olwen, you look well and content."

She is more lovely than anything that I have ever set my eyes on, but there is time enough for her to find that out.

"But, dear Ann, how sad you are!"

"It is nought but my mourning. Are you as happy as you were with Mrs. Hill?"

"Yes, indeed. The mistress is always kind; she never scolds but she is half laughing herself, though sometimes she talks until my head spins."

"And the master?"

"I keep clear of him for fear of his terrible temper."

"Is he unkind to you?"

She shakes her head.

"No, never, but he talks rough and looks miserable. He swears away to himself in Welsh all day long."

"Maybe he isn't swearing if you cannot understand his tongue."

"Oh yes, he is, between his teeth," says Olwen laughing, "and Miss Evans says, 'Dal dy dafod' (hold your tongue)."

Willy Preece told me the meaning of that. I cannot help but smile.

"Then you don't like the master?"

"No, he is too rough. Nobody likes him in these parts."

"It does seem nobody has a good word for him."

"He is terrible hard on his men, Ann, and on his animals too, if it suits him. Last week he flogged one of the horses up the hill with a load of roots that Willy said was more than enough for two. The mistress put her fist through the wire net over the larder window, she was that upset. 'For shame, brother!' she screamed out in English so that all the world could hear."

"What did he say?"

"He shouted something and threw the whip into the pigsties. I couldn't understand because they always speak Welsh to each other.

"Oh, Ann, the mistress is a good woman; she sings hymns beautiful and plays the harmonium in the parlour on Sunday afternoons."

"And does the master sing hymns too?"

Olwen laughs out loud.

"No, he goes to sleep! Ann, they say Welsh folk are near, yet your mother was Welsh and she was kind to me, while Shepherd will never give me a word. Miss Evans is good to everybody, even tramps and beggars. Many of that sort come round for meals regular as washing days: they are given everything we have ourselves; they sit on the cobbles outside the back door, and when they have finished they hand me the dish and go off without a word."

"And what does the master say to that?"

"The mistress always tells me to look out for him; if I see him coming they make off to hide, for he makes trouble when he catches them. He come in sudden through the dairy door once when there was a tramp that Miss Evans was giving bread and butter; we pushed the tramp into the larder while the master passed, and when we went to let him out we found he had gone with sausages and two pounds of butter that was put by for young Mrs. Williams because her husband had been poorly."

"I should think Miss Evans gave over a bit after that."

"No, she said there are good and bad tramps, same as other folk."

She gets up to go, but I catch at her.

"Wait, Olwen—tell me, you must have heard—is it true that my father drinks overmuch these days?"

"Folk say he does."

"Can't you tell me any more than that?"

"Yes, only don't look at me so sharp, dear Ann, and I'll tell you all I know. The day after Shepherd found scab in the sheep I was washing potatoes in the brook, and I heard Mrs. Hill talking to the mistress.

" 'Why doesn't your brother get rid of him?' she asks. 'He was never an overpatient master, by all accounts. Only last week Tom found Shepherd in the hedge, sleeping it off.' "

"Go on, Olwen bach, what more?"

"I splashed my hands in the water so they should know someone was there, but they went on talking. The mistress answered:

" 'My brother wouldn't hear of it, no more would I. The man was here for years before us.'

" 'Yes,' says Mrs. Hill, in a kinder voice, 'he has passed most of his life in that cottage, and he was born in the workhouse at Salus.'

"I could not help but hear, Ann!"

"What of that?" I says.

Olwen puts her hand on mine.

"Miss Evans goes on: 'He brought his wife there, out of Wales. Oh, we Welsh aren't as black as you paint us, Mrs. Hill. My brother is a hard man in many ways, but he would never get rid of John Goodman.' "

I do not know what comes over me that I cry out:

"Ni fedrwch gael ei debyg yn Lloegr!" (In England you will not find the like.)

Olwen stares at me.

"Why, what does that mean?"

"I hardly know myself."

At dusk I pass the master in the fields.

"Nos da, Ann Goodman."

"Nos da, Evan ap Evans."

I sit waiting for my father to come in until midnight, then I take the lantern and go to look for him. There is no moon. Beyond my lantern-light it is pitch-dark, and as I reach the bottom it begins to rain. My father is lying on the far side of the stream as still as if he were dead; neither shakes nor shouts rouse him up. I leave him, and run back to Cotterill's for Willy Preece. He is coming down the granary steps very softly, with his fishing rod in his hand, and he calls out my name, affeared at seeing me out at this hour when only poachers are abroad.

"Hush!" I whispers, with my eyes on a lighted

window. "Come and help me to carry my father up the hill."

As we creep out of the yard the master's dog gives a yowl that brings him to the window, candle in hand.

"Who's there?" he calls.

"Run! He'll be down in another minute!" says Willy.

My father has not moved; together we get him home, though the hill has never seemed so long. We look down on him, full length on the settle, and Willy tells me he will never be fit for work in the morning.

"I'll be there to do his share."

"But, Ann, it's not a woman's work."

"I have done it before now."

Willy says no more, he has other things afoot. He goes away quietly, but not to his bed.

In the morning my father is still sleeping as I go out, turning the key on him. All the men stare when they see me coming with the buckets and no shepherd. They ask where he is.

"At home, as you know very well. There's not an hour's work in him, so I'll do it for him. Now let us settle to."

None gainsays me.

Ill-luck will have it that the master comes to look at the sheep.

"No shepherd this morning, Preece?" he asks,

lifting his brows. Then he catches sight of me, and coming over stands before me.

"Ann!"

"Good day, Master."

"Give over this minute."

"That I will not."

"Thou must," says he, "I'm going to do the work myself. But thou shalt hand me the stuff."

"Master, let me do it. It is my father's work, and he is asleep in the kitchen at home. Let me."

"What is that to me?" he cries. "Stand out of the way, Ann bach, and thou shalt see what a fine shepherd was lost to make an ordinary farmer."

He strips off his coat and rolls up his sleeves: to see him set about it I remember my mother was used to say that as a young boy he was a shepherd on the mountains.

"Art happy to be home?" he asks.

"Yes."

"Wert content to see me this morning?"

"I never was more vexed," I says, half laughing.

"From my heart I thank thee," he says under his breath.

When I get home I find my father mixing ointment. "You can be useful, it seems," he grunts. "You had best come down with me every day. If they do well, they will be over it in a fortnight."

"One thing, I know, they will never do well without a shepherd. The way those boys handle them is pitiful to see."

"What! After all I have taught them! I'll show them round," my father cries angrily.

To-day I let my father know I am not going back to Twelve Poplars before the spring.

"Do as you please," he answers.

It is hard that whatever I do should be of so little account.

The master is ploughing. The crows follow the furrow, flying round him, and settling on the red earth where he has passed.

His eyes are on his work; only at the turn he sees me stood watching him in the shadow of the hedge, and as he moves down the field his words come back to me, though they are softly spoken in the tongue he was born to:

"What art thou doing there all alone?"

It is the truth that I answer:

"Waiting for thee."

It is dark when he leaves the plough and, coming to me, looks down in my face:

"Fy nghariad, the waiting is over," he says, and with his two hands draws me to him.

We shall be married before the trees are bare, for there is no need of waiting.

338

In a letter Mary tells me Gabriel left Tan y Bryn last week without warning.

Autumn has come: her sheep are from the mountains, and Morgan is threshing the barley in the long dark evenings.

It seems like some peace at last!

(END OF ANN'S BOOK)

Evan ap Evans was never married to his shepherd's daughter; before the trees were bare, she was lying in Salus churchyard, and his name and Gabriel Ford's were on the lips of all the countryside.

There is a stone on the river bank with a rail around it to keep off the cattle. It was placed there by the master opposite the deep pool where Ann was found, her body wrapped in water weeds, her head no more than an inch or two from the surface.

On her temple was a great wound that cried aloud for justice. The cry was taken up all along the Border, and rang in the ears of Evan ap Evans, who loved her, as he avowed, above all things on earth.

Suspicion was divided between him and Gabriel Ford, but while the Welshman was at hand to bear the load of it with all eyes fixed upon the hideous burden, the Englishman, from the time he left Tan y Bryn, was never again seen by the living. None knew of his goings and comings, and only the testimony of Mary Maddocks saved Evan ap Evans from

339

arrest. But while he was not held guilty in the eyes of the law, neither lack of evidence nor lack of motive could shield him from the rage of the country-folk; his violence and the distrust which his ways had fostered, gave rise to wild brutal rumours which even to-day are looked upon as truth.

Though Gabriel was undoubtedly the murderer and Evan ap Evans the lover, his unpopularity reached a climax which, together with a grief so sharp that he could no longer endure the neighbourhood, caused him to part with Cotterill's.

He died, it is said, in Canada.

These are the facts which can be gathered from the tangle of traditions and tales in a district where suspicions are truths and rumours evidence, facts which are borne out in the little ruled book where Gabriel is branded and where a darker pen runs beside Ann's quill, tracing a noose which, had it lain to hand, would have hanged him as surely as he deserved such a death, and which is like a long-hidden key to a door that has rotted away.

In this book some may see only the evidence of a guilt which never came to light until its power was as dead as the hand that wrote it, or at the most, the insignificant prelude to a commonplace disaster. Also there may be those who will discern the subtler underlying narrative that bound the days together, the record of a mind rather than of actions, a mind which though clear in itself was never conscious of the two nations at war within it. Here is represented the entire history of the Border, just as the living Ann must have represented it herself—that history which belongs to all border lands and tells of incessant warfare.

Wales against England—and the victory goes to Wales; like Evan ap Evans, the awakened Celt cries: "Cymru am byth!" with every word she writes.

Those that can follow this will see that the story begins and ends with the book; for them there will be no need to follow the bodily fate of the men and women who people it. Complete and triumphant, it stands untouched by word of mouth fed from the rusty memories of folk long since dead who would have decked it out according to their own opinions and allotted tails and haloes as their lively fancy pleased.

All old stories, even the authenticated, even the best remembered, are painted in greys and lavenders —dim, faint hues of the past which do no more than whisper of the glory of colour they once possessed. Yet live awhile in these remote places where these pale pictures were painted, and something of their first freshness will return to them, if only in the passing of a homestead or the mowing of a field. You will come to know how the dead may hold tenure of lands that were once theirs, and how echoes of their lives that are lost at a distance linger about their door-ways. Here among the hills and valleys, the tall trees and swift rivers, the bland pastures and sullen woods, lie long shadows of things that have been.

But new furrows are ploughed in old fields, harvests are sown and gathered and names that sprang from the red earth itself have died away to a faint murmur which only native ears attuned may hear.

It is well that men's doings, like the leaves after their season, fall to the earth, and beneath the boughs crowded with fresh green growth, lie buried and forgotten.

by

JACK GRIFFITH

*

SOMETHING TO BE THANKFUL FOR

Two men came from the direction of the coal-face of the mine. Although the working day was but half through, they were dressed to go out. They were young, and hurried along, one behind the other, quickly and silently, their electric lamps hanging low. The second man had injured his left hand which he kept nursed between his half-buttoned waistcoat and his shirt.

They entered the empty "parting", a junction which widened out into two rail-tracks for the exchange of empty trams for full ones to be taken in a "journey" of a dozen or so back to the pit-shaft. Their lights attracted the attention of a man who sat in a frail structure, built around a small engine, and courteously called "engine-house". The man's name was Idris. He was the fireman, the official in charge of that district of the pit. Waiting until the two men came alongside, he stepped out, his lamp lifted so that the light fell upon their faces.

"Where you goin'?" he asked sharply.

343

"Out," was the reply of the man who led the way. His name was Twm.

"Who told you you could go out?"

"You did."

"Me?"

"Yes, you. Bloody 'ell, it was only ten bloody minutes ago that you tol' me to go out with Will 'ere, after 'e smashed 'is 'and."

The fireman remembered. His many duties and the eternal demand for a never ceasing supply of coal kept him in a state of constant worry. He had forgotten the damaged hand reported to him.

"Oh, yes, yes," he assented. "Take 'im out, Tommy bach, take 'im out. 'Ow is it now, Willy bach, 'ow is it now? 'Urtin' much?"

"Beginnin' to 'urt like 'ell," Will replied. "The feelin's comin' back now."

"Look after it, Willy bach," the fireman advised, trying to appear sympathetic. "Look after it. Twm will take you out."

The two men commenced to ascend the gradient connecting two level galleries broken from each other by a fault.

"Off 'is bloody onion," was Twm's comment when they got beyond hearing distance.

They reached the top of the rising ground and continued their way along the main heading. They kept their heads low for fear of striking them against the timber ranged frequently across the road at varying heights in support of the roof. Their heavy lamps were held without swinging, Twm shielding his from the eyes of the man behind. Although the steel haulage-rope was motionless and half-hidden in the grey-black dust of the floor, they sprang over it quickly each time a bend in the heading made it necessary to cross to the other side. When the journey would commence its way in, the resultant tightening of the rope might pull it up to the roof and down again, like the plucked string of a giant banjo. Of course, it might not, but if it did when they were in the act of crossing. . . .

At last the rope became taut and gave a low growl as it rubbed along the sleepers supporting the tram-rails. The men continued their way, for the pit was nearly a mile off and the journey had only just left it. Twm, however, swayed the beams of his lamp upward slightly in order to see on which side of the road the manholes lay. The law demanded that manholes should be placed at a distance of every ten yards or so, and be three feet in depth. Theoretically they should be like a row of sentry boxes dug into the earth, but actually they were often no more than frames of timber receiving the name of "man-hole" out of sheer courtesy. Often, despite the law, they stored a coil of wire-rope, a bag of cramps or a roadman's tools. Frequently they were knee-deep with fine, soft, powdery stone-dust which restrained men from entering because of a dislike for plunging

345

their feet into the dust and having it fill their boots.

After a while the rope ceased to move along the ground; it moved silently a few inches in the air. The journey was near. The hollow sound of empty trams, whose wheels bumped over the rail-ends, came to meet the two men.

"She's gettin' close," Twm said; "better get in this man'ole."

The one they entered was fairly big. Will, with his injured hand, got innermost; while Twm stood at the mouth, leaning against the post that supported the side of the aperture away from the pit.

The journey came by. A light on the first tram showed that the rider, the man who changed the ropes from one journey to another, was at the front instead of the back end. This was to avoid crawling through limited space and tearing clothes and fraying temper when the destination was reached.

"Hoi, Steve," Twm shouted as the light went past.

" 'Ow do, Tommy boy?" the rider replied, recognizing the voice. "Where goin'?"

"Takin' Will. . . ."

Twm suddenly stopped speaking as a post, loaded in one of the trams, seemed to flick the prop he leaned against. The timber, longer than the tram, had been put in pointing in the wrong direction, the way the journey was going. This was dangerous, for the slightest roll might turn the outer end to one side and jam it.

346

Anything might result; a fall of earth, a broken rope, a disabled engine. Now, the timber had not jammed but seemed to have merely flicked the post beside Twm's head.

The journey went on, and Will, mourning over his injured hand, waited for his companion to continue their way out. At last he looked up questioningly. Twm stood leaning against the post, head down and cap pulled over his eyes. His lamp hung upon the leather belt that supported his trousers. It was half hidden by his jacket. He was very quiet.

"Put a move on, Twm," Will said at last, unable to understand the delay.

Twm made no reply; nor did he move. Will experienced a strange, unpleasant thrill that seemed to grip his stomach muscles.

"Come on," he said, and his voice was shrill and forced. "What the 'ell is the matter with you?"

He reached out a timid, uninjured hand to the shoulder that seemed to loom large before him—yet an incredible distance away. He touched it.

"U-ugh! Christ!" he cried, leaning back instinctively. Twm fell forward to the ground. The cap rolled off, exposing what had once been a face. Now it was a shapeless mass of flesh and thick, welling blood. With his sound hand Will rolled him over. Blood and flesh had flowed and dripped upon the muffler and waistcoat. He twisted the signal wires together until the bell in the engine-house rang unceasingly. The engine was stopped and the journey-rope rumbled into stillness.

Will lifted his lamp to where Twm's head had been when the timber in the tram had struck it and glanced off. The post was thick with blood and skin, and in the centre, where a piece of the bark had been chipped away, the white of the wood beneath made the crimson appear paler. When Steve, looking for the cause of the stopping of the journey, found him some time later, Will was sitting on the floor with his back against the same post.

The mine manager was sitting in his lodge at the bottom of the pit when Steve reported the incident to him. He was very tired, and dried sweat and dirt had caked upon him. He made no comment for some time after Steve had departed, but merely looked idly round the white-washed lodge with its awkward table almost too big to be passed, the iron door that swung slightly open from a useless cupboard containing only a damp smell and a portion of obsolete blue-print and the grimy dog-eared, thin-leaved report books. The lodge was lit by an electric bulb protected by a wire net. It smelt of mice.

The manager had been worried before this occurrence had happened. Now. . . . He dropped his head on his arms as they rested upon the table. The peak of his cap got caught as it touched his forearm, and the cap rolled off, baring the hair rapidly and prematurely becoming grey. The upper portion of the forehead was clean compared with those parts that had been unprotected by the cap.

On the other side of the table the under-manager ate the bread and butter and cheese that had been left over from his lunch. He had worked in the mines for over fifty years, and was nearly twenty years older than the manager.

"Well, John," the manager said, lifting his drawn, bleak face towards his assistant, "have you ever known such a run of damn bad luck?"

The under-manager made no reply. He tapped the crumbs out of his now empty food-box and placed it carefully in the pocket of an overcoat that hung on a nearby nail. Then, taking a piece of cheese he had put aside, he carried it to a fuse-box fastened to the wall near the door. Above the box was a mouse-hole. He laid the cheese carefully before it.

"Sorry I'm late to-day, mouse bach," he said, then returned to his seat.

Soon a little grey-brown nose peeped from the hole, and two black eyes like tiny boot-buttons glittered for a moment. With a squeak the nose, eyes and cheese vanished.

"Well," the manager repeated, "have you?"

"I've known men killed in the pit before," the other grunted. "And it's not so bad—only somebody's goin' to ketch it for sendin' that timber in the wrong way."

349

"Don't I know it," the manager agreed, picking up his cap and replacing it upon his head. "My name raked in the muck again. Another inquest. Three hundred pounds compensation—six if the company's proved liable. Extra cost for the company, and I'm the one to get the blame."

Again he buried his head in his arms. The other man reached a hand across and squeezed his shoulder sympathetically.

"Don't worry about the money," he said. "I know the boy. There's no one dependin' on him, so it will only cost about ten pounds for buryin' 'im." His face hardened into a grimly amused smile as he added: "It saves the company a lot of expense that they haven't got to pay for people's feelin's, don't it?"

The manager lifted his head again. His expression was even more bleak and tragic.

"Yes," he agreed bitterly. "I suppose that *is* something to be thankful for."

by

IFAN PUGHE

*

THE WILD HORSES AND FAIR MAIDENS OF LLANGANOCH

I took up the scythe and left my father's house and walked away towards the mountain. There I would find a stone upon which to sharpen my scythe, and as I carried it on my shoulder it seemed heavy, but the blade shone in the morning light, and once I felt the beautiful cool of it against my face, and it was so cool it was like the slated floor in the outer kitchen where I had taken meal and bread and strong tea that morning. "With the sky looking as blue as Our Lady's mantle," my father said, "it should be a splendid day for the corn." I said nothing to that for I am not one to doubt his word. I would go ahead first, he following with the other men. It would be hot to-day. Of that I was certain. Already I could glimpse the far-off haze drawing nearer and nearer like the most delicate veil, and the heat was already coming towards me from all that mass of quivering life which my cold scythe would cut down to-day. But I was not thinking upon that, only upon certain young pines and firs

351

which were growing on the hill. Father said as they were my children I should look after them. So now, as I proceed on my way I will go to them. There is nothing so lovely as their morning bow to me as I approach in the face of a light wind. But first I must get the stone with which to sharpen the scythe. When the scythe sings to the touch of the finger-nail then all is good in it, its heart is stout, its blade strong, its swing from the shoulder as light as a feather. I walked on and I kept looking up at the sky and was certain it would be terribly hot. Laughing I felt in my pocket to see if the cold tea in the bottle was still there. Now I began to ascend. My feet sank in all the wild riot of flowering and lush grasses, and I could hear the faintest sound coming to me, like fairy music and I knew it was the pines and firs. A light breeze was coming down now and I took my fill of it greedily for the day would be long, and there might not be another breeze as this seemed like the last wave of coolness coming down from that mountain. Here is the rock. Here is the hole wherein I have planted my stone. I sat down and began to sharpen the scythe. I thought of Mari and I also thought of my father and the dead foal. These were like wounds and I stood between them, and soon my thoughts were tuned up to the rhythm and hum and momentum of my stone against the steel. Thinking of Mari I was sad for though she is a fair maid she is also fickle as the books say of them. But the foal. I said to myself, "I hope my father's angry thoughts are now cold in his head", for I had no mind to work the long day with him near me and thought of that poor foal singing in his head. Behind me I heard faint sounds of voices on the air and I knew that my father and the other men were coming that way. So I got up at once and shouldering the knife I went higher. Now I could see my children, the young pines and firs, and somehow on that height there was still a light wind and there they were bowing and waving towards me as I drew nearer. I would pass through their ranks, descend again and come out at the east corner of the cornfield. The voices of the following men became louder and more distinct the higher I climbed and I heard the name Llanganoch and I knew they would be discussing the coming fair on Friday. Yes. On Friday. It was on a fair day that I had had the trouble with Mari. She was twenty now and I liked her brown eyes and the colour of her hair, like the corn I would be cutting that day. I knew I would like to be well away from my father's house and married to Mari with a home of our own and we would clean and drain the land and sow and reap. But I also knew my father was against this. I was between the wound of her and my father's wound. I would say nothing. I would not see Mari, she could go her own way now. I sat down by some gorse bushes, it looked like a thread of flame all along the hillside, these lovely golden blooms. But now the men were getting nearer

M 353

so I rose again and climbed higher. At last. I was
stood underneath my pines and firs. I looked at them
as they swayed in the wind. I shut my eyes and thought
how Mari was just as these young trees, waving first
this way, then that, bowing low, then tossing their
heads at me. "Perhaps my father is wrong," I was
saying to myself, and the cracked weather-glass full
of deceit, for up here the wind is rising and after all
it might blow the whole day. The corn would dance
fickle and unthinking as Mari, and the living field as
it moved with the press of wind would not be so easy,
the dancing corn would not lie easily enough for the
swing of the scythes. When I opened my eyes the
wind was stronger and there were my pines and firs
like mad children racing towards the blue skies, racing like wild and helpless ships towards some distant
horizon, a horizon that was like Mari too, for she had
the essence of deceit in her blood also. I looked at
"my children". Alive, dancing, and full of song.
Waving, waving, bowing, lashing this way and that,
heads down, unthrust under the belly of wind.
"Blow, blow," I shouted, and my voice was wizened
down to a little squeak as the wind whipped up my
words. "Blow, blow." Tall young pines, tall young
firs, graceful with the grace of blue sky above them
and the dark strong earth beneath them. Lovely as
the heads of all the young maidens in Llanganoch.
Heads thrusting themselves to the sky. "Higher,
higher," I cried, and my voice was melting upon air

quicker than the thought in my head. "Dance, dance," I said, and the heads swayed this way and that, and the long bodies swayed too, and the grace and strength of wild horses was in them and I knew the sap was rising and the richness about them was in essence of air and riot of colour all about and the deep strong smell of air, and just below them all the witches of nettles that grow about these parts. I looked at my trees a long time and all joy was in looking at them, I could see them growing taller and taller, stronger and stronger, so one day their combined strength would hold the wind back from rushing to the valley below. I had planted them, they were mine. "Good-bye," I cried to them as I picked up my scythe and walked down towards the field. Already I could hear their loud voices, and as I came clear of the wood I saw the bright flash of their knives in the sunlight and one with bent back had a white and blue kerchief about his neck and I knew it was my father. So I hurried to him and I said, "Which end shall I go, father?" He raised himself, wiping black sweat from his face, saying it was hot below here and that I would go to the east end of the field and work towards him. I knew then that his anger had not cooled. He had carried the dead foal to this cornfield and it would be a burden on him all that day, and the air would hold it for us all. "Yes, father," I said, and walked off to the east corner. I ran my hand along the blade and I knew it was ripe for the touch, so bending I began to work. As I swung I thought of the wounds between which I was now standing, and it seemed in my mind as though this mass of corn, this swaying trembling, living corn was a vast desert, obstacle between me and my own happiness. If, I thought, if I mow this field clean I will have made a road nearer to my happiness, yet curiously my heart was heavy as the blade swung and cut down the golden dancing ears of wheat, and more. This waving corn was the waving hair of a young girl, not Mari, but a young girl whom I had never seen in my whole life. Once I paused, my knife in air, thinking of this. Perhaps there was a young girl somewhere, and her young head was covered with hair like the colour of the corn. My heart felt suddenly lightened then and my fancy was in a moment carefree and joyous. So I swung again. Towards eleven we stopped work and stood in our different corners and drank our tea, and wiped sweat from our faces. Whilst I was stood there I looked towards the mountain again and there were my pines and firs doing the maddest dance I have ever seen and I wondered at that for below here the air was quiet and the heat burdensome to one. My father shouted to us then to begin again. Before I began I felt my blade and all its coolness had gone. It was warm, and along its surface glistened its own strange sweat, and I was curious as to this, for the like had not happened to me before. The scythe like me had worked hard that morning, but now I did not like its touch. I saw out of the corner of my eye my father watching me, and such was his mood that day that I had no mind to work more that morning. Again I felt the blade and the sweat of it was upon my fingers. A strange thing it seemed, but a strange day, for the trees above seemed like many young girls to me, and the corn before me like the matted tresses of them all. I was suddenly sad. I threw down my scythe and walked towards the gate, and I heard my father call. I heard him halloo through his cupped hands, and the other men shouted too, loud and long that my father said I was to come back but I walked on, never turning my head until I had reached the wood. My steps were heavy, for all the time Mari was in my head and I felt sick and unable to do anything then for love of her. I lay down underneath my trees and closed my eyes and thought of her. The weather-glass had lied, the foal tricked my father and Mari, but then my thoughts ceased altogether and as I wiped my face it was the sweat of this wound that came from it, for I was crying to myself yet did not know it. To-morrow I was resolved to be up early, to take my scythe and my bundle and leave my father's house for ever.

by

BLANCHE DEVEREUX

*

THE BULL GIANT HEAD

Oh, yes! there was a great, splendid herd, once, of most beautiful cattle, all white, every beast, with red ears and red spots upon their bodies, that did vanish away from Brecknock in a cloud of dust, and did go to Llundain city in England, and to the King's wife at Castell Windsor. All but one bull, the most famous bull in the world; and I, Goronwy ap Evan, do know—blessed be Dewi and Eigan the virgin!—the whole story of that little bull.

On the low pastures that lie between the Hay and the hill Wenallt, and on the high summer pastures in the valleys of the Black Mountains, fed the herds of the Lady Maud Waleri, wife of the Syr William de Breuse, Lord of Brecknock, and of English Hay and Welsh Hay; and an arrow's flight from the east gate of Castell Hay the Lady had many beast-houses, with a big stone wall built round them that had iron spikes in it to keep out all sorts of robbers. The better these cattle were fed and tended, and the more carefully I, Goronwy ap Evan, chief herdsman, selected sire and dam, the bigger they became, and broader, and their flesh richer and sweeter, when they did be to be eaten, and with each new generation their coats were more and more spangled red, and less and less like the white coats of the old ancient wild cattle.

One summer's day the Lady de Breuse sent me word that I should collect every one of her cattle, bulls, cows, and calves, and bring them down by the east gate of Castell Hay. Four hundred in all she had. So I, and Rhys ap Howel, and Evan Coch, and the rest of my assistants, in one day did gather all these together and did drive them down. Those our beast-houses would not contain we put in pens in the shade.

An hour before middle day the Lady came from the castle. Her cows, her calves, and her young bullocks she looked at with me; and then I took her in turn to each of her bulls; and last of all she did come to the best bull of all.

Oh, dear! How shall I tell you how beautiful he was, the best of all bulls? A great frame he had, as if he had been a dragon, and a chest as broad as the chests of two men standing side by side, and a coat all glossy like a ripe chestnut that do be split and do show the creamy-white kernel. Head of a giant he had, and a wide forehead all tight little curls. Very furious was the little bull that day. He was tethered, and he bellowed, and rattled with his horns at the manger.

The Lady smiled to see him over the strong half-door. "You do well to keep him shut away," she said to me.

"Yes, indeed," I answered. "Nuisance he was to get here. Yesterday he chased Morgan ap Owen, and Elen wife of Einon The Cockett."

She began to twist her hands together.

"Goronwy," said she, "what would you do if I told you to take all these fair cattle of mine to Llundain in England and give them as a present to another lady?"

I was never afraid of the Lady Maud, although most of the people round by here did tremble before her eyes when she did look at them. She had a powerful and impatient tongue; but that was because she was a very clever lady.

"By the Well of Eigan!" I cried, "I would rather see their dead carcases lying about this ground than send them to England—and indeed I would rather be lying in my own grave than lose the little bull Giant Head, the best of all bulls."

Said the Lady Maud: "I am in a great difficulty."

A handsome woman she was—yes, with dark, bright eyes; but to-day there were big black hollows underneath them, and there was less of the high, commanding way she used to have about her, and she was somehow soft and gentle. Tired she is, I said to myself; it is all her terrible journeyings. She and the lord Syr William have been padding the hoof for many months in all sorts of old foreign countries, thought I; and three days ago she did return to the Hay without her husband, to find it in the hands of a constable sent by King John, who has held her castle over a year in the King's name! As I looked her up and down, puzzled I was about something that seemed to be missing. In her dress, I thought.

"Now listen," said she. "Syr William must pay to the King a fine of many thousand marks, and I have promised that it shall be paid; but indeed I have not the money, and my Lord is in Ireland. The King's constable wishes me to stay here, where he can have me under his eye; but I have persuaded him just now to go to Bredwardine on an errand for me, and as soon as we have dined I and my son will be off over the hills to Abergavenny, to ask my Lord's tenants there to give us the lend of what they can spare. But this is the worst of my troubles: the Queen, the Frenchwoman, is jealous. She stirs up the King John continually against my Lord and me, because there are two things she envies me. One is my great, sweet mountain herd. The other. . . ."

"Is it the green jewels?" I asked. "This is the first time I have seen the Lady not wearing them."

"You have it!" she cried, in her own proud way once more. "Shall Queen Isabel have the emeralds of Breuse? I have hidden them where that lazy French-woman will never be able to find them. They may be sparks of the charcoal of hell—I think they are some-times, such ill-fortune has followed me since I first clasped them about my neck—but they are the royal treasure of my Lord's own family.

"So, when I give the command," said Maud Waleri, and her two eyes became one dark blaze that caught hold of my eyes, "you and Evan Coch, and what others you shall choose, shall take my white-and-red cows with their calves and the bulls into England, and you shall bring them to Castell Windsor, and present them humbly to Isabel the King's wife, that she may win her husband to lift his oppression from the Syr William and from me. Shall you not, good little Goronwy?"

The green jewels it was to be, and not the white-and-red cattle.

Said I: "If the Lady Maud is in trouble and difficulty, and if she do command me to give the little cattle to the Woman of Castell Windsor, I shall do as the Lady Maud wishes."

With a great sigh she turned round, and she saw passing along an alley between the pens Evan Coch, red to the shoulders as he always was after slaughtering.

"Have you butchered?" said she.

"Yes, yes!" I replied. "Old Spotty Nose—ugly old brute he was. But he will do to feed the men of the castle six days from now, on the feast of John the Saint."

"Here is my son," said the Lady; and she left me, walking with her eldest, Syr William the young, with

the crooked eyebrow—Gwilym Gam we did call him
—whom we liked as much as we did fear his next
brother, Giles, the Bishop of Hereford.

"Goronwy ap Evan!" Evan Coch shouted to me,
"come you on now, wash your hands and face, and
leave the others to see to the cattle. There are black
puddings at the castle, at the low table, for the servants."

Well, I did go with Evan Coch into the hall of
Castell Hay. There were very good black puddings
that day, made with barley. When the middle-day
meal was over, the Lady Maud and her son Gwilym
Gam, and most of the people she had lately brought
with her, mounted their horses in the big courtyard
and the east gate was open before them that they
might ride by the Gospel Pass to Abergavenny. Suddenly we heard a noise of horses outside, clatter-clatter.
Some men rode in at the east gate, and the first of
them was a small, angry man with a bright red coat
covering his armour, and a face very nearly as red—
the King's constable, supposed to be at Bredwardine.
They came right into the court, and drew up in a
little clump before the Lady and her party, who sat
upon their horses before the hall door.

"What is this, my Lady de Breuse?" this one in
the red coat did splutter. "You prepare to go on a
journey without a word to me, who have lodged you
three nights in this castle, which I hold in the name
of the King. Know, then, Lady Maud, that I will not

363

have you move beyond the castle and the township of La Haye."

"There is pressing need that I should go," said the Lady Maud. "You cannot in courtesy, sir, detain a lady seeking to travel peaceably about the business of her husband."

"My lady," said he, "last time you roved abroad between the castles of your traitor lord, there was burning at the good town of Leominster. I am resolved to keep both you and your son prisoners until I have word from the King how he will deal with you. Shall I set you free to stir up the mountain robbers to rapine and arson," said that bad Syr Constable, "and to scour the pilgrims' road for idle Welsh vagabonds?"

The east gate was still open; the Lady's men held it and the portcullis, awaiting her command to shut or lower.

"Dewi Sant and Deiniol!" said I to myself, "if we could drive them out? But it will take more than men to drive out these ones."

Then I, Goronwy ap Evan, did slip out of the courtyard, not by way of the open gate, but by a little door I know of, that lets you out by the Lion tavern beyond the castle walls. Straight to my beast-house I did go. My dark handkerchief I tied about the eyes of my little bull, Giant Head; I put a strong halter upon him, took another halter upon my arm, and a prickly goad in my hand, and I brought him, the best of all bulls, to the castle gate. About the gate were the

Lady's men. Wink I did at Piers, the master of the archers, and he let me pass in without one word.

"You have even eased me of half my duty," the King's constable was saying, "for I must deliver your whole herd of milk-white cattle, madam, to our Lady the Queen——"

I led my Giant Head until he faced the King's men: quick as a salmon do jump, I whisked my kerchief from his eyes, I slit the bands of his halter with my small knife, and darting round behind him, I gave him a sting with my goad.

Roaring as the wind do roar in the valleys as it tugs at the roofs and doors of the houses, the little bull, with his head lowered, rushed as the wind do rush at the King's constable in the scarlet coat. Syr Constable's horse whipped round, and galloped in a mad clatter out of the castle gate. A proper clamour there was. How the horses did shriek! Suddenly one of the constable's servants, running, tripped up: our little bull had him on his horns. He tossed him, and the man fell again on the cobblestones. Someone did dash a bucket of water in the bull's face, and two or three other of the constable's men picked up their comrade and ran out after the rest. I think he had a broken neck: as they carried him his head did shiggle. The constable's people were outside the gate by now. The Lady's people were inside: they crashed down the portcullis, and with great bangs they shut the inner and the outer gates.

Giant Head had his horns caught in the portcullis bars. I had picked up the hammer of Owen Saer, and with it I did hit the bull smartly upon the forehead; oh, no! not to kill him; only to stun him for a little, so that I could put my extra halter upon him.

"Oh, madam!" cried Gwilym Gam from the outer rampart; "they cover the ground! They will not draw rein, I'll wager my sword, till they sight Pain's Castle."

"Come down, my son; we must be starting," said the Lady. "If we keep an even pace, we shall be at Abergavenny before nightfall. But first, I thank you, Goronwy ap Evan, my herdsman; I thank you heartily for a happy thought. And now, Goronwy, do me another service; while you are free to go, take you my five hundred cattle from here, as I have commanded you. Syr Hugh Sollars, seneschal of this castle, you shall send Syr John Walbeoff and an armed company with my cattle and Goronwy, Herdsman, away by the road of the Valley of the Dwr to Castell Windsor, in England; and you, John Walbeoff, shall, with your gravest courtesy, make plain to Queen Isabel that this herd is the free gift and gentle offering of Maud of Hay, and neither levy nor tribute."

"That old fellow was dead, like," came into my mind. I stood holding my bull by his halter, and I spoke to them.

"The Lady Maud de Breuse has commanded me

366

to take her white-and-red cattle to the King's wife in England. This bull, now, little Giant Head, has broken the neck of that bad old man, her enemy: I saw his head shiggle. Will the Lady de Breuse not tell me how true it is—and Syr Gwilym also, and Syr Hugh Sollars, steward of the manors of English Hay and Welsh Hay—that by the laws that the great Syr Bernard, the Red King's cousin, brought out of France, any beast that have killed a man shall be forfeit to the lord of the place where he have killed that man. Gift to God he shall be called. And you, men of the Welshery, shall say that King Howel has written, even a stranger's blood you shall pay for in a fine of cattle! Pay to our own Lord we must then; how can we pay that constable, and he our enemy? The bull Giant Head is a dangerous animal, very savage: even I, Goronwy ap Evan, am afraid of him when he is in his senses. Is it right, now," I said, "that such a bull—the spit of him I never saw before —should go from here out of these manors?" And I looked very hard into the Lady Maud's eyes.

The good gentlewoman! Suddenly her eyes did soften and pucker; she had taken my meaning, God be with her! the lovely lady.

"It is all as you say," she answered. "I charge you, Syr Hugh the steward, and you, my good Goronwy, to do justice on Giant Head the bull, in the name of the Syr William de Breuse, lord of English and of Welsh. Farewell, my people," she said, and passed out of Castell Hay with her son and all her train.

"Look you," I said to Hugh Sollars and the rest, "she has given judgment, the Lady of Hay. Giant Head I will slaughter. We will roast his old carcase, make a nice feast in honour of our Lady's deliverance."

"Ach y fi!" I cried, "I have forgotten my big sharp knife. Well, well! kill him round by my beast-houses I will. Hasten, make a fire; fetch you the iron stanchions and the spit."

Evan Coch and Rhys ap Howel, they and I led the little bull out at the gate. When we did get behind the old beast-houses, Evan brought me my knife and my steel.

"Go to the devil, head of a pig!" I whispered. "Have we not slaughtered enough for one day? Giant Head shall live to be a prince and a father of cattle."

A big fire they made in the castle courtyard, and they roasted Spotty Nose, that ugly old brute, and ate the meat, drinking ale and apple-cider, and there was dancing and singing.

Syr Hugh the Steward stood by silent and watched our doings, but during the roasting he called for Syr John Walbeoff and a guard of armed men and sent them with the Lady Maud's herd, just about five hundred, and Evan Coch, and Rhys ap Howel, and my other under-herdsmen, away along the road of the valley of the Dwr. They were going to the Woman of Castell Windsor, the King's bad wife. Good thing it was that there was much dust upon the road, that did rise up and cover them soon from sight. I could not bear to see their tails go from me, my beautiful beasts!

But Syr Hugh never asked me for what was better than all the cattle I had parted with.

The next morning, early, while the stars were still shining, I did lead the little bull, muzzled, up into the hills along the Gospel Pass. But, oh! my ill-luck! Owen Saer, the Lord's carpenter, came towards me singing, from courting his sweetheart. "Do you drive hell-hounds, now that you have no cattle?" said he, with a loud laugh. "Or has the flesh of Giant Head the Mighty, that I have eaten, given me power to see his spirit?"

"Shut your face, Owen Saer!" I answered. "There is foolish enough you are, I believe, to think that the best bull in Brecknock would go to the King of England's silly old park, where the grass is always yellow, and never do grow more than half an inch high!"

"Well, well!" he said. "Goronwy ap Evan, you are very clever. I have a nice little heifer, whatever, and all in good time I shall remember your bull."

Giant Head and I, we kept along the foot of the mountains, until we came to the white house of the gentleman Cadwgan ap Rhys, which his family had lived in since Adam was a little boy. I told my secret to Cadwgan ap Rhys, and he agreed to keep the little bull in his own beast-houses, and to let him run sometimes in the island of pasture that he had fenced in among the common rough grazing.

Summer passed, and autumn came; then we had the winter. The Lady Maud did not return to the Hay, and we had no news of her.

In the second summer of Giant Head's hiding, I was walking one morning along the Gospel Pass alone, when round a corner, like, I met a party of men on horseback. The leader of them had his face shaven, and wore a long gown and a very strange big hat of felt, with a golden cross stuck up in front of it. And this man called my name:

"Goronwy! Goronwy ap Evan! Come you here!"

Like a weasel I sprang up the bank—there were hazel bushes to catch hold of. No stranger was the bald-face, but Giles de Breuse, the Bishop of Hereford.

"Come you down, Goronwy ap Evan," he called, "and make speech with me, or by Dewi the Saint and by Brychan the King! I will curse you so that you shrivel where you do hang crouching!" So I came slipping down till I stood at his feet. "I have need of beef for my table," said Giles the Bishop, "and they do say that you, Goronwy, have not many miles from here a famous bull that will just suit my purpose. You must take me where he is; and any questions I shall ask you you must answer, for I am your lord and your master, instead of my father Syr William, who is dead in Normandy, and of my mother Dame Maud, whom they starved to death in Castell Windsor, with my brother William."

"Lost is Giant Head!" thought I; but I made no lamentation; very terrible was the Bishop.

"Oh, dear! Yes, yes!" I did say. "Please to come with me."

We went the shortest way to Cadwgan ap Rhys's island of pasture, and there, with some of Cadwgan's cattle, was my little bull, cropping the fresh green grass.

Then the Bishop suddenly burst out laughing.

"Goronwy, you rogue, you capital rascal!" cried he to me, "I have dreamt of this sight! Breeder of cattle was my mother, and breeder of cattle will I be. You shall take this bull, the Giant with the Giant Head, to my park of Sugwas, and it will not be long before I have cattle to rival the lost herd of the Lady Maud. You, Goronwy, shall have five acres of land down by the Great Way to the ford of the Wye, to hold free, and when you are old you shall live upon them in a white house, in riches."

I don't know what became of my first herd, that did go to England, to that proud old wife of King John. That Queen Isabel had a bad time, they do tell me, when her husband was dead; maybe she did slaughter all the beasts she had to keep her from starvation. The worst of luck to her, alive or dead. She starved the Lady of the Hay, Maud Waleri.

The small herd that I and the Bishop did breed from Giant Head was divided when Giles de Breuse did come to die: the new Bishop of Hereford took one half, and the other half went to Reynald, the brother of Giles who came after him as lord of Brecknock. No, no! I didn't hate the Bishop. Did he not give me five acres of land to hold free? Now, all you people, I have told you the story why we still have cattle, white with red ears and much red upon their bodies, in Brecknock, and round by Hereford.

by

D. J. WILLIAMS
Translated from the Welsh by
LL. WYN GRIFFITH

★

A GOOD YEAR

The rent of Pant y Bril was fifty shillings a year, and as Rachel relied upon a calf to provide the money, the day the cow calved was one of the great days of her year: not the greatest of all, for that honour fell to the day of sale. Once only did the cow fail her, and it took the best part of her life to recover from that disaster.

She talked so much about the price she hoped to get that the neighbours—some of them owning many calves—could almost reckon their profit or loss for the year according to the price of Rachel's calf. If she got fifty-two and six, it would be a good year and every one paid his way; fifty-five shillings meant a year of prosperity, and some unexpected weddings. But if the bargain were struck on Rachel's small hard hand at forty-seven and six, a lean year followed, and if the price fell as low as forty-five shillings, it was high time to hold a service of intercession.

Rachel pondered deeply upon these matters as she knit her stocking in the garden immediately after dinner, the fleeting warmth of an April day quickening her ruddy complexion. Her dog, Cora, with her tail curled into a small yellow ring on her back, sniffed here and there, finding more delight in this riot of smells than in the scraps of dinner she had just finished. Spring and its magic were in the air: wherever she looked, Rachel saw young growth, on currant bush, gooseberry, and the red rose climbing up the house. She looked at it all, this miracle of sudden birth, as if she saw it for the first time, unconsciously drawing it all into her own life. Could she hope for spring in herself, or must she dwell for ever in that long autumn that cut short the summer of her youth, fifteen years ago, when she was left a childless widow mourning the gentlest of husbands? Fifteen years of hard scraping for food, of sacrifice of body and of soul. She had made the best of it, in spite of lapses. But had not King David himself sinned and repented and found forgiveness, as the preacher said on Sunday? And now she felt so cheerful and contented, untroubled by her past, that she knew that her sins were forgiven her.

She glanced at her clothes: a short white shawl on her shoulders, a well-ironed check apron neatly pleated, and her brightly shining shoes. Before coming out, she had looked into her mirror and found that the crowsfeet under her eyes were less noticeable than usual. In the gentle warmth of the day, with young life budding round her and permeating the world, she felt ten years younger.

A moment later her mind went back to the sermon, and she blushed a little, without knowing exactly why. And then came another impulse, equally inexplicable, to return to the house for her coarse apron and her clogs and to clean the pigsty. None too soon, as she had noticed in the morning when she fed the pig. But before she made up her mind, a gruff voice greeted her over the garden gate and startled her, and she turned cold and virtuous within.

"And how's my bonny to-day?" the words came thickly, with a beery richness. "Here I am again. . . . I'll buy your calf from you."

"I might have known that this lump of a fellow would turn up," said Rachel to herself as she tried to hide behind a currant bush, and her eyes fell guiltily upon her neat black shoes.

"Ah-ha! Playing hide and seek, my pretty? Let's have a look at you . . . aren't we grand to-day? Just look at her!" said Tim as he placed his elbows on the bar of the gate. He knew well enough that he commanded the garden, and he thought of the gold that lay snugly in the long grey purse in his trouser pocket. A cunning rogue, turning up each spring, long before the snowdrops, to enquire into the fate of the first-born calf.

"I'm not selling the calf this year, to you or anybody else," said Rachel. She had been forced to leave the shelter of the currant bushes, and her anger had driven the blood to her cheeks. "Clear off. . . . I'm finished with you!"

"Did you ever hear the like? Going to retire and live on your means like Griffiths Ty Sych, I suppose! But maybe you're going to rear him . . . Rachel Ifans, Pant y Bril, Mark One X Bull!" Tim roared with laughter at his own joke.

"You fool! It isn't a bull calf, and as the cow's getting old, I'm going to rear it."

"I don't know about the cow," said Tim, his small black eyes twinkling dangerously. "I know you're getting younger each year. Let's have a look at your new shoes . . . let me see if they fit properly. And I want to see how you got those pleats in your apron," he added as he tried clumsily to open the gate.

"If you come one step nearer, I'll set the dog on you!" shouted Rachel. But Cora was too intent upon her own business in the hedge even to protect her mistress.

"No use calling Cora . . . she knows me well enough," said Tim. "Come, my beauty, let's have a squint at your calf. We'll strike a bargain soon enough." He nodded his head towards the cow-house.

Suddenly a clod of earth flew past him, followed by a second and a third.

"Just you dare to come here again until I send for

you, you scoundrel," shouted Rachel, ablaze with righteous indignation. And Tim, cunning as he was, saw that he was on the wrong tack this time. He retreated, mumbling to himself about the strange ways of women.

As soon as she saw that he had gone, Rachel went into the house, relieved at her success in casting Satan out of the garden, but weeping a little in her excitement. Sitting by the fire, she succeeded even in conquering that uneasy conscience which had pricked her ever since last Sunday's sermon. But in her joy she forgot that the devil is never so dangerous as in defeat; before the warmth of her gratitude had cooled, new thoughts began to stir. A vision of Tim, dark and ungainly, striding up the lane with the soil falling about his ears. She began to laugh riotously at the thought that a slip of a creature like herself had sent him flying. What would the neighbours say?

But after all, why should they know? Many worse than he, all said and done, although his tongue was as rough as his beard. But he had no right to comment on the fact that she was wearing her best shoes . . . she wore them for her own pleasure, not for his. If he came back that night—as he might well do, for he never bought a beast without going away once or twice or even thrice, to screw down the price by a few coppers—if he returned, she'd salt him well in the matter of money.

The lamp was on the table, and Rachel sat meditating in the dusk. Perhaps she had been over-hasty and had missed her market: the rent was long over-due. Suddenly she was roused by noises in the cow-house. Walking along the passage from the kitchen to the stalls, she saw Tim feeling the calf's ribs. The calf arched his back in gratitude.

"Not a bad calf, Rachel, I must say," said Tim as he came out, ignoring the events of the afternoon.

"He's all right, but his price is beyond you," Rachel replied significantly.

"Come now, don't be awkward. Tell me your price and we'll make a deal of it. It's getting late, and I've a long way to go."

"No need for you to have come back," said Rachel briskly.

"Don't waste time. I know you're dying to get rid of the calf . . . you wouldn't have slept to-night if I hadn't turned up. Seeing it's you, I'll give you fifty shillings."

Rachel was surprised at his opening bid. "I won't get forty for it," he continued, "not after I've dragged it twenty miles to Carmarthen fair next Saturday . . . not a chance."

"Fifty-five," she answered stiffly.

"Tell you what I'll do . . . we'll split. Give me half a crown and a cup of tea. . . . I've a great thirst on me."

"Fifty-five," said Rachel obstinately. "And not a penny will I bate even if you stay the night."

378

"No, no . . . never mind the half-crown. A cup of tea is all I want."

"You're talking nonsense," she replied.

They haggled long over the remaining half-crown, although Rachel was anxious to close.

"Since you're so obstinate, you can have your half-crown," said Tim, tired of it all. "Give me your hand, and we'll close it on fifty-five."

She snatched her hand away.

"You and your dirty tricks . . . fifty-five? I said sixty-five all along. Fifty-five, indeed!" She laughed into his face and ran back into the house.

"You fool," she continued, holding the door half open. "If you hadn't been so cheeky about my best shoes, you'd have had the calf for fifty shillings, and luck-money as well. Did you think I put my best clothes on because you were coming?"

"Heaven alone knows," Tim replied.

"I know well enough, I'm telling you. And it's my turn now . . . you can have the calf for sixty, and maybe I'll throw in a cup of tea. Make up your mind quickly before I shut the door."

"You can keep your calf till his horns grow through the roof," said Tim.

She slammed the door.

Tim had not gone far before he was caught in a heavy shower. He turned up the collar of his coat and took shelter beneath a holly tree, his mind in a turmoil: angry with Rachel for fooling him, still more angry with himself. The sky darkened and the wet clouds raced. More rain to come. On his right, long miles of cross-country trudging over moor and marsh. On his left, an arm of lamplight reaching out towards him and the rain falling across it. There was Rachel in her clean apron and her bright new shoes that cost her so much, laying the table for tea. Pride, Avarice and Ambition struggled within him as the rain poured down upon his head.

Suddenly he heard the click of the door-latch, and a wide shaft of light penetrated through the rain. He saw Rachel peering into the dark, her hand shading her eyes.

"Three pounds is a terrible price to pay for a wee thing like that," said Avarice.

They still talk of it as the most prosperous year the country ever knew.

by

RICHARD PRYCE

*

A HEWER OF STONE

When Mrs. Pugh of Maen Gorsedd, the gossip with the heart of gold, said of Evan Radnor that he was "stead-fast" as his own gravestones, and quite as solid, she spoke of the stonemason's moral worth. But the gods have a way of playing with the words of men. They heard, perhaps, the words that were spoken at the bar of the Cambrian Arms, and chose to be literal, and laughed in their sleeves.

"Solid as his gravestones, is he? H'm! We shall see!"

Evan Radnor, who dwelt a few miles off, at Aber-llwyn, was monument-maker to the neighbourhood. His name was to be seen in the corner of most of the recent slabs and crosses in the churchyard of his own village and those of the district, and a headstone of his engraving had found its way even into the cemetery at Borderhampton.

He was hale and hearty at fifty-eight, which was his age at the time that a certain order reached him. He was short of stature and lean, but exceedingly wiry. He had never had a day's illness in his life. His temper was even, and his temperament cheerful. Nor did he know that he had nerves.

A sardonic pleasantry was the jest the gods conceived.

Evan was working in the strip of garden which ran from the front of the house, where stood the stones and monuments that were at once his sign and his stock-in-trade, to the back of it where were the yard and the shed. It was late summer and evening. There had been rain earlier in the day—the heavy rain of August that does not fall till the drops are large—and the earth smelled fresh and moist as the stonemason turned it with his spade. There were many scents in Evan's garden; the scent of the rose was one of them, of heliotrope another, of honeysuckle a third; but sweetest of all was the scent of lavender. Mrs. Radnor, when she came out to exchange a word with her husband, picked a sprig of it and crushed it between the hard finger and thumb of a hand which was yet very gentle, and held it to her nose.

"It makes me remember things," she said, and did not know that she would never again smell lavender without thinking of this evening.

"You store a sight of things in your head, mother, I know."

"O-oh!" said Mrs. Radnor, with vowels long drawn out, but not very full in sound, "I do indeed."

She smelled the flowers again and fell into reverie.

She was a somewhat gaunt woman, whose frame had, with years, exchanged the willowy slimness which had been its chief allurement, for a thinness which showed itself in a sharpness of outline and angle. She held herself erectly, and the stonemason often said that "Mother" had still the proud look which had once made him think her "bigsorted", and thus delayed his courting.

"An' me waitin' for him to speak!" Mrs. Radnor of the misleading carriage had upon occasion made admission.

"Where's Robert, mother?"

Mrs. Radnor did not answer, and presently the stonemason repeated his question. He looked up as he spoke and noted his wife's abstraction.

"If you anna' dreamin', mother! Well, indeed."

"It's this here lavender," she said, and heard footsteps on the gravel. It was her son who was approaching.

"Just askin' for you," said his father. "You hanna' forgotten that copin's got to go round to-night."

"No. I'll see to it now. I've brought you a customer, father. He's lookin' at the stones now."

Mrs. Radnor recalled her wandering thoughts.

"O-oh," said Evan. "Give me my coat, mother. It's on the barrer there. Who is it, Robert? Here, wait, it's ketched my sleeve. That's better. What's he want?"

But the stonemason did not wait for an answer. He hurried up the path, taking off his spectacles as he went. Mrs. Radnor turned to her son.

"Who is it?"

"Indeed, I don' know. He's stranger in these parts, I believe. He was just reached the gate as I come down the road. It's a headstone, I think he said, but, indeed, I didna' stop, for father likes to take his own orders."

Robert gave a little laugh, as one who recognizes a pardonable weakness and humours it.

"Father is rare and executive," said his mother. She took her long words from the local paper, and sometimes they meant what she meant them to mean, and sometimes they didn't. She had been heard to say that, if she were not satisfied with Evan for a husband, she must be an epicure indeed!

"Supper's all ready," she said presently. "Me an' father waited for you. You've been over at Derwen, I suppose?"

(Where lived Bessie Morgan, who, all going well, would one day be Mrs. Robert.)

Robert nodded.

Mrs. Radnor remembered the talk that ensued.

"Father'll take you into partnership before long, you'll see."

Robert's face lit up.

"O-oh!"

"Don't you say nothin'."

384

"Has he said anything, then?"

His mother looked wise; inscrutable also.

"Well, indeed———" he began and paused.

"Don't you jump to no conclusions, look you," said Mrs. Radnor. "He lets a word or two drop now and again, that's all."

"I should like to be by, indeed, to pick 'em up then," said Robert.

"Do you think I don't save 'em and put 'em together!" said his mother. " 'Father,' I say, 'and what was that you were sayin' about Robert the other day an' the half-share,' or, 'I told Bessie you said Robert was gettin' so useful to you in the business, you'd have to do something for him.' "

"What did father say?"

"Well, indeed, I belief he told me it was well I didn't have to ride upon my own tongue, for she'd run away with me one of these days."

"You canna' get a taste out of nothin'," said Robert, laconically.

"You have patience. Father likes to manage things his own way. You work on steady for a month or two, an' father'll find something to say to you, I know. I wouldn't speak to him just yet."

Robert strolled into the yard. There his mother heard him moving the truck, in preparation, probably, for "taking round" the coping of which his father had spoken. He was a good lad. She could hear her husband's voice and the voice of the stranger in the front garden. A belated bee buzzed past on hurrying wings. A breath of wind was laden with all the scents of the garden. There were people who liked towns. . . . Mrs. Radnor thought then that she would like to see what manner of man engaged Evan in conversation, and she took a few steps in the direction of the pair.

But it was "Good evening to you, mister, and thank you"; "Good evening," and the click of the gate's latch as she came round the corner of the house. Evan stood watching the retreating form of his client. He did not see his wife as she came up and joined him. Mrs. Radnor saw a broad back disappearing at the bend in the road. She would have liked to run to the turn to gaze after the departing customer, but she never forgot the pride of her bearing, and denied herself many small pleasures on its dignified account.

"Not anyone as I know!" she said.

Evan started and looked round. He shook his head.

"Where from?"

"White Valley."

"A grave?"

"Plain headstone."

He divested himself of his spectacles, shutting his eyes as the long metal prongs trailed across his face. Then he folded them up slowly.

"Anything the matter, father?"

"No, mother. What should be?"

386

"I don't know, indeed."

Mrs. Radnor looked at her husband enquiringly. "I only thought——"

"Well, mother?"

"O-oh, I don't know," she said again. "I think too much—like I talk."

The stonemason began absently to retrace his steps towards the spot where he had been working when the stranger's arrival had interrupted him. Robert came towards him out of the yard, to the entrance of which he had wheeled the truck whereon lay the coping-stones that were ready for delivery.

"Do you come in to supper, there's good people," said Mrs. Radnor. "Leave them plants, Effann, you'll easy spare five minutes in the mornin' to finish there. Besides, it is gettin' dark, and Robert's got to go with them things."

Evan began to put away his gardening tools with the desultoriness of preoccupation.

He went then to the pump and washed his hands. He shook them and went, holding them out before him, to the lean-to scullery at the farther side of the house, where he dried them; after all of which he joined his wife and son at supper.

Mrs. Radnor paused abruptly in something she was saying as he came into the room.

Evan ate in silence for some moments. "Well, I'm d'd!" he said then (he never permitted himself to profess himself damned). "Well I'm d'd. It will be for all the world like cutting my own gravestone."

Mrs. Radnor put down her knife and fork. Robert looked at his father for explanation, and from him to his mother.

Evan slowly took his spectacles from their big case and put them on. He fumbled in his waistcoat pocket and produced thence the crumpled slip of paper on which were written the directions his client had left with him.

He read aloud: " 'Here lies all that is mortal of Evan Radnor, servant of the Lord'," and looked first at his wife and then at his son over the rims of his spectacles.

Mrs. Radnor was the first to speak after that. She asked many questions. Who was this Evan Radnor, deceased? He came from Carnarvon. He was a corn-factor by trade, and had died soon after buying the business in White Valley which had brought him to the neighbourhood. Could he be any "relationn"? Evan had tried to make out. His own great-grand-father had had two sons. One of these (his grand-father) had been a builder in Borderhampton; of the other (his great-uncle) little was known, except that he followed the sea. He had died, Evan thought, of fever in the West Indies; but he might have left issue. Who came to order the stone? A nephew of the dead cornfactor. No; in conclusion, Evan didn't sup-pose the families were connected, though it might be that they were.

Mrs. Radnor had been looking over her husband's shoulder, having risen from her chair to fetch a plate from the dresser. She had paused behind him on her way back to her place. Now a sudden exclamation broke from her. She put down the plate hurriedly, and took the slip of paper from his hand.

"What's the matter?" said Evan, sharply. Already his nerves were disquieted, and the suddenness of the little cry that left her lips startled him. "What's up, mother?"

As he waited for her answer an inward irritation, traceable also to nervousness, manifested itself in an expression of impatience upon his usually placid face. Robert was looking at his mother, too, and expectantly.

"Well?" said Evan, "well?"

Mrs. Radnor folded the paper across. "I wouldna' touch it," she said. "There's no good in it. I wouldna' have nothin' to do with it."

"Why not, indeed? What more have you seen in it? Come, speak up, mother."

But Mrs. Radnor shook her head. "I wouldna' touch it," she said again.

Evan unfolded the paper. Robert rose, pushing his chair back, and came and stood behind his father as his mother had stood. Evan glanced up over his spectacles as if his son's movement disturbed him. He flattened out the sheet of paper, however, and proceeded to read it again. He was reading

389

to himself, but he formed the words with his lips:
" 'Here lies all that is mortal of Evan Radnor,
servant of the Lord. Born 21st January 18——' "

He had got so far when Robert moved from behind his chair. He looked up, and saw the young
man exchange a glance with his mother. Robert saw,
then, what his mother had seen. The stonemason
gave a little snort and returned to the paper he held.
It was a second or so before he seemed able to concentrate his attention upon the words.

" 'Born 21st January 18——' " he read again and
looked up.

Why, that was his own birthday—day and year!
Unconsciously he had read the line aloud. Mrs. Radnor and Robert looked at him responsively as people
who, having guessed a riddle or knowing its answer,
look at one who at length has solved it.

"Send it back, Evan," said Mrs. Radnor, "send it
back, and write and say you canna' do it. Say you've
got too much to do, indeed, and there's an end of it.
Let him take the job elsewhere. There's Mr. Williams
over at Derwen as 'd do the job, an' welcome, and
there's Griffiths at Borderhampton. Or if that's too
far, there's someone in White Valley, sure to. What's
he want to come to you for? Don't you have nothin'
to do with it, for, indeed, it's not in nature."

At this the stonemason, the chafing of whose nerves
had been cumulative perhaps, broke into choler.

"Well, indeed," he said, "an' what old wife's

foolery is this? Canna' two men have the same name an' be born on the same day but there must be all this set out about it? What did he come to me for? Well, p'raps my work is as good as Mr. Williams's at Derwen or Griffiths's of Borderhampton, as you are so anxious to recommend. I must come an' ask you an' Robert here, I s'pose, before I take an order."

"Fie, father, fie!" said Mrs. Radnor. "You've got no call to get angry. You know very well as I never want to be consulted. You do things your own way, I always say, an' it'll be a good way, I know. Come, come, eat your supper, there's a good man. That's your own favourite pie as you're so fond of. Robert, give your father the cider."

Robert took the cue from his mother and helped to change the subject. That last cask, he said, sparkled uncommon. It was better than the stuff they sold at the Dragon, and he wasna' sure, indeed, that Mrs. Pugh could beat it over at Maen Gorsedd.

For the time the matter dropped. Later in the evening, when Robert had gone out and Mrs. Radnor was working, the stonemason himself returned to it. He was a little bit ashamed of his hastiness, Mrs. Radnor thought. Yet even now something of irritation seemed to temper his contrition. He had been sitting in silence on the settle with a newspaper in his hands, but he had not been reading, and an inability to fix his thoughts upon the news, coupled with the knowledge that the thoughts of his wife, evenly as she plied her needle, were occupied with the same subject as his own, acted and reacted upon his mind till he found himself compelled to speak. Mrs. Radnor divined something of the state of his feelings. She must see, he said, that any reluctance she might feel to his executing the order which he had received that day could only have its being in superstition. (Evan's word was "stuperstition"—perhaps as the result of some unconscious association of superstition with stupidity—but apparently he thought it a good word, for he used it three or four times.) There could not, come to think of it, be any ill-omen in the chance of a man being called upon to carve the monument of an unknown namesake. Could there, when you came to consider?—unprejudiced, mind! Besides, what was to be would be. And as to the coincidences of the year and day of birth, why, as to that, indeed, there were only three hundred and sixty-five days in the year on which you could be born, and thousands of people had to be born every day—millions, perhaps! And it would never do to refuse orders. There was Robert to think of. The lad was growing up, and his father was bound to provide for him, and there was Bessie Morgan. It was very important to keep the business together. Moreover he, Evan Radnor, had been recommended to Mr. Hughes, his client, who was a stranger to the neighbourhood; and it would not do to fail him. Besides (there were many "besides" in the stonemason's argument), it was partly the fact

of the coincidence of the names that had decided
Mr. Hughes to employ Evan Radnor in preference
to other monument makers of the locality. Mr.
Hughes had but recently come to White Valley to
look after his uncle's affairs. The late Evan Radnor
(servant of the Lord) had been dead nearly a year,
and the living Evan Radnor did not think it would
do to delay the erecting of the stone which was to
mark his resting-place by refusing to undertake it.

Mrs. Radnor was silent for a few moments.

"You know best, father," she said then.

"Well, of all the obstinate. . . ."

The stonemason broke off as his wife met his eyes
with a look of wonder.

Evan was not himself.

Mrs. Radnor slept ill that night. She had a suspicion that Evan had slept ill also, and she found
presently that he too had heard the rain that fell
so abundantly between the hours (the church clock
struck them) of twelve and two.

Then for a strange moment the husband and wife
exchanged glances that were questions, as a shrug of
the shoulders or a raising of the eyebrows may be an
epigram, but neither answered the other's unspoken
thought.

The morning passed and the afternoon and evening. Evan was silent and gloomy. Nothing was said
about the discussed stone. Mrs. Radnor felt that she

was to understand that her husband intended to undertake the order. She would have liked him to tell her definitely that he had decided to do so. She had always had his confidence. But she was a sensible woman, and she did not dwell upon the little disagreement they had had, nor did she magnify the incident out of its just proportion. She went round into the shed, upon one pretext or another, twice or thrice in the course of the next few days to see if the thing was begun, but when she saw that her husband watched her with an enquiring look that reminded her of a look she wished somehow to forget, she forbore to try personally to gratify what, after all, was only curiosity. However, she was above such petty taking of offence, as, in many another woman, would have shown itself in ostentatiously washing the hands of a matter wherein her wishes were to be disregarded, and she asked Robert if the work was to be put into execution at once.

"Father hanna' said anything," said Robert. "There's two or three jobs as'll come before it, I believe. I've seen him lookin' at the paper, and pencillin' a thing or two, but, indeed, I don't know what to make of him just now."

"Oh!"

"He's like as if he was thinkin' of summut else all the while. An' you'd call father accurate, wouldn't you? But he's makin' mistakes."

"Mistakes!" said Mrs. Radnor.

Robert nodded.

"He was puttin' 'Miriam' instead of 'Marian' on old Mrs. Edwards yesterday, an' blowed if he wouldna' have done it again if I hadna' been lookin' at him. There's a funny letter in her name now, I can tell you. It's a 'a' as was very near being a 'i', I know."

Mrs. Radnor's face expressed her concern.

"An' it's not like father to be short either," said her son, "but he was down on Thomas Jones like a cartload of bricks about one of the tools as he thought he had lost, and as couldna' be found. He was wrong about it too, for it was in the office where father put it himself."

"Oh, he's never a hard master," said Mrs. Radnor.

"Nor yet he oughtn't to be to Thomas Jones," said Robert, "who's as good a workman as father's ever likely to find, an' better than most, I'll lay."

"He don't bear any malice, I know."

"Father?"

"No, Thomas Jones."

"No, but indeed he looked surprised."

Mrs. Radnor kept these things in her heart. But she thought she understood.

More certainly was she convinced that she understood, when, signs still manifesting themselves of something unusual and foreign to his nature in the present state of Evan, glimpses of that nature, the kindly nature she knew so well, allowed themselves to be seen, as sunlight through clouds.

Mrs. Radnor tried now to be more than ordinarily gentle and considerate in her manner towards her husband, for she knew that his soul was vexed within him, and she half suspected that a morbid and superstitious fear, coupled with a determination not to yield to it, had part in the causes that produced his abnormal demeanour. She would have liked to be with him a great deal at this time, but now it was that there occurred a thing which kept them presently to a great extent apart.

There broke out at Aberllwyn an epidemic of scarlet fever—the epidemic that occasioned the year which held it to be known afterwards as "the fever year". Three people sickened simultaneously: the wife of Abel Cadwalladr at the shop and post-office, one of Mr. Owen's little girls at the Red Dragon, and Thomas Jones who worked for the stone-mason.

Before a week was over, seven people lay sick of the fever within a stone's throw of the house. Robert had been at work in the shed for a long day in close proximity to Thomas Jones, whose case was serious; and Mrs. Radnor looked anxiously at her son from time to time. The illness spread throughout the village. The school was closed. On the ninth day after the succumbing of Thomas, Robert, after a night of restlessness and fitful slumber, woke with an inflamed throat and an aching head.

He attempted to get up as usual; but the room

turned round. He put his hand over his eyes and sat on the edge of his bed. He could not hold up his head; it was heavy as lead. His limbs, too, were aching. He slipped back into bed and pulled the clothes once more about him. He did not need the doctor to tell him what ailed him.

The day before, the stonemason had been notably silent and gloomy. Mrs. Radnor liked to remember afterwards that for a time, at least, he was stirred out of his moodiness to show a keen solicitude for his son's welfare. Moreover, news of a message he sent to Thomas Jones reassured her. It bore testimony to the kindness of his heart. Thomas had that day been pronounced to be right bad, and when people are said to be right bad at Aberllwyn, you may know that they are thought to be sick unto death.

"Thomas was fine an' pleased, indeed," Mrs. Jones said to the doctor (who was Mrs. Radnor's informant), in telling him of the stonemason's promise, that, in the event of his workman quitting this for another world, a stone should be erected over his grave by his sorrowing employer. "If he gets well," Mrs. Jones added, "I suppose we shall lose it; but, indeed, we canna' have everything in this life," with which conclusion the doctor very properly agreed, hazarding, as his opinion, that a gravestone in this life would be a somewhat embarrassing thing to have. Evan Radnor was soon to be in a position to judge, and would have been able, perhaps, to tell him already, what sensations would accompany so grisly a possession!

Mrs. Radnor, sitting by Robert's bed, found that her thoughts sped over to the shed where her husband worked and lived. Stringent efforts were beginning to be made by the local authorities to allay the spread of the infection, and the stonemason had consented to have a bed made up for himself in the little office that adjoined his workshop. Here he lived isolated from the house, for the doctor having chanced to say that no one coming from the sickroom should mix with those uninfected, or hold communication with them except in the open air, Mrs. Radnor steadfastly (and, perhaps, in truth, under attending circumstances, somewhat superstitiously), kept herself away from him. As often as she could spare a few moments she came and talked to him from the yard. At any other time she would have believed that his years would protect him, but at the back of all her meditations just then were the words that she had read upon paper, and that her husband, she supposed, was now graving on stone, and she would have him run no risks.

" 'All that is mortal'," she said to herself, and shuddered. " 'All that is mortal of Evan Radnor, servant of the Lord'."

The long nights, with their intervals only of sleep —for Mrs. Radnor was nursing Robert unaided— and the knowledge that a pestilence stalked through

the village, attuned even the healthy mind to thoughts
of death. Mrs. Radnor, creeping on tiptoe to the
window, looked out. Thence she could see the stones
and monuments which stood for samples of her husband's wares in the garden below. Some of these
(trades were handed down from generation to generation in Aberllwyn, as in other remote country dis-
tricts) were the handiwork of other days. A Radnor
with the fantasy almost of an Albrecht Dürer, had
here left a record of no mean art in the skulls, and
crossbones, and urns, and weeping figures in low
relief that Mrs. Radnor knew so well by heart that,
though the darkness hid the gruesome designs, she
could picture them all. Never before had a gravestone seemed to her a grim or a sinister object. As a
child she had played in the old churchyard under the
hill, and run a chubby finger round the outlines and
into the hollows of many a dismal decoration; and to
her, as a woman, and the wife of a maker of monuments, the sight of them had been no more than the
sight to a miller's wife of sacks of flour, or, to a
brewer's wife, of casks. She had regretted with Evan
—who, conscious of a measure in himself of his
ancestor's cunning, would fain have carved skeletons,
and hour-glasses, and broken columns—a day when
gravestones admitted of greater elaboration. But now
of a sudden the very stones seen dimly through the
darkness took fearful shape for her. And her husband
was dwelling amongst tombstones; cooking his food

on the workman's brazier that was used generally for
melting lead to fill in their inscriptions of mourning;
sleeping almost amongst them; and one of them must
seem to him (if as yet he were working at it) to be for
the recording of the death of himself. She shuddered
again and held her breath. Then restlessness possessed her sick son, and the remainder of the night
was passed in ministering to him.

The next day brought Bessie Morgan and comfort of its own. Bessie was book-keeper at the hotel
at Derwen, and her time was not at her unfettered
disposal, or, it may be believed, not many hours
would have elapsed after hearing of Robert's illness
before she came to see his parents and gain news of
him at first hand.

Letters had passed between them, and the carrier
who took the two places on his rounds twice a week
had been anxiously questioned.

But, as she explained to Robert's mother, the sight
of the house where he lived seemed to bring her
nearer to him than all the messages, written or verbal,
that had ever been framed.

Mrs. Radnor talked to her from a window,
Bessie, with an anxious face, standing below in the
garden.

"An' indeed you ought not to come to Aberllwyn
at all, Bessie," Mrs. Radnor said, when she had given
her as reassuring an account of Robert's condition as

was possible. "With all this sickness about it'd be best to keep away."

"Oh, I couldn't sit at home," said Bessie, "and Robert ill."

Mrs. Radnor withdrew her head from the window and presently looked out once more.

"He's sleepin' still," she said; "he's sleepin' like a baby. He hardly closed his eyes last night. Indeed, I'd a job to keep the bedclothes on him. Toss an' turn it was, an' not a bit of comfort to be got out of his pillow. But he's sleepin' now uncommon."

"Is there nothing I could do?" said Bessie.

"Yes," said Mrs. Radnor. "Go an' make Mr. Radnor his tea, Bessie. It'll please him, an' he'll be glad of a bit of company. It's dreadful lonely for him havin' to live out of the house, an' I canna' leave Robert for more than a few minutes to go an' see to him, an' I know my poor old man misses me."

Bessie nodded responsively and went round to the shed. Evan looked up as she came in. He was strange at first in his manner, she thought. He threw a cloth over something at which he was working, and presently began to work at something else. Bessie noted his action, but she asked no question, though it struck her even at the time that what he had been doing he did not wish her to see. Afterwards she would tell how his eyes went from time to time to the stone he had shrouded. She would tell, too (when later all were telling what they knew), of an abstraction in his mien that seemed to her altogether foreign to it; and how she had found herself looking at him at intervals just as he looked at the shrouded stone. But she behaved as if she noticed nothing. She was deft and handy, and she glanced about to see what she could do for him while she waited for the kettle to boil. First she put his temporary bedroom to rights, re-making the bed (he had made it for himself, and it looked so lumpy and ill-balanced that she declared the clothes would have been off him a dozen times in the night if he had tried to sleep in it as it was); and folding such things as lay about and settling them neatly upon a chair. Then, in the garden she gathered flowers, some of which she arranged in a glass for the stonemason, and others (kissing these furtively) she made up into a nosegay for Robert. They came from his father's garden, and so were his own to all intent—but what of that? Her love was entwined round them with the string that bound them.

She made the tea presently, and all the time, though her heart was full of anxiety, she presented a brave front.

The stonemason relaxed. One would have said that some spell was broken—that he had shaken himself free of a weight which oppressed him.

When the time came for her to go, she put on her hat which she had removed when she came in. The stonemason watched her.

"Good-bye, Mr. Radnor. I don't suppose I shall be able to come over again this week, but Mrs. Radnor's promised to write, and if anything was wrong, she's promised she'll let me know."

"Her'll let you know. You needna' fear."

"And I'll come over the first day I can. Good-bye, Mr. Radnor."

She was at the threshold.

"Bessie, Bessie, my dear!"

"Yes, Mr. Radnor."

"We'll just send a bit of a word up to Robert— just something as'll please him, maybe."

She looked at him wonderingly. He followed her to the door, and thence preceded her.

He was about to call his wife, gently, by name, when Mrs. Radnor put her head out of the window.

"He's awake, Bessie, an' I told him you was here, an' he sends you his love, an' says, indeed, if you want to please him, you munna' be comin' over to Aberllwyn with all this fever about."

"Oh," said Bessie, tears starting to her eyes.

"It'd make him anxious dear, wouldn't it, father?"

"She's quite right," said Evan to Bessie.

"Think, dear, if you was to get it too, how unhappy it'd make him—an' him lyin' here an' not able to stir."

"Tell him I won't come, then," said Bessie. "I couldn't have at once, for I shan't get out in the afternoon again this week, but I thought I might on

Tuesday or Wednesday. I won't if he wants me not to; but you will write, won't you, Mrs. Radnor?"

"Yes, I'll write, indeed."

"Tell him something else, too," said Evan, who moved forward and looked up at his wife. "Tell him to get well as soon as ever he can, for there's a partnership in the business waitin' for him to step into."

Bessie blushed a rosy red.

"Kiss him, my dear," said Mrs. Radnor, from the window. "I canna' come down, or I'd do it myself. Kiss him for me and for yourself too, Bessie."

Evan stood for some moments at the gate looking after Bessie as she went up the road. Mrs. Radnor watched him from the window. He turned presently to go back to the shed, and she saw the strange expression his face had worn of late settle upon it once more.

Robert was less restless that night, but Mrs. Radnor was unable to take advantage of her opportunities for sleep. She knew that Evan Radnor, working alone at the headstone which proclaimed Evan Radnor to be dead, was haunted by a numbing dread. What a fearsome thing to be recording, as it must seem, and insistently it must seem, of yourself. She thought of the words and the personal look of the letters that would get a grip of you as you worked. Evan Radnor; you were Evan Radnor; and Evan Radnor was dead. She stirred in her chair and looked over her shoulder. Bits of the Burial Service forced their way into her mind, and hummed and jigged there. She felt as if she were Evan, and that the thoughts that had possession of her to-night in the sickroom, where the clock ticked out the moments, and the candle was shaded from the bed, were not her thoughts but his, and he was alone with the terrible stone.

"Lord, let me know mine end," ran the thoughts that were not her thoughts, "and the number of my days, that I may be certified how long I have to live. . . ."

Evan had attended many funerals, but she had not. How, then, did her recollection of the Service, from *the Priest and clerks meeting the corpse at the entrance of the churchyard* to "be with us all ever more, Amen", seem to be so little defective?

". . . We therefore commit his body to the ground, earth to earth" (and the rattle of the pebbles in the handful of mould sprinkled upon the coffin), "ashes to ashes, dust to dust. . . ."

It was Evan thinking, not she.

She could not sit still. She looked at her son and saw that he was sleeping peacefully. She stole from the room to her own and enveloped herself in the first thing she could find. It was a waterproof cloak, and incidentally she thought it would shut away the infection which must attach itself to the other garments she was wearing. She was frightened. She must see Evan. The church clock struck three as she stole down to the shed. She had meant to go in, but she changed her mind and went round to where there was a little window in the office.

She tapped and said "Evan! Evan!" just above her breath.

A smothered exclamation and a hurried movement within told her that she was not wrong in thinking he did not sleep.

"Evan," she said again. "It's me—mother."

The window was opened. There was light enough for Mrs. Radnor to see her husband's startled face.

"There's nothing the matter," she said quickly. "Robert's sleepin' beautiful. He's a deal easier to-night. I believe, indeed, what you said to-day did him more good than all the medicine he's took yet. It's not Robert——"

She paused, at a loss to proceed.

"I couldna' sleep," she said then, "an' somehow I knew you wasna' sleepin' either, an' it come over me as I must just see you."

"No, I wasna' sleepin'," said Evan.

Mrs. Radnor's face grew very tender. Tears sprang to her eyes.

"What is it, father? What is it, Evan? Won't you tell me, indeed?"

The stonemason's hand was thrust out and held hers.

"I canna' sleep for thinkin' of it," he said, in a

voice which trembled. "You was right, mother. Indeed, if I'd known how it'd been I wouldna' touched it. It's me, mother. You were right. It's me!"

She could not speak for some moments.

"That's all silliness an' nonsense," she said then, "of course. But we can write an' say we can't take the order."

"It's done," said Evan. "I finished it before I went to bed, an' I canna' sleep because it's there."

"Oh," said Mrs. Radnor, "then you'll get it off to White Valley in the mornin'."

"I hope so, indeed. To-day's the 6th of September. It's to-day I want over."

"Why?"

"I wish it wasna' finished, or that I'd got it done last week," Evan said, speaking as if to himself. "I thought I'd 'a been able, too, but I hadna' got time; and then—somehow I had to finish it." He stopped, and pointed towards the shed. "He died the 6th of September."

Mrs. Radnor gave a little start, before with an effort she pulled herself together.

"What of that?" she said; "the year'd be wrong any way."

"Yes, the year'd be wrong," said Evan.

"Besides, it's foolishness," said Mrs. Radnor. "You said it was, an' it is. We'll laugh at all this when the stone's stuck up safe in White Valley."

"If it ever is," said Evan; "for you'd keep it, mother, if anything was to happen."

"Hush, father, hush! It'll go there right enough to-morrow, and we'll laugh, you'll see. Good night, my dear old man."

She came back to say: "Evan, woman never had a better husband," and then she stole away.

But it was the gods who laughed, nor was the year wrong. It needed at most but a slip of the chisel to make the past year the current one, and had not Robert said that his father, contrary to habit, was making mistakes! It was still the 6th of September when the day broke. No one saw the accident happen. The stonemason was alone in the shed; it is supposed that in trying to transfer the stone to the truck. . . .

They lifted the heavy slab off his bruised form, and felt with trembling hands for a beat of his heart.

But Mrs. Radnor had no need to be told that he was dead. The fact was graven in stone; and the words which recorded it may be read any day in the churchyard at Aberllwyn, where the story is told to all new-comers, and where you may hear, moreover, that in the dispute which ensued for the possession of the stone (Mr. Hughes holding that a commission was a commission), it was on the point of the mistake in the date that Mrs. Radnor gained the day and the monument which her husband was thus said to have carved for himself.

by

RICHARD HUGHES WILLIAMS

Translated from the Welsh by
Ll. Wyn Griffith

*

SIÔN WILLIAM

A cold wet day, driving the quarrymen into their rough shelters, their faces grey and disconsolate.

"If the weather doesn't mend", said one of them, standing by the door with an old sack over his shoulders "we'll starve like church mice, every one of us."

"True enough," replied an old man, his body bent with years of labour. "True enough . . . all who aren't starved already."

They were puzzled by his answer. Easy enough to talk about starving, but why should Siôn William use these words?

"What do you mean, Siôn?" asked one of them suddenly.

"Nothing," he replied with a shrug of his shoulders.

"Why did you talk about starving, then?"

"Why did Huw mention it?" asked the old man.

"He was only joking."

"That's all I was doing. Do you think I'm too old to make a joke? I'll soon be too old to do anything but die."

"No, no, you've got it all wrong," the quarryman replied kindly. "I'd as soon hear you joking as any man here, but. . . ."

"But what?"

"Never mind."

"I want to know what you're getting at."

The quarryman began to talk to one of the others, thinking that that was the best way of changing the conversation.

But Siôn William was not to be put off so easily, and tugging at his beard he moved towards him.

"Guto," he said.

The quarryman pretended not to hear him.

"Guto Jones," he continued.

There was no reply.

"D'ye hear me, Guto?"

"What's the matter with you?"

"Nothing," replied the old man, his eyes afire.

"Why don't you leave me alone, then?"

"I want to ask you a question."

"What is it?"

"Do you think I'm starving?"

Guto Jones scratched his head: he was cornered.

"I never said a word about you," he replied.

"You answer my question. Do you think I'm starving; me, Siôn William?"

Guto Jones whistled.

"Get out my light," he answered.

"Soon as you answer my question," said the old man. "Am I starving?"

"You know best."

"I know that, but I know that you and all the rest think I'm starving, yes, starving. Well, you're wrong as wrong, I'm not starving; by heck I'm not. I'm rich, that's what I am, I'm a wealthy man."

When he had finished, Siôn William sat down on the bench, exhausted.

"What time is it, boys?" he asked a few minutes later.

"Nearly midday," one of them replied.

"Is it?" said the old man, somewhat perturbed. "I feel sleepy. Didn't sleep well last night. Don't wake me, boys."

He fell asleep—at least, he shut his eyes and breathed heavily.

Dinner-time came, but he did not wake up, and the quarrymen looked at one another as they ate their bread and butter. Another hour passed by, with Siôn William still asleep, and as it was still raining, some of them got ready to go home.

"We'd better wake the old man," said Guto Jones.

At this, Siôn William opened his eyes and looked about him, dully.

"What time is it, boys?" he asked.

"Three o'clock," one of them replied.

"Three?"

"Yes."

"And I haven't had my dinner!"

"Better late than never."

Once again a perturbed look came into Siôn William's eyes.

"Don't think I'll bother to eat now. Might as well let it be till I get home. Besides, my food is in the shed up aloft."

"If it's any use, I've got a spare piece of bread and butter," said Guto Jones. "It'll save you going up for yours."

The old man looked keenly at him.

"Well, if you've got one to spare," he replied, "I'll have it. Save me going up, and I'm getting a bit old for climbing ladders."

Guto Jones gave him the piece of bread and butter, and he ate it with relish.

"Have another?" asked Guto. "Save me carrying it home. Maybe I'll be glad of one of yours some day when I've left mine in the shed."

"That's right enough," said the old man. "Give and take, that's what it is in this old world, isn't it?"

"True."

When he had finished eating, the old man pulled out his pipe, filled it cheerfully, and began to smoke.

"Guto!" said he, touching his sleeve.

"What's the matter now?"

"I've got a mighty fine chisel here."

"What about it?"

"Nothing . . . would you like it?"

"But you'll want it yourself."

"No, I don't think so."

"Why not?"

"To tell you the truth, I'm going to retire."

"Retire?"

"Yes. Didn't you hear me say I'm a wealthy man?"

"Yes, but. . . ."

"But what? Don't you believe me?"

"Yes, but. . . ."

"That's enough of that, Guto. If you don't want the chisel, there's plenty that do."

"I know. But you'd better not give your tools away just yet."

"And me retiring? I shan't want them any more. Don't you understand me?"

"Oh yes, I do."

"Take this chisel, then. Would anybody like this old sack?"

"You'd better keep that, anyway . . . that will always come in handy."

"No, I don't think so. I'll have to get a mackintosh when I retire."

"It will come in for something else."

"No. I'll leave it here. Somebody will be glad of it. Good-bye, Guto."

The next day, Siôn William did not appear, and they all inquired after him.

"He's retired," said Guto, quite seriously.

The quarrymen laughed.

"All very well for you to laugh," said Guto. "But I'm telling you the truth. You won't see him in the quarry again."

"How is he going to get food?" asked Huw Huws.

"He's got money."

They laughed again.

"He told me so himself."

"Perhaps he's saved a bit," said Huw. "He was a mean old boy."

"Take more than saving to get rich in a quarry," said Dic Ifan. "My wife's as careful a woman as you'd find, but I'm not sure I'll die outside the workhouse."

"Anyway, the old man's retired. He told me yesterday he was going to, and he was a bit high and mighty about it, too."

Nothing more was said, but Guto Jones decided to call on the old man that night, and he asked Huw Huws to go with him. About eight o'clock, they stood at the door of his cottage.

"He's not for wasting money," said Huw Huws. "There's neither light nor fire inside."

"Perhaps he's gone to bed."

"Maybe . . . give him a knock."

There was no answer.

"Give it a kick," said Guto.

No one answered.

"Give it another."

414

The door of the next cottage opened.

"Heaven above! What's the matter?" asked a middle-aged woman.

"Where's Siôn William?"

"You're a nice pair, you are!" she replied.

"What do you mean? Out with it, or shut up!"

"Call yourself men!" she continued. "Letting the old man die on his feet."

"Die?"

"Yes . . . that's all there is to come to him, I'll warrant."

"Where?"

"In the workhouse, of course."

"Who's in the workhouse?"

"Siôn William . . . since this morning."

The two quarrymen looked at each other.

"I ought to have known that there's nowhere else a quarryman can retire to," said Guto Jones, looking down at his sleeve.

by

DYLAN THOMAS

*

THE ORCHARDS

He had dreamed that a hundred orchards on the road to the sea-village had broken into flame; and all the windless afternoon tongues of fire shot through the blossom. The birds had flown up as a small red cloud grew suddenly from each branch; but as night came down with the rising of the moon and the swinging-in of the mile-away sea, a wind blew out the fires and the birds returned. He was an apple-farmer in a dream that ended as it began: with the flesh-and-ghost hand of a woman pointing to the trees. She twined the fair and dark tails of her hair together, smiled over the apple fields to a sister figure who stood in a circular shadow by the walls of the vegetable garden; but the birds flew down on to her sister's shoulders, unafraid of the scarecrow face and the cross-wood nakedness under the rags. He gave the woman a kiss, and she kissed him back. Then the crows came down to her arms as she held him close; the beautiful scarecrow kissed him, pointing to the trees as the fires died.

Peter awoke that midsummer morning with his lips still wet from her kiss. This was a story more terrible than the stories of the reverend madmen in the Black Book of Llareggub, for the woman near the orchards, and her sister-stick by the wall, were his scarecrow lovers for ever and ever. What were the sea-village burning orchards and the clouds at the ends of the branches to his love for these bird-provoking women? All the trees of the world might blaze suddenly from the roots to the highest leaves, but he would not sprinkle water on the shortest fiery field. She was his lover, and her sister with birds on her shoulders held him closer than the women of LlanAsia.

Through the top-storey window he saw the pale blue, cloudless sky over the tangle of roofs and chimneys, and the promise of a lovely day in the rivers of the sun. There, in a chimney's shape, stood his bare, stone boy and the three blind gossips, blowing fire through their skulls, who huddled for warmth in all weathers. What man on a roof had turned his weathercock's head to stare at the red and black girls over the town, and, by his turning, made them stone pillars? A wind from the world's end had frozen the roof-walkers when the town was a handful of houses; now a circle of coal table-hills, where the children played Indians, cast its shadow on the black lots and the hundred streets; and the stone-blind gossips cramped together by his bare boy and the brick virgins under the towering crane-hills.

The sea ran to the left, a dozen valleys away, past the range of volcanoes and the great stack forests and ten towns in a hole. It met the Glamorgan shores where a half-mountain fell westward out of the clump of villages in a wild wood, and shook the base of Wales. But now, thought Peter, the sea is slow and cool, full of dolphins; it flows in all directions from a green centre, lapping the land stones; it makes the shells speak on the blazing, half-mountain sand, and the lines of time even shall not join the blue sea surface and the bottomless bed.

He thought of the sea running; when the sun sank, a fire went in under the liquid caverns. He remembered, while he dressed, the hundred fires around the blossoms of the apple trees, and the uneasy salt rising of the wind that died with the last pointing of the beautiful scarecrow's hand. Water and fire, sea and apple tree, two sisters and a crowd of birds, blossomed, pointed, and flew down all that midsummer morning in a top-storey room in the minister's house on a slope over the black-housed town.

He sharpened his pencil and shut the sky out, shook back his untidy hair, arranged the papers of a devilish story on his desk, and broke the pencil point with a too-hard scribble of "sea" and "fire" on a clean page. Fire would not set the ruled lines alight, adventure, blazing, through the heartless characters, nor waters close over the bogie heads and the unwritten words. The story was dead from the devil up; there was a burning tree with apples where a frozen tower with owls should have rocked in a wind from Antarctica; there were naked girls, with nipples like berries, on the sand in the sun, where a cold and unholy woman should be wailing by the Kara Sea or the Sea of Azov. The morning was against him. Peter struggled with his words like a man with the sun, and the sun stood victoriously at high noon over the dead story.

Put a two-coloured ring of two women's hair round the blue world, white and coal-black against the summer-coloured boundaries of sky and grass, four-breasted stems at the poles of the summer sea-ends, eyes in the seashells, two fruit trees out of a coal hill: poor Peter's morning, turning to evening, spins before you. Under the eyelids, where the inward night drove backwards, through the skull's base, into the wide, first world on the far-away eye, two love trees smouldered like sisters. Have an orchard sprout in the night, an enchanted woman with a spine like a railing burn her hand in the leaves, and her sister-stick hold you close as her bones; man-on-fire a mile from a sea have a wind put your heart out: Peter's death in life in the circular going down of the day that had taken no time blows again in the wind for you.

The world was the saddest in the turning world, and the stars in the north where the shadow of a mock

419

moon spun until a wind put out the shadow, were the ravaged south faces. Only the fork-tree breast of the woman's scarecrow could bear his head like an apple on the white wood where no worm would enter, and her barbed breast alone pierce the worm in the dream under her sweetheart's eyelid. The real, round moon shone on the women of LlanAsia and the lovetorn virgins of This street.

The word is too much with us. He raised his pencil so that its shadow fell, a tower of wood and lead, on the clean paper; he fingered the pencil tower, the half-moon of his nail rising and setting behind the leaden spire. The tower fell; down fell the city of words, the walls of a poem, the symmetrical letters. He marked the disintegration of the ciphers as the light failed, the sun drove down into a foreign morning, and the word of the sea rolled over the sun. Image, all image, he cried to the fallen tower as the night came on, whose harp is the sea? whose burning candle is the sun? An image of man, he rose to his feet and drew the curtains open. Peace, like a simile, lay over the roofs of the town. Image, all image, cried Peter, stepping out through the window on to the level roofs.

The slates shone around him, in the smoke of the magnified stacks and through the vapours of the hill. Below him, in a world of words, men on their errands moved to no purpose but the escape of time. Brave in his desolation, he scrambled to the edge of the slates, there to stand perilously above the tiny traffic and the lights of the street signals. The toy of the town was at his feet. On went the marzipan cars, changing gear, applying brake, over the nursery carpets into a child's hands. But soon height had him and he swayed, feeling his legs grow weak beneath him and his skull swell like a bladder in the wind. It was the image of an infant city that threw his pulses into confusion, and the slates and the cirrus-clouded sky into a strange perspective. There was dust in his eyes; there were eyes in the grains of dust ascending from the street. Once on the leveller roofs, he touched his left breast. Death was the bright magnet of the streets; the wind pulled off the drag of death and the falling visions. Now he was stripped of fear, strong, night-muscled. Over the housetops he ran towards the moon. There the moon came, with a hill for a mouth, in a colder glory than before, attended by stars, drawing the tides of the sea. By a parapet he watched her, finding a word for each stage of her journey in the centred sky, the strange land at night where the seasons pass over in a black drift, and the scythe-sided grasses in the lunar country drop with the dawn. He eyed the moon, calling her same-faced, wondering at her many masks. Death-mask and dance-mask over her mountainous features transformed the sky; she struggled behind a cloud, and came with a new smile over the wall of wind. Image, and all was image, from moon to yard, from Peter, ragged in the wind, to the appalling town. All was a moving shadow and the ghost of matter, he on the roofs invisible to the street, the street beneath him blind to his walking word. He looked upon the moon again, dead as her stars. His hand before him was five-fingered life. Image, and all was image, as, man among ghosts, he climbed again from the parapet to the level tiles.

A baby cried, but the cry grew fainter. It is all one, thought Peter, the loud voice and the still voice striking a common silence, the dowdy lady flattening her nose against the panes, and the well-mourned lady. The word is too much with us, and the dead word. Cloud, the last muslin's rhyme, shapes above tenements and bursts in cold rain on the suburban drives. Hail falls on cinder track and the angelled stone. It is all one, the rain and the macadam; it is all one, the hail and cinder, the flesh and the rough dust. High above the hum of the houses, far from the skyland and the frozen fence, he questioned each shadow; man among ghosts, and ghost in clover, he moved for the last answer.

The bare boy's voice through a stone mouth, no longer smoking at this hour, rose up unanswerably: Who walks, mad among us, on the roofs, by my cold, brick-red side and the weathercock-frozen women walks over This street, under the image of the Welsh summer heavens walks all night loverless, has two sister lovers ten towns away. Past the great stack forests to the left and the sea his lovers burn for him endlessly by a hundred orchards. The gossips' voices rose up unanswerably: Who walks by the stone virgins is our virgin Peter, wind and fire, and the coward on the burning roofs.

He stepped through the open window.

Red sap in the trees bubbled from the cauldron roots to the last spray of blossom, and the boughs, that night after the hollow walk, fell like candles from the trunks but could not die for the heat of the sulphurous head of the grass burned yellow by the dead sun. Half-flying there, he rounded, half-mist half-man, all apple circles on the sea-village road in the high heat of noon as the dawn broke; and as the sun rose like a river over the black-headed hills so the sun sank behind a tree. The woman pointed to the hundred orchards and the blackbirds who flocked around her sister, but a wind put the trees out, and he woke again. This was the intolerable, second waking out of a life too beautiful to break, but the dream was broken. Who had walked by the virgins near the orchards was a virgin Peter, wind and fire, and a coward in the destroying coming of the morning. But after he had dressed and taken breakfast, he walked up This street to the hilltop and turned his face towards the invisible sea.

Good morning, Peter, said an old man sitting with six greyhounds in the blackened grass.

Good morning, Mr. David Davies, said Peter.

You are up very early, said David Two Times.

I am walking towards the sea.

The wine-coloured sea, said Dai Twice.

Peter walked over the hill to the greener left, and down behind the circle of the town to the rim of Whippet valley where the trees, forever twisted between smoke and slag, tore at the sky and the black ground. The dead boughs prayed that the roots might shoulder up the soil, leaving a dozen channels empty for the leaves and the spirit of the cracking wood, a hole in the valley for the mole-handed sap, a long grave for the last spring's skeleton that once had leapt, when the blunt and forked hills were sharp and straight, through the once-green land. But Whippet's trees were the long dead of the stacked south of the country; who had vanished under the hacked land pointed, thumb-to-hill, these black leaf-nailed and warning fingers. Death in Wales had twisted the Welsh dead into those valley cripples.

The days was a passing of days. High noon, the story-killer and the fire-bug—(the legends of the Russian seas died as the trees awoke to their burning)—passed in all the high noons since the fall of man from the sun and the first sun's pinnacling of the half-made heavens. And all the valley summers, the once monumental red and the now headstone featured, all that midsummer afternoon were glistening in the seaward walk. Through the ancestral valley where his fathers, out of their wooden dust and full of sparrows, wagged at a hill, he walked steadily; on the brink of the hole that held LlanAsia as a grave holds a town, he was caught in the smoke of the forest, and, like a ghost from the clear-cut quarters under the stack roots, climbed down on to the climbing streets.

Where are you walking, Peter? said a one-legged man by a black flower-bed.

Towards the sea, Mr. William Williams.

The mermaid-crowded sea, said Will Peg.

Peter passed out of the tubercular valley on to a waste mountain, through a seedy wood to a shagged field; a crow, on a molehill, in Prince Price's skull cawed of the breadth of hell in the packed globe; the afternoon broke down, the stumped land heaving, and, like a tree of lightning, a wind, roots up, forked between smoke and slag as the dusk dropped; surrounded by echoes, the red-hot travellers of voices, and the devils from the horned acres, he shuddered on his enemies' territory as a new night came on in the nightmare of an evening. Let the trees collapse, the gusty journeymen said, the boulders flake away and the gorse rot and vanish, earth and grass be swallowed down into a hill's balancing on the grave that proceeds to Eden. Winds on fire, through vault and coffin and fossil we'll blow a manful of dust into the garden. Where the serpent sets the tree alight, and the apple falls like a spark out of its skin, a tree leaps up; a scarecrow shines from the cross-boughs,

425

and, by one in the sun, the new trees arise, making an orchard round the crucifix.

By midnight two more valleys lay beneath him, dark with their two towns in the palms of the mined mountains; a valley, by one in the morning, held Aberbabel in its fist beneath him. He was a young man no longer but a legendary walker, a folkman walking, with a cricket for a heart; he halted by Aberbabel's chapel, cut through the graveyard over the unstill headstones, spied a red-cheeked man in a nightshirt two foot above ground.

The valleys passed; out of the water-dipping hills, the moments of mountains, the eleventh valley came up like an hour. And coming out timelessly through the dwarf's eye of the telescope, through the ring of light like a circle's wedding on the last hill before the sea, the shape of the hundred orchards magnified with the immaculate diminishing of the moon. This was the spectacle that met the telescope, and the world Peter saw in the morning following upon the first of the eleven untold adventures; to his both sides the unbroken walls, taller than the beanstalks that married a storey on the roof of the world, of stone and earth and beetle and tree; a graveyard before him—he thought each inch of the ground bird-boned as a lord-and-lady flower—the ground came to a stop, shot down and down, was lost with the devil in bed, rose shakily to the sea-village road where the blossoms of the hundred orchards hung over the wooden walls, and sister roads ran off into the four white country points; a rock line thus, straight to the hilltop, and the turning graph scored with trees; deep down the county, deep as the history of the final fire burning through the chamber one storey over Eden, the first green structure after the red downfall; down, down, like a stone struck with towns, like the river out of a glass of places, fell Peter's footholding hill. He was a folkman no longer but Peter the poet walking, over the brink into ruin, up the side of doom, over hell in bed to the red left, till he reached the first of the fields where the unhatched apples were soon to cry fire in a wind falling westward to the sea. A man-in-a-picture Peter, by noon's blow to the centre, stood by a circle of apple trees and counted the circles that travelled over the shady miles into a clump of villages. He laid himself down in the grass; and soon fell back, bruised to the sun; and he slept until a handbell rang over the fields. It was a windless afternoon in the sisters' orchards, and the fair-headed sister was ringing the bell for tea.

He had come very near to the end of the indescribable journey. The fair girl, in a field sloping seaward three fields and a stile away, laid out a white cloth on a flat stone. Into one of a number of cups she poured milk and tea, and cut the bread so thin she could see London through the white pieces. She stared hard at the stile and the pruned, transparent

hedge, and as Peter climbed over, ragged and un-
shaven, his half-stripped breast burned by the sun,
she rose from the grass and smiled and poured tea
for him.

This was the end to the untold adventures. They
sat in the grass by the stone table like lovers at a
picnic, too loved to speak, desireless familiars in the
shade of the hedge corner. She had shaken a handbell for her sister, and called a lover over eleven
valleys to her side. Her many lovers' cups were empty
on the flat stone.

And he who had dreamed that a hundred orchards
had broken into flame saw suddenly then in the windless afternoon tongues of fire shoot through the blossom. The trees all around them kindled and crackled
in the sun, the birds flew up as a small red cloud grew
from each branch, the bark caught like gorse, the
unborn, blazing apples whirled down devoured in a
flash. The trees were fireworks and torches, smouldered out of the furnace of the fields into a burning
arc, cast down their branded fruit like cinders on the
charred roads and fields.

Who had dreamed a boy's dream of her flesh-and-
ghost hand in the windless afternoon saw then, at the
red height, when the wooden steproots splintered at
the orchard entrance and the armed towers came to
grief, that she raised her hand heavily and pointed
to the trees and birds. There was a flurry in the sky,
of wing and fire and near-to-evening wind in the

going below of the burned day. As the new night was built, she smiled as she had done in the short dream eleven valleys old; lame like Pisa, the night leaned on the Welsh walls; no trumpet shall knock the west walls down until the last crack of music; she pointed to her sister in a shadow by the disappearing garden; and the dark-headed figure with crows on her shoulders appeared at Peter's side. This was the end of a story more terrible than the stories of the quick and the undead in mountainous houses on Jarvis hills, and the unnatural valley that Idris waters is a children's territory by this eleventh valley in the scaward travel. A dream that was no dream skulked there; the real world's wind came up to kill the fires, and where two sisters had stood together, twining together the fair and dark tails of their hair, a scarecrow pointed to the extinguished trees. He heard the birds fly down, unafraid of the cross-wood nakedness under the rags, on to his lover's shoulder. He saw the fork-tree breast, the barbed eye, and the dry, twig hand.

by

HYWEL DAVIES

*

THE FIVE EGGS

When the chapel wedding was over in the valley, old William called at his mother-in-law's bit of a farm to collect the cow which she was giving away with the bride. He harnessed Shoni the horse in the cart, gave a leg up to his wife, who sat stiff as a ram-rod on the plank seat, and tied the end of the halter round the cow's neck to the back of the cart. Then he cried "Gee up, Shoni," and they set off for home. Old William walked behind, for the horse knew the way up the steep road to the top of the Yellow Mountain as well as he any day.

Old William walked behind, he did, putting a horny forefinger now and again below the ring of grey beard which stretched from ear to ear and giving a tug at his tight collar. Ay, there was the cow, splaying her legs before him as she walked, and there was his virgin bride of forty-five, her black back humping below the ring of blowing pansies in her hat, and there was Shoni, snoring and roaring in his windpipe as he tugged up the road cut deep between the hedges.

He stretched out a hand and pinched the cow's rump.

"It's a bit old the cow is, Mair," he called out.

"It's a bit old we are all getting, William bach," she cried back, but not turning her head.

"That is truth," William agreed, but he had a bad feeling that his mother-in-law had cheated him.

It was a fine spring morning, with a small wind moving in the hedges. The cocks were crowing in the valley.

Towards the top of the hill they went past the farmhouse of Gellywern. Dan saw the pansies bobbing above the hedge and fired a gun into the air. Bang, went the gun, and the birds stopped singing.

"A good wedding to you," shouted Dan at the gate as they went past, his red face laughing at them.

William waved his whip towards him.

Soon they were out on the flat bleak heather-land at the top of the Yellow Mountain, where the bogs are and the water is rusted with red. On a rise away to the right William pointed out his little house, the windows as small and shut-looking as a man's eyes when the sun is in them. Round the house were a few sheds, with zinc roofs.

"There is a great need for something to eat on me," shouted Mair. "I hope there is the filling of a belly at your house, husband."

"I have a hole to be filled too," said William. "There is bread and butter and five eggs."

"Three to me and two to you," said Mair.

"Am I not the man?" asked William.

The cart creaked to a stop in the yard. William unharnessed Shoni and turned him and the cow loose into the field. Mair ran indoors, stepped out of her black skirt and tied an apron over her red flannel petticoat. She hung up her hat on a peg behind the door and soon had the table laid and the eggs on the boil.

"Busy like a good wife you are," said William, undoing the stiff collar round his neck.

"Near ready are the eggs," said Mair. "Three to me and two to you."

"What's got into the woman?" cried William. "Sure it is two to you and three to me."

A look of thunder came into her face.

"Said I not three to me?" she shouted.

"Saying is not doing, wife. Are they not the layings of my own hens, and gathered fresh this morning with my hands?"

"This is why you have called me from my mother," she cried. "Man, go away with you and leave me peace for my three eggs."

Out the eggs came from the saucepan, huddling white and close together on the wood of the table.

William picked them up with his large hands and put them all five in his pocket.

"Advice must we have," he said, and went out

through the door. In the yard he put his fingers to his mouth and shrilled three whistles.

"Dan will be with us in a little minute now," he said when he got back to the kitchen. "Wife, get you the bread and butter cut."

"Is it me you are ordering about?"

"A word in the ear is better than a clout," said William.

But there she sat, with a brow like a ploughed field. William cut himself a slice of bread the thickness of a hand, buttered it, and started eating. In a while she did likewise.

"Little wife of my bosom," he cajoled, "a sad thing it is to start our two lives together in this wise."

"Och, so it is," she agreed.

"In this question of the eggs now, it is reason which should reign."

"It is truth you speak there, husband."

"So let it be," said William, passing over two eggs to Mair and keeping three for himself.

"Where is my other egg, the little husband?"

"Why, three for me and two for you," said William, exasperated.

"Agree with that I never will," shrilled Mair.

But there was Dan the farmer, with his red face. He saw how it was in the twinkle of an eyelid. What a story to tell homing from chapel, or on Saturday in the market, or at the Eisteddfod! Yes, sure, a rich man of words would he be the rest of his days, with plenty of men listening. Over his tongue it would come like a never-stopping waterfall.

"Woe is me, you see how it is, old neighbour," said William.

Dan sat on the skew and spat into the fire.

"It's justice I do want," cried Mair, "three eggs to me and two to him."

"Depends it does", said Dan judiciously, "on who is top dog in this marriage."

Mair and William hung their heads, not looking at each other. Hadn't they known from the beginning it was that, a fight to be top dog. And here was this gross fool of a red-faced jackass saying it out loud.

"A dull-headed fellow you are, Dan," said Mair sharply.

"From a religious point of view now," Dan went on happily, "there is that bit about for better or for worse, until death do you part."

"His side you are taking then?" said Mair with a high voice. "It is not death that do be parting us, but eggs."

"In truth, in truth," murmured Dan placatingly.

"A shameful thing indeed it is to quarrel before neighbours," said William, combing his beard with his fingers. "Little wife, now, come you over here and we will talk."

Dan watched them with crafty eyes. Not a bit of this salty story must he miss. Saying tidy, consoling things old William was by the dresser, and soothing down was that hag, Mair. But not a word could he hear. Yes, now he was taking her by the arm and turning her round. Pity indeed to be peacemaking, without a smart smack of a tail to the story.

"Ay then, Mair dear," William was saying out loud. "Reasonable you are, so let us to the food. Three eggs for me."

There was the fat in the fire again and words being thrown like stones.

"Back to my mother I go in a minute," shouted Mair. "Go you now at once and put your wheezy Shoni in the shafts, and do you be tying my cow behind quickly."

And by God, there was old William going out, too, and catching the horse, and putting harness on him, and stepping him back into the shafts, and now he was calling the cow, "Trwydi fach, Trwydi fach," and putting a halter round her neck and tying the end of it to the back of the cart. Was justice to be done ever to a story as skittish as this!

Ay, Lord help us, old William was sitting down side by side with Mair and crying "Gee up" to the horse, and Shoni legging it out smartly.

Dan took to the road in pursuit. It was not a thing to be missed.

Down in the valley again William spoke his mind.

"Shameful it is, leaving me the day of your wedding, Mair fach. Great will be your shame, and lonely indeed will I be on the Yellow Mountain. Little wife, not good is it for man to live alone. A despised virgin you will be until you are under the earth."

"That is my thought too," said Mair gently.

Coming round a corner of the road, the sweat dripping from his nose, Dan saw them turning back, and stopped like a shot rabbit.

"Is it settled then?" he shouted, showing his disappointment.

"Yes indeed," said Mair; "three eggs to me and two to him."

"The devil to you, woman," cried William. "Round with you, Shoni horse, to her mother with her."

William did not open his mouth again until they came to her mother's house, though Mair was sniffling in her nose.

"Down you get, virgin," he shouted. "Put your old feet to earth."

But Mair did not move.

"Heard you not me, wife?"

But not a word in answer. It was all a silence, Shoni hanging his head down, the cow without a whisk in her tail, Mair sitting like a stone, William looking up, and Dan not breathing at all.

"Turn you the horse round and go home," said Mair meekly.

"It is three eggs to me then?" William asked.

Mair put her skirt up to her eyes and started crying. She wept a long time with a loud noise.

"It is three to me?" William asked again.

"Eat you all bloody five," she whimpered at last.

THE FIVE EGGS

Mair put her skirt up to her eyes and started crying. She wept a long time with a loud noise.

"Is there——" He said, then stopped again.

"Eat you all bloody five," she whimpered at last.

by

HILDA VAUGHAN

*

A THING OF NOUGHT[1]

To her neighbours she was known as Megan
Lloyd. In my memory she lives as Saint Anne.

Years after I had lost her, I was wandering through
the Louvre, and came upon the picture attributed to
Leonardo. I stood before it, happy; and my eyes
filled with tears. Megan Lloyd, when I knew her,
was older than this wise and gracious mother of the
Virgin. Her hair was white as lamb's wool; her face,
like a stored apple, seamed with fine wrinkles. Yet
there was her familiar smile, full of tenderness and
understanding.

She is in my mind now, seated, like Leonardo's
homely saint, in the open. Often I saw her moving
about the farmhouse kitchen, or sitting beside the
white-washed hearth, her fingers, as she stooped to
warm them, cornelian red in the glow of a peat fire.
Sometimes she had a grandchild in her lap, and
another in the cradle that her foot was rocking with
slow rhythm. But I remember her best as I saw her

[1] First published in book form by Lovat Dickson Ltd.

often during my last summer in Wales, out of doors, her faded lips parted a little to the hill wind.

She sat on an oaken chair upon the stretch of sward surrounding Cwmbach homestead, where hissing geese paddled to and fro, bobbing their heads on long necks. From the neighbouring buildings, white as mushrooms in the green landscape, came the cheerful noises of a farmyard and a house full of lusty children. Her eldest son, dark and dour, clothed in earth-brown corduroys, her busy shrill daughter-in-law, her tribe of swarthy grandchildren, to me were present only as a background to Saint Anne. They and their home were like the walled towns, the cavalcades of horsemen, the plumed trees, behind the central figure of the Madonna in some fifteenth-century altar piece. They had no connection with my tranquil saint. Their toil and clatter, their laughter, quarrelling and crying did not disturb us, who were the only two human beings of leisure in the countryside.

I was idle and self-tortured throughout that long hot summer. The harsh gales of spring were raging through my mind, unemployed and as yet empty of experience.

She was profoundly calm; serene as an autumn evening after a tempestuous day, when the wind has fallen and the dead leaves lie still.

It was with difficulty that she dragged herself abroad. Her fingers were twisted with rheumatism;

439

she could no longer work. She could not even see to read her Bible. So, during these last months of her life, she sat, content to wait for death, with hands folded, while she watched the shadows of the hills on either side of Cwmbach as they stole across the narrow valley.

The shade of the eastern hill dwindled behind the house as the sun reached its zenith; that of the western hill advanced when the sun began to sink. Little Cwmbach was so strait that only for an hour at noon was its whole width lit by sunshine. The mountains rose like walls on either side, shutting out the world. Down in the dingle lay the solitary farm and a stern chapel, square and grey, with the caretaker's cottage clinging to its side, as a white shell to a strong rock. An angry stream, hurling itself against boulders, foamed between these two dwelling places, and a thin ribbon of road wound its empty length up over the pass, where the hills converged.

Day after day I climbed across a waste of heather, moss and bog, and, scrambling down the channel of a waterfall, flung myself at Saint Anne's feet. I was eighteen. The universe to me was the stage upon which my own tragedy was being acted. I talked by the hour about myself and my important emotions. She listened with inexhaustible patience. When I told her that no one had ever loved or suffered as I did, she smiled, not with derision, but sadly, as one who knew better.

440

If I looked up at her and found her smiling in that fashion, I fell silent. Then, after a while, she would begin to talk. It was thus I came to know her lover, her husband and her child. Her words were few, but they had magic to conjure up the dead. I knew so well their looks, their manner of speech, their gestures; it is hard to believe that never in my life did I see them, save through her eyes, or hear their voices except as an echo in her memory.

She was eighteen when she went to Pontnoyadd fair and fell in love with Penry Price, son of Rhosferig. He was tall, broad-shouldered, wind-tanned, blue-eyed. His laughter had reached her, gay and good-natured, so that she loved him before ever she set eyes upon his beauty. She edged her way forward through the press of admiring yokels by whom he was surrounded. He was in his shirt-sleeves, hurling a wooden ball at an Aunt Sally. With a superb swing he brought his right arm back and flung the ball with such force that the coconut he aimed at flew out of its stand and broke to pieces. A chuckle of applause arose from the spectators. He turned round to smile at them, displaying teeth white and strong as those of a young savage. Picking up another ball, he threw it with all his might, smashing the target as before. One after another, he brought the coconuts down, until a heap of broken winnings lay scattered at his feet. The owner of the booth watched him with apprehensive

admiration, and the murmuring of the onlookers rose
at last to a shout. Megan could not take her eyes off
him. His cap and coat lay on the ground. The sun
on the bright hair gave him the splendour of a war-
rior in a helmet of gold. His shirt-sleeves were rolled
up, and the hairs on the back of his freckled arms
glinted like a smear of honey. The sweat of exertion
made his shirt cling close. She could see his muscles
swell. To her, who seldom looked on any young man
but her own weakling brother, this hero of the fair
appeared a god. She held her breath with joy when
he turned round and began to distribute his earnings
to the children in the crowd. *"There now!"* she
thought, proud as a mother. He was as good and
generous as he was strong and handsome! "Any gal
'ould have been bound to love him," she was wont
to tell me, "he was such a *man*. There was summat
about him of a child, too."

Soon he caught sight of her brother, who had
brought her to the fair, and greeted him with a slap
on the shoulder.

"This is my sister as you are not knowing," announced the boy, pushing Megan forward.

Looking down at her eager face, Penry flushed
self-consciously. "And shy, also, like myself," she
thought. "Who ever 'ould have guessed it!" Should
he treat her to a ride on the roundabout, he asked,
stammering. She was too excited to answer, but nodded her head, whilst her colour came and went and

her green eyes sparkled, like dew on spring's first grass.

She went with him, elated by the scene—the white tents pitched upon the wet and shining field; the dizzy kaleidoscope of colours formed by roundabouts flashing with brass and gipsies' choice of paint; the throng of country folk, forgetful to-day of their Puritanism; the discordant clash of three or four organs playing different tunes, of bells ringing and people laughing, talking, shouting; the holiday jostling and fun of it all.

"There's pretty you are," said a young man, ogling her. She was glad that Penry heard, and marched her off quickly. She glanced at him from under her straw bonnet. Perhaps she really was good to look upon? Devoutly she hoped so. Her hair was parted demurely in the centre, brushed down each side of her oval face, and twisted in a neat coil at the nape of her neck. She wore her Sabbath gown of black alpaca, and the shawl of white cashmere with a red fringe in which her mother had been married. In a new pair of slippers "her feet beneath her petticoat like little mice stole in and out". To the front of her tight-fitting bodice was pinned a posy of cottage garden flowers. Her breasts were small and firm as apples; her waist was slim. She looked winsome, and Penry thought so, evidently, for he stayed close to her the rest of the day, and showed her the many delights of the fair: the gipsy fortune-teller, who promised each of them

443

a faithful and pretty sweetheart; the monstrous fat
woman in tights and spangles, the shooting gallery
where goldfish could be won; the acrobats and jug-
glers, the wrestlers and daubed clowns. By all these
pagan wonders Megan was enchanted. She drove
home that evening beside her sleepy brother in the
jolting farm-cart with her heart beating and her
temples throbbing. For nights after, she dreamed of
Penry. The sound of footsteps, a knock at the door
brought hot colour to her cheeks.

He came on the fifth day. It was the Sabbath. She
was trying to read the Psalms, but closed her Bible
quickly as she saw him vault down from his pony.
He asked leave to stable it at Cwmbach farm. "I have
come to hear the preacher at your chapel," he explained to her brother, who grinned.

Penry flushed, and her father replied: "He's a tidy
minister, but I never heard tell as he was noted for
his eloquence. . . . Still, you're welcome, young man."

So Penry stayed to tea, and at dusk walked over to
chapel side by side with Megan. There, in a dream
of Paradise, she listened to him singing in his hearty
bass voice.

"What a voice he was havin'," she would say.
"Goin' through me it was, deep down into my heart.
Onst I had heard him sing, it was as if I was belongin'
to him ever after. He was *here*—always." And she
would lay her gnarled hand, with wrinkled skin loose
on the knuckles, upon her shrunken breast.

I did not dare look up at her when she spoke of her lover's singing. At such times I knew that tears were trickling down her cheeks. Of all the suffering through which she had passed, she could speak in her old age dry-eyed; but not of that happy voice, to remember which was ecstasy.

"They was all listenin' to him in chapel; and praisin' his singin' after. But *I* wasn't able to say nothin'. Feelin' too much, I was."

After that first Sunday, he came again often from his father's farm which lay twelve miles away over the wind-scoured hills. He was a general favourite, whom Megan's parents welcomed to a meal and heard with indulgent disapproval when he told of fights, fairings and poaching. They were strict Calvinistic Methodists. A pious gloom hushed their home when Penry was not in it. To Megan he seemed a dazzling shaft of sunshine which had pierced its way into the darkness of a tomb.

"I was livin' in a family vault afore he came," she said to me once. "Indeed, he was my Saviour, bringin' me hope o' a glorious Resurrection. God forgive me if I do take His name in vain. 'Tis not in blasphemy. For Penry was my life, as Christ is the life o' good religious Christians."

She spoke to him seldom, being content to listen to his voice, and to his laughter that made her happy, hot and afraid. It was to her he spoke when he addressed her parents or her brother. His tales of

445

daring escapades were told to them in order to amuse
her. When she joined, whole-hearted, in their reluc-
tant mirth, he grew still gayer. Sometimes he and she
exchanged a glance full of understanding.

So she existed from week to week, going about her
drudgery in a trance, waiting for Sunday till she
should live again. Monday and Tuesday were hateful
days, empty and cold. On Wednesday anticipation
began to revive. Was it not already the middle of the
week? Throughout Thursday and Friday her impatience mounted. On Saturday she was secretly dis-
traught. Tired though she was by long hours of
labour, she could scarcely sleep that night, but lay
tossing in the darkness, asking herself again and
again: "Will he come to-morrow? Will he come?"
If he came, she was supremely blissful, until the hour of
his dreaded departure. If he did not come, the day was
leaden with disappointment, and another week of inter-
minable length dragged itself out like a life sentence.

One Sunday Penry knocked at the door of Cwmbach farmhouse.

"There he is," cried Megan, springing up.

She had been trying for hours to hide the fact that
she was on the alert for his approach. When her
mother looked at her with a smile and a sigh, she
hung her head, abashed.

"Come you on in, boy," her father called, and
Penry strode into the kitchen.

His manner was preoccupied. He neither laughed

nor boasted during dinner. The old people noticed nothing amiss, since he spoke with his usual candour when they asked him any question. Only Megan, who knew every fleet change of expression in his eyes, grew troubled. Watching him anxiously, she pushed away her food untouched. His glance avoided hers, until, as they rose from table, she laid her hand timidly on his wrist. She had never touched him before, and she withdrew her fingers as though the contact had burnt them. He stood rooted, gazing down at her. She could have fainted, fearing that he was about to take her in his arms before them all. For an instant he seemed to struggle with himself whilst she held her timid breath. Then, turning away with a frown, he addressed the others.

"I have been thinkin'. 'Tis like this. A boy as is the youngest o' five and livin' at home like I am, he isn't gettin' no manner o' chance to earn money—not even gettin' the wages of a workin' man, he isn't." He stared at the stone-flagged floor between his feet. "Workin' like that for twenty or thirty years maybe, and left with nothin' after."

Megan's father nodded. "Yes, yes. When there is more nor one or two sons, 'tis better for the younger ones to get out o' the nest."

"Well, now, I am havin' an uncle in Australia," Penry resumed gloomily, and Megan's eyes grew wide with fear. "Writin' to mother he was some years ago, and sayin' 'send you out one o' the lumpers, and

447

I'll see as he shall do well'." Megan's lips parted, but
no sound came from them. "I've a mind to go out to
my uncle," Penry announced, his tone challenging
anyone to stop him. Megan leant for support against
the dresser and became aware that the kitchen had
grown dark. The speech of her parents and brother
had a muffled sound as though it came from a long
way off. They were agreeing with Penry, but she
could scarcely make out what they said. Her life
seemed to be coming to an end. She had turned so
white that at last her mother noticed it.

"Whatever's on you, fach?" she cried, and all eyes
were turned on the girl where she stood, still as a
figure of stone.

"I am all right," Megan murmured, "only—'tis
terrible cold in here."

She moved unsteadily towards the door and went
out into the pale sunshine of early spring that turned
to a sad yellow the stretch of sward before the house.
The smell of moist earth and the sound of many
streams were in the air. The hills, that had been
brown and sombre all the winter through, were beginning to grow green, except where a patch of snow
still lingered in a hollow. Everything was awakening
to new life. Yet Megan felt as though her blood were
ebbing away.

After a while she heard her mother's voice calling
from the small window overhead. " 'Tis time to get
ready for chapel."

"I am not going," she answered, and remained motionless, staring at the wide sweep of open hillside across the valley. From the time she was a little child, the vastness of the hills had brought her comfort in distress. At this moment she could not endure to have them shut out from her sight. So she stayed while the little group of black-clad figures came out of the house, and made their way soberly across the valley.

When the landscape was once more empty, and the silence of the hills unbroken but for the voices of wind and waterfall, Penry also came out of the house, and laid his hand on Megan's shoulder. She started and, turning round, looked up at him with eyes full of suffering. He was gazing at her as he had done when she touched his arm in the kitchen, and her heart began to beat again violently.

"Why are you goin' away?" she made bold to whisper, with a catch in her throat.

"Because it was comin' to me, sudden like, when last I seed you, that I couldn't live no more without you."

She gave a sob of joy and wonder. "But you are goin' away from me where I 'ont never see you."

"Only to make a home for you there, Megan fach," he answered, and his eyes travelled caressingly over her face, the silky lustrous brown hair around it, the curves of her slender neck. Then, because he could find no words to say, he picked her up in his arms, and carried her into the house. There he set her on his knee. She sat very still for a long while, with her head drooped on his shoulder. Fear and suffering no longer existed for her; nor did time. In a moment she had been raised from the depths of despair to giddy heights of happiness beyond belief. The upward flight had left her weak, and with a queer sensation of dizziness. She clung silently to Penry, and listened to the throbbing of his heart close to her own. The strength of his muscle-hard arms around her was consoling. They gave her a sense of safety. Nothing, she fancied in this hour of ecstasy, could ever take her from him. She was profoundly content.

After a while, his hand stole up to her small chin and raised her face gently to his. Their lips had never met before. They did not soon part.

Penry came again to Cwmbach oftener than hitherto; and, since the young people were from henceforth admitted to be "courting", they were allowed to sit up together, according to custom, long after the rest of the household had gone to bed. They sat hand in hand in the glow of a peat fire, and talked in whispers. What they said would have conveyed nothing to anyone else, for they had much to tell which neither could put into words. They looked, sighed, smiled and kissed. Sometimes they laughed low, and sometimes they clung together throughout a long silence. They understood each other perfectly. Their love filled the world for them. There was no serpent in their Eden. Even the thought of the impending parting did not greatly dismay them—they passed it over, and looked forward already to the time when they should meet again and be always together. They believed that such love as theirs must needs triumph over poverty, and that neither time nor distance could make it grow dim. Talking thus, they would throw more peat on the embers. The fire would leap up and the light of it flicker on the low ceiling. Wicked little shadows would run hither and thither, as if mocking the lovers and their happy fancies. But they did not heed—being too glad for fear, until their eyelids grew swollen for lack of sleep and dawn looked in upon them, ghostly grey.

"Cold," Penry would say with a sudden shiver. "Is it?" Megan would ask. "I wasn't noticin'."

It was not until the autumn, when Penry had gone away, that Megan began to realize the meaning of that dread word "parted". Then her longing to see him and to hear his voice became a physical torment, and she would lie awake at night struggling with her sobs, telling herself in vain that this separation was but for a little time.

The winter set in pitiless. For months the pass at the top of the valley was snowbound, and even the pious few who attended Alpha chapel in lonely Cwm-bach were kept from their devotions. Megan went about her household duties day by day, silent and subdued, finding the weeks and months of waiting, which were to have sped by so swiftly, intolerably long. She wrote to Penry every Saturday night; but letter-writing was to her a labour, exceedingly slow and toilsome; and when the ill-spelt letters, that had cost such pains, were returned to her long after, with "Not known at this address" scrawled on them, she abandoned herself to despair. It seemed as though she would never hear from Penry, never be able to reach him, now that the unknown had closed upon him. She tormented herself with the thought that he had died on the voyage out; until at last, almost a year after he had gone away, she received his first letter. It was despondent in tone, but still she hugged it to her as evidence that he was still alive, and not irrevocably lost to her.

He had arrived in Australia, so he wrote, to find that his uncle was dead, and that no work was to be obtained in that locality. There had been a succession of droughts, and prospects were very bad; still, he had managed, after great difficulty, to find temporary employment on a sheep ranch. He feared that making a home for his Megan would prove a longer business than they had thought, but, if she would wait for him, he would never give up the struggle.

Wait for him? What else could he fancy there was for her to do? What was she living for but the time when they should meet again? She laughed at him for imagining that she could ever give any other man a thought. She carried his letter about inside her bodice, and slept with it under her pillow, until it was tattered and crumpled. Then, lest she should wear it out altogether, she put it away in the oak chest where she kept the coloured daguerreotype he had sent her of himself before he sailed from Liverpool. It was her most cherished possession, too well beloved to be exposed; to be taken out and looked at only by lamplight and in secret.

Another year went by, and another; and after that, in her loneliness and disappointment, Megan lost count of the seasons that divided her from her lover, and, at length, even from hope. She heard from him at rare intervals. Now he was doing well, and would soon have earned enough to come and fetch her. Now another drought had ruined his employer, and he was again cast on the world, searching for work, whilst his precious store of savings, that meant happiness for them both, dwindled.

He had been gone seven years when she received a short, barely legible letter, written in pencil, much blurred, and in a laboured, childish hand. Luck was against him. She must wait for him no longer. He had been almost starving for the last month, rather than break into the store of money he had laid by. He had enough to come and fetch her now, but where was the good in bringing her out to a country in which he had no home to offer her? Every enterprise he touched failed. He had begun to think that he brought ill-fortune with him wherever he went. "Like Jonah in the Bible," he wrote. "I won't never bring you, my love, to ruin, you may be sure. So better think of me as dead." There followed a cross and his signature.

This was the last letter she ever received from him. With tears dropping on to the paper, she wrote to tell him that she would never give him up. The pathetic smudged little missive was returned unopened. He had apparently gone away, leaving no address, no indication of his whereabouts. She heard from him no more. She could not hope to obtain news of him, for she knew no one in that far-distant country. He was now utterly lost to her, as though he had passed over to another world. "Indeed most likely the boy is dead," her parents told her, and at last she came to believe that it was so.

It was then that the new minister came to Alpha chapel. He was unmarried, and lived alone with the deaf caretaker in the barnacle cottage clinging to the bleak wall of his house of prayer. The fame of his preaching spread abroad, and people came from far over the hills to be denounced and edified by him.

He was not old; nor did he look young. His aspect was austerely virginal, for he was tall and very thin, with a pale face, and black eyes, in which burned fanatical fire. A spiritual descendant of Savonarola, he loathed the sins of humanity, and saw terrible visions of an avenging God. He would have made a "bonfire of vanities" and condemned to the flames

whatever ministered to the gaiety of life. Religion
and self-denial were to him inseparable. He was
ready, in the name of his faith, to endure torture or
to inflict it. Yet even he was moved to pity by the
sight of Megan's pale face. He learned her story
from the lips of her parents, at whose house he became a frequent visitor. She herself never spoke to
him of her sorrow until one day he met her coming
home from market alone, and laid his lean hand on
her shoulder.

"My sister," he said abruptly, "I know why you
are sad." "Oh," she cried, flushing, "I do hope as I
don't let everyone see how 'tis with me. I am tryin'
not to hurt others by the sight o' my sorrow. Indeed
and I am." "Yes, yes," he answered, looking into
her eyes. "I know. You endeavour to be brave; but
you cannot always succeed, is that not so?" She
nodded. "Do you know why?" he resumed. "Because
you are proud."

She stared at him, astonished.

"Proud," he repeated. "And spiritual pride is sinful. In your secret arrogance, you strive to bear the
burden of your grief alone." He had intended to
preach her a sermon on the duty of casting her care
upon the Redeemer, but the grandiloquent words,
long premeditated, died on his lips. He found himself saying instead, quite simply: "Won't you make a
friend of me, and tell me all about it?"

She was too overwhelmed to reply; so he took the

market basket out of her hands, saying as he did so: "I can carry this home for you, at any rate."

Lonely and unused to kindness as she was, she felt her eyes smart with tears of gratitude. "You are wonderful good to me," she murmured, "and you such a great preacher too."

"We are all alike sinners in the sight of God," he answered, resuming once more the lofty tone that became his calling.

The following Sunday, Rees Lloyd preached upon the Christian virtue of resignation. His thin fingers strayed along the edge of the pulpit, as though they groped for something to hold fast. His gaze seemed to pierce through the white-washed wall on which it rested, as if beyond it he beheld a sublime vision. He was in a gentler mood than usual. No longer concerned with death and judgment and the vengeance of an Old Testament Deity, but full of pity for the afflicted. "Blessed are they that mourn for they shall be comforted," he quoted, and again: "It is good for me that I have been in trouble; that I may learn Thy statutes." "Without suffering", he cried, "there is no understanding; be not rebellious then, but resign yourselves to the hand of the Lord, knowing that whom He loveth he chasteneth, that His loved ones may be refined as is gold by the fiery furnace."

The black-clad congregation sat spellbound, listening to the vibrations of the preacher's voice as it rose to a shout or sank to a penetrating whisper.

Down the weather-beaten face of an old man, who had lost his wife and child, tears fell. A girl, who had crept into the back of the building, huddled up in a shawl, shrinking from the contemptuous glances of her respectable neighbours, sobbed unrestrainedly. All who had suffered loss and grief were moved by the sermon. But Megan was afraid, knowing that this eloquence was directed towards herself.

"Did you like what I said to-day?" the preacher asked her that evening when he came to Cwmbach farm. "Yes, indeed," she answered, "it was beautiful." "Oh," he said impatiently, "but was it *helpful?*"

They were standing beside the hearth in the kitchen, apart from the others, who were busy at the supper table. Megan gave him a look at once timid and thankful.

"Yes," she breathed, scarcely above a whisper, "it do help me somethin' wonderful to know as you are feelin' for me."

"I would give my life to help you," he whispered back, with such fierce intensity that she shivered and hung her head. "Look at me," he commanded in a low tone, but she dared not raise her eyes to his.

"Supper is ready," her mother announced, and Megan turned away quickly with a breath of relief. She could not define her attitude towards Rees Lloyd, his absorption in the things of the spirit, his devotion to his faith, the stirring tones of his voice, the penetrating gaze of his eyes, fascinated her; yet she feared him personally, and was never at ease in his presence. When he was near her she would have been glad to escape; but because he, of all souls in this indifferent world, had offered her his sympathy, she felt the need of him when he was gone. Her hopeless love for Penry was in no way abated; but daily the minister took a larger share in her thoughts.

Soon after this, the caretaker of Alpha chapel died. The elders who gathered together at the funeral were concerned as to what should be done. It was not easy to find anyone who, for the pittance so poor a community could offer, would live alone in the valley where was only one other dwelling. "If only the preacher were married," one of them said, "he and his wife could have the house by the chapel for theirselves."

"Yes, yes," they all agreed. " 'Tis pity as he isn't married to a tidy 'oman as 'ould look after the place for us."

When Rees Lloyd came to Cwmbach farm that night, Megan's father repeated to him what the elders had said. They were sitting round the kitchen table in a circle of light thrown down by a heavily shaded lamp. The rest of the room, with its low raftered ceiling and stone-flagged floor, was in semi-darkness; only a red glow shone from the hearth and was reflected in the gleaming eyes of cats that slunk about in the shadows. All the brightness in the room was concentrated on the open pages of the Bible, which lay on the table beneath the lamp. Rees Lloyd, with his hand resting upon the book, arose. His head and shoulders disappeared in the twilight above the lamp. His pale face was still visible, ghostly, with eyes shining in the gloom. He remained thus whilst the grandfather clock ticked through a whole minute, and all the while he looked fixedly at Megan. The old people sat in hushed expectancy, with faces upturned; but their daughter kept her gaze on the Bible and the taut hand clenched in the harsh light upon its sacred pages. She dared not look Rees Lloyd in the face. At length he turned his burning glance on her parents.

"Behold your daughter," he said, in slow deliberate tones. "This is the Lord's call to her." "No, no," she cried, starting to her feet, "not that." "Yes," he persisted, "the Lord has need of you for His service. You cannot deny His call."

She looked about her distractedly, seeking a way of escape. The others remained awestruck, listening to his voice that compelled them in the darkness.

"Here is your appointed task in life," it continued. "I am a minister of the Most High; I need your help, and in helping me you will serve Him also. He is calling to you, Megan, to forget yourself and your personal sorrow; to live only for others, and for His greater honour and glory." She made no reply. "God is calling to you," cried the voice, louder and more insistent than before: "He is calling to you through me, because it shall be given to me to lead your wandering soul into the safety of His fold. Will you not come?"

She turned away into the darkness, and hid her face in her hands. "Answer," he commanded. "I do want to serve God," she whispered at last, "but indeed, indeed, I can never be your wife." "Are you mad, gal?" cried the old people both together. For answer she wrung her hands. Then the voice from the darkness spoke to her more gently.

"I know what you are thinking of, Megan. You have not forgotten your first love." She inclined her head. "But I have need of you," cried the voice, vibrating with passionate appeal. "I love you." And after a tense silence, imploringly—"Will you not come?"

Slowly, reluctantly, as if drawn towards him against her will, she stole into the circle of lamplight, and placed her cold hand in his upon the Bible.

When they were married she crossed the narrow valley from her old home to her new. There she took up the work of the chapel caretaker, and cooked the minister's meals, and kept his cottage in order, waiting on him day by day. He believed that in doing this she was serving God; and he made her also believe it. Therefore she was content with her lot, and her husband in his possession of her. He had not known carnal love before, and he abandoned himself to it, indifferent to the feelings of the woman who submitted herself to his caresses.

So the weeks wore by, each like the last, marked by Sundays when up the valley and down over the pass the faithful came to worship, black as rooks. When they were gathered together in chapel, they sang their melancholy hymns, set to music in the minor key, older than Christianity, old almost as the race; and Rees Lloyd thundered at them from his high pulpit.

After the people had gone away, the shadow of the western hill stole across the emptied valley, and every trace of the congregation was gone. It seemed to Megan that with the next Sunday might come a fresh generation, for a week and an age were as one to the mountains that had looked down unmoved on the passing of one race after another.

To her husband she did not tell these fancies. It would have been difficult for her to put them into words, though as a girl she had managed to convey all she felt to Penry. But he and she had been as children together, holding hands on the threshold of a darkened room, peering awestruck into the unknown. Rees Lloyd, on the contrary, appeared to her to possess vast learning, gained from his score of theological books, which she dusted reverently every day. His positive assertion and ease of self-explanation made it almost impossible for her to converse with him at all. She spoke to him always with hesitation, struggling to translate her thoughts into the intricacies of language—a language seldom used by the people around her except to communicate the needs of daily life. To have contradicted any of her husband's dogmatic pronouncements would have been open heresy, and she dared be a heretic only in secret. She admired him. She sat demurely listening to his eloquence Sunday after Sunday, aware that his knowledge of many matters was as great as was her ignorance. Yet in the wisdom of her humility, she guessed that he was well instructed rather than wise. His wrath against sinners made her sigh. For his famished lusting after her body she felt a shrinking pity.

He had gone one day to preach at a distant chapel. She stood with arms folded on the stone wall before their home, and mused upon the strangeness of their marriage. Her gaze was on a point where, at a bend in the valley, the road was lost to sight. Something about that lonely road, leading away into a world she had never seen, fascinated her. She often stood thus, staring. To-day she felt unable to take her eyes off it, though it was time she locked up the house and crossed over the stream to her former home. Whenever her husband was away, she returned to Cwmbach farm "for company"; but this evening the profound stillness held her entranced. As she lingered in the mellow golden sunlight, a speck appeared upon the road and grew presently into the figure of a man. When he had come closer, she saw that he was unusually tall, and was swinging along at a great pace. He carried a stick in one hand, and a bundle slung over his shoulder. He drew near rapidly, and she noticed that he wore no hat and that his fair hair and beard glistened like honey in the sun. Her curiosity was awake now, for a stranger was seldom seen in the Cwm. She leant over the wall, intently watching his approach. As he came closer still, she could see that his face was sunburnt, making his blue eyes appear startlingly light; they were fixed upon her. Something stirred within her breast, as though her heart, long dormant, had awakened, and begun once more hotly to beat. The rugged strength of this strange man's features was familiar. The upward tilt of the chin, though hidden by a luxuriant beard, recalled a favourite pose of *someone* whose face she had once known——someone——who was it? The next instant the ground beneath her feet seemed to have given way.

"Did you ever dream as you were fallin' off of a tremendjous high place?" she asked me when she was describing the sensations of that moment. "That's how I was feelin', and I wasn't wakin' up neither, as you are doin' after a bad dream. I seemed to go on fallin' and fallin' for a long while, and then to hang in the air, as if there wasn't nothin' below me nor above, nor on either side. It was the sound of his voice as brought me back to myself, at last—— the same voice, strong and deep as ever, not changed even so much as his face was. Only I was havin' a terrible feelin' as if I was listenin' to the dead; and I was tryin' to pray—'God help me, God help me'. But there didn't seem to be a God no longer, seein' as *this* had happened."

She sat twisting her fingers together when she told me this. "What did *he* say to you?" I asked at last, caressing her knee. " 'Megan,' he was sayin', coming close up against the other side o' the wall, 'are you rememberin' me?' I was leanin' against the wall, my strength havin' gone clean from me, and lookin' up into his face. I knowed it well, every line of it. It seemed 'twas only yesterday as he'd gone away—only there was more power in his face like, and lines round his eyes, as wasn't there before. Very thin and strong it looked, not so round and boyish; but hand-somer nor ever. I wasn't answerin' him for a while, but was lettin' my eyes have their fill of what they'd been weepin' for many a long year. When I could find my voice, I was answerin': 'I am rememberin' you right enough—*Diar Anwl*, could I ever forget you?'

" 'You *did* forget me, whatever,' says he, 'when you married another man. They told me down in Pontnoyadd how 'twas; but I 'ouldn't believe them, no, not one of 'em, till I saw it with my own eyes.' He was lookin' at the ring on my hand, as I held by the wall for the weakness in my knees. I looked down at it too, and I turned as cold as if I'd been standin' on top o' the hills in a bitter winter. I couldn't speak for a long while after, to tell him how I comed to get married; but we was lookin' at each other all the time, quite still, and frightened like, same as people that had seen a corpse candle."

She could not tell me, but I knew what turmoil of emotions assailed her during this silence that seemed to her tormented soul to last through an eternity. For she knew, as she looked upon Penry, that there was the man who had possessed her heart entirely from the day on which she had first set eyes on him; and that she had no love for her husband, with whom she must live out her days to the end. She looked back on her own passive calm of a few moments ago, as though she were looking across a gulf of time, knowing that the relative contentment of her first months of married life could never again be hers. *He* had returned. He would go away, no doubt, suddenly as he had come, and she would most likely never see him in this world again. But in these threatened moments, as she stood scrutinizing his face, the ecstasy and passion of first love, the yearning of years of hope deferred reawakened within her; and she knew that never for an instant could she forget him again. The memory of her promise to "love, honour and obey" another man tormented her. Honour and obey—yes, she could continue to do that, but *love*—was it possible to keep such a promise? Was it right to force anyone to make it? Could she ever again suffer the caresses of Rees Lloyd? At the thought of them she sickened. The future appeared to her so unbearable that she prayed God to take pity on her and let her die, now, whilst she stood looking up at the man whom she adored. But God was without mercy, since He had suffered her to betray Penry's trust. Why had she received no warning that he was yet alive? Why had she not waited for him just a few months more? Wherein had they both deserved this cruel suffering? Was there no compassion, no justice even, in the universe?

I do not know to what depths her soul went down during that long silence. She spoke to me of it once only, and then in broken sentences. She was never quite at home in English, and there are feelings too deep for any language to convey. It was forty years afterwards that she related to me this episode in her life, but as I looked up into those quiet deep-set eyes of hers, I saw such a haunting of anguish that I turned away.

At last they began to talk. Simply, in a few words, they told each other what had happened. Soon after Penry had written her the last letter she received, he had succeeded in finding work with a man who paid him good wages and treated him as a friend. He still had those cherished savings of his. Grown reckless with ill-fortune, he sank them all in a speculation into which he and his employer entered together. To his delight and astonishment, the concern prospered. Soon he had doubled his small hoard and wrote to tell Megan that a turn had come in the tide of his affairs, that he would be home within the year to fetch her. That letter, which should have reached her just before her marriage, miscarried.

"Duw, Duw," she cried, wringing her hands, "why was I never gettin' it? I didn't hear from you, *diar anwl*, and the years was passin' by, and they was all tellin' me as you were dead."

"I do wish as I had died out there," he answered, "I can't go back to the place where I've made a home for you; nor I can't bear to stay here where you are livin' as another man's wife." "What will you be doin', then?" she asked him. " 'Deed and I don't know," he answered wearily. "Maybe as I 'on't be livin' long."

It was then that she clasped his hand in hers. At the contact, fire seemed to run through her veins. Another silence fell between them, but this time there was a different look in their eyes. She forgot all her misery, her dread of the future. She lived exultantly in the present.

A moment, or an hour, may have passed; and then Penry leant across the wall, and taking her face between his hands, he kissed her on the lips.

She did not remember when he let her go, nor if any more was said between them. I do not think that they spoke again. It never seems to have entered their heads to go away together. She had married Rees Lloyd, and was bound.

How he left her, Megan could never recall. When she regained full consciousness, after the delirium of that kiss, he was already a long way off, striding up the valley towards the pass. She was still standing where he had found her, leaning against the inside of her little garden wall. Nothing had changed visibly, except the shadow of the western hill, which now lay across the Cwm. As Penry disappeared from sight, the last glint of sunlight vanished from the tops of the hills.

Not until many hours later did Megan re-enter her house. She remained standing motionless until it became too dark to trace the white line of road in its ascent of the distant pass. Even then she stayed on, staring into the deepening gloom. She was not aware as yet of being acutely miserable. The magnitude of the blow she had received had stunned her, and left her unable to act, or even to think.

Perhaps she would have remained like this all night, had not her parents sent their servant girl to enquire why she had not come to supper. "I 'on't be comin' to-night," she managed to say, when she became conscious that someone was addressing her. " 'On't you be afraid to sleep here alone?" the girl asked. "No," she answered, "I'm not afraid of anything as can happen to me — now." It was the sound of a human voice, reminding her of a life which must be resumed, that awoke her from her lethargy.

When she was alone once more, she began to pace up and down in the darkness, sobbing inconsolably like a child. Nothing broke the silence of the hills, that loomed above her, black, on either side, but the pitiful sound of her crying, and the faint sighing of the night wind.

For hours she walked to and fro, and cried, and wrung her hands. When dawn was turning the sky to a chill grey, she dragged herself into the house, and up the stairs, and fell, exhausted by suffering, on to the bed. She must have fallen asleep immediately, and have stayed in the drugged slumber of worn-out grief, for it was noon when she was awakened by her husband and her mother.

Rees Lloyd had called for his wife at Cwmbach farm that morning; but she was not there. "There's odd she was last night, too," the servant girl had told him, "like as if she's *seen* something." He had turned to his mother-in-law anxiously and asked her to come over at once to his home with him. They set off together in haste, fearing that Megan might have been taken ill. On their way across the valley they encountered the postman, who passed Cwmbach twice a week on his rounds. He was excited, and shouted to them from a distance. "Have you seen Penry Price, son of Rhosferig as used to be?" Megan's mother stared aghast. "The Lord forbid," she cried. "Isn't he dead this long while?" "Nor, nor," answered the postman, coming up to them, triumphant

469

that he should be the bearer of sensational tidings. "Alive he is, and they do tell me as he was in Pont-noyadd yesterday. The folks there was tellin' him as your gal was married to Mr. Lloyd here, but he 'ouldn't believe it. 'Megan's not one to forget,' says he, so he was comin' up by here to see for hisself." "Coming here?" Rees Lloyd interrupted. "Yes, yes," the postman affirmed. "Up this road he did come sure. John Jones as was ploughin' close by seed a great tall man passin' by in the afternoon. Findin' out his mistake he was, no doubt," the postman added, grinning at the old woman. "Your gal's done a deal better for herself by marryin' a wonderful gifted preacher like Mr. Lloyd here. She's not havin' no cause to look back, she's——" But Rees Lloyd waited to hear no more. He seized his mother-in-law by the arm, and hurried her on towards his cottage. She stole a glance at his white face and thin tight lips, and was so much alarmed that she began to wail: "Duw, Duw, why has Penry come back to trouble us all?" Rees Lloyd made no reply, but jealousy and fear tormented him, and he hastened his pace, dragging the breathless whimpering old woman after him. When they reached the house, he flung open the door which he found ajar, and called in a harsh voice: "Megan, Megan, where are you?" There was no answer and, dreading to find her gone, he rushed upstairs, and burst into the bedroom.

There he found her, fully dressed, but with her

hair dishevelled, lying asleep upon the bed with shadows under her closed eyes. The lids were swollen with much crying. The fit of murderous jealousy that had possessed him when he heard of her sweetheart's return left him as suddenly as it had come. "Megan fach, poor Megan fach," he whispered, and her mother, who had followed him into the room, echoed "Poor Megan fach, she must have seen him; but indeed," she added, "Megan's allus been an honest gal, and she 'on't think no more about him, now that she's married to you; only do you be gentle with her, Rees bach." "I'll be gentle," he promised, struggling to quell another pang of jealousy at the thought that his wife should have been so deeply affected by the return of Penry.

At that moment Megan opened her eyes. At first she was only vaguely conscious of great unhappiness; then, as her mother began to talk, she recalled what had happened the night before, and turning her eyes away from her husband, she hid her face in the pillow. "I do wish as I might die," she thought. She lay there too unutterably weary and miserable to move; whilst Rees Lloyd stood watching her, with hatred and pity, love, desire, and jealousy coursing each other through his tortured being. The old woman rambled on, incessantly repeating the phrases about duty and the will of God which she had heard so often in chapel; and outside the little window of the darkened room, the autumn sunshine gilded the hills, and the larks and meadow pipits soared up singing joyfully into a blue sky.

"Let me be," Megan pleaded at last, "just for a little while." At length they left her alone. Later in the day her husband brought her a cupful of something to drink, liquid which might perhaps have been tea, though it had no flavour. He forced it between her lips. She shrank from physical contact with him; but this act of kindness on his part gave her a sort of desperate courage to go on living.

When he left the room, she rose unsteadily, and began to wash her tear-stained face and arrange her disordered hair. It surprised her to find how easily these things could be done, mechanically, whilst the spirit was far away. Having set the bedroom to rights, with the precision of a machine, she went downstairs, and began, as though nothing unusual had occurred, to cook her husband's supper. He asked her no questions, but his sombre eyes followed her wherever she went, with the devotion and suspicion of an ill-treated, hungry dog.

In the weeks that followed, she often saw this expression in his gaze, invariably fixed upon her; and she grew increasingly to pity the man of whom formerly she had been afraid. In pitying him she found some solace from her grief. So she picked up the broken thread of her life, and was busy as ever about the house and the chapel, all day long. Only at night when her husband had fallen asleep was she able to abandon herself to her sorrow.

There came a day when Rees Lloyd was sitting moodily before the fire with a book of sermons lying unread on his knee. Megan had grown so thin that he had sent her to Pontnoyadd to see the doctor. As he awaited her return, forebodings of disaster assailed him. There had always been something elusive about his wife, he reflected bitterly. Even before the accursed return of Penry Price, she had never seemed wholly to belong to himself. Now perhaps she would cheat him altogether by dying, daring to die for love of another man! It was unjust, he swore, clenching his hands in impotent anger. She had only set her eyes on this interloper once since he left her eight or ten years ago. "Whilst I," cried Rees Lloyd to himself, "I am close to her day and night, watching over her, ready to spend all I have on her, if only she would love me as I love her." And then he added threateningly: "And I am her lawful husband. I have a *right* to her affection." It appeared to him dishonest of her to pine away as she was doing, for this Penry—a vagabond, with no claim on her affection.

Rees Lloyd angrily closed his book. He could not read. When Megan was not there to distract him in person, her sorrowful face haunted his imagination. She, who in the early days of their marriage had quenched his desire when need be, and at other times occupied a safe place in the background of his

473

thoughts, had, through this unforeseen catastrophe, forced herself into his every thought and dream, awake or sleeping. He could no longer concentrate his attention upon his preaching or his prayers. He had chosen her for his helpmate; it was her wifely duty to succour and soothe him, that he might the better serve God. Now that she came between him and his devotion she was beginning to assume the aspect of a temptation sent him by the Devil.

He rose and was frantically pacing up and down the little kitchen, trying to banish her image, when she herself came softly into the room. He turned on her his black eyes full of lustful hostility. For answer she smiled at him, yet he fancied hardly so much *at* him as *through* him, as though she were smiling at another whom she saw in his place. He scowled, suffering from a sense of unreality, wishing that she might fade away, if only he could be released thus from the nightmare in which he had been living. But she laid her hand on his shoulder. "I am goin' to have a child," she announced quietly.

For a moment he was too greatly surprised and overjoyed to speak. Then he took her in his arms and triumphantly kissed her. "Now you will be mine," he said, "wholly mine." She made no reply. "When you are the mother of my child, Megan fach, you will learn to care for *me* only," he assured her.

"You are very kind to me," she murmured, absently. She was thinking of the child she might

474

have borne, had she been the wife of Penry—blue-eyed and golden haired, splendid to look upon, like himself; and she fancied that she could hear again the infectious happy laugh she remembered so well from her girlhood.

The days passed monotonously, and Megan went about her work as before. But now she wore a mysterious smile, as if she were picturing to herself something which greatly pleased her. She had set herself, scarcely conscious of what she was doing, to form the child of her dreams. Throughout her waking hours she dwelt on her memories of Penry. She rehearsed every word he had spoken to her; she recalled every characteristic gesture, every tone of his voice. They were all stored up in her heart, these precious things. The years had but overlaid them with the dust of lesser matters. When she came to search them out once more, scenes and incidents of her early courtship became distinct again, as on the day when they took place. Her picture gallery of beloved memories grew more vivid as her time drew near.

When her household work was finished, she would put a chair outside the cottage, close to the wall on which she had leant when Penry had returned. She knew the exact spot on which their hands had met; and there, evening by evening in the winter's dusk, she rested her clasped hands, as she sat picturing that last meeting in all its details. Sometimes she fancied even that she felt his parting kiss on her lips. Then, for a long while, she would sit motionless in silent ecstasy, with her eyes closed.

When she had married, she had put away the little coloured daguerreotype of Penry with her other relics of him. She had not thought it right to cherish, yet lacked the heart to destroy them. Now she brought out his portrait, and, carrying it about in her pocket, looked at it secretly a hundred times a day.

Her husband, unsuspecting, watched her covertly, and rejoiced that she should have become, it seemed, not merely content, but cheerful. He was considerate to her in a clumsy fashion. She, in return, was in all things a dutiful, submissive wife. In all things, that is, but her thoughts. These she kept to herself, as the silent hills about Cwmbach have kept the secrets of ten thousand years.

Rees Lloyd and all his kith and kin were swarthy of skin, dark-haired, black-eyed, with the long narrow skulls of a race older even than the Celt. Megan's hair was nut-brown, smooth and silky to touch. Her eyes were the colour of the peat streams that ran down her native hillsides, neither altogether brown, nor green, nor amber, but each in turn, according to the light in which you saw them. The child that was born to these two some nine months after the return of Penry was blue-eyed and had a crop of close yellow curls all over his head. When Megan's mother took the crumpled scrap of flesh out of the doctor's hands, she stared at him with grave misgiving; after which she hastened to tell her son-in-law that his firstborn "favoured" a maternal great-grandfather, the only one of her family whom she could recollect to have had blue eyes. She assured the neighbours that the likeness was remarkable. As the ancestor in question had been dead and buried for half a century, they could not contradict her. Nevertheless, the matrons who went to see Megan's baby whispered together about it as they came out of chapel.

Rees Lloyd had a puzzled, incredulous way of staring at the infant; and Megan from the moment when he was put into her arms, as she lay half dead with pain and exhaustion, loved him idolatrously. She would sit for hours in silent adoration of the child in her lap.

Had Rees Lloyd been a Catholic, he might have accepted this miracle, which filled his wife with glad devotion, and have been content to play the role of meek Saint Joseph. But being a Calvinistic Methodist, he indulged in no specially tender sentiment about the Holy Family. Moreover, he believed in no miracles excepting those recorded in the Bible. Such things had happened once; this he was constrained to believe on Divine Authority; but that nothing miraculous could possibly occur nowadays, his common sense assured him.

It was not long before rumours of what was being said by his congregation reached his ears, and he began to brood over the shameful suspicion that tarnished his home. He sat watching his wife in her contemplation of the child, and struggled to put all thought of the slander from him as unworthy. He had, however, been trained in the school of thought which holds the human heart to be full of wickedness and guile; and he was afraid of his own more generous instincts. He dared not trust the evidence of his eyes, or believe in the innocence of a possible sinner merely because she had every appearance of innocence. Megan's untroubled manner towards him, and her frank steadfast gaze, became at last, to his fevered imagination, proofs of her deceitfulness. He said not a word to her of this; but he began to preach sermons more threatening than any of his former ones on the need for repentance and of public confession. On the deadly sin of adultery he waxed especially eloquent, and the denunciation of those who transgressed the seventh commandment became his obsession. So great was his fervour and eloquence that women sobbed aloud, and men rose to confess to fornication before an hysterically excited congregation. Strange things came to light in Alpha chapel. The impressionable young were overwrought; the elders shook their heads. Weak brethren, they declared, committed sins in order to enjoy the notoriety of penitence. Some were even so wicked as to invent sins which they had not committed. But though sober-minded persons disapproved, the chapel collections increased, the groaning and crying of "Amen" rose louder, and

Rees Lloyd thundered ever more savagely his terrible threats of death and judgment and everlasting fire.

Only the woman at whom all this fury was directed, who dominated his every thought, who filled his being with impotent rage, sat beneath his pulpit unmoved and placid, as if in her childlike innocence, above the storm of his anger, she heard the calm music of celestial things.

When the child, whom they had christened Ifor, was two years old, Megan gave birth to another son. He was as swarthy as a gipsy. His mother gave him the same dutiful care which she paid to his father. She spared herself no trouble in the service of these two. Nothing was lacking to them but the warmth of her love. That was all for her firstborn, and Rees Lloyd hated her daily more and more.

He found her one day, seated beside the kitchen fire, giving her breast to the black-eyed baby in her arms. He stood staring down at her in a gloomy reverie, when the sound of Ifor's crying reached their ears from the walled-in space before the cottage. In an instant Megan was on her feet, and taking the baby from her breast, rolled it up hastily in a shawl and left it to whimper in its cradle, whilst she hurried out to comfort her loved one.

A gust of fury shook Rees Lloyd. He followed his wife out through the doorway, and the sight of her holding the golden-haired child in her arms drove him to the verge of madness. "Put down that bastard," he shouted at her, "put it down, or I'll kill the both of you."

She gave him a terror-stricken look, but clung closer to the child. "Do you hear me?" he cried hoarsely. "You will drive me to murder, flaunting your shame before me as you do!"

"It isn't true," she said in a low voice, facing him unflinchingly. For a moment he towered over her, clencing and unclenching his hands as though he would strangle her. Then he turned abruptly away, and strode off bareheaded into the hills. Megan crouched down upon the doorstep with Ifor folded close to her heart; and the wailing of the neglected baby rose unheeded from the house.

When Rees Lloyd returned home that evening after hours of prayer and wrestling with himself in the solitude of the mountains, he came up to Megan and laid his hand on her shoulder. "I will not blame you," he said, in a voice from which all the life was gone. "God knows, we are all miserable sinners, and in danger of hell fire; yet the worst of us may be saved, at the last, by repentance. Confess your sin, and I will forgive you, as I hope myself for pardon."

"I am not guilty of what you do think," she answered resolutely.

He turned away from her sharply with a gesture of despair. She followed him across the room, moved to compassion by the sight of his suffering. "Maybe I have done wrong," she murmured, "without

knowin' as I did it." He turned and looked at her
with revived hope, waiting for her confession. "But
if I sinned," she continued softly, " 'twas only in
thought. I have allus been keeping my marriage
vows, and actin' honest by you." "Look at the child,"
he interrupted her with renewed anger. " 'Tis the
child of my dreams," she whispered. He stared at
her uncomprehending, and turned away in disgust.

That night he said no more, but throughout the
years that followed he returned to the subject which
poisoned his mind, with reiterated demands for her
confession. "I am not guilty as you do think," was
all she would vouchsafe him, and he with growing
conviction would answer: "You lie!"

She bore him three more children, all dark as her
second, and she listened patiently to his cruel denunciations, his reproaches, his appeals to her to
repent. She suffered his moods of passionate desire,
and his violent reactions of loathing and self-con-
tempt; and the whole wealth of her love was poured
out upon Ifor and the memory of Penry. She was far
less unhappy than the man who lived to torment her
and himself; for her life was one of resignation, whilst
his was a self-created hell of hatred and suspicion.

When the imprisoned winds came howling down
the Cwm one night in December, a wizened old man
knocked at Rees Lloyd's door. Megan opened it a
crack, and a wreath of blue smoke and peat ash went
swirling round the kitchen. Rees Lloyd raised his

head, as he sat before the fire with a book on his knee. He listened to the whispering of his wife and the man who stood in the darkness outside. Unable to hear what they were saying, he felt an angry suspicion that they were discussing something of which they did not want him to know. He was ready to believe any ill of Megan, since she had so repeatedly lied to him.

Presently she closed the door on the storm and the firelit room grew warm and still once more. When she came back into the light he saw that her face was pallid and her lips were quivering. She stared past him with dilated eyes; then caught up a shawl and wrapped it round her shoulders. "I must be goin' to Graigfawr," she announced. "What!" he cried, "going up to the top of the valley on a night like this?" "Yes, yes, there is someone dyin' there as do want to see me."

He asked her no more questions, but let her go out alone into the darkness. Driven by an ill presentiment, he rose and followed her stealthily up the road that was just visible beneath his feet.

The wind came raging down between the hills on either side, and lashed the rain and icy sleet into his face. His hands grew numb with cold; at times he could scarcely draw his breath; still he struggled on, now and then catching a glimpse of the two figures ahead of him. Once the sound of their voices was blown back on the tempest. "Hurry, hurry," Megan cried in agonized appeal. "He may be dead afore we can get there." The old man shouted at her: "I am goin' as fast as I can. I can't do no more." The force of the wind had almost overmastered him and he staggered. She caught him by the arm, and dragged him along. She was endowed with superhuman strength, and would have fought her way through fire and water to the place where Penry lay dying.

Two shepherds had found him lying at the foot of a steep rock, off which he had stepped, blinded by the treacherous mist. They had carried him to a neighbouring farm; and there he lay in an upper room, barely conscious when Megan entered. His eyelids fluttered and lifted slowly at the sound of her voice. His blue eyes seemed to have turned black, for the pupils were dilated to take in the last of light. His face was corpse-pale; but at sight of her, a faint smile hovered over it. She knelt down beside the bed, and motioned away the farmer and his wife who had followed her in to the dimly lit room. They stole out on tiptoe. On the narrow landing at the top of the stairs they encountered the minister, with burning eyes fixed upon the door through which his wife had passed. No one had seen him enter the house, and they exclaimed in suprise and fear at sight of him.

"Go downstairs," he commanded, "and leave me be. I will keep watch here."

They obeyed him in awed silence; and when he was left alone in the dark, he crept close to the door

Q*

through which came a faint crack of light. He knelt down beside it, listening, with murder in his heart. Megan was speaking in low tones. She was telling the dying man the story of the miracle. Her husband could see her, through the crack in the door, kneeling beside the bed, her eyes fixed adoringly on the white face upon the pillow. The haggard man, with blood-stained bandages about his head, did not stir; but he was fully conscious now, and his wide eyes shone with fever's brilliance in the light of the single candle.

"How is it possible you comed to bear a child like me?" he murmured. His lips hardly moved. The words seemed to form themselves in the air. "We were never doin' no wrong, you and I, Megan."

"All things are possible to the spirit," she answered, "as we are readin' in the Bible. The old folk too, they are tellin' us stories of things they have seen as aren't of this 'orld. I am not laughin' at the old stories, as some are doin'. Folks as have had a bit of education, they aren't willin' to believe in anything as they can't understand. But the wisest are them as are full o' wonder still, like little children." And she added: "There is nothin' so strange but what it may come to pass." This was the summing up of her faith.

Penry nodded his assent, and there seemed to be no further need of speech between them.

They remained silent for a time, gazing at each other with comprehension in their eyes.

At length he murmured dreamily: "Your love is

484

wonderful strong, Megan. I do feel as 'twill go with me where I am goin', slippin'—away———"his voice became barely audible, "away, into—I am not knowing what."

She bent over him, but could not catch the last words formed by his lips. They had turned the colour of skimmed milk. Silence reigned. He seemed to have fallen asleep, but when she pressed closer to listen to his breathing she found that it had ceased. She rose quietly and turned away from the bedside. She was not frightened, nor appalled by any tragic sense of loss, for she had suffered all the agonies of parting with him whilst he was yet alive. Rather, she was glad that she had come in time to say to him what she had said. "He might never have known," she thought; and then she added: "but wherever his soul has gone, it must have known *there*." To her the things of the spirit were stronger and more real than those of the flesh. Had she not proved it to be so?

In the chill of dawn, when she came out of the room where the dead man lay, she saw her husband seated at the head of the stairs with his head buried in his hands. He rose, shivering, as he heard her footsteps behind him, and turning, looked at her with mournful eyes.

"Forgive me," he said, and suddenly kneeling down at her feet, he put the hem of her coarse skirt to his lips and kissed it reverently. She drew away with an exclamation of surprise and self-depreciation, and taking his hand in hers, raised him and led him downstairs. He wrapped his own coat round her shoulders and her shawl over her head before he took her home; but he did not speak of what had happened that night.

It lay like a mysterious gulf between them, which nothing could bridge. It had been, for him, a revelation of the inexplicable. A chasm had opened under his feet where had been the solid ground of his harsh and concise beliefs. Doubts of all sorts came thronging up from this abyss, doubts as to the finality of his theological creed, the justice of his denunciations, the infallibility of the Bible, or at least of his rendering of it. From that hour until the day of his death he was assailed by questions innumerable and unanswerable. He became daily more morose and absorbed in uncertainty, but gentle in his manner towards Megan, whom, in the light of the miracle, he had ceased to regard as his possession. He was no longer consumed by the flame of jealousy as when he had fancied her unfaithful; but he regarded her as irrevocably lost to him, a saintly being whom he had no right to touch, and for whose love he dared never hope, in this world or the next.

He died of pneumonia before the spring came. As Megan sat at his bedside, he gasped out: "You are wiser than I am, *diar anwl*. I have been preaching to others about the will of the Lord; but you have kept silent and listened whilst God spoke to you." "No,"

she said, "I have only listened to my own heart."
"Perhaps," he murmured, "God speaks to us through
our hearts." He lay still for a time, struggling for
breath; his frail hands clenched, and a line between
his brows. He was grappling with a difficult, new
thought. At last he said: "I don't know"; and later
on he repeated very sadly: "I don't know . . . after
all——"

These were the last words spoken by the preacher
who had gained so great a reputation for fiery eloquence and dogmatic fervour. The minister who
preached his funeral oration had much to say on the
tenacity of Rees Lloyd's faith, in an age of scepticism.
"He stood fast in the true faith," cried the preacher,
"he was never, for a moment, troubled by doubts on
religion, nor on the right conduct of life. He *knew*
the right from the wrong. He never admitted that
there could be more than one path, the old and narrow road, to Heaven."

The black-clad crowd that had gathered from far
and near to attend the funeral, nodded and murmured "Amen". Only one woman amongst them
knew the torment of uncertainty through which Rees
Lloyd's soul had passed before it left his body; and
she was the wife whom for years he had hated for a
sin of which she was not guilty. The tears ran down
her face as she sat listening to the sermon; but not,
as her neighbours fancied, because she had lost the
husband whom she had betrayed. "I was under-

standin' him, at the last," she told me. "And what you do understand you do forgive."

Before the year was out she had lost Ifor also. "When he comed to die, I was like a mad 'oman. Sittin' over the fire in my old home here, where I've been ever since, and rockin' myself back and fore, day and night; not able to eat, nor to sleep, nor even to cry for days together; but moanin' to myself and prayin' God in my heart to let me join him. The light was clean gone out o' my life with his honey-sweet hair and that laugh o' his, for all the 'orld like the laugh o' Penry. Father and mother they was takin' it to heart somethin' terrible. 'Ticing me to eat with this and that, and settin' the other children on my lap to try and make me pay heed to them; but nothin' 'ouldn't rouse me. Dyin' I should have been, for I hadn't no wish to go on livin', if they hadn't got me out one day into the sunlight.

"It was springtime, and everything was fresh, and newborn like. The hills was standin' there as calm and grand as ever; and it comed to me, all of a sudden, that we was like their shadows, as do pass to and fro across the Cwm, and are leavin' no trace of theirselves behind."

I remember that the shadow of the western hill had almost touched our feet as she reached this point in her story. We were still bathed in the afternoon sunlight, Saint Anne and I, but the grass before us lay dark as emerald velvet in the shade.

"Yes," I said, looking up in wonder at her tranquil old face, "but did that make you want to go on living?" She shook her head. "I did not *want* to live," she said, "but lookin' up at those ancient old hills, it seemed to me such a small little thing to live out my short span, patient like, to the end o' my days."

Those words sent a chill through my being. I remember thinking how endlessly long were her seventy years of life. They do not appear to me so now.

"And then", the sound of her soft Welsh voice broke the stillness, "little Emrys as is a grown man and farmin' here now, was fallin' down on the path by my feet, and cryin' something pitiful. I was pickin' him up, and comfortin' him. And after that I was goin' back to my work. There was four little uns to mind, and that kept me from thinkin' overmuch of the one I'd lost. Not that they was ever the same to me, as he'd been; but they had need o' me none the less." After a pause, she added: "They are married and with children o' their own now, all dark-eyed, same as poor Rees. Mother died soon after I was comin' back to live here, and I was lookin' after father, as was gettin' simple. Then I was keepin' house for my eldest boy, after father was taken too, until the lad was marryin'. Then again there was his children to see to. . . . Yes, yes, I've been busy with one thing and another. And now I'm gone old," she

said placidly, watching the shadow of the hills opposite steal across her feet, and creep inch by inch up
her dress. "I am sittin' here day after day, rememberin' all as is past. There is no trace of Penry, nor of
little Ifor, they are gone—like shadows o' the hills."

When I raised my eyes to hers again, the sunlight
had disappeared from Cwmbach.

Saint Anne is gone now also. Last summer I
tramped up the road that leads through the imprisoned valley. I found it unchanged. The great green
hills stood sentinel on either side. There was the
square grey chapel, and the caretaker's cottage, and
Cwmbach farm, nestling in its hollow on the opposite
side of the angry torrent. Nothing broke the well-
known stillness but the sleepy trickling of many
streams, that in winter are foaming spates, and the
sound of my own footfall along the stony track. I
came to the fold gate. There I disturbed a tribe of
black-haired urchins, swarthy as Spaniards, who were
playing upon the strip of sward on which Saint Anne
used to set her chair. The sight of these children
brought back my own girlhood, so that I called to
them by name—"Gladys, John Owen, Rees *bach*".
Then I saw that they were watching me with shy
curiosity. After a moment they ran away and hid
from the stranger.

As I trudged on towards the pass, the shade of the
western hill stole across the road behind me, seeming

to blot out all trace of my passage; and I remembered the words of the Psalmist that my father had taught me in the Book of Common Prayer: "Man is like a thing of nought; his time passeth away like a shadow."